MARY SHELLEY'S

FRANKENSTEIN

THE GRAPHIC NOVEL

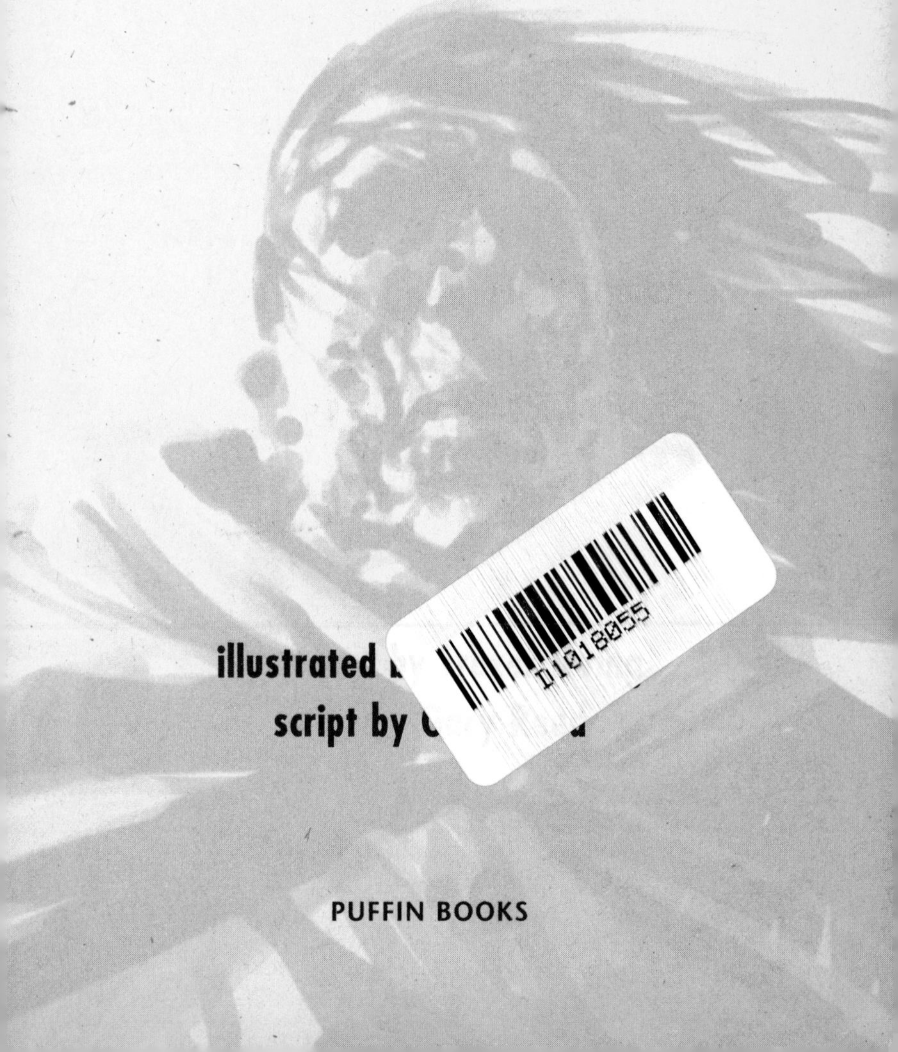

illustrated b[illegible]
script by C[illegible]d

PUFFIN BOOKS

PUFFIN BOOKS
Published by the Penguin Group
Penguin Young Readers Group,
345 Hudson Street, New York, NY 10014 U.S.A.
Penguin Group (Canada). 10 Alcorn Avenue, Toronto, Ontario, Canada M4V 3B2
(a division of Pearson Penguin Canada Inc.)
Penguin Books Ltd, 80 Strand, London WC2R 0RL, England
Penguin Ireland, 25 St. Stephen's Green, Dublin 2, Ireland
(a division of Penguin Books Ltd)
Penguin Group (Australia), 250 Camberwell Road, Camberwell, Victoria 3124,
Australia (a division of Pearson Australia Group Pty Ltd)
Penguin Books India Pvt Ltd, 11 Community Centre, Panchsheel Park,
New Delhi – 110 017, India
Penguin Group (NZ), Cnr Airborne and Rosedale Roads, Albany, Auckland 1310,
New Zealand (a division of Pearson New Zealand Ltd)
Penguin Books (South Africa) (Pty) Ltd, 24 Sturdee Avenue, Rosebank,
Johannesburg 2196, South Africa

Registered Offices: Penguin Books Ltd, 80 Strand, London WC2R 0RL, England

First published by Puffin Books, a division of Penguin Young Readers Group, 2005

10 9 8 7 6 5 4 3 2 1

A Byron Preiss Book
Byron Preiss Visual Publications
24 West 25th Street, New York, NY 10010

Illustrated by Frazer Irving
Script by Gary Reed
Lettering by Ryan Yount
Series Editor: Dwight Jon Zimmerman
Series Assistant Editor: April Isaacs
Interior Design by M. Postawa & Gilda Hannah
Cover Design by M. Postawa

Puffin Books ISBN 0-14-240407-1

Printed in the United States of America

MARY SHELLEY'S

FRANKENSTEIN

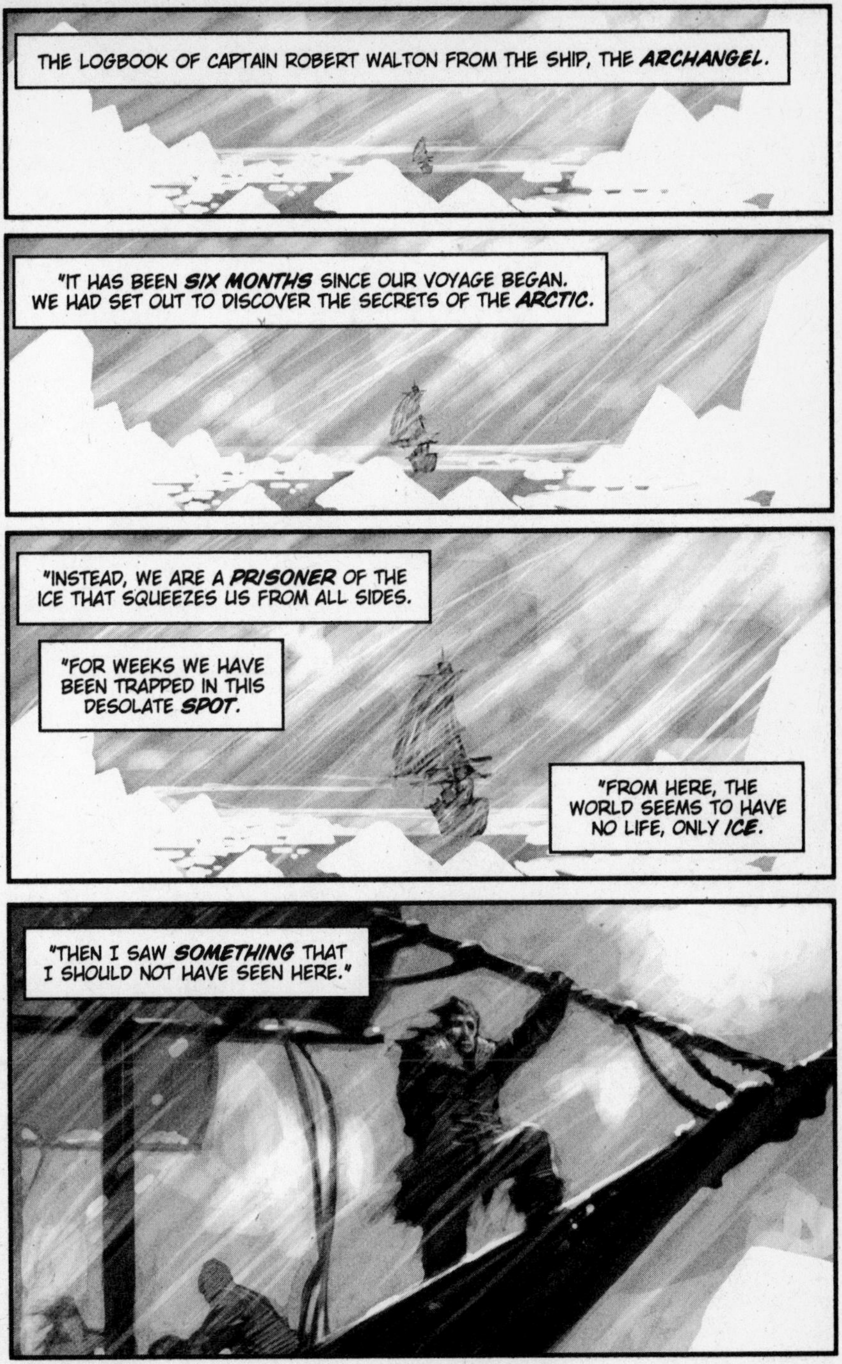
THE LOGBOOK OF CAPTAIN ROBERT WALTON FROM THE SHIP, THE ARCHANGEL.
"IT HAS BEEN SIX MONTHS SINCE OUR VOYAGE BEGAN. WE HAD SET OUT TO DISCOVER THE SECRETS OF THE ARCTIC.
"INSTEAD, WE ARE A PRISONER OF THE ICE THAT SQUEEZES US FROM ALL SIDES.
"FOR WEEKS WE HAVE BEEN TRAPPED IN THIS DESOLATE SPOT.
"FROM HERE, THE WORLD SEEMS TO HAVE NO LIFE, ONLY ICE.
"THEN I SAW SOMETHING THAT I SHOULD NOT HAVE SEEN HERE."

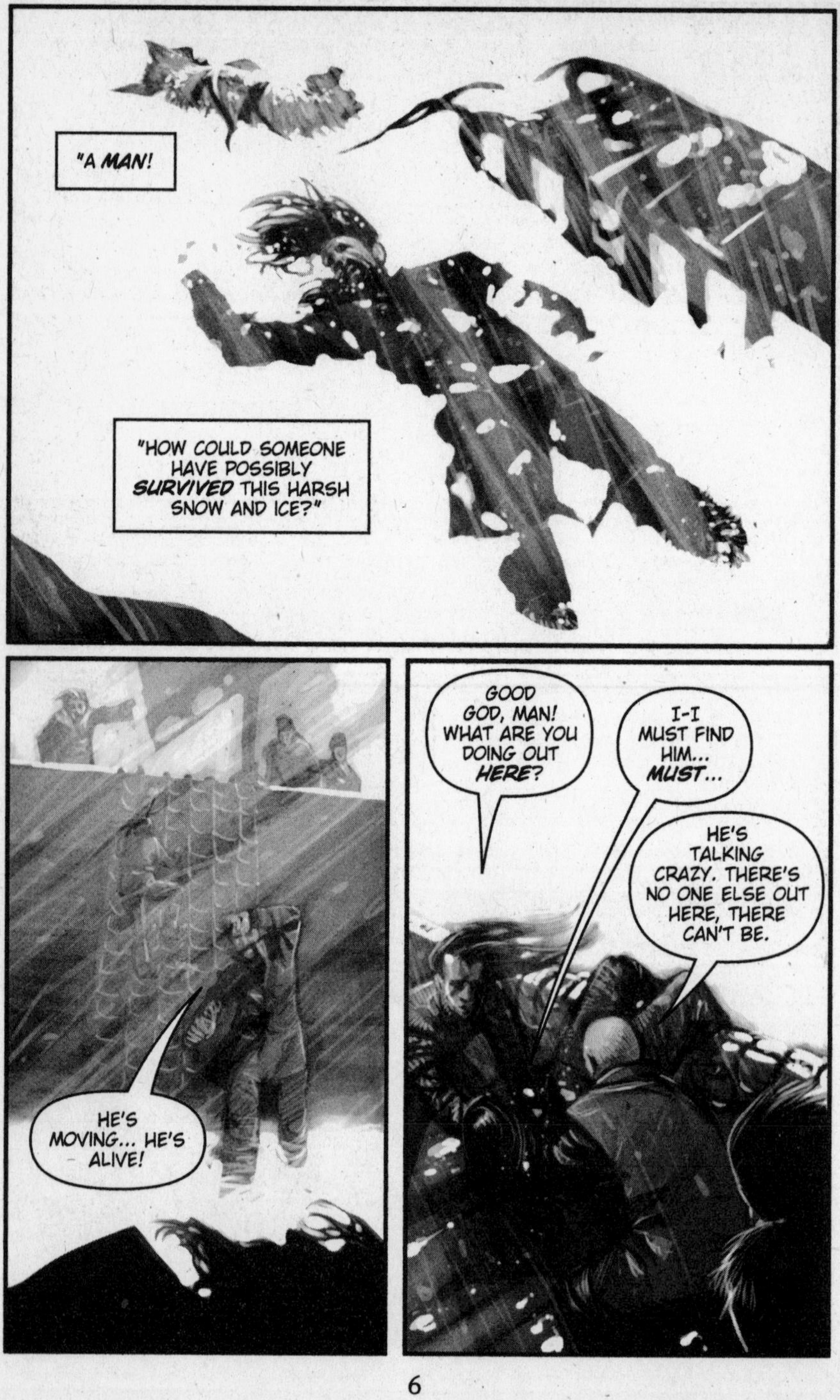
"A *MAN*!
"HOW COULD SOMEONE HAVE POSSIBLY *SURVIVED* THIS HARSH SNOW AND ICE?"
HE'S MOVING... HE'S ALIVE!
GOOD GOD, MAN! WHAT ARE YOU DOING OUT *HERE*?
I-I MUST FIND HIM... *MUST*...
HE'S TALKING CRAZY. THERE'S NO ONE ELSE OUT HERE, THERE CAN'T BE.

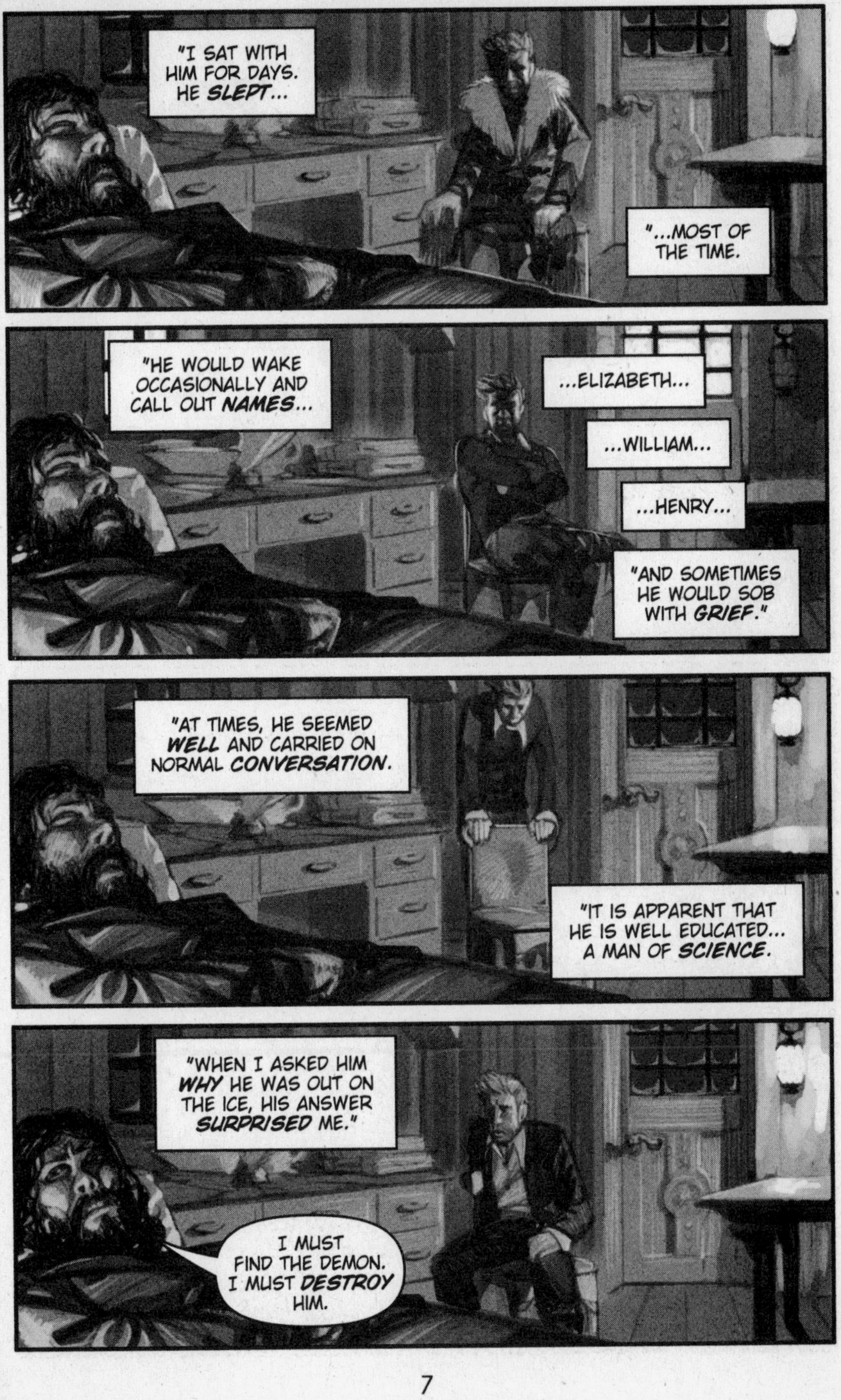
"I SAT WITH HIM FOR DAYS. HE SLEPT...
"...MOST OF THE TIME.
"HE WOULD WAKE OCCASIONALLY AND CALL OUT NAMES...
...ELIZABETH...
...WILLIAM...
...HENRY...
"AND SOMETIMES HE WOULD SOB WITH GRIEF."
"AT TIMES, HE SEEMED WELL AND CARRIED ON NORMAL CONVERSATION.
"IT IS APPARENT THAT HE IS WELL EDUCATED... A MAN OF SCIENCE.
"WHEN I ASKED HIM WHY HE WAS OUT ON THE ICE, HIS ANSWER SURPRISED ME."
I MUST FIND THE DEMON. I MUST DESTROY HIM.

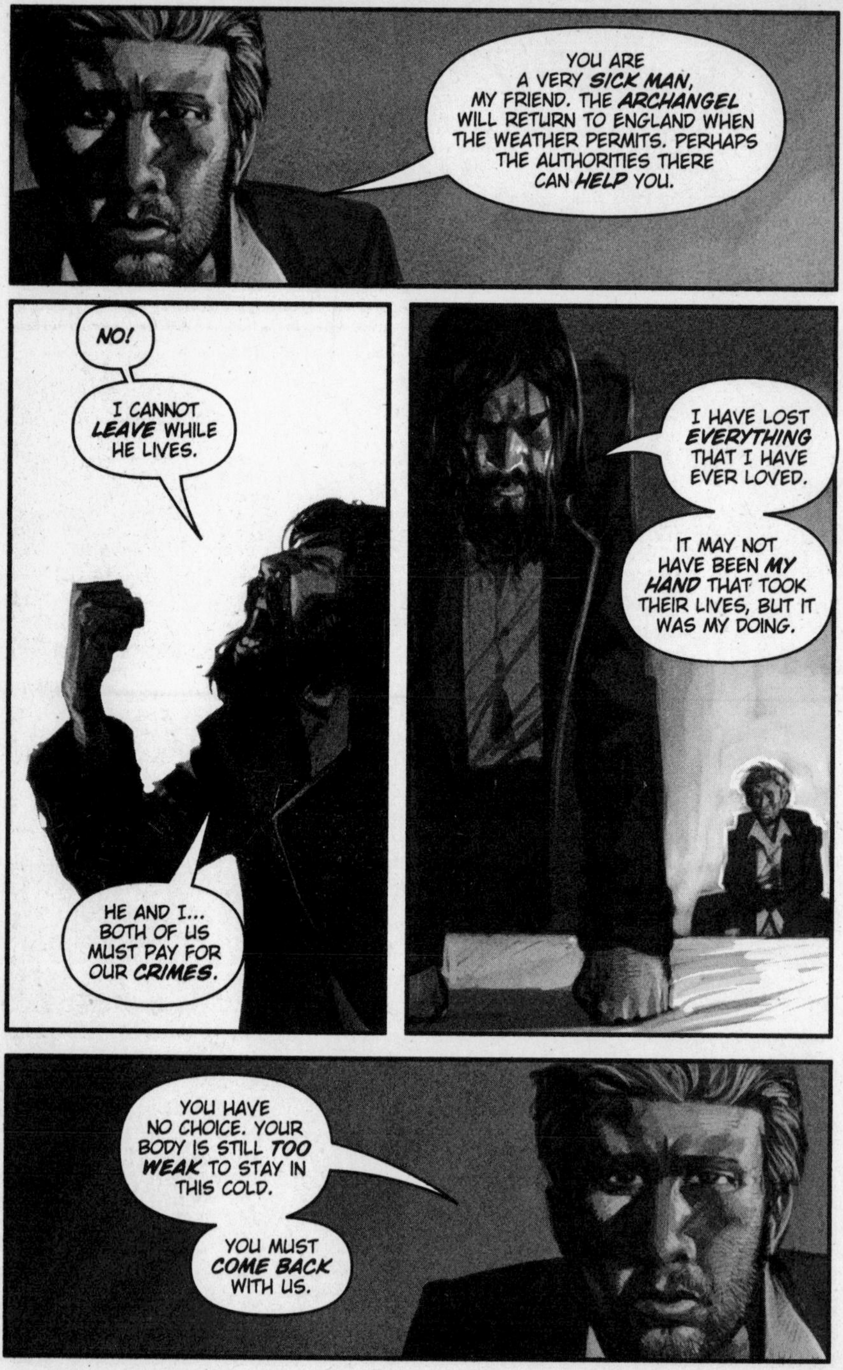
YOU ARE A VERY SICK MAN, MY FRIEND. THE ARCHANGEL WILL RETURN TO ENGLAND WHEN THE WEATHER PERMITS. PERHAPS THE AUTHORITIES THERE CAN HELP YOU.
NO!
I CANNOT LEAVE WHILE HE LIVES.
HE AND I... BOTH OF US MUST PAY FOR OUR CRIMES.
I HAVE LOST EVERYTHING THAT I HAVE EVER LOVED.
IT MAY NOT HAVE BEEN MY HAND THAT TOOK THEIR LIVES, BUT IT WAS MY DOING.
YOU HAVE NO CHOICE. YOUR BODY IS STILL TOO WEAK TO STAY IN THIS COLD.
YOU MUST COME BACK WITH US.

I WILL NOT BE ACCOMPANYING YOU...

...ON YOUR RETURN *HOME*, CAPTAIN WALTON.

MY *JOURNEY* MUST END HERE BECAUSE MY *FATE* IS SEALED.

I DO NOT THINK I WILL LIVE MUCH LONGER. THE *WEIGHT* OF ALL THOSE WHO DIED IS TOO MUCH FOR ME.

I MUST TELL YOU OF MY CRIMES, OF THE *TERRIBLE THINGS* THAT I HAVE DONE.

IT IS NOT FORGIVENESS THAT I SEEK, ONLY THAT YOU KNOW THE *TRUTH*.

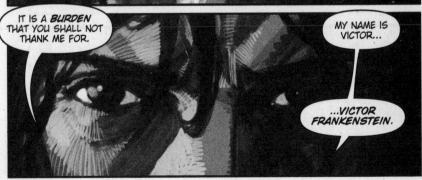

IT IS A *BURDEN* THAT YOU SHALL NOT THANK ME FOR.

MY NAME IS VICTOR...

...*VICTOR FRANKENSTEIN*.

9

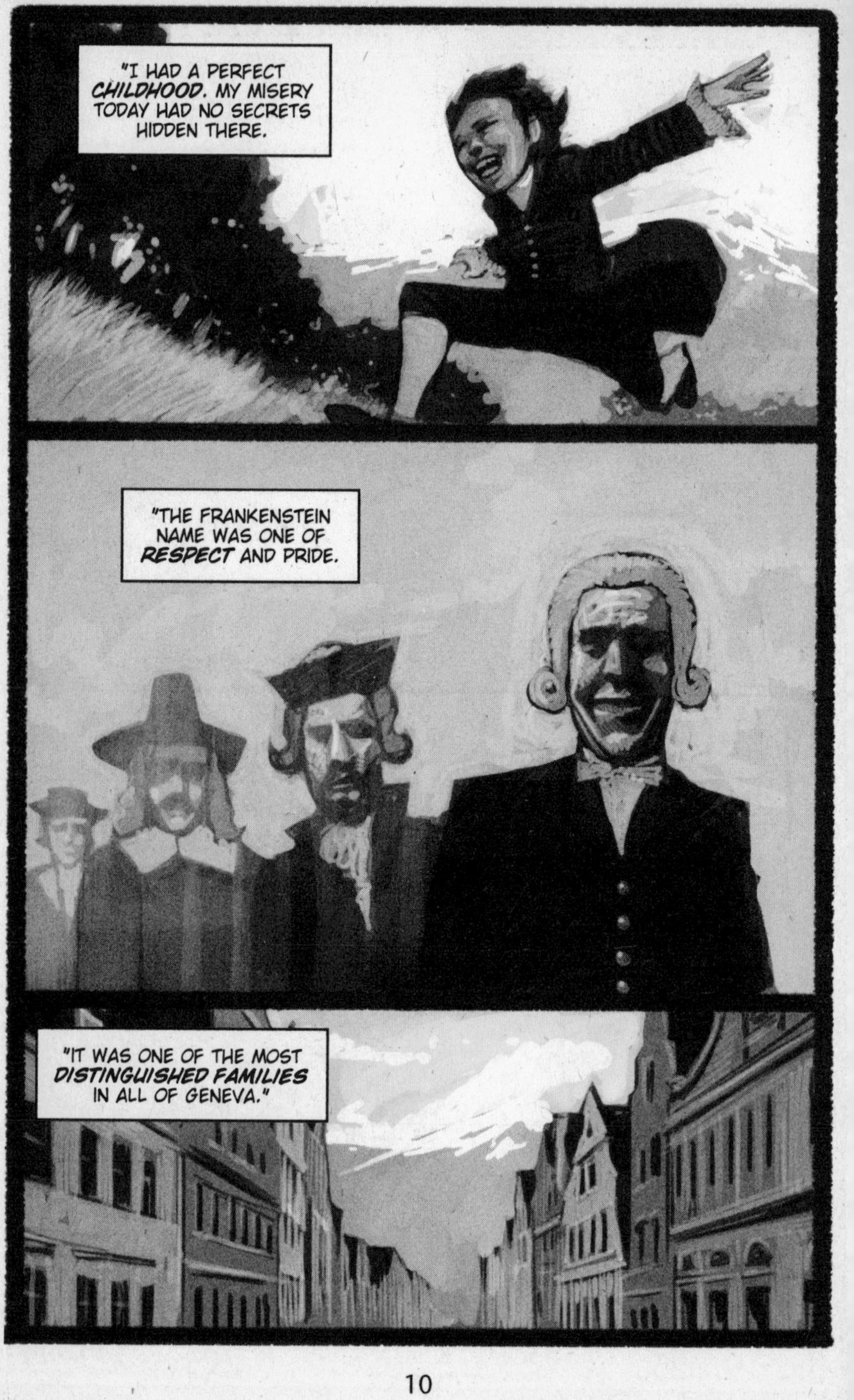
"I HAD A PERFECT CHILDHOOD. MY MISERY TODAY HAD NO SECRETS HIDDEN THERE.
"THE FRANKENSTEIN NAME WAS ONE OF RESPECT AND PRIDE.
"IT WAS ONE OF THE MOST DISTINGUISHED FAMILIES IN ALL OF GENEVA."

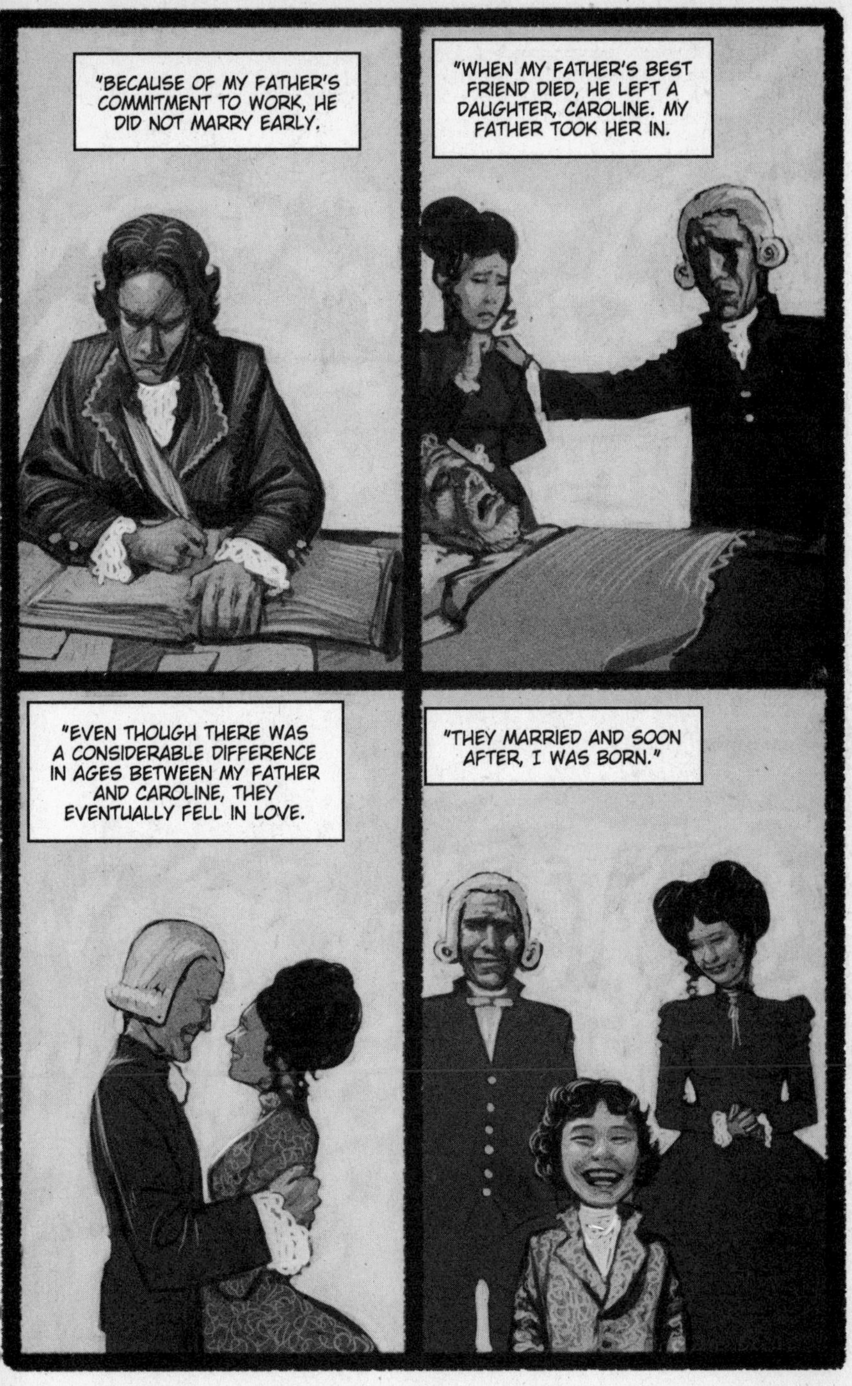
"BECAUSE OF MY FATHER'S COMMITMENT TO WORK, HE DID NOT MARRY EARLY.
"WHEN MY FATHER'S BEST FRIEND DIED, HE LEFT A DAUGHTER, CAROLINE. MY FATHER TOOK HER IN.
"EVEN THOUGH THERE WAS A CONSIDERABLE DIFFERENCE IN AGES BETWEEN MY FATHER AND CAROLINE, THEY EVENTUALLY FELL IN LOVE.
"THEY MARRIED AND SOON AFTER, I WAS BORN."

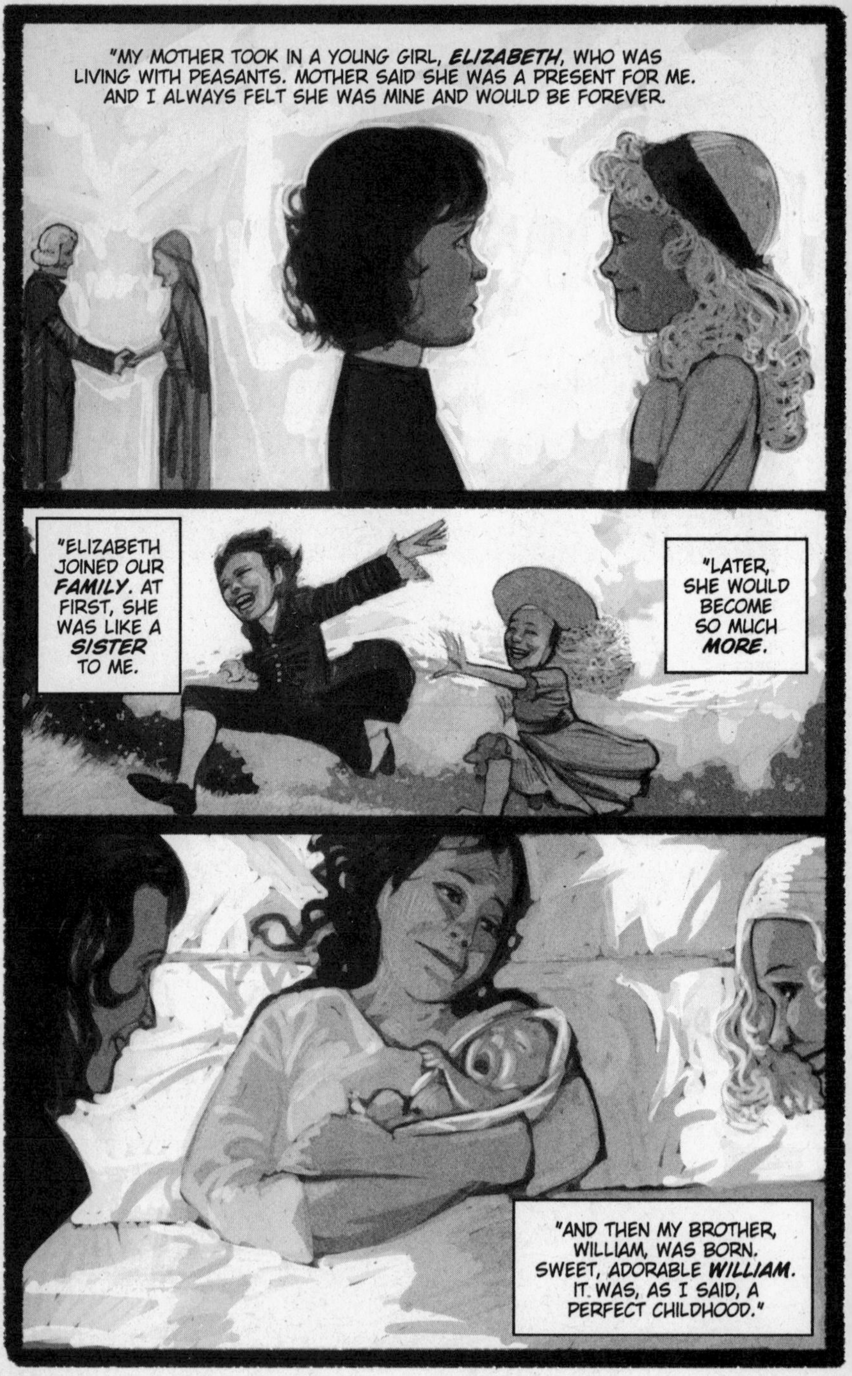
"MY MOTHER TOOK IN A YOUNG GIRL, ELIZABETH, WHO WAS LIVING WITH PEASANTS. MOTHER SAID SHE WAS A PRESENT FOR ME. AND I ALWAYS FELT SHE WAS MINE AND WOULD BE FOREVER.
"ELIZABETH JOINED OUR FAMILY. AT FIRST, SHE WAS LIKE A SISTER TO ME.
"LATER, SHE WOULD BECOME SO MUCH MORE.
"AND THEN MY BROTHER, WILLIAM, WAS BORN. SWEET, ADORABLE WILLIAM. IT WAS, AS I SAID, A PERFECT CHILDHOOD."

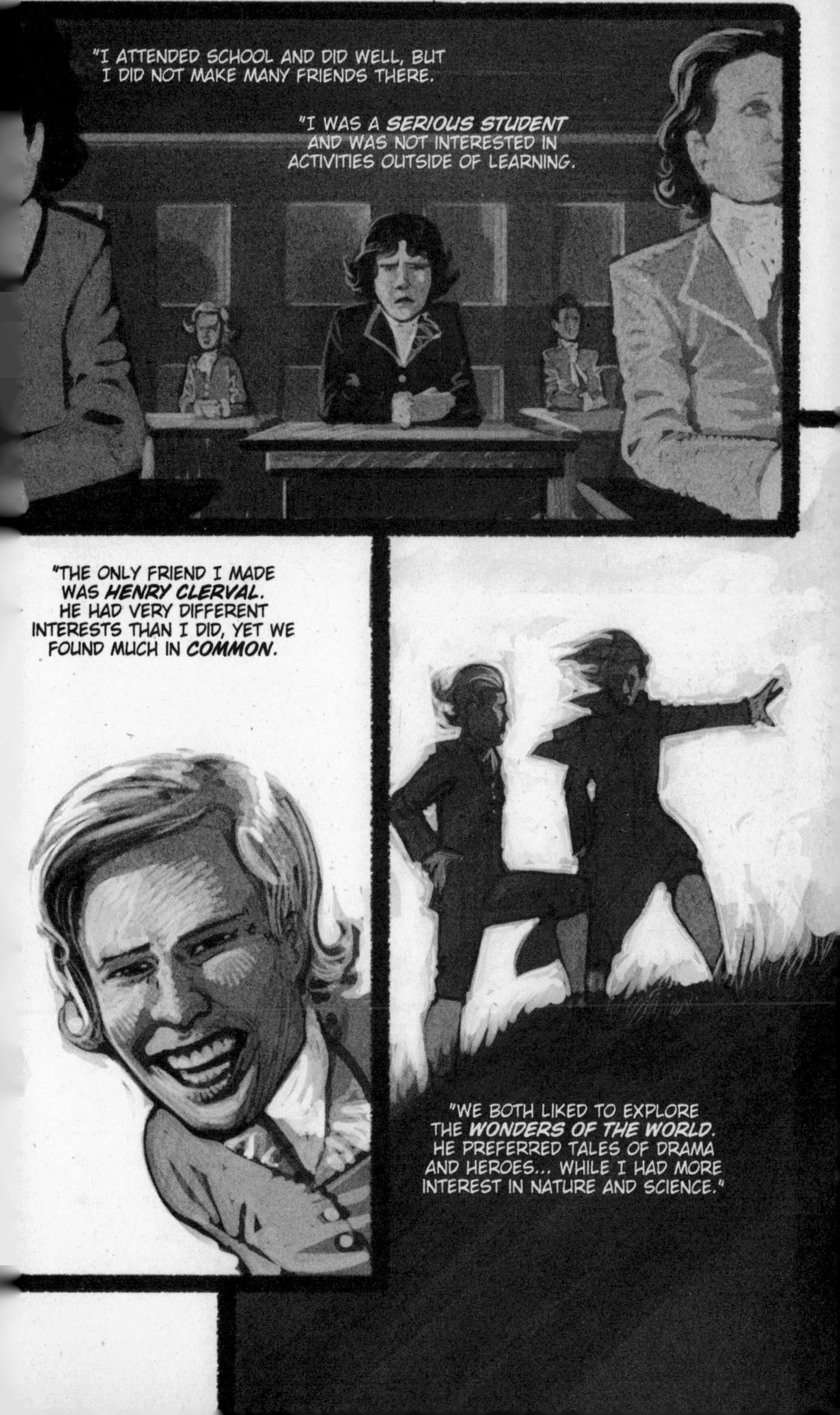
"I ATTENDED SCHOOL AND DID WELL, BUT I DID NOT MAKE MANY FRIENDS THERE.
"I WAS A SERIOUS STUDENT AND WAS NOT INTERESTED IN ACTIVITIES OUTSIDE OF LEARNING.
"THE ONLY FRIEND I MADE WAS HENRY CLERVAL. HE HAD VERY DIFFERENT INTERESTS THAN I DID, YET WE FOUND MUCH IN COMMON.
"WE BOTH LIKED TO EXPLORE THE WONDERS OF THE WORLD. HE PREFERRED TALES OF DRAMA AND HEROES... WHILE I HAD MORE INTEREST IN NATURE AND SCIENCE."

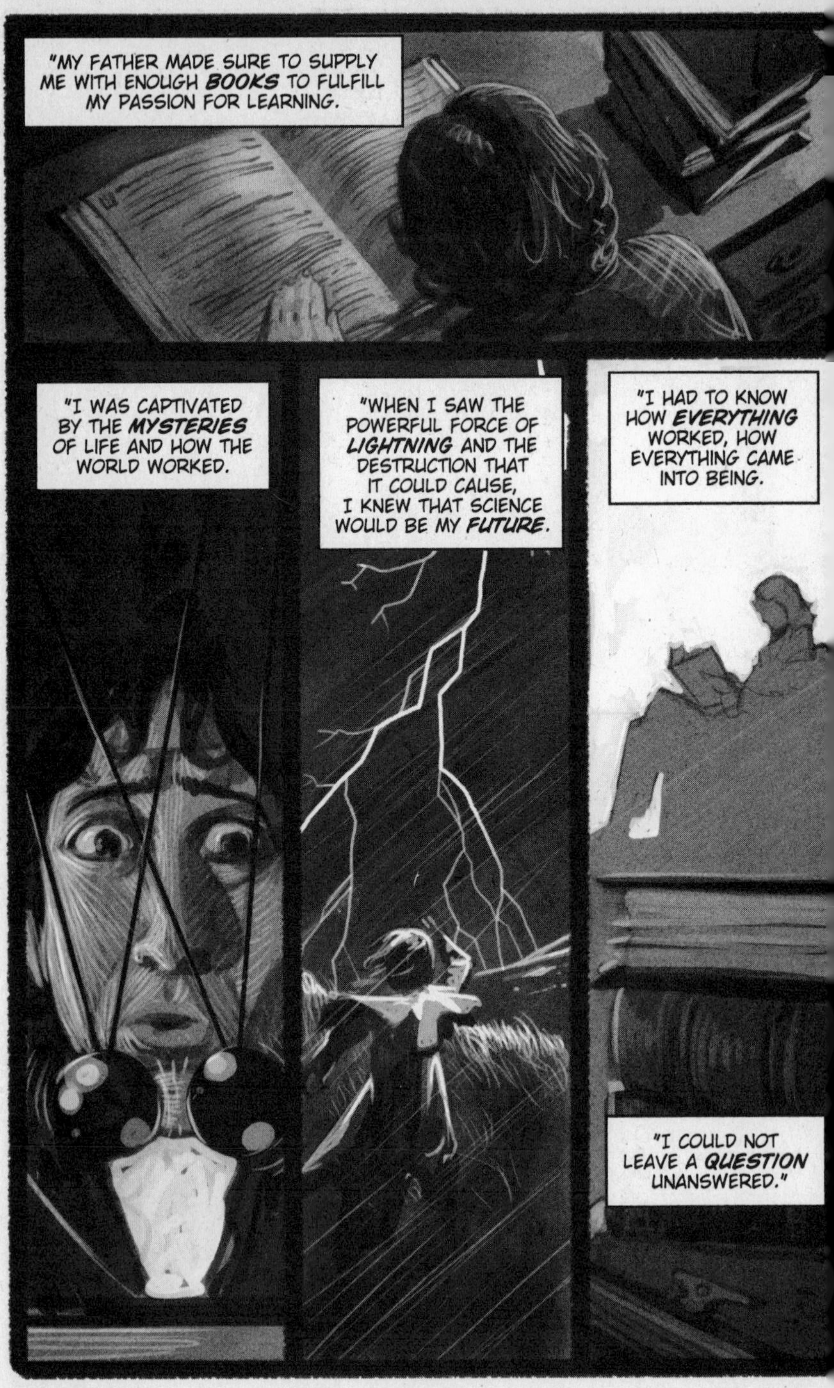
"MY FATHER MADE SURE TO SUPPLY ME WITH ENOUGH **BOOKS** TO FULFILL MY PASSION FOR LEARNING.
"I WAS CAPTIVATED BY THE **MYSTERIES** OF LIFE AND HOW THE WORLD WORKED.
"WHEN I SAW THE POWERFUL FORCE OF **LIGHTNING** AND THE DESTRUCTION THAT IT COULD CAUSE, I KNEW THAT SCIENCE WOULD BE MY **FUTURE**.
"I HAD TO KNOW HOW **EVERYTHING** WORKED, HOW EVERYTHING CAME INTO BEING.
"I COULD NOT LEAVE A **QUESTION** UNANSWERED."

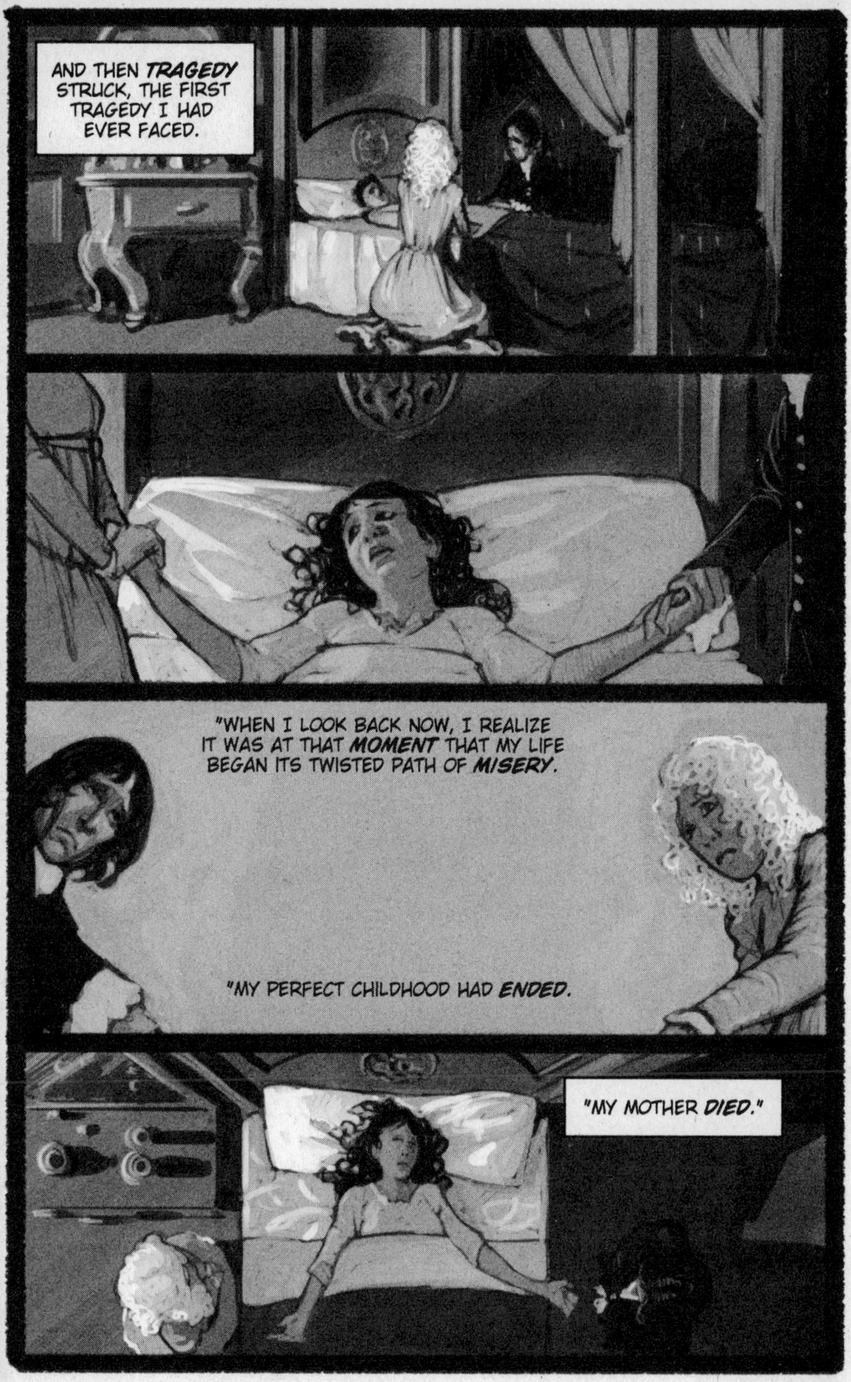
AND THEN TRAGEDY STRUCK, THE FIRST TRAGEDY I HAD EVER FACED.
"WHEN I LOOK BACK NOW, I REALIZE IT WAS AT THAT MOMENT THAT MY LIFE BEGAN ITS TWISTED PATH OF MISERY.
"MY PERFECT CHILDHOOD HAD ENDED.
"MY MOTHER DIED."

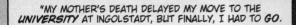

"MY MOTHER'S DEATH DELAYED MY MOVE TO THE *UNIVERSITY* AT INGOLSTADT, BUT FINALLY, I HAD TO *GO*.

"I HAD TO LEAVE MY FATHER AND MY *FAMILY*... MY DEAR FRIEND, HENRY...

"BUT IT WAS *ELIZABETH* THAT I WOULD MISS MOST.

"WE HAD TALKED OF *MARRIAGE* BUT MY EDUCATION HAD TO COME FIRST. I HAD THE NORMAL FEARS OF YOUTH BUT WAS ALSO EXCITED ABOUT WHAT I WOULD *EXPERIENCE* AT INGOLSTADT."

16

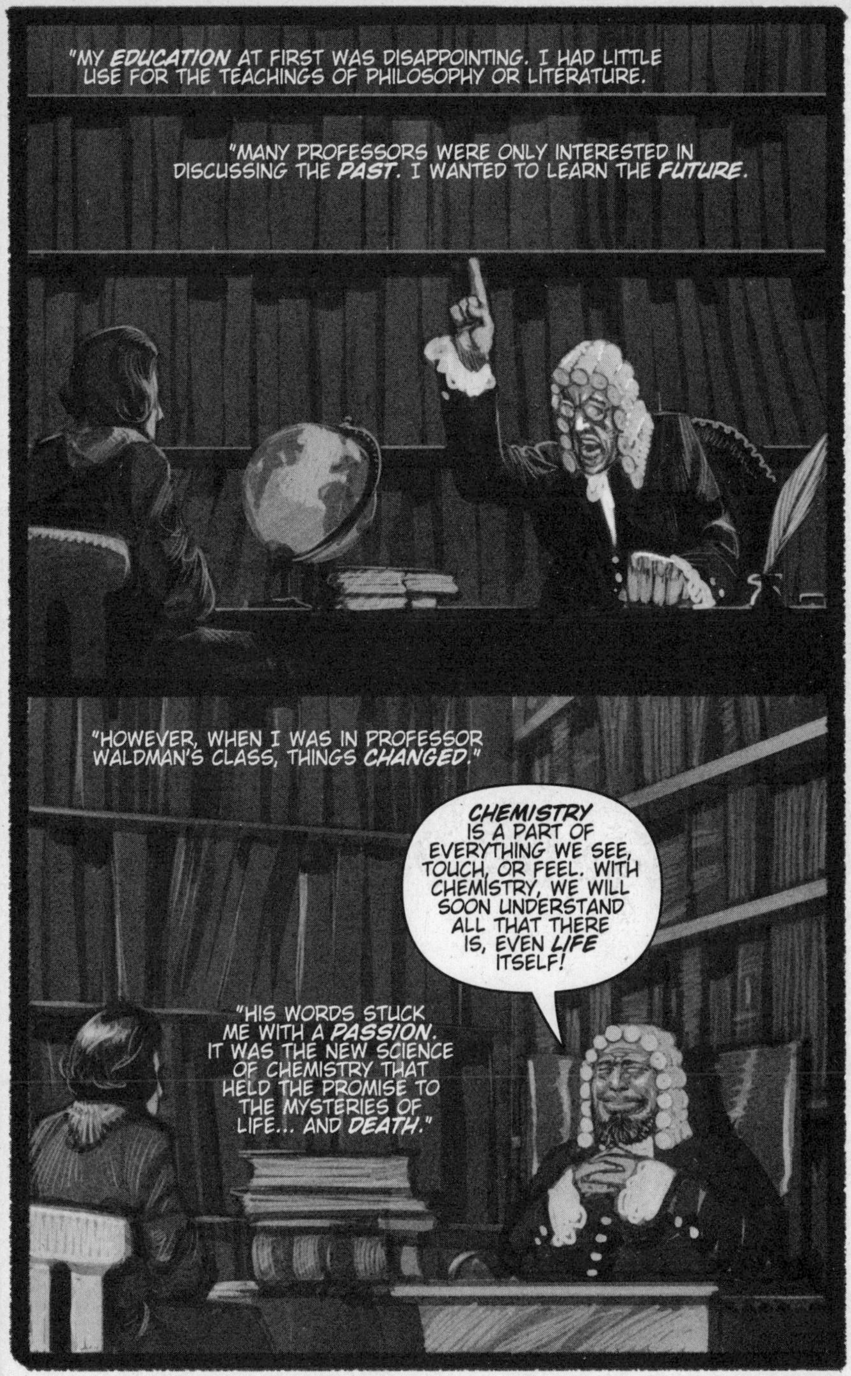
"MY EDUCATION AT FIRST WAS DISAPPOINTING. I HAD LITTLE USE FOR THE TEACHINGS OF PHILOSOPHY OR LITERATURE.
"MANY PROFESSORS WERE ONLY INTERESTED IN DISCUSSING THE PAST. I WANTED TO LEARN THE FUTURE.
"HOWEVER, WHEN I WAS IN PROFESSOR WALDMAN'S CLASS, THINGS CHANGED."
CHEMISTRY IS A PART OF EVERYTHING WE SEE, TOUCH, OR FEEL. WITH CHEMISTRY, WE WILL SOON UNDERSTAND ALL THAT THERE IS, EVEN LIFE ITSELF!
"HIS WORDS STUCK ME WITH A PASSION. IT WAS THE NEW SCIENCE OF CHEMISTRY THAT HELD THE PROMISE TO THE MYSTERIES OF LIFE... AND DEATH."

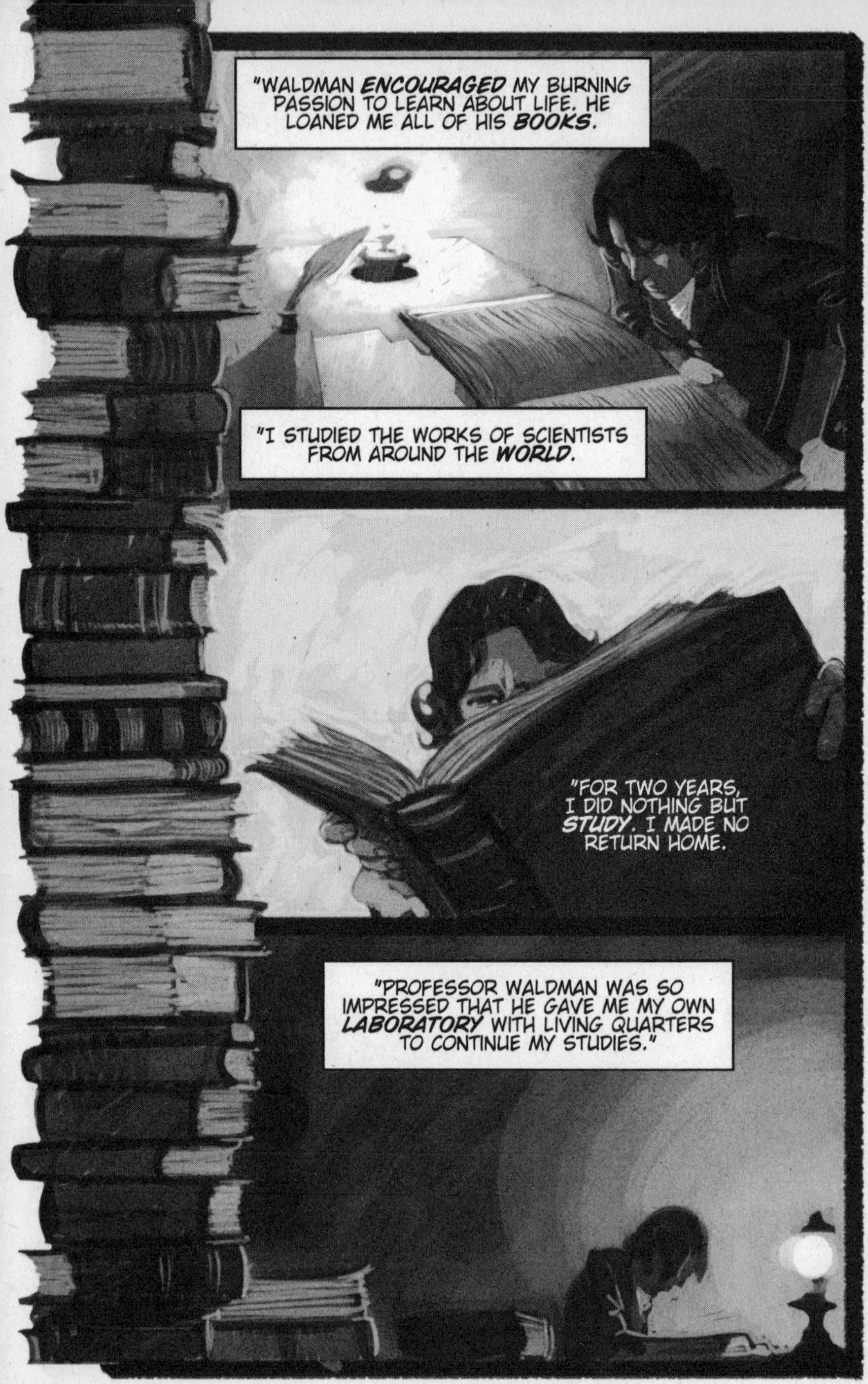
"WALDMAN ENCOURAGED MY BURNING PASSION TO LEARN ABOUT LIFE. HE LOANED ME ALL OF HIS BOOKS.
"I STUDIED THE WORKS OF SCIENTISTS FROM AROUND THE WORLD.
"FOR TWO YEARS, I DID NOTHING BUT STUDY. I MADE NO RETURN HOME.
"PROFESSOR WALDMAN WAS SO IMPRESSED THAT HE GAVE ME MY OWN LABORATORY WITH LIVING QUARTERS TO CONTINUE MY STUDIES."

"I STUDIED HOW LIFE WORKED... AND WHAT CAUSED *DEATH*.

"I SAW THAT EVEN LIFE WAS MADE OF CHEMICALS AND HOW CHEMISTRY COULD UNLOCK MANY *SECRETS*.

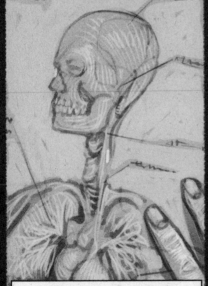

"I HAD A PASSION TO UNCOVER THE *MYSTERIES* OF THE HUMAN BODY.

"AND SLOWLY, I BEGAN TO DEVELOP AN *IDEA*. AN IDEA THAT WOULD SOLVE THE RIDDLE OF LIFE."

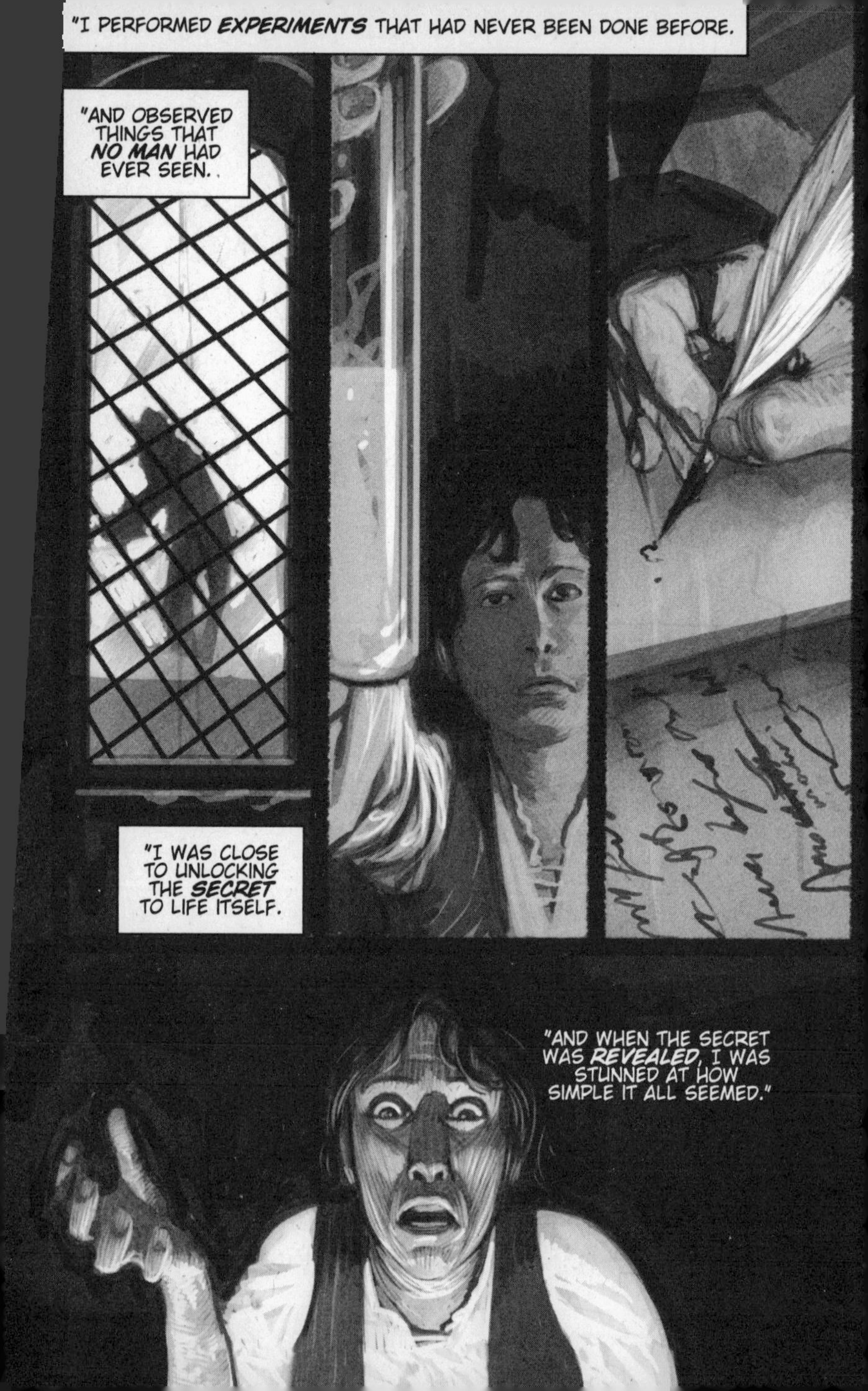
"I PERFORMED EXPERIMENTS THAT HAD NEVER BEEN DONE BEFORE.
"AND OBSERVED THINGS THAT NO MAN HAD EVER SEEN.
"I WAS CLOSE TO UNLOCKING THE SECRET TO LIFE ITSELF.
"AND WHEN THE SECRET WAS REVEALED, I WAS STUNNED AT HOW SIMPLE IT ALL SEEMED."

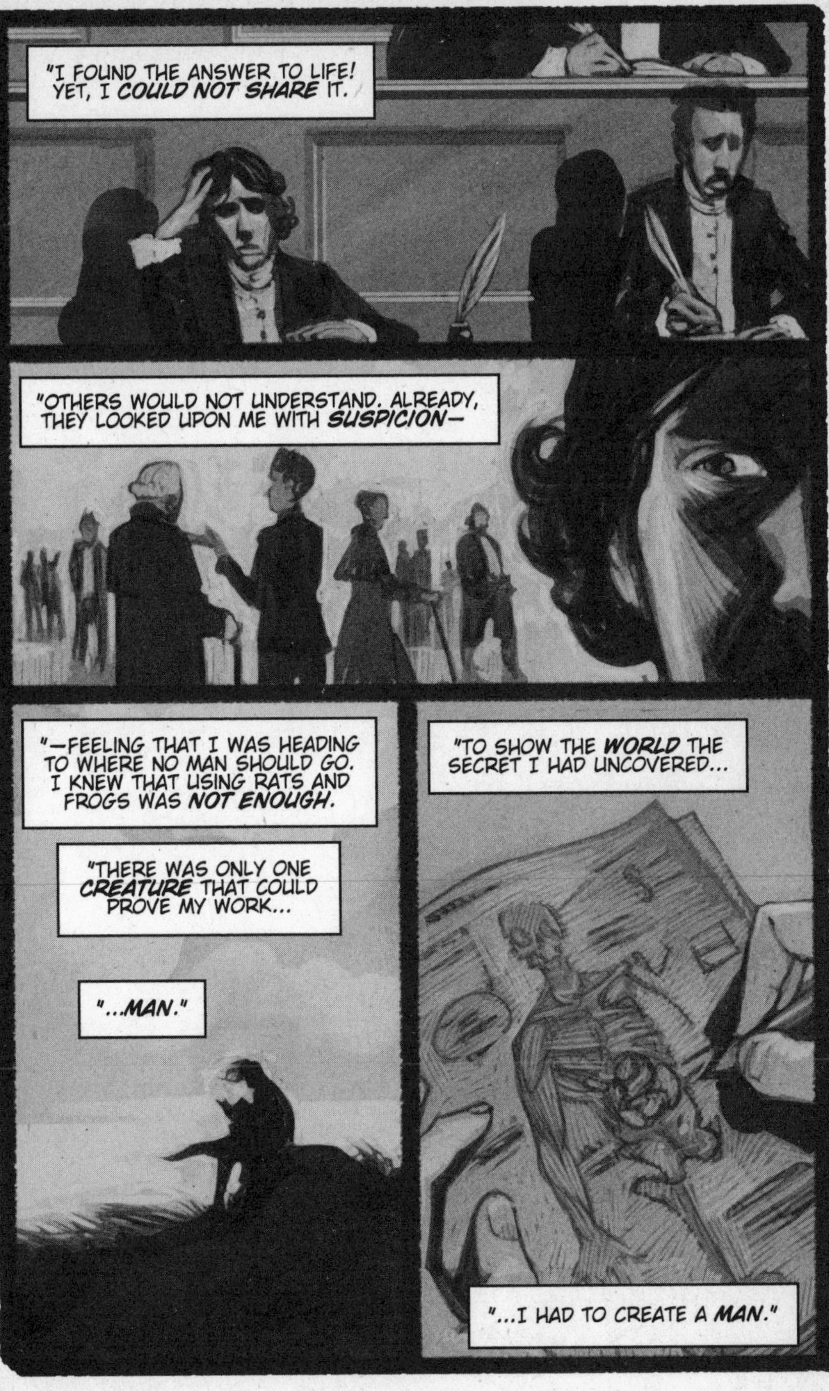
"I FOUND THE ANSWER TO LIFE! YET, I COULD NOT SHARE IT.
"OTHERS WOULD NOT UNDERSTAND. ALREADY, THEY LOOKED UPON ME WITH SUSPICION—
"—FEELING THAT I WAS HEADING TO WHERE NO MAN SHOULD GO. I KNEW THAT USING RATS AND FROGS WAS NOT ENOUGH.
"THERE WAS ONLY ONE CREATURE THAT COULD PROVE MY WORK...
"...MAN."
"TO SHOW THE WORLD THE SECRET I HAD UNCOVERED...
"...I HAD TO CREATE A MAN."

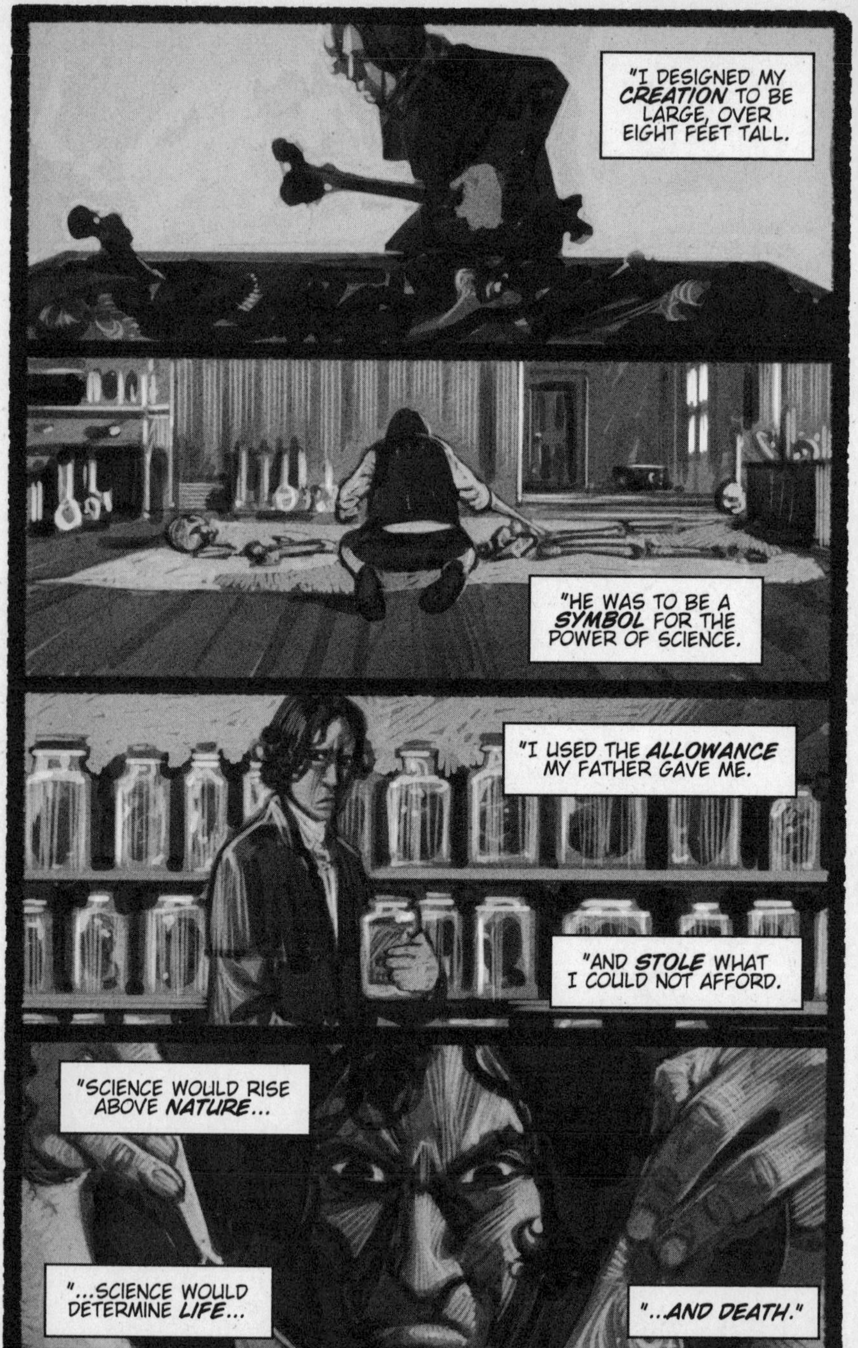
"I DESIGNED MY CREATION TO BE LARGE, OVER EIGHT FEET TALL.
"HE WAS TO BE A SYMBOL FOR THE POWER OF SCIENCE.
"I USED THE ALLOWANCE MY FATHER GAVE ME.
"AND STOLE WHAT I COULD NOT AFFORD.
"SCIENCE WOULD RISE ABOVE NATURE...
"...SCIENCE WOULD DETERMINE LIFE...
"...AND DEATH."

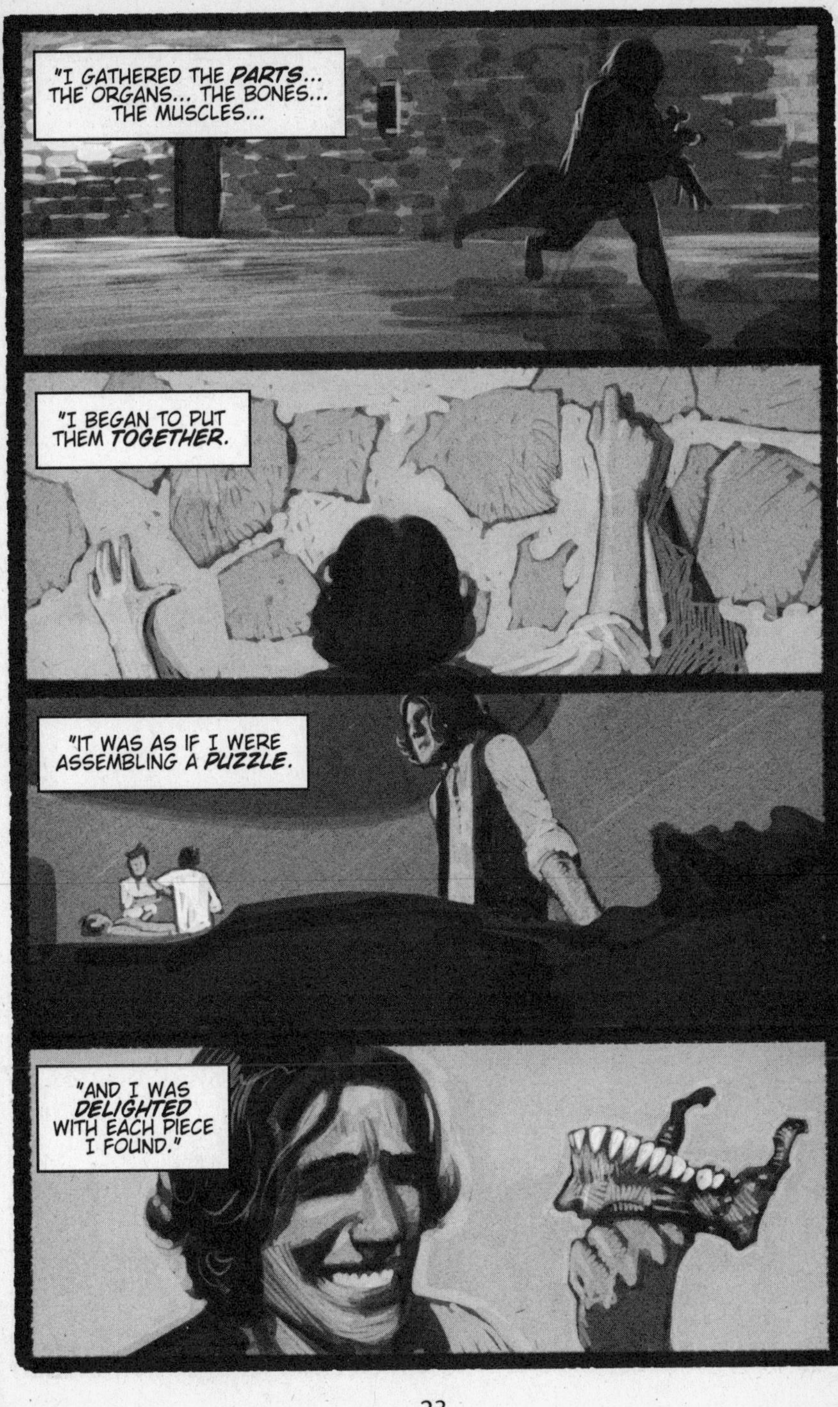
"I GATHERED THE **PARTS**... THE ORGANS... THE BONES... THE MUSCLES...
"I BEGAN TO PUT THEM **TOGETHER**.
"IT WAS AS IF I WERE ASSEMBLING A **PUZZLE**.
"AND I WAS **DELIGHTED** WITH EACH PIECE I FOUND."

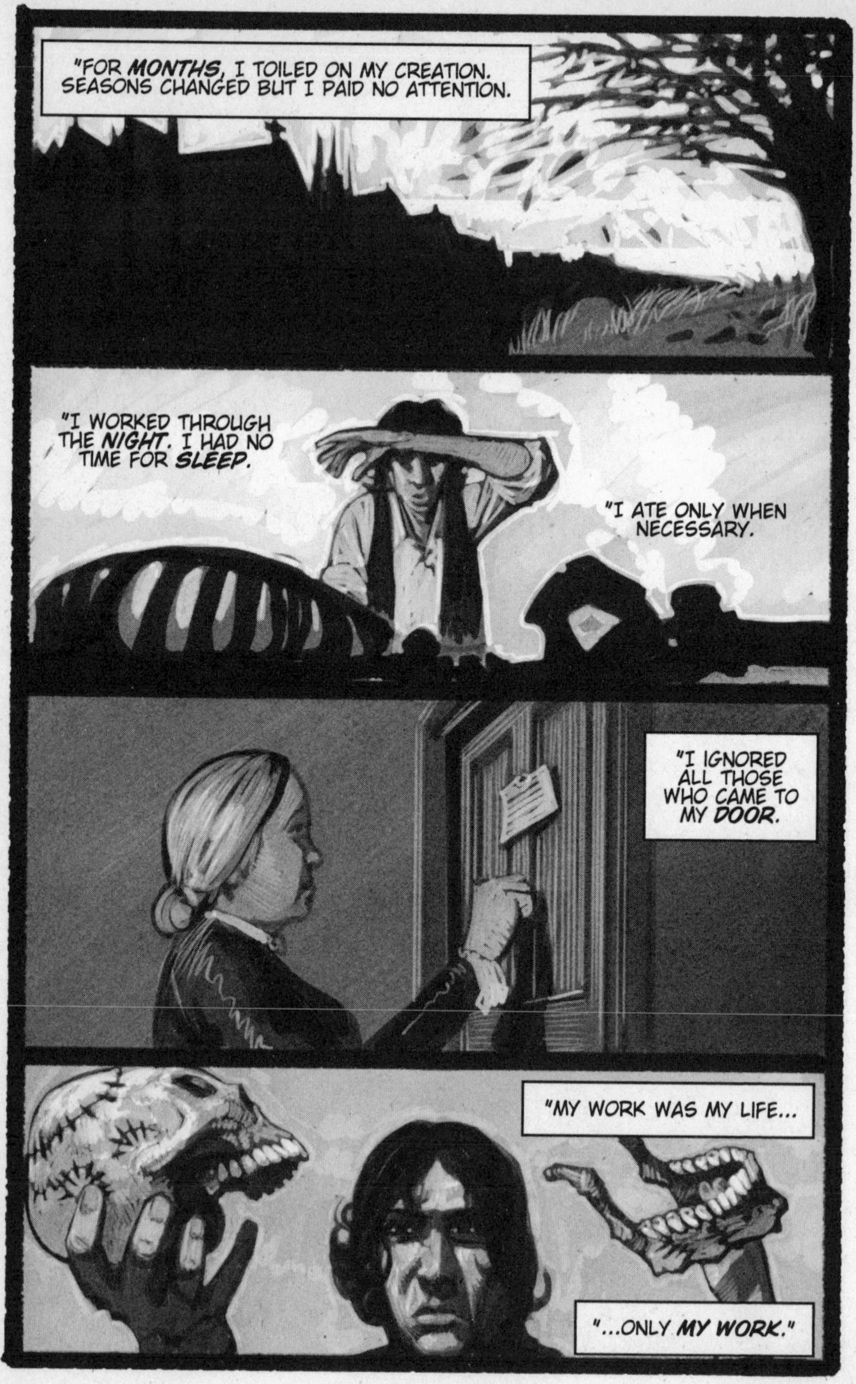
"FOR MONTHS, I TOILED ON MY CREATION. SEASONS CHANGED BUT I PAID NO ATTENTION.
"I WORKED THROUGH THE NIGHT. I HAD NO TIME FOR SLEEP.
"I ATE ONLY WHEN NECESSARY.
"I IGNORED ALL THOSE WHO CAME TO MY DOOR.
"MY WORK WAS MY LIFE...
"...ONLY MY WORK."

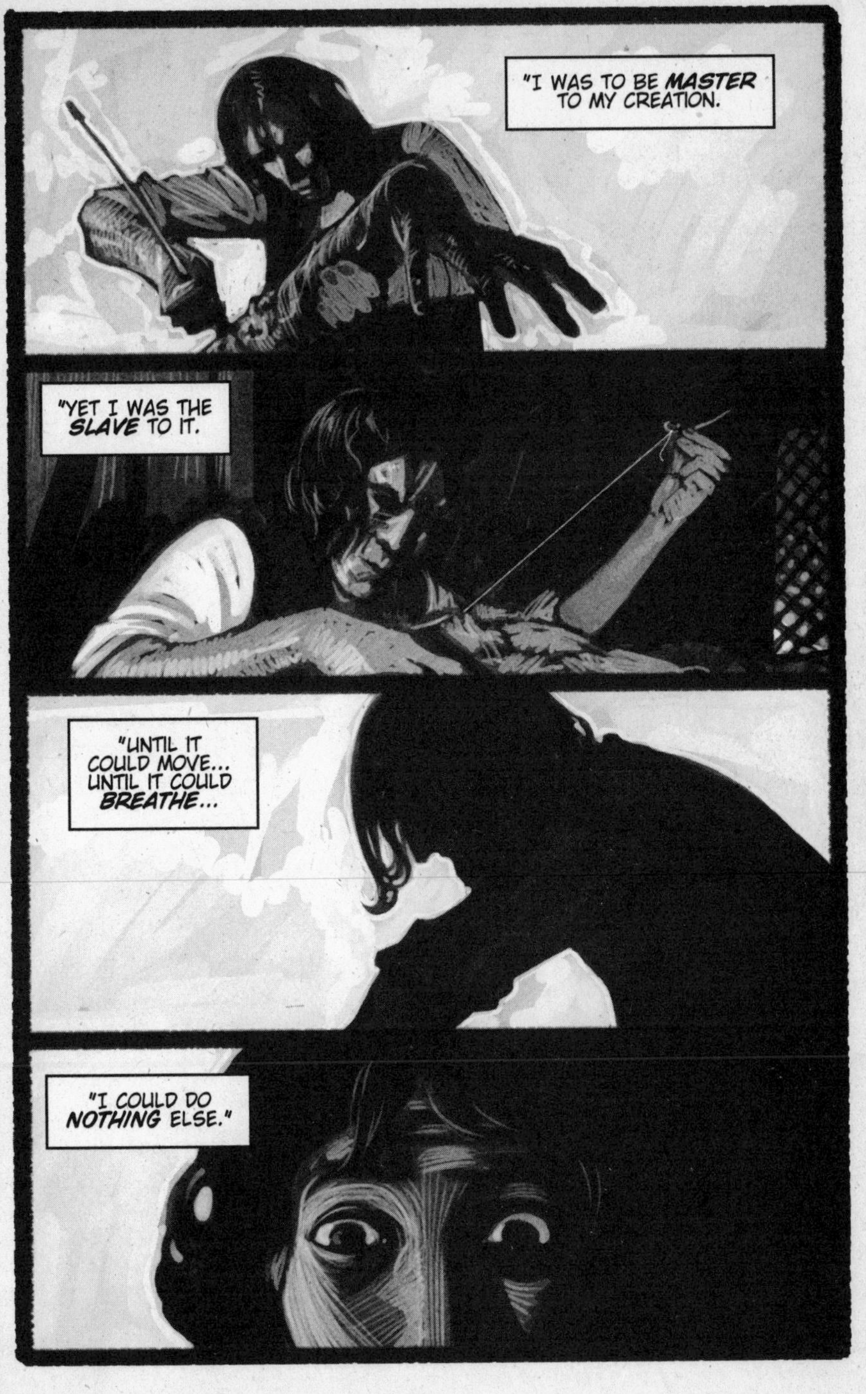
"I WAS TO BE MASTER TO MY CREATION.
"YET I WAS THE SLAVE TO IT.
"UNTIL IT COULD MOVE... UNTIL IT COULD BREATHE...
"I COULD DO NOTHING ELSE."

"IT WAS A DREARY NIGHT IN NOVEMBER WHEN I FINISHED.
"I COLLAPSED IN EXHAUSTION.
"ALL I COULD DO THEN WAS WAIT...
"...WAIT TO SEE IF MY CREATION WOULD STIR WITH LIFE."

"I WAITED WITH ANXIOUS *AGONY*.

"THEN... THEN, ITS EYES *OPENED*.

"I HEARD A *DEEP BREATH*... A GULPING BREATH...

"...AND MY CREATION... MY *PERFECT* CREATION...

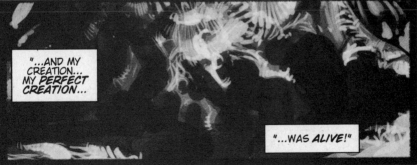

"...WAS *ALIVE!*"

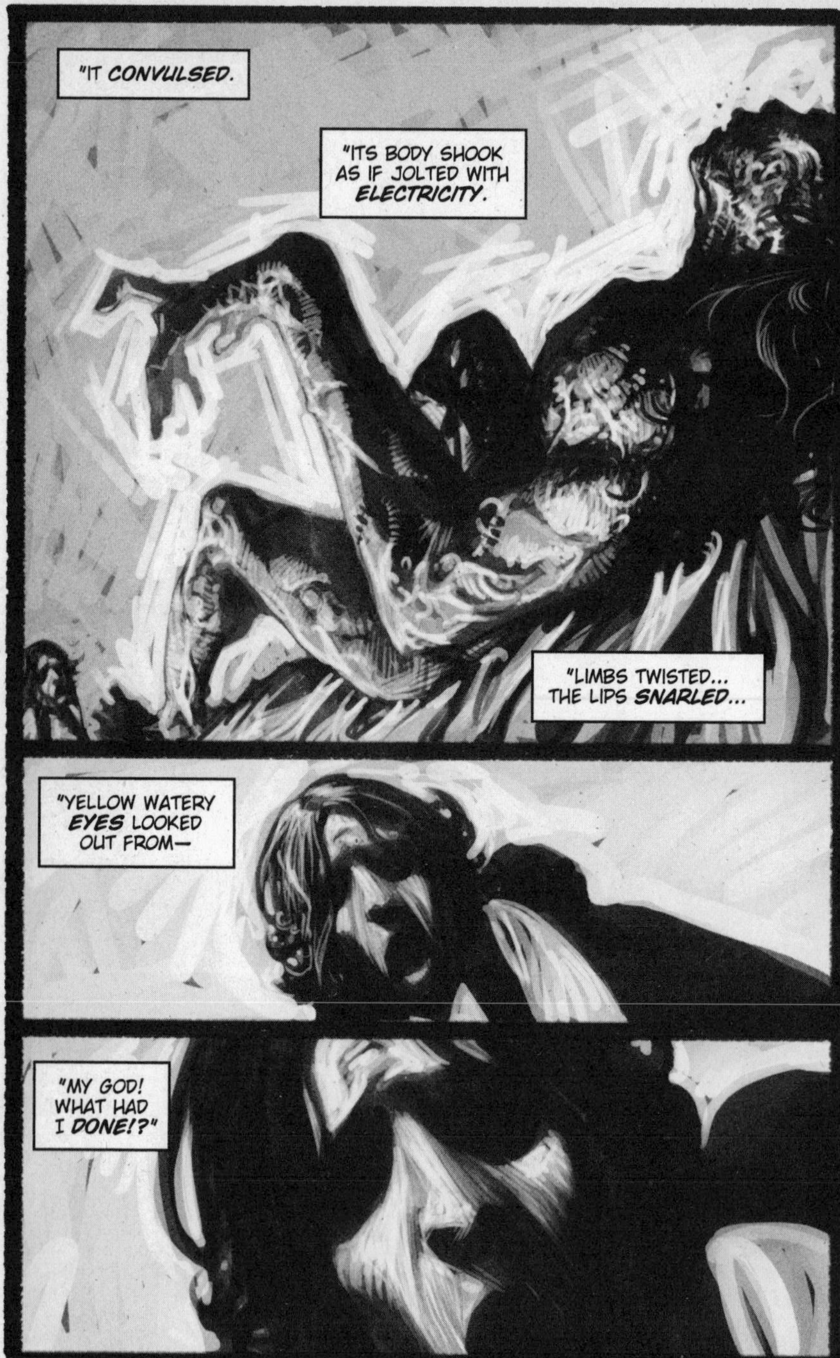
"IT CONVULSED.
"ITS BODY SHOOK AS IF JOLTED WITH ELECTRICITY.
"LIMBS TWISTED... THE LIPS SNARLED...
"YELLOW WATERY EYES LOOKED OUT FROM—
"MY GOD! WHAT HAD I DONE!?"

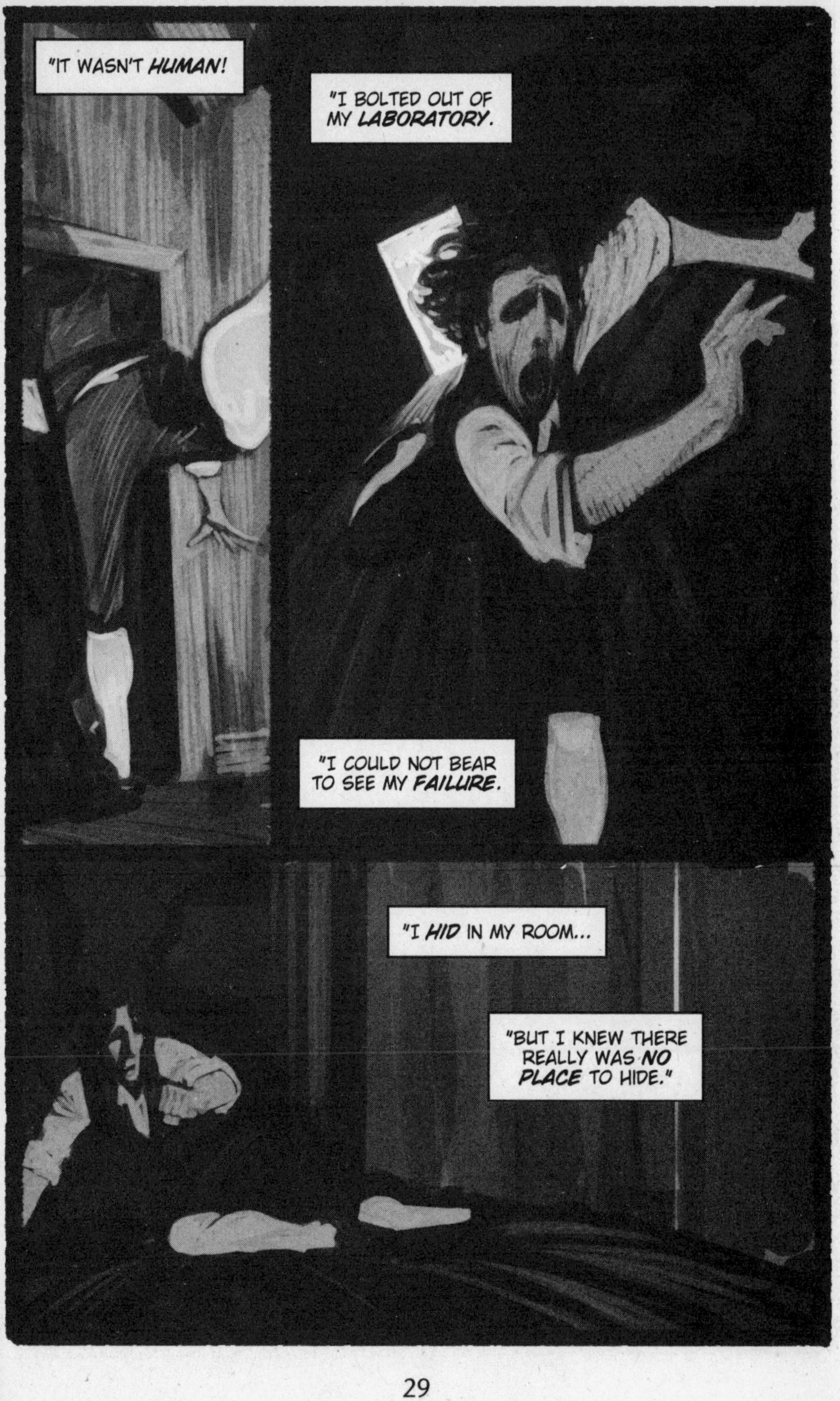
"IT WASN'T HUMAN!
"I BOLTED OUT OF MY LABORATORY.
"I COULD NOT BEAR TO SEE MY FAILURE.
"I HID IN MY ROOM...
"BUT I KNEW THERE REALLY WAS NO PLACE TO HIDE."

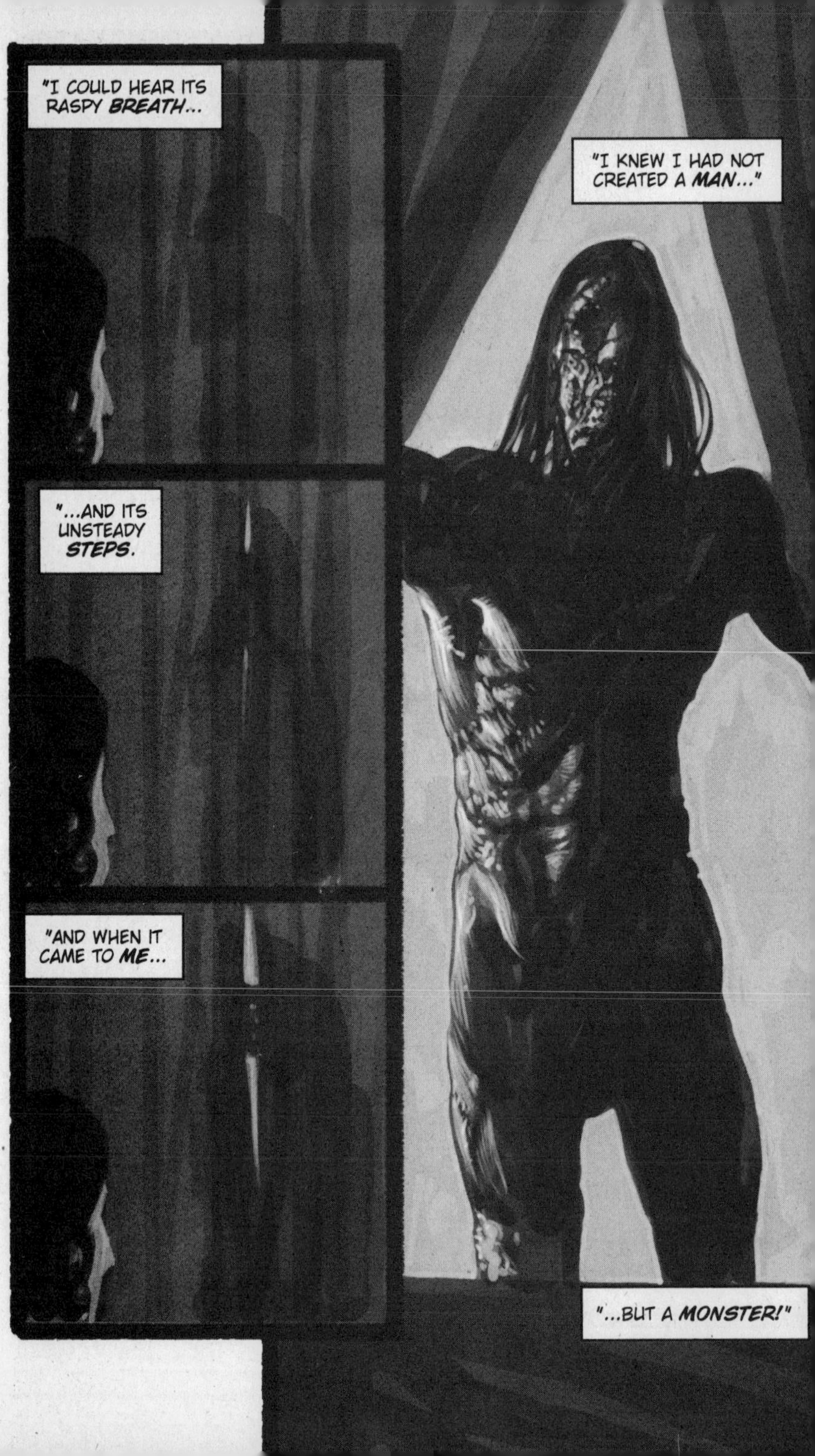
"I COULD HEAR ITS RASPY BREATH...
"I KNEW I HAD NOT CREATED A MAN..."
"...AND ITS UNSTEADY STEPS.
"AND WHEN IT CAME TO ME...
"...BUT A MONSTER!"

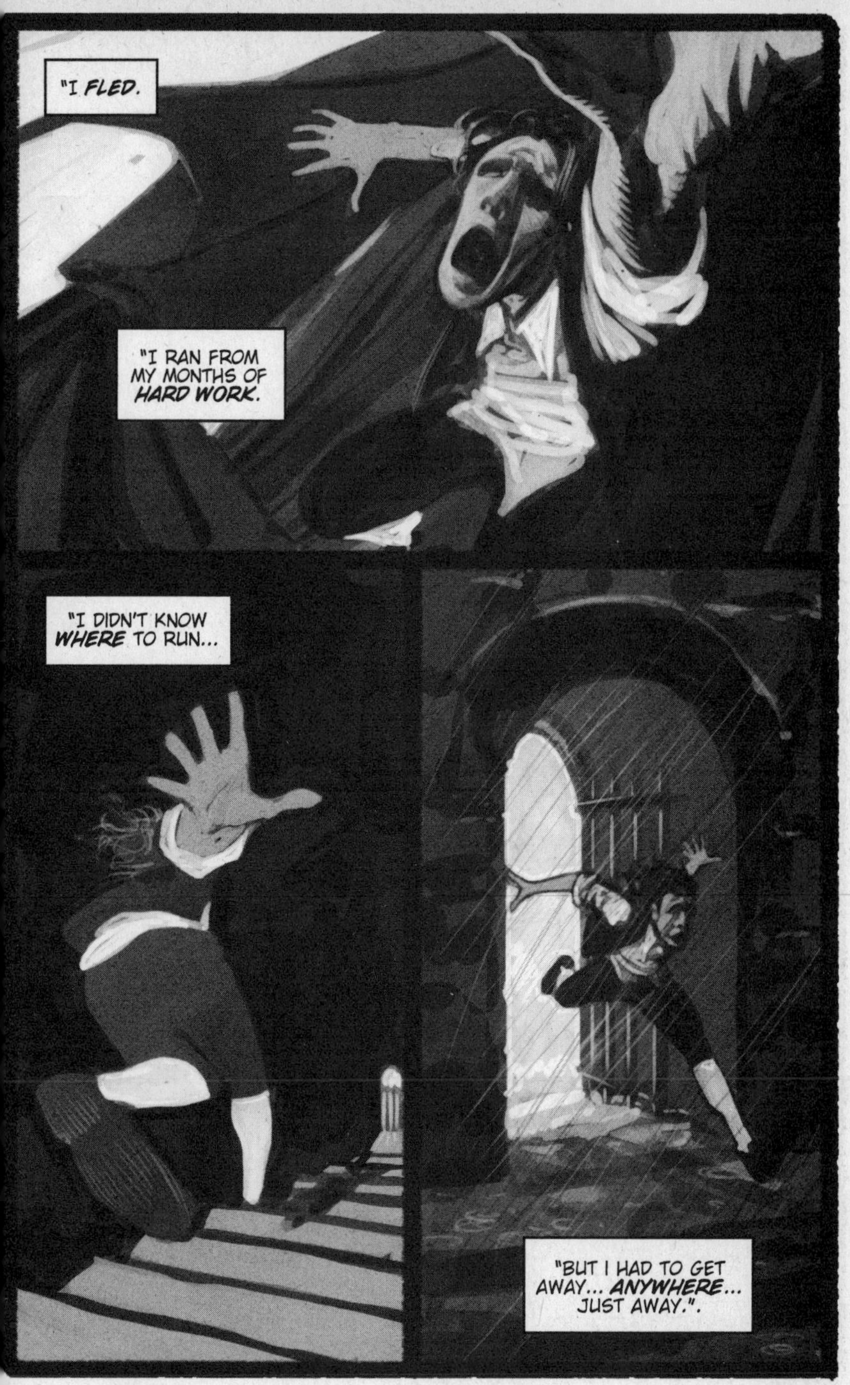
"I *FLED.*
"I RAN FROM MY MONTHS OF *HARD WORK.*
"I DIDN'T KNOW *WHERE* TO RUN...
"BUT I HAD TO GET AWAY... *ANYWHERE*... JUST AWAY.".

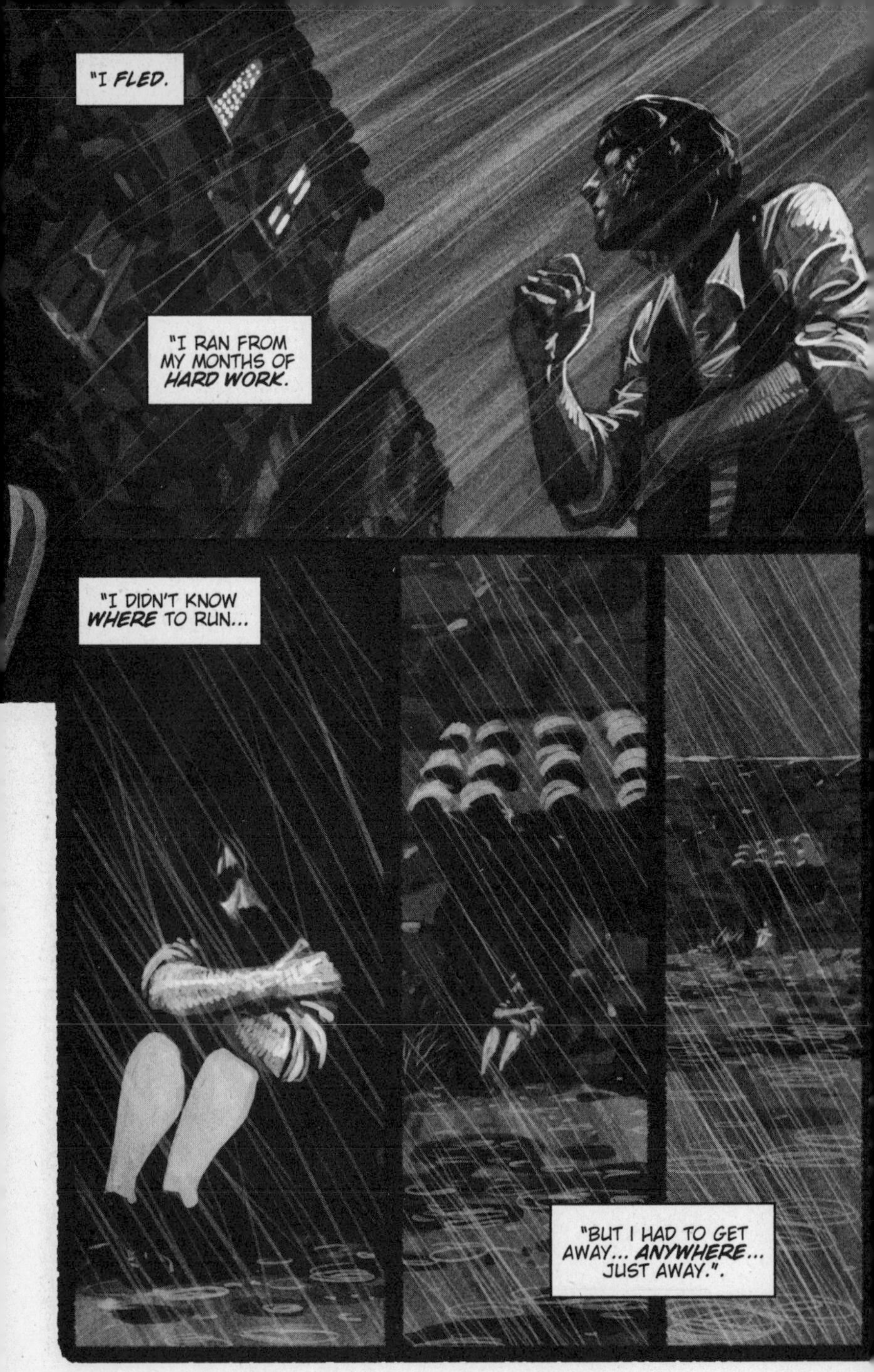
"I FLED.
"I RAN FROM MY MONTHS OF HARD WORK.
"I DIDN'T KNOW WHERE TO RUN...
"BUT I HAD TO GET AWAY... ANYWHERE... JUST AWAY.".

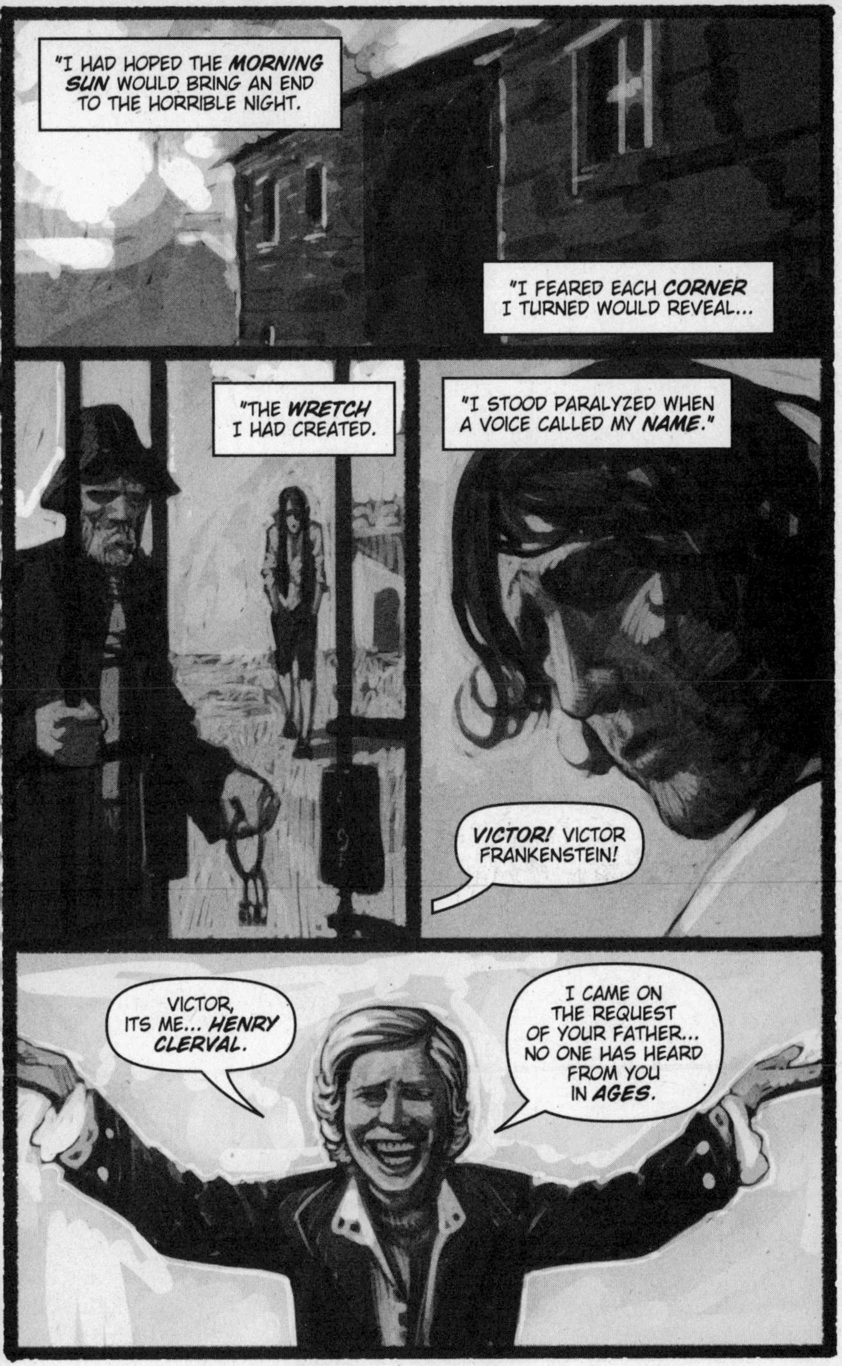
"I HAD HOPED THE MORNING SUN WOULD BRING AN END TO THE HORRIBLE NIGHT.
"I FEARED EACH CORNER I TURNED WOULD REVEAL...
"THE WRETCH I HAD CREATED.
"I STOOD PARALYZED WHEN A VOICE CALLED MY NAME."
VICTOR! VICTOR FRANKENSTEIN!
VICTOR, ITS ME... HENRY CLERVAL.
I CAME ON THE REQUEST OF YOUR FATHER... NO ONE HAS HEARD FROM YOU IN AGES.

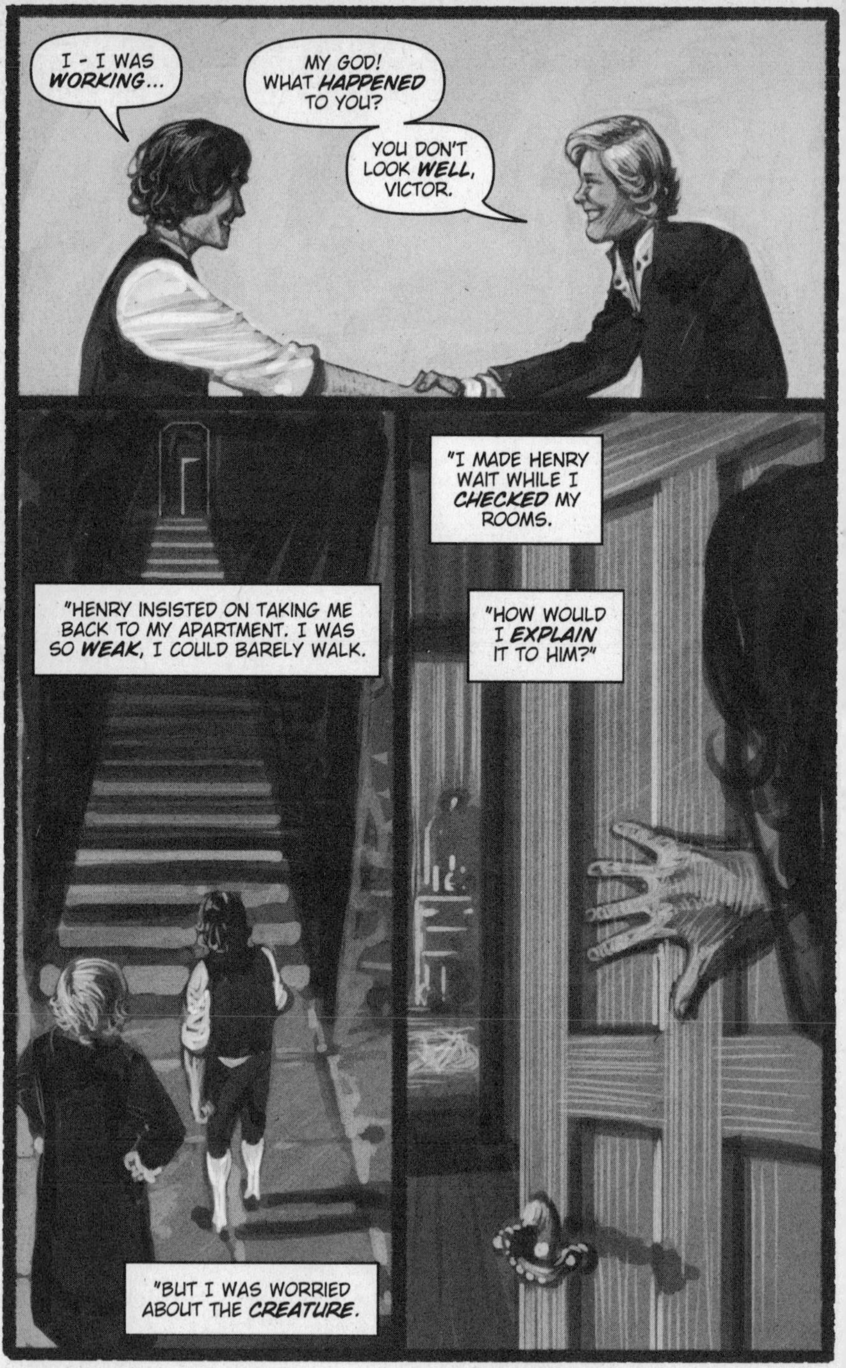
I - I WAS WORKING...
MY GOD! WHAT HAPPENED TO YOU?
YOU DON'T LOOK WELL, VICTOR.
"HENRY INSISTED ON TAKING ME BACK TO MY APARTMENT. I WAS SO WEAK, I COULD BARELY WALK.
"BUT I WAS WORRIED ABOUT THE CREATURE.
"I MADE HENRY WAIT WHILE I CHECKED MY ROOMS.
"HOW WOULD I EXPLAIN IT TO HIM?"

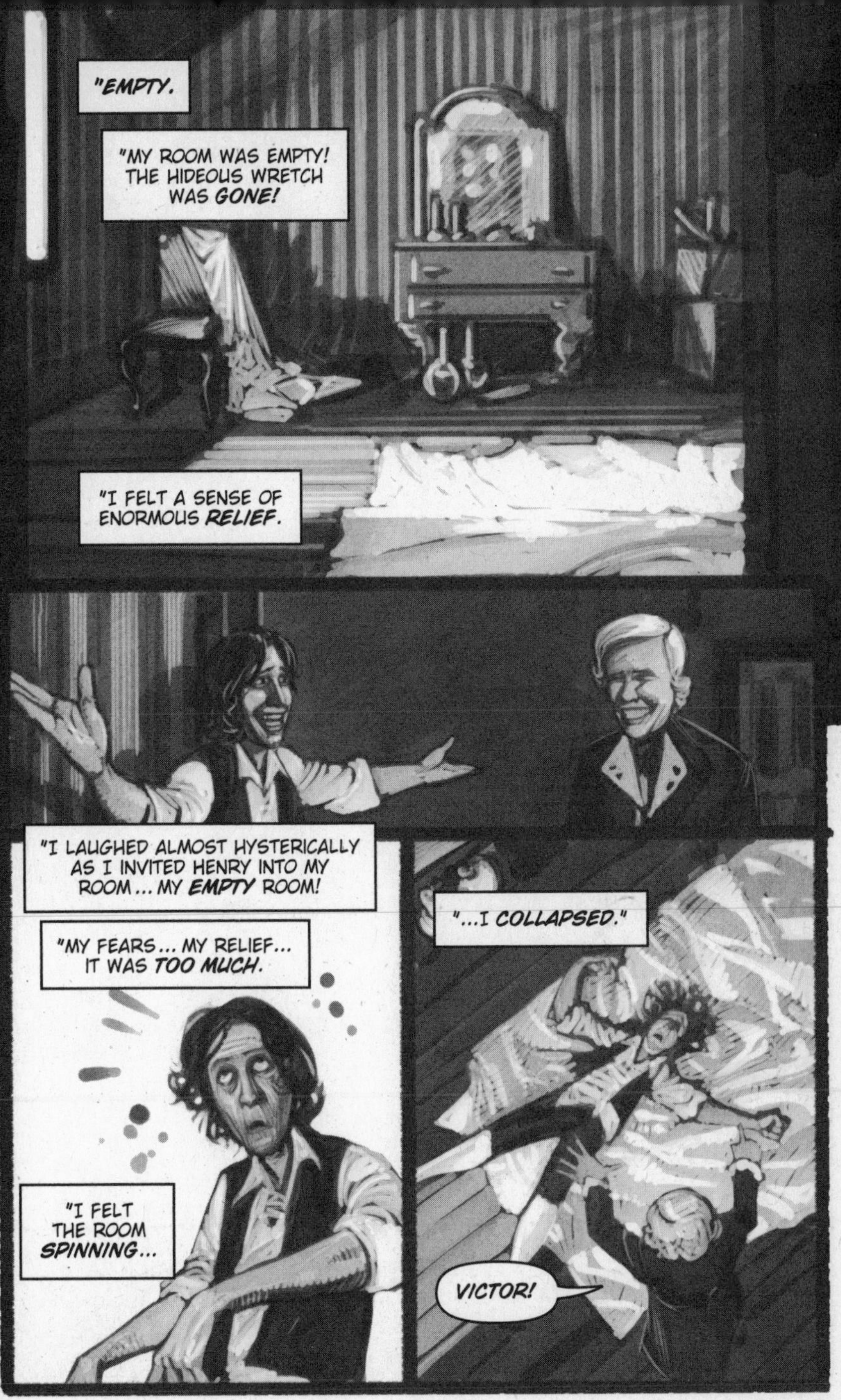
"EMPTY.
"MY ROOM WAS EMPTY! THE HIDEOUS WRETCH WAS GONE!
"I FELT A SENSE OF ENORMOUS RELIEF.
"I LAUGHED ALMOST HYSTERICALLY AS I INVITED HENRY INTO MY ROOM... MY EMPTY ROOM!
"MY FEARS... MY RELIEF... IT WAS TOO MUCH.
"I FELT THE ROOM SPINNING...
"...I COLLAPSED."
VICTOR!

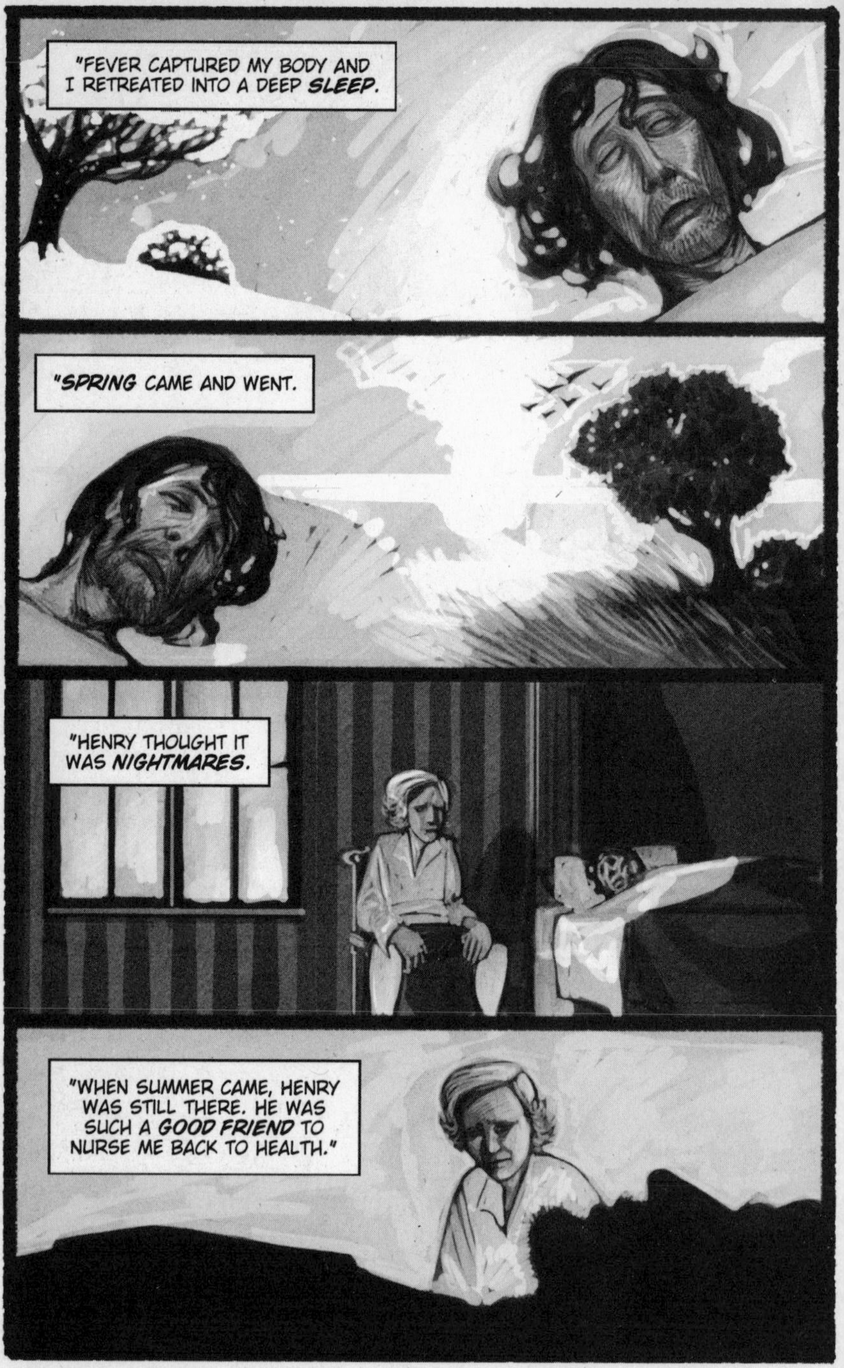
"FEVER CAPTURED MY BODY AND I RETREATED INTO A DEEP SLEEP.
"SPRING CAME AND WENT.
"HENRY THOUGHT IT WAS NIGHTMARES.
"WHEN SUMMER CAME, HENRY WAS STILL THERE. HE WAS SUCH A GOOD FRIEND TO NURSE ME BACK TO HEALTH."

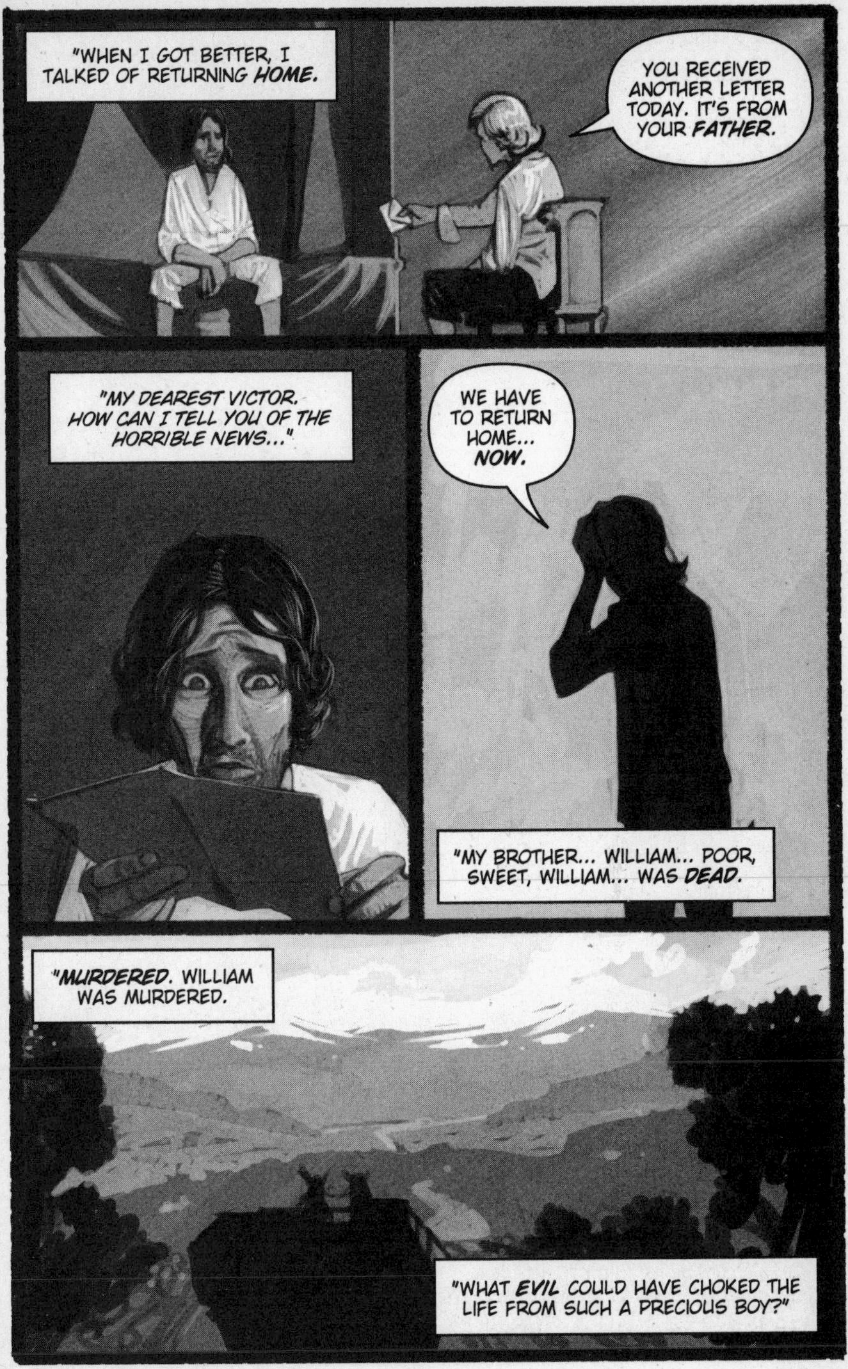
"WHEN I GOT BETTER, I TALKED OF RETURNING *HOME*.
YOU RECEIVED ANOTHER LETTER TODAY. IT'S FROM YOUR *FATHER*.
"MY DEAREST VICTOR. HOW CAN I TELL YOU OF THE HORRIBLE NEWS..."
WE HAVE TO RETURN HOME... *NOW*.
"MY BROTHER... WILLIAM... POOR, SWEET, WILLIAM... WAS *DEAD*.
"*MURDERED*. WILLIAM WAS MURDERED.
"WHAT *EVIL* COULD HAVE CHOKED THE LIFE FROM SUCH A PRECIOUS BOY?"

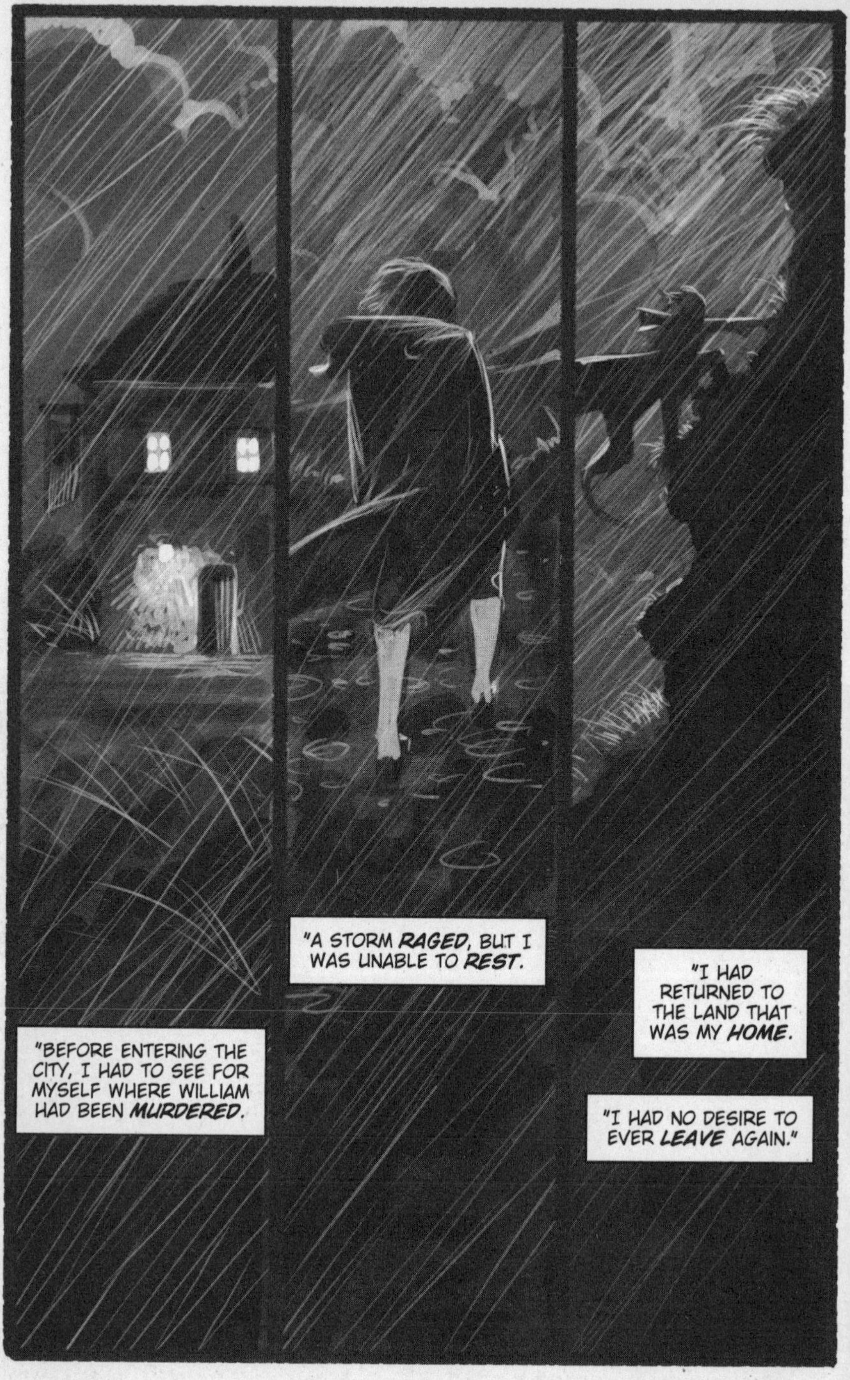
"BEFORE ENTERING THE CITY, I HAD TO SEE FOR MYSELF WHERE WILLIAM HAD BEEN MURDERED.
"A STORM RAGED, BUT I WAS UNABLE TO REST.
"I HAD RETURNED TO THE LAND THAT WAS MY HOME.
"I HAD NO DESIRE TO EVER LEAVE AGAIN."

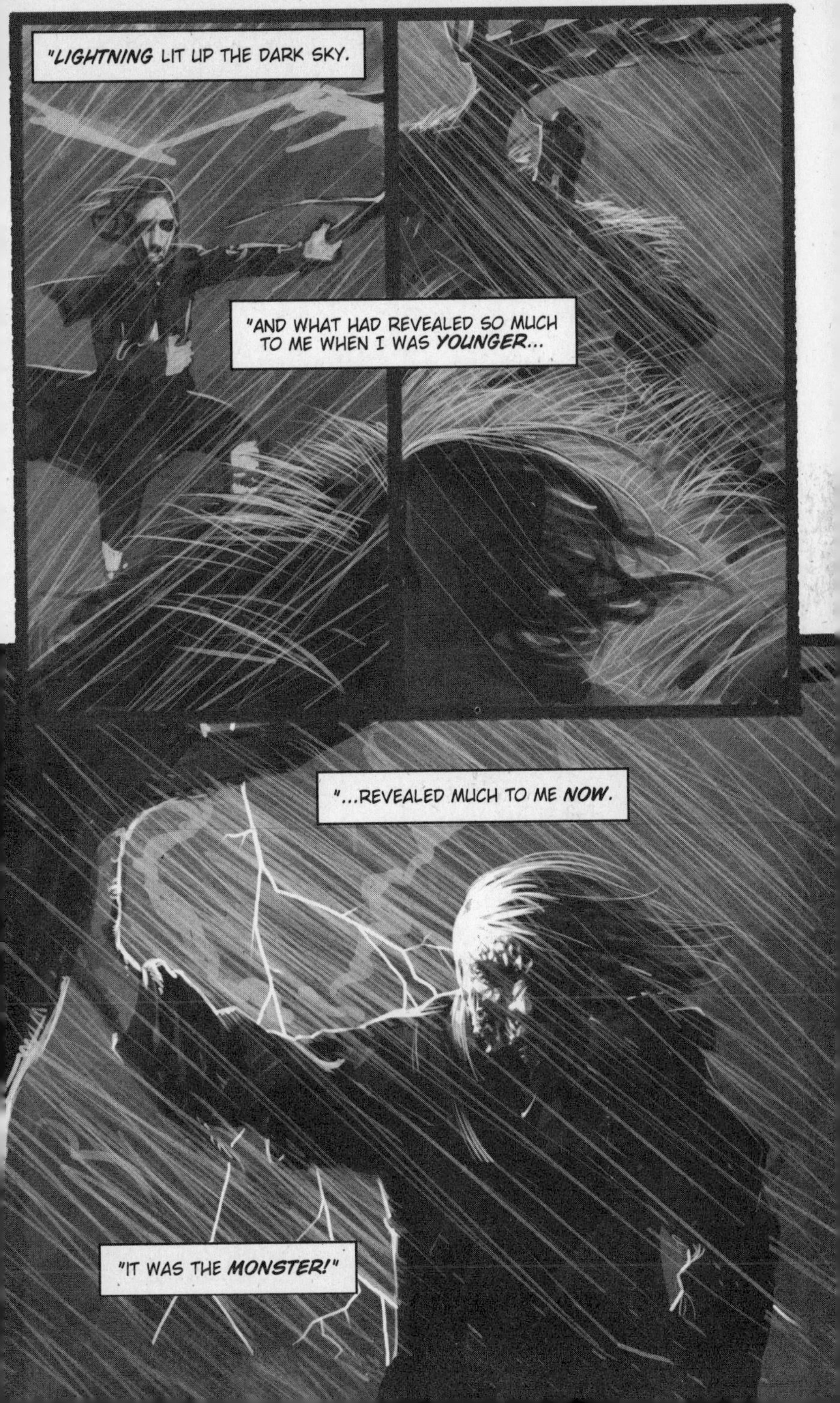
"LIGHTNING LIT UP THE DARK SKY.
"AND WHAT HAD REVEALED SO MUCH TO ME WHEN I WAS YOUNGER...
"...REVEALED MUCH TO ME NOW.
"IT WAS THE MONSTER!"

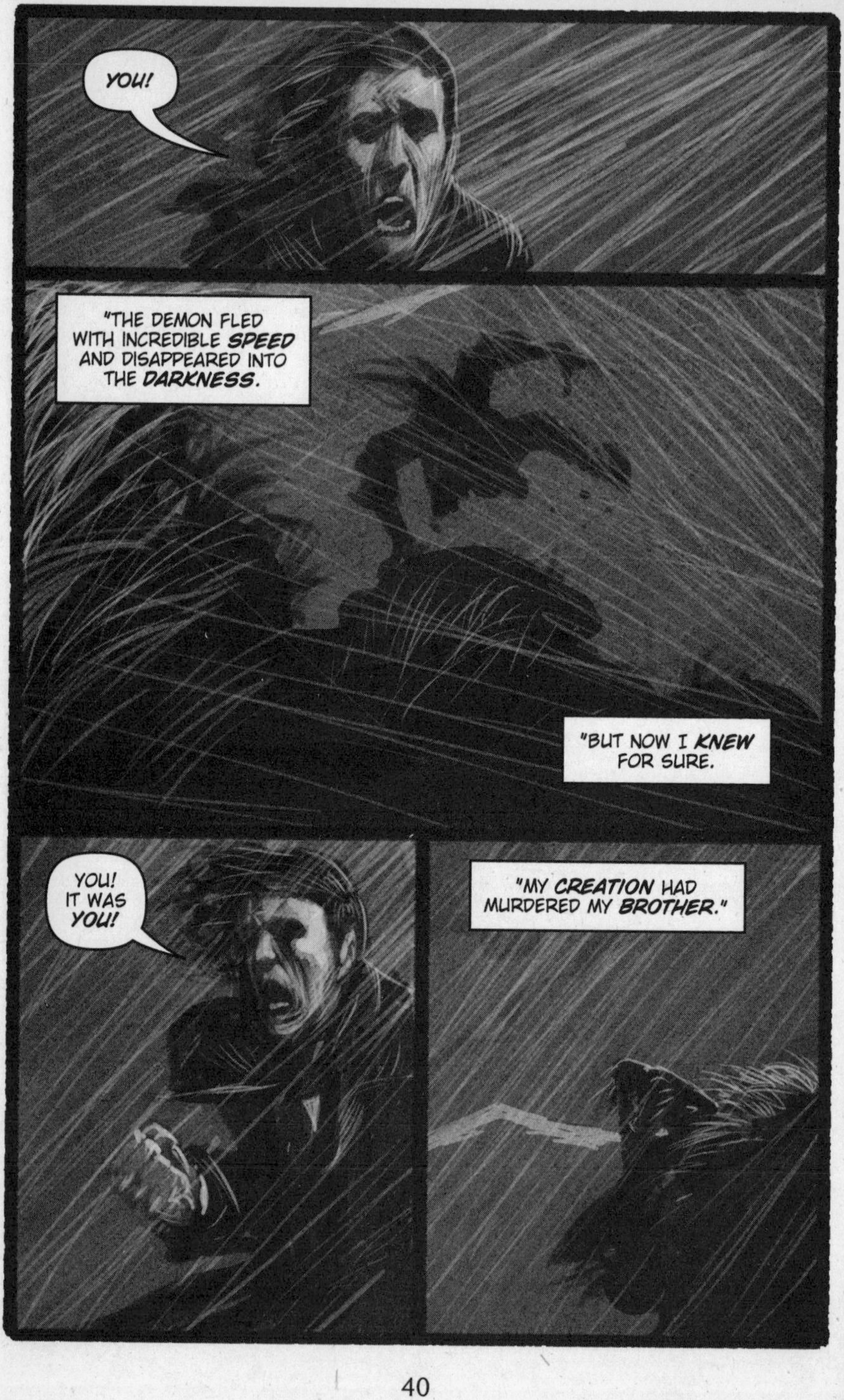
YOU!
"THE DEMON FLED WITH INCREDIBLE SPEED AND DISAPPEARED INTO THE DARKNESS.
"BUT NOW I KNEW FOR SURE.
YOU! IT WAS YOU!
"MY CREATION HAD MURDERED MY BROTHER."

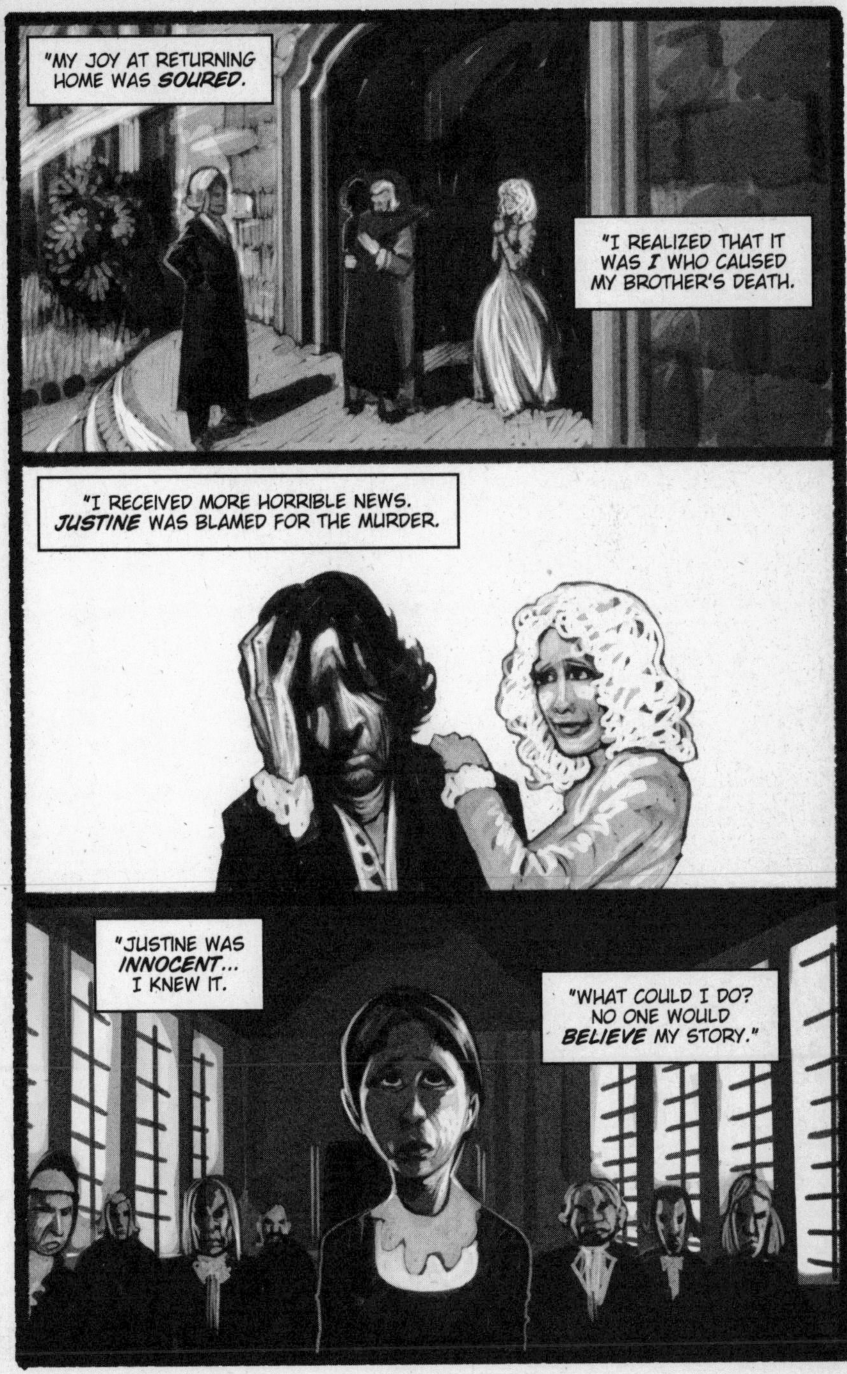
"MY JOY AT RETURNING HOME WAS SOURED.
"I REALIZED THAT IT WAS I WHO CAUSED MY BROTHER'S DEATH.
"I RECEIVED MORE HORRIBLE NEWS. JUSTINE WAS BLAMED FOR THE MURDER.
"JUSTINE WAS INNOCENT... I KNEW IT.
"WHAT COULD I DO? NO ONE WOULD BELIEVE MY STORY."

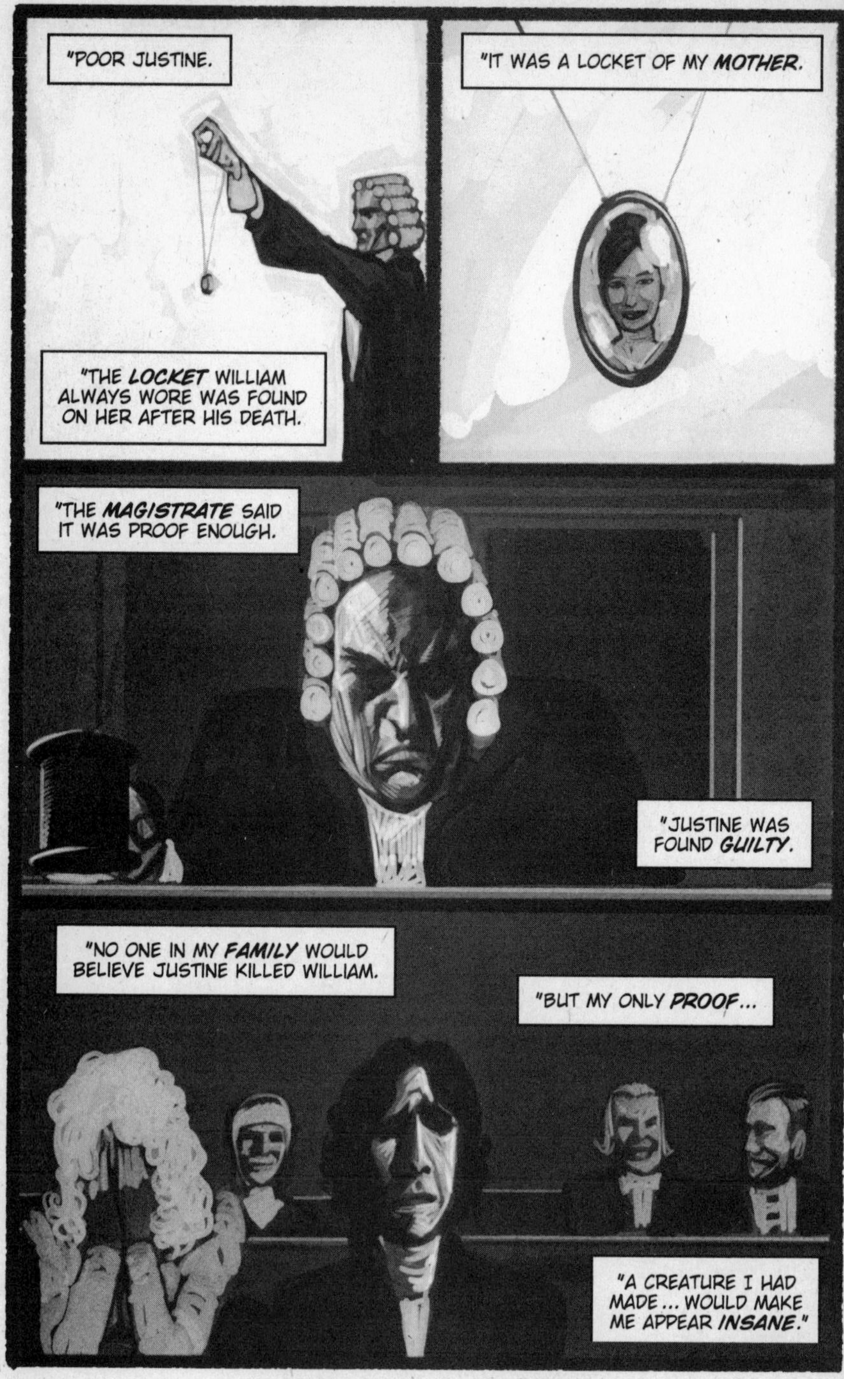
"POOR JUSTINE.
"THE LOCKET WILLIAM ALWAYS WORE WAS FOUND ON HER AFTER HIS DEATH.
"IT WAS A LOCKET OF MY MOTHER.
"THE MAGISTRATE SAID IT WAS PROOF ENOUGH.
"JUSTINE WAS FOUND GUILTY.
"NO ONE IN MY FAMILY WOULD BELIEVE JUSTINE KILLED WILLIAM.
"BUT MY ONLY PROOF...
"A CREATURE I HAD MADE ... WOULD MAKE ME APPEAR INSANE."

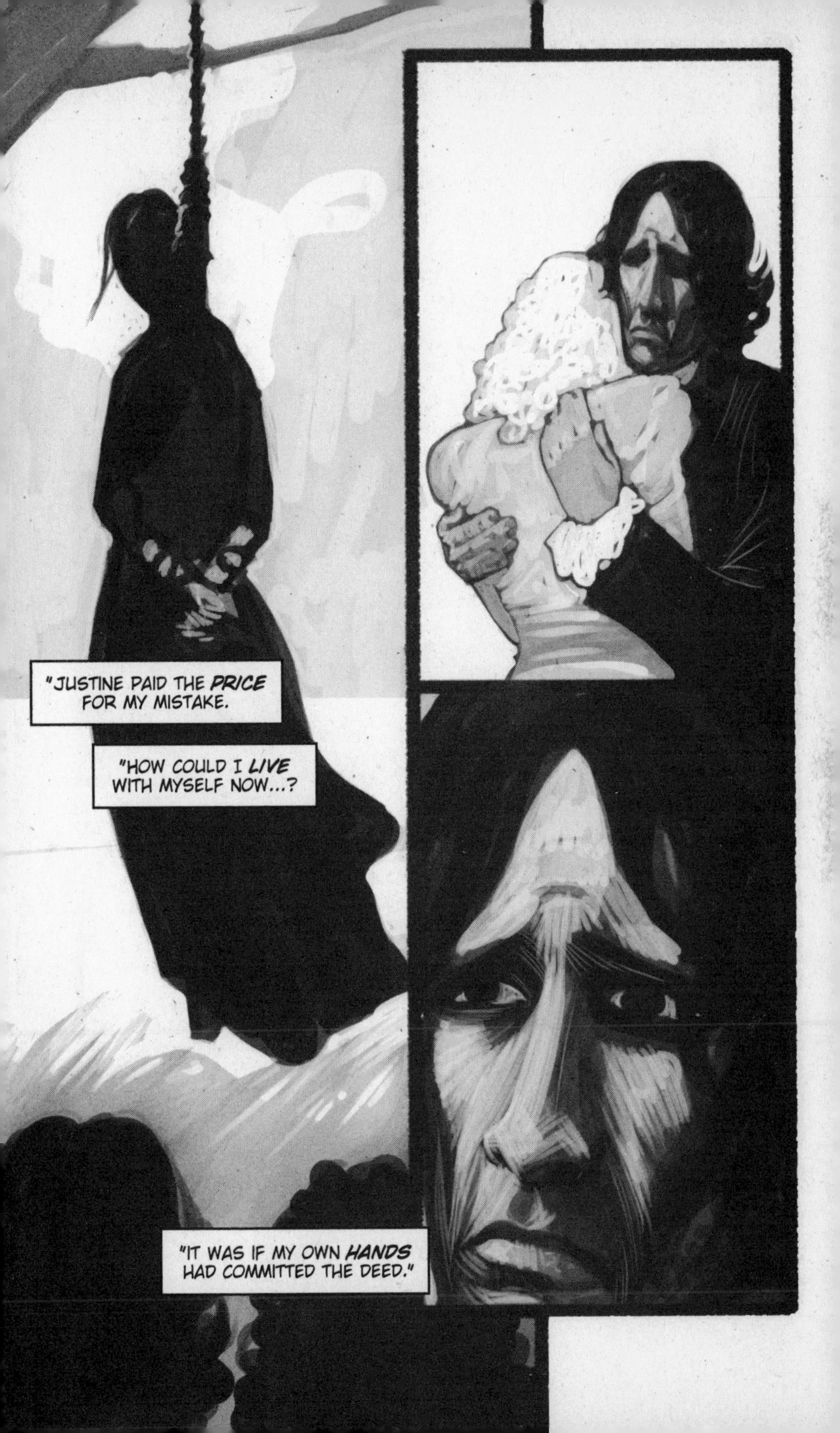
"JUSTINE PAID THE PRICE FOR MY MISTAKE.
"HOW COULD I LIVE WITH MYSELF NOW...?
"IT WAS IF MY OWN HANDS HAD COMMITTED THE DEED."

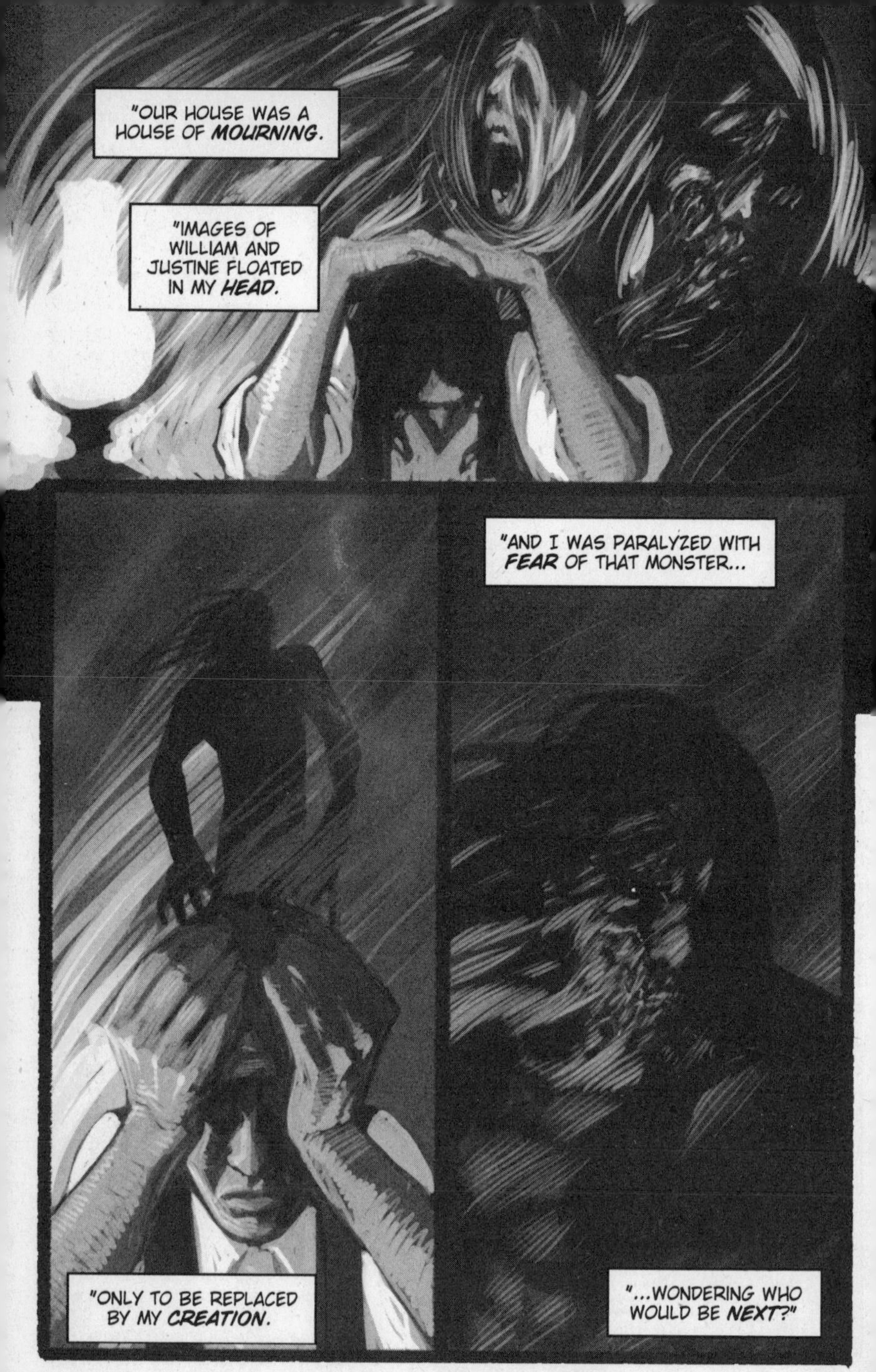
"OUR HOUSE WAS A HOUSE OF MOURNING.
"IMAGES OF WILLIAM AND JUSTINE FLOATED IN MY HEAD.
"ONLY TO BE REPLACED BY MY CREATION.
"AND I WAS PARALYZED WITH FEAR OF THAT MONSTER...
"...WONDERING WHO WOULD BE NEXT?"

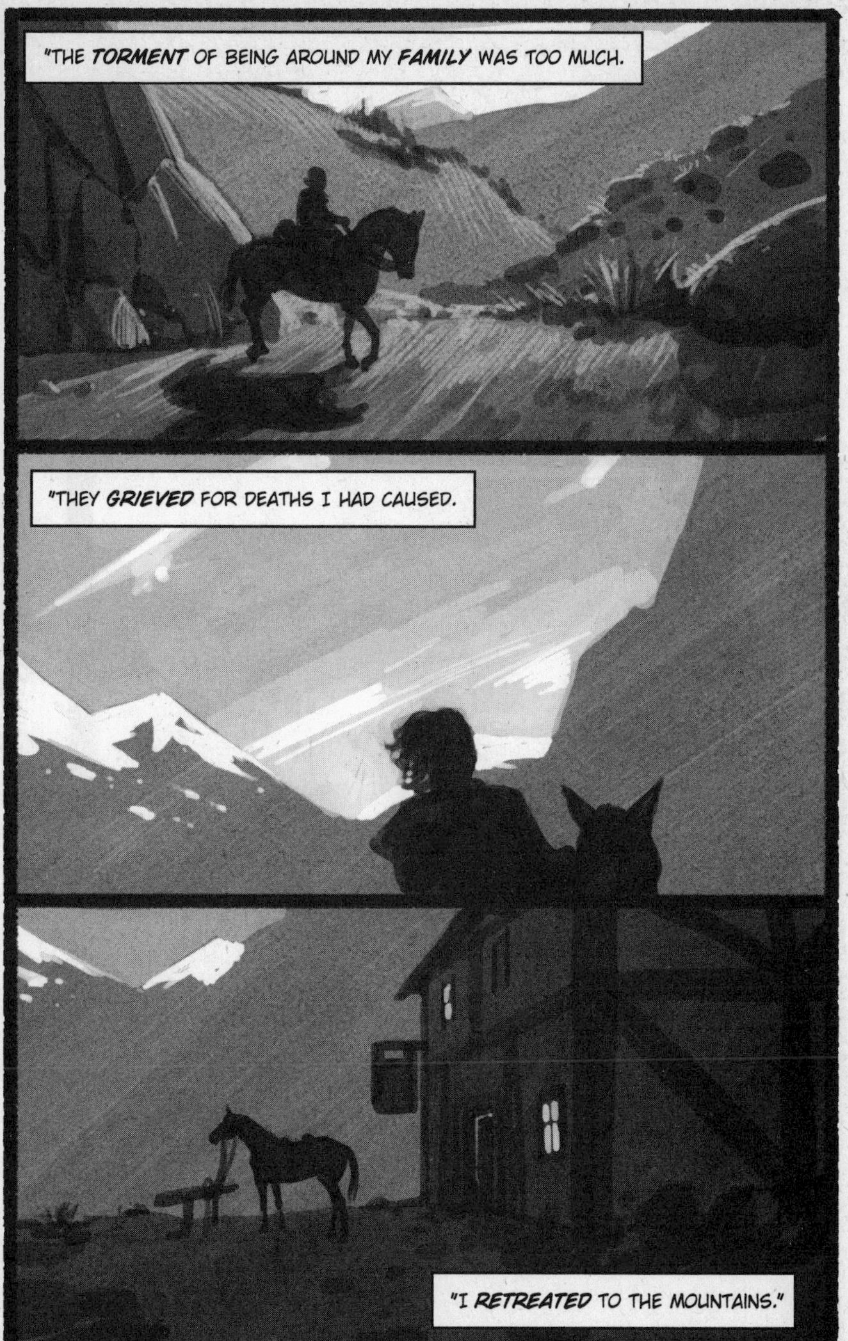
"THE TORMENT OF BEING AROUND MY FAMILY WAS TOO MUCH.
"THEY GRIEVED FOR DEATHS I HAD CAUSED.
"I RETREATED TO THE MOUNTAINS."

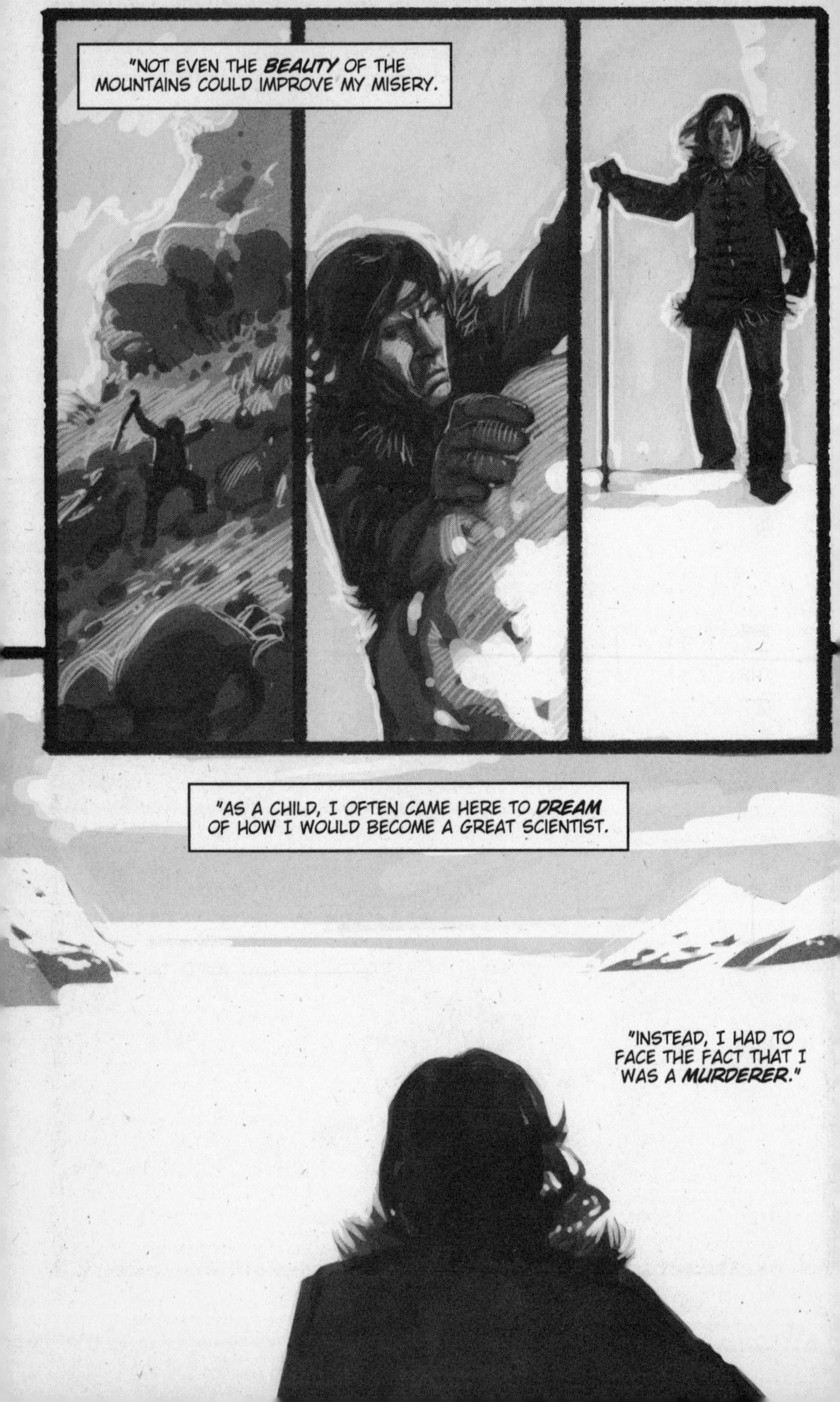
"NOT EVEN THE BEAUTY OF THE MOUNTAINS COULD IMPROVE MY MISERY.
"AS A CHILD, I OFTEN CAME HERE TO DREAM OF HOW I WOULD BECOME A GREAT SCIENTIST.
"INSTEAD, I HAD TO FACE THE FACT THAT I WAS A MURDERER."

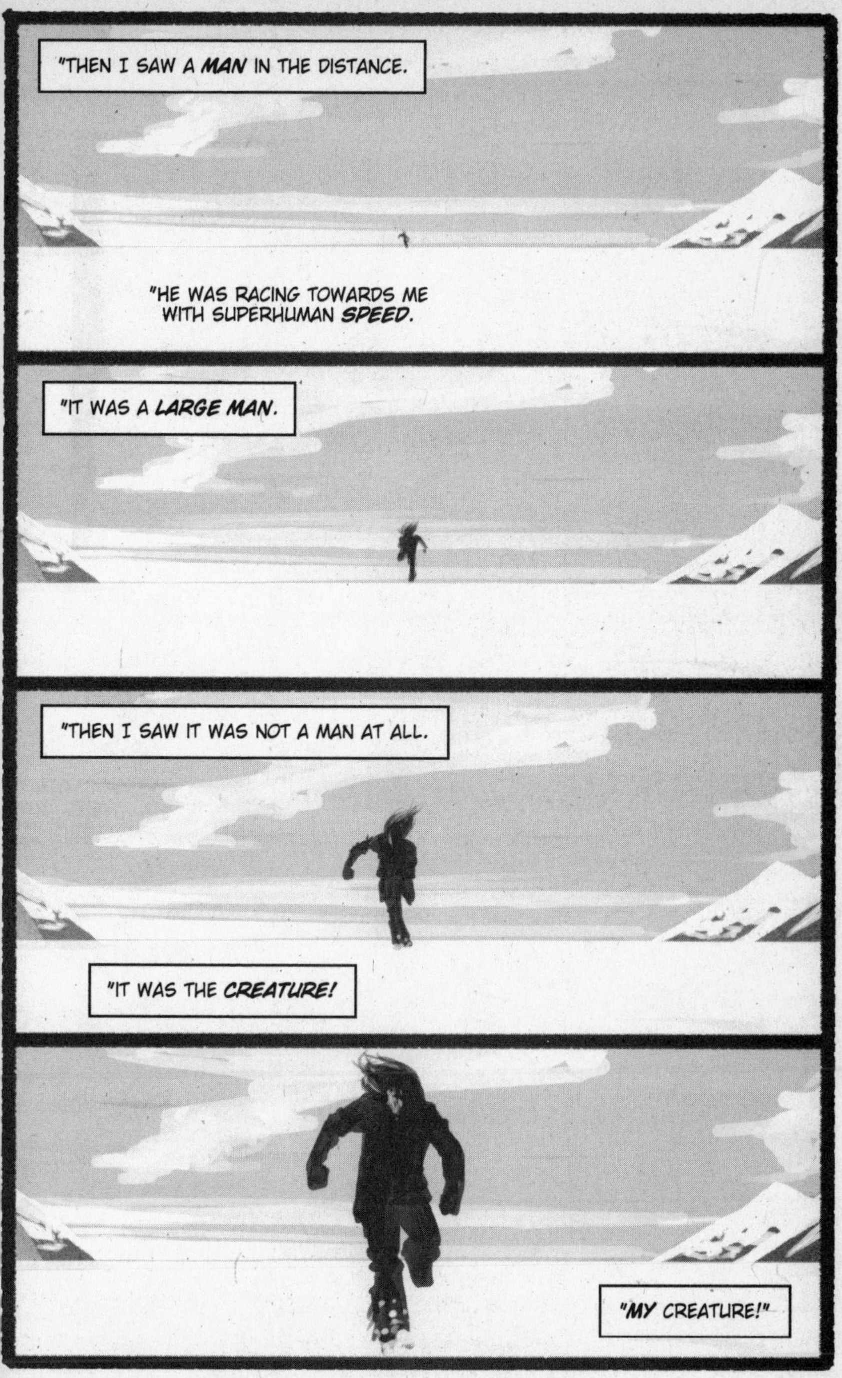
"THEN I SAW A MAN IN THE DISTANCE.
"HE WAS RACING TOWARDS ME WITH SUPERHUMAN SPEED.
"IT WAS A LARGE MAN.
"THEN I SAW IT WAS NOT A MAN AT ALL.
"IT WAS THE CREATURE!
"MY CREATURE!"

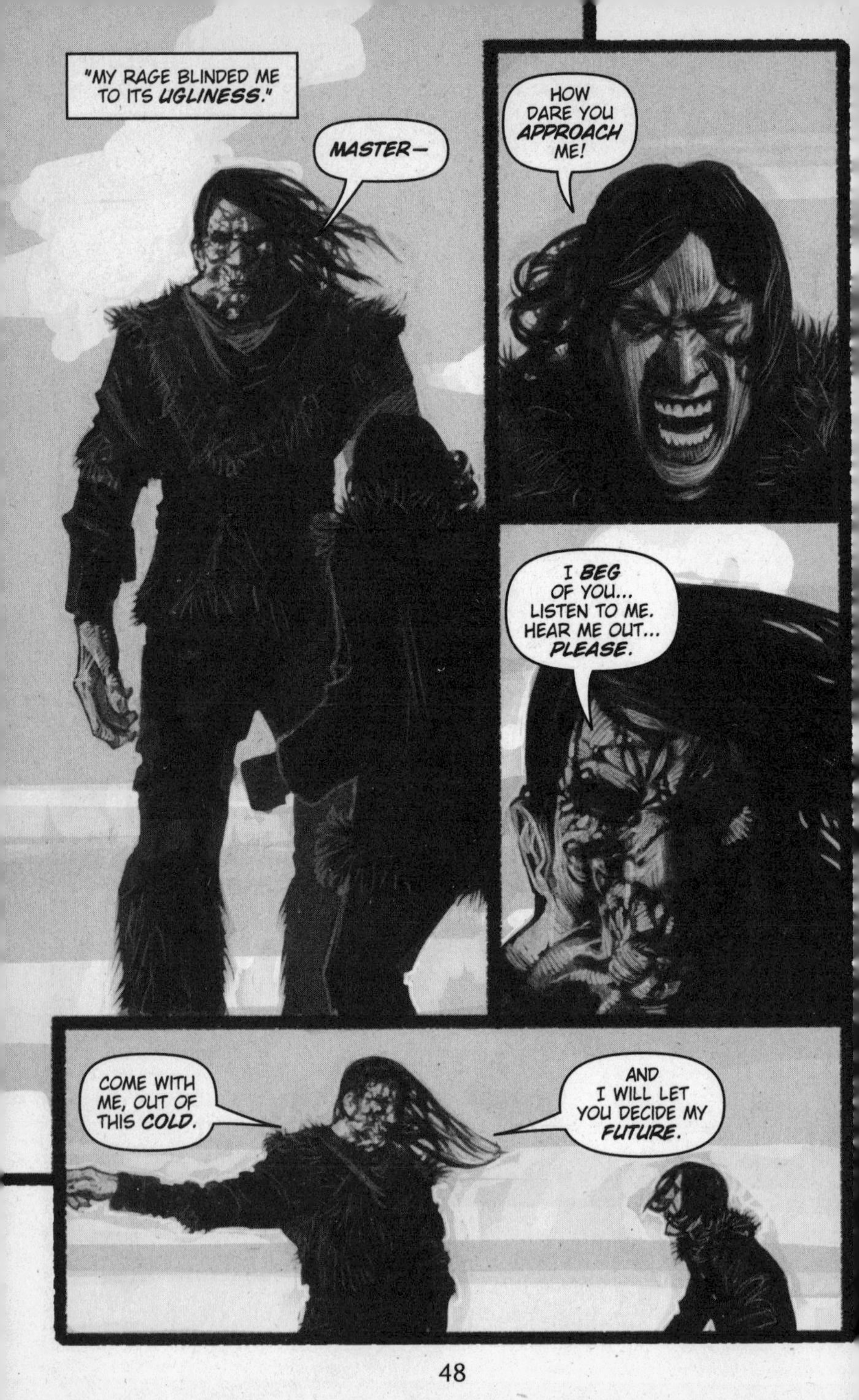
"MY RAGE BLINDED ME TO ITS UGLINESS."
MASTER—
HOW DARE YOU APPROACH ME!
I BEG OF YOU... LISTEN TO ME. HEAR ME OUT... PLEASE.
COME WITH ME, OUT OF THIS COLD.
AND I WILL LET YOU DECIDE MY FUTURE.

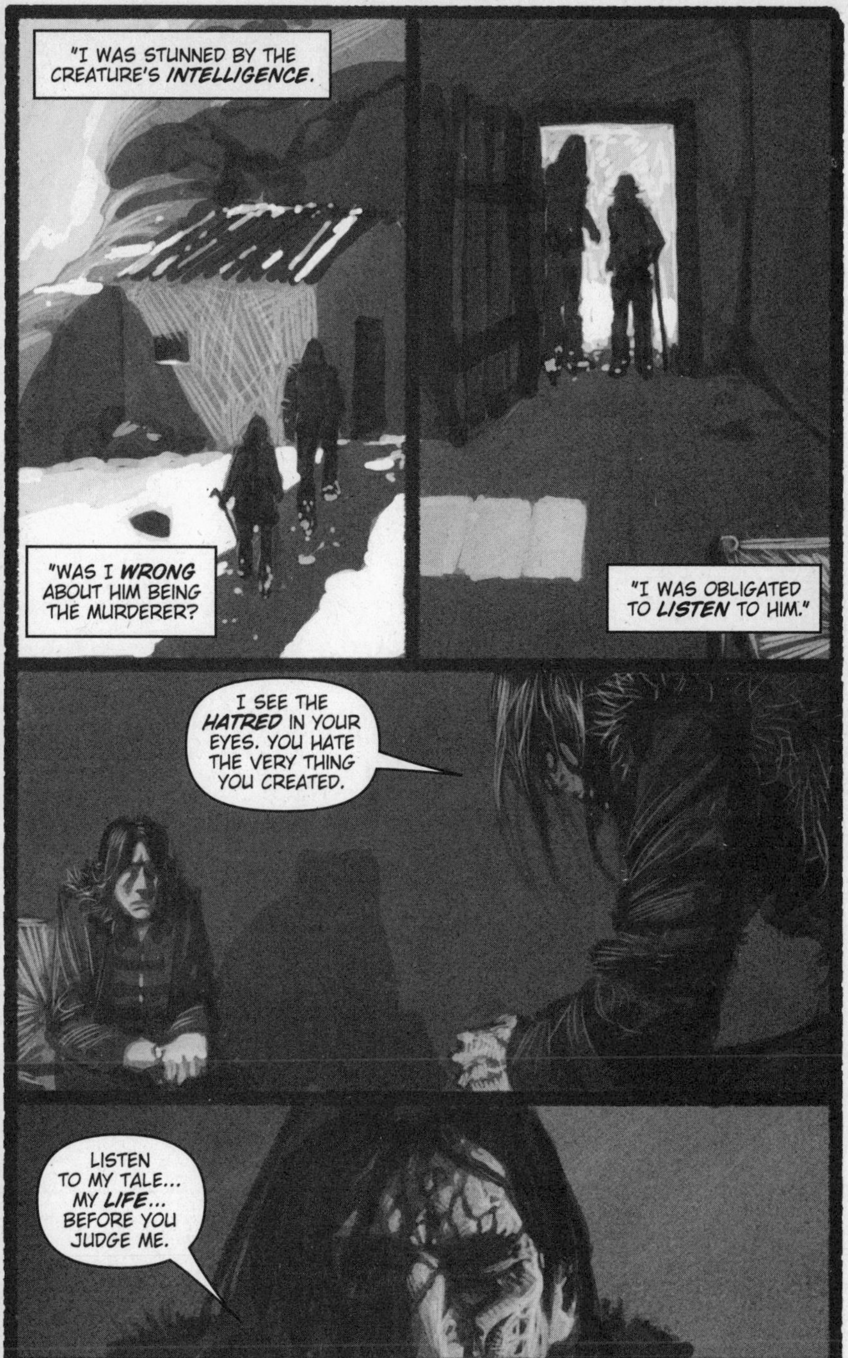
"I WAS STUNNED BY THE CREATURE'S INTELLIGENCE.
"WAS I WRONG ABOUT HIM BEING THE MURDERER?
"I WAS OBLIGATED TO LISTEN TO HIM."
I SEE THE HATRED IN YOUR EYES. YOU HATE THE VERY THING YOU CREATED.
LISTEN TO MY TALE... MY LIFE... BEFORE YOU JUDGE ME.

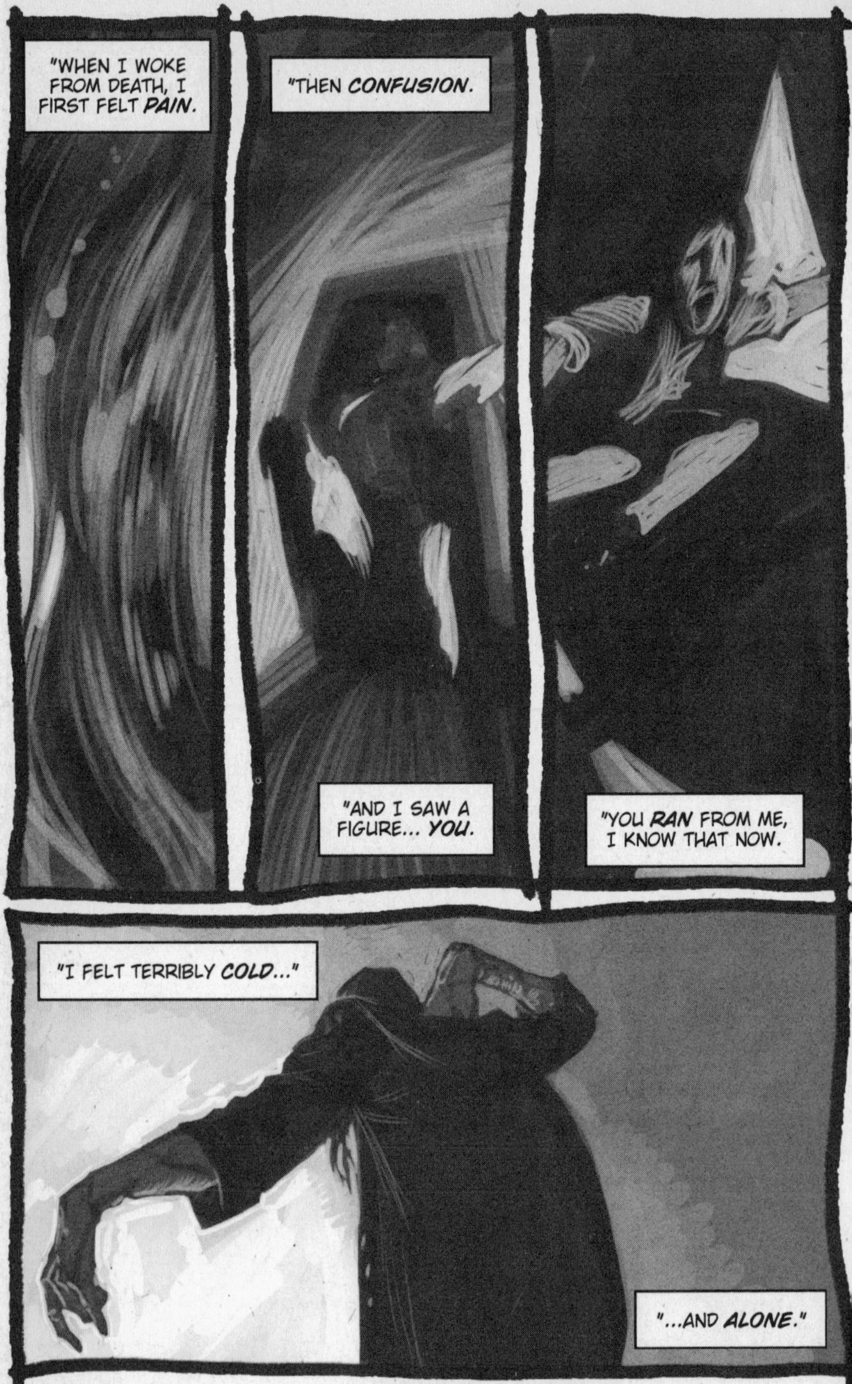
"WHEN I WOKE FROM DEATH, I FIRST FELT PAIN.
"THEN CONFUSION.
"AND I SAW A FIGURE... YOU.
"YOU RAN FROM ME, I KNOW THAT NOW.
"I FELT TERRIBLY COLD..."
"...AND ALONE."

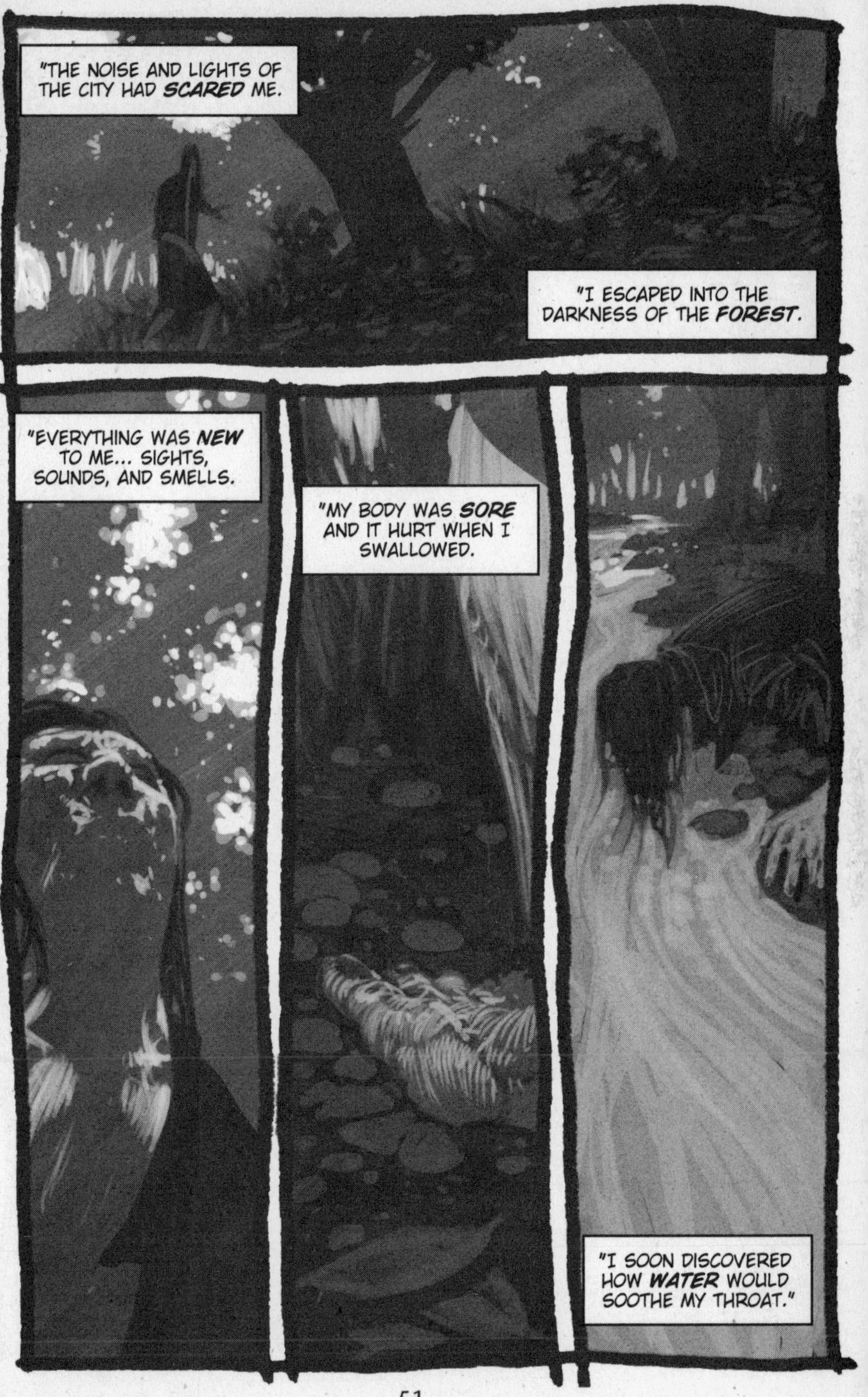
"THE NOISE AND LIGHTS OF THE CITY HAD SCARED ME.
"I ESCAPED INTO THE DARKNESS OF THE FOREST.
"EVERYTHING WAS NEW TO ME... SIGHTS, SOUNDS, AND SMELLS.
"MY BODY WAS SORE AND IT HURT WHEN I SWALLOWED.
"I SOON DISCOVERED HOW WATER WOULD SOOTHE MY THROAT."

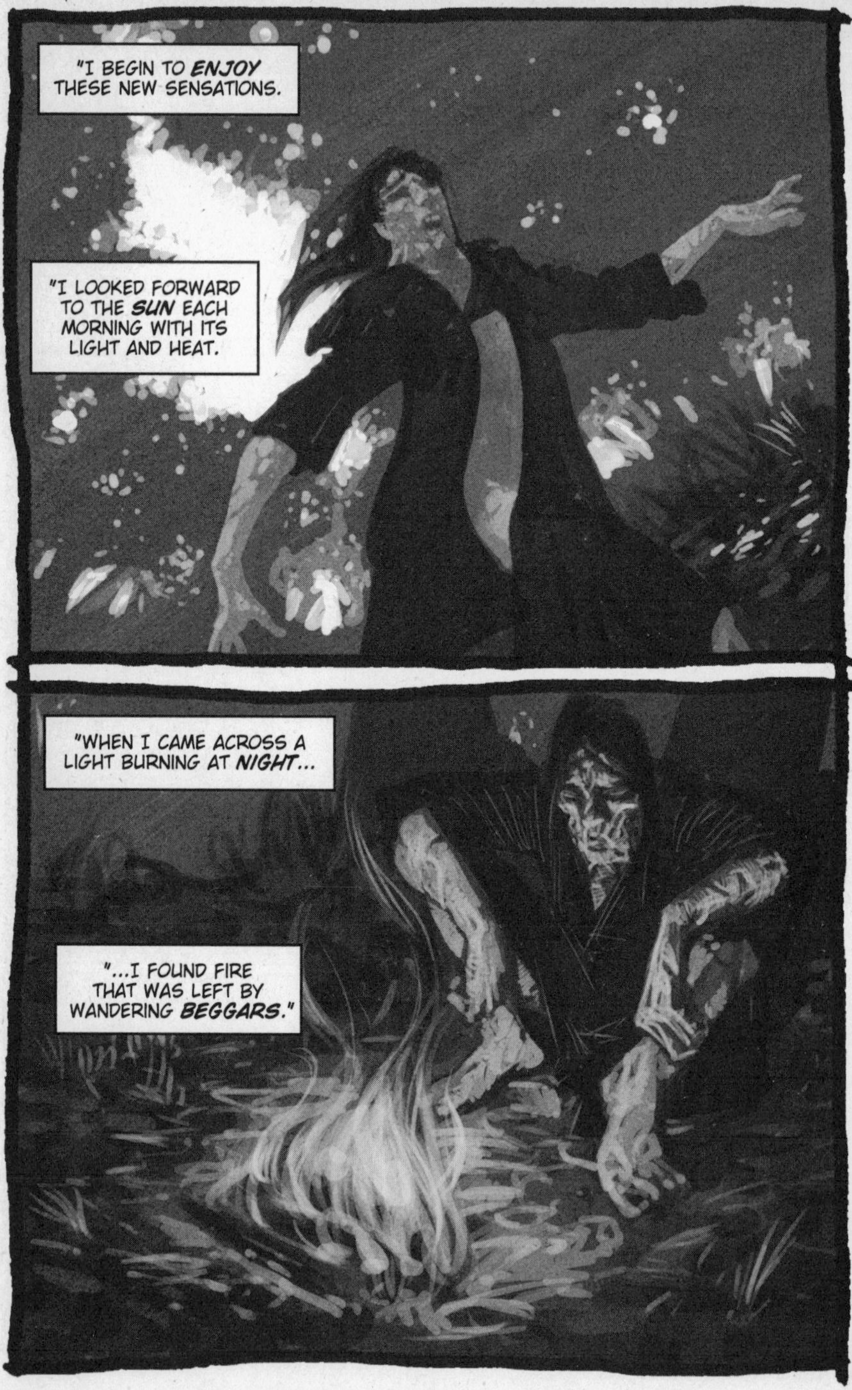
"I BEGIN TO ENJOY THESE NEW SENSATIONS.
"I LOOKED FORWARD TO THE SUN EACH MORNING WITH ITS LIGHT AND HEAT.
"WHEN I CAME ACROSS A LIGHT BURNING AT NIGHT...
"...I FOUND FIRE THAT WAS LEFT BY WANDERING BEGGARS."

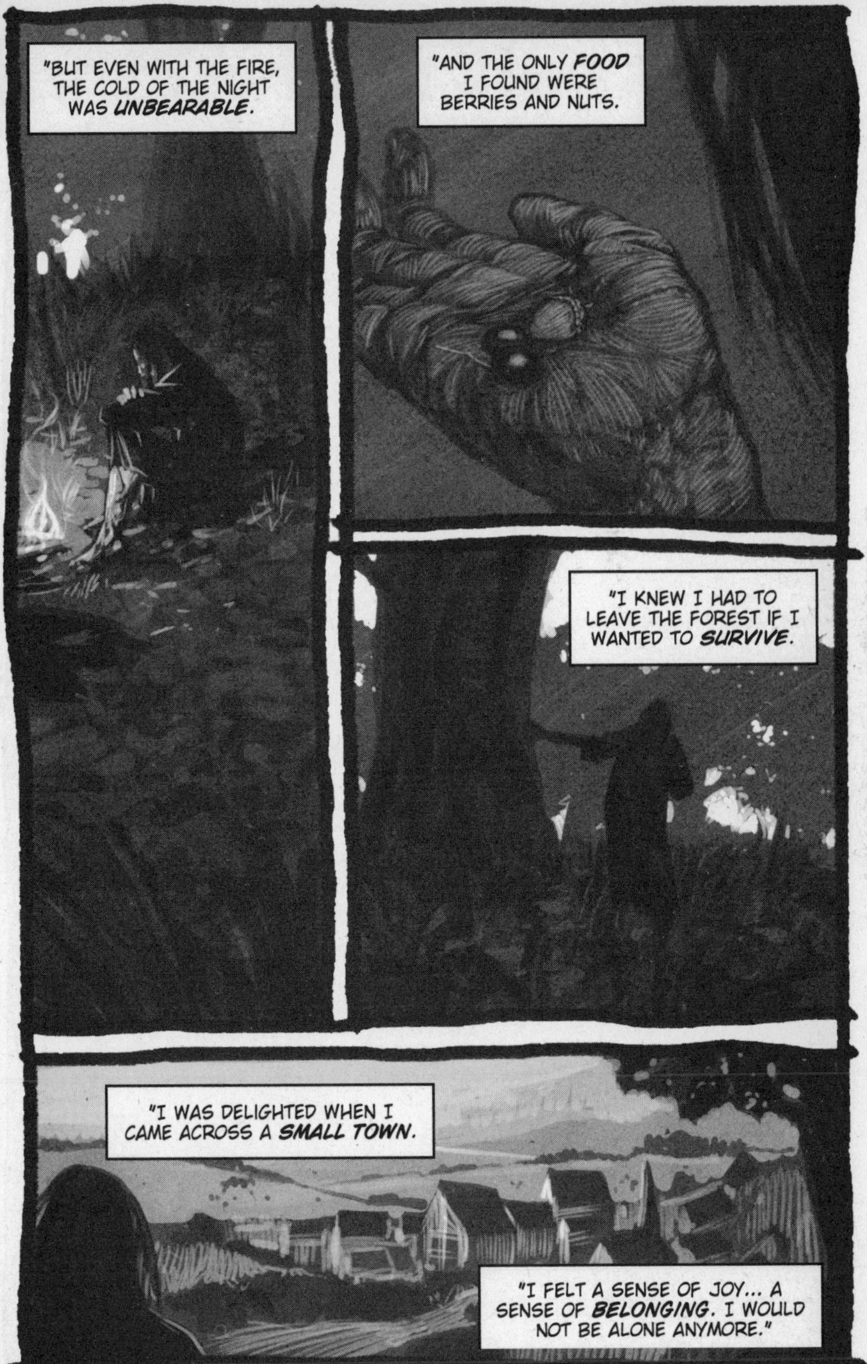
"BUT EVEN WITH THE FIRE, THE COLD OF THE NIGHT WAS UNBEARABLE.
"AND THE ONLY FOOD I FOUND WERE BERRIES AND NUTS.
"I KNEW I HAD TO LEAVE THE FOREST IF I WANTED TO SURVIVE.
"I WAS DELIGHTED WHEN I CAME ACROSS A SMALL TOWN.
"I FELT A SENSE OF JOY... A SENSE OF BELONGING. I WOULD NOT BE ALONE ANYMORE."

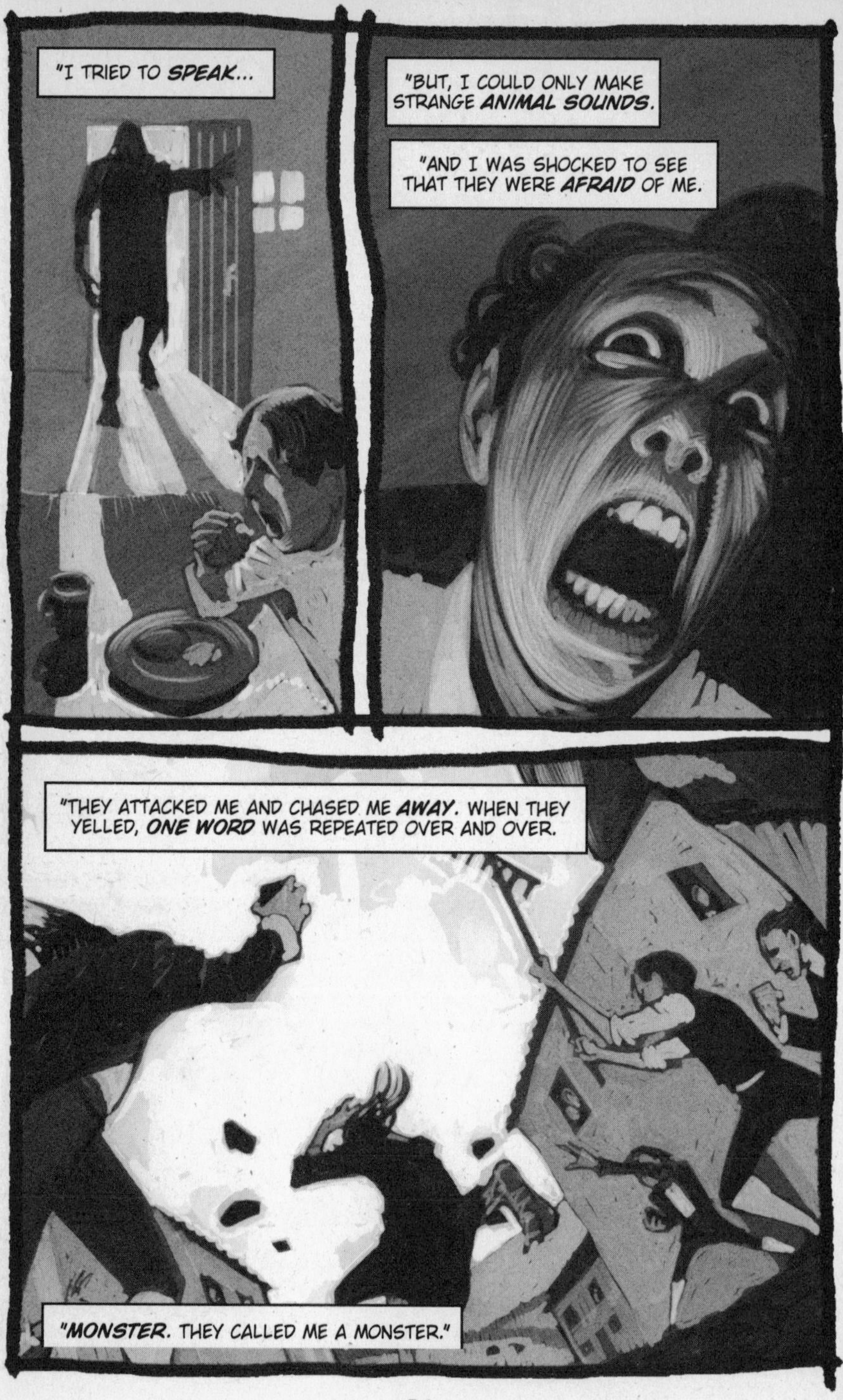
"I TRIED TO SPEAK...
"BUT, I COULD ONLY MAKE STRANGE ANIMAL SOUNDS.
"AND I WAS SHOCKED TO SEE THAT THEY WERE AFRAID OF ME.
"THEY ATTACKED ME AND CHASED ME AWAY. WHEN THEY YELLED, ONE WORD WAS REPEATED OVER AND OVER.
"MONSTER. THEY CALLED ME A MONSTER."

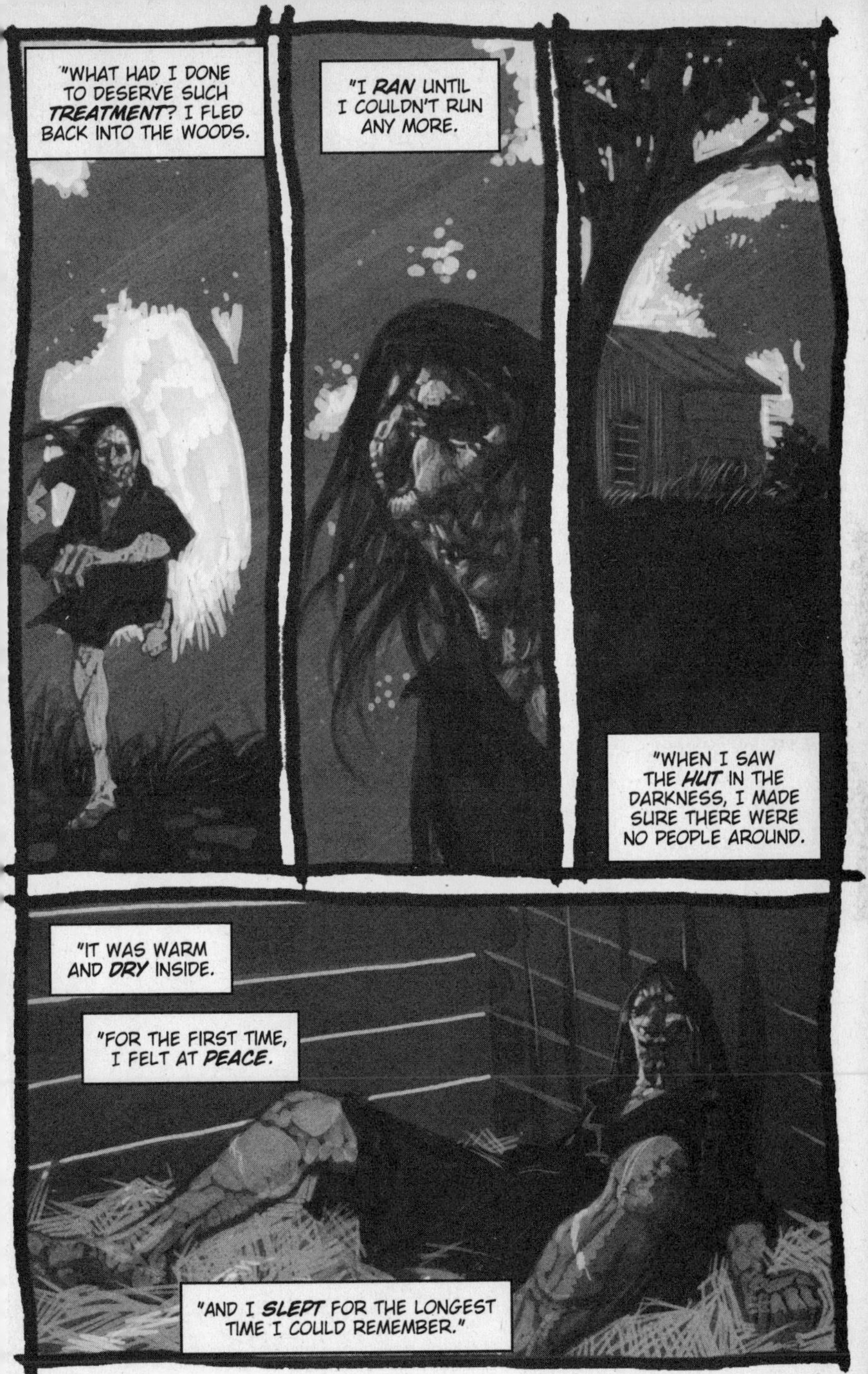
"WHAT HAD I DONE TO DESERVE SUCH TREATMENT? I FLED BACK INTO THE WOODS.
"I RAN UNTIL I COULDN'T RUN ANY MORE.
"WHEN I SAW THE HUT IN THE DARKNESS, I MADE SURE THERE WERE NO PEOPLE AROUND.
"IT WAS WARM AND DRY INSIDE.
"FOR THE FIRST TIME, I FELT AT PEACE.
"AND I SLEPT FOR THE LONGEST TIME I COULD REMEMBER."

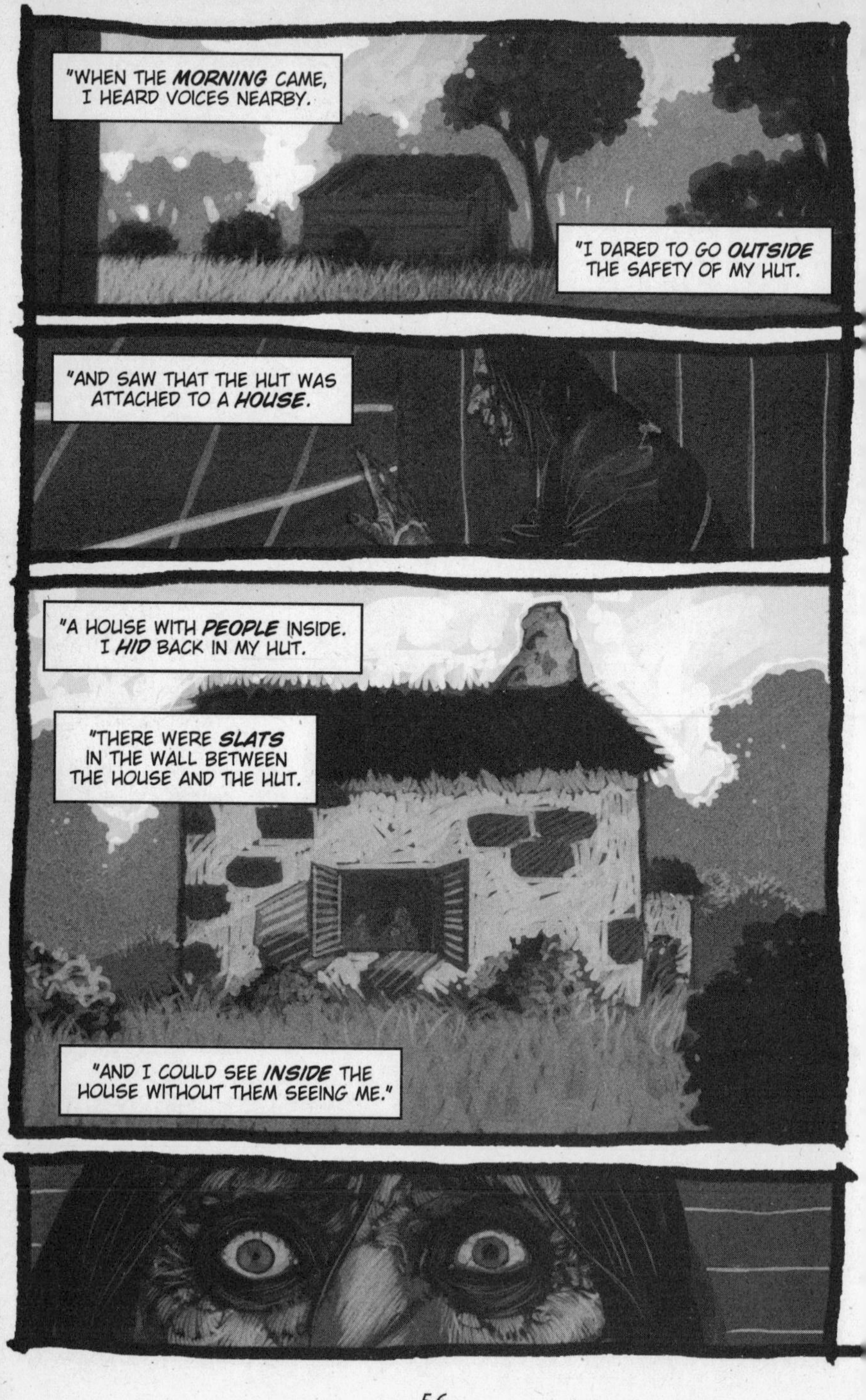
"WHEN THE MORNING CAME, I HEARD VOICES NEARBY.
"I DARED TO GO OUTSIDE THE SAFETY OF MY HUT.
"AND SAW THAT THE HUT WAS ATTACHED TO A HOUSE.
"A HOUSE WITH PEOPLE INSIDE. I HID BACK IN MY HUT.
"THERE WERE SLATS IN THE WALL BETWEEN THE HOUSE AND THE HUT.
"AND I COULD SEE INSIDE THE HOUSE WITHOUT THEM SEEING ME."

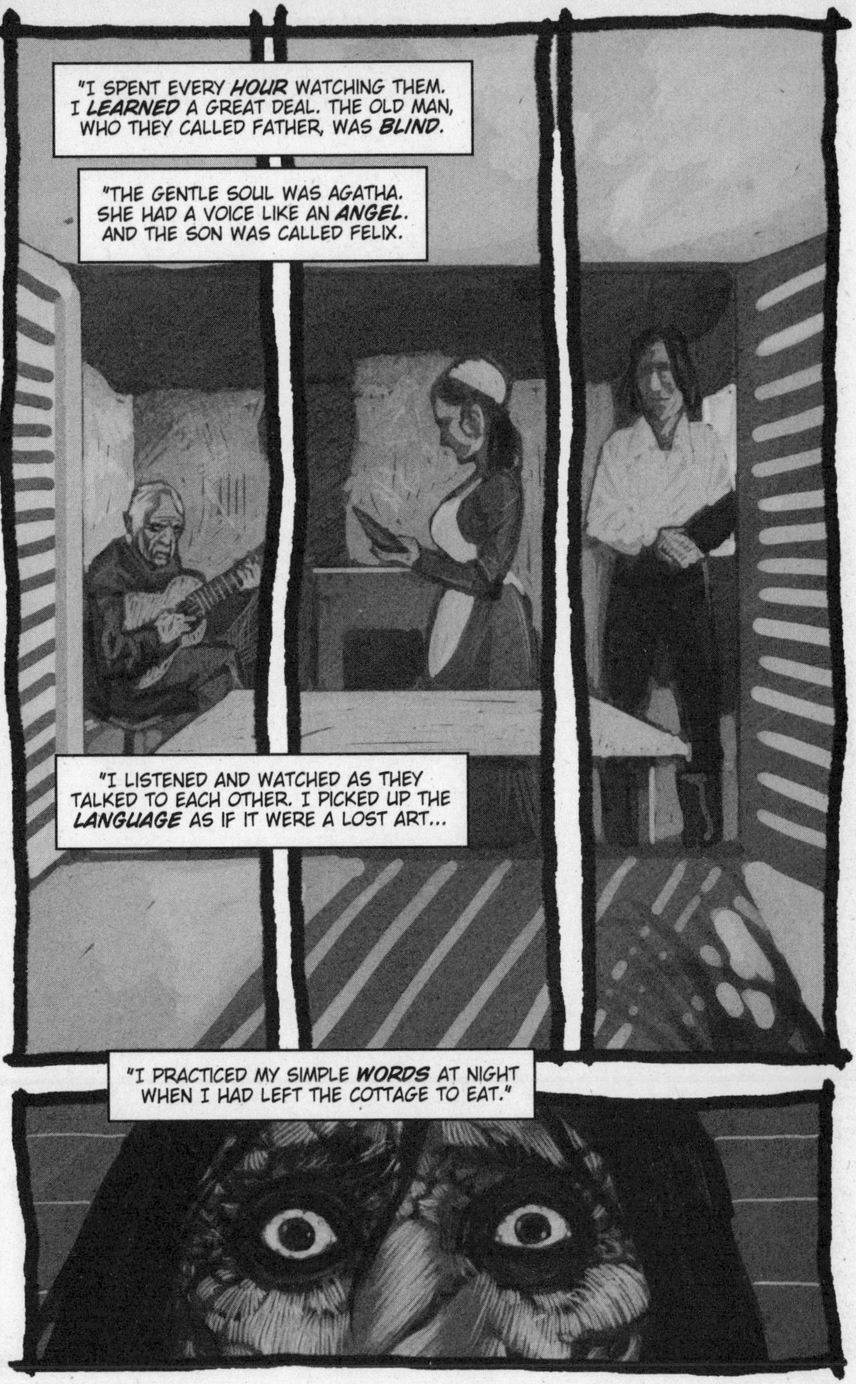
"I SPENT EVERY HOUR WATCHING THEM. I LEARNED A GREAT DEAL. THE OLD MAN, WHO THEY CALLED FATHER, WAS BLIND.
"THE GENTLE SOUL WAS AGATHA. SHE HAD A VOICE LIKE AN ANGEL. AND THE SON WAS CALLED FELIX.
"I LISTENED AND WATCHED AS THEY TALKED TO EACH OTHER. I PICKED UP THE LANGUAGE AS IF IT WERE A LOST ART...
"I PRACTICED MY SIMPLE WORDS AT NIGHT WHEN I HAD LEFT THE COTTAGE TO EAT."

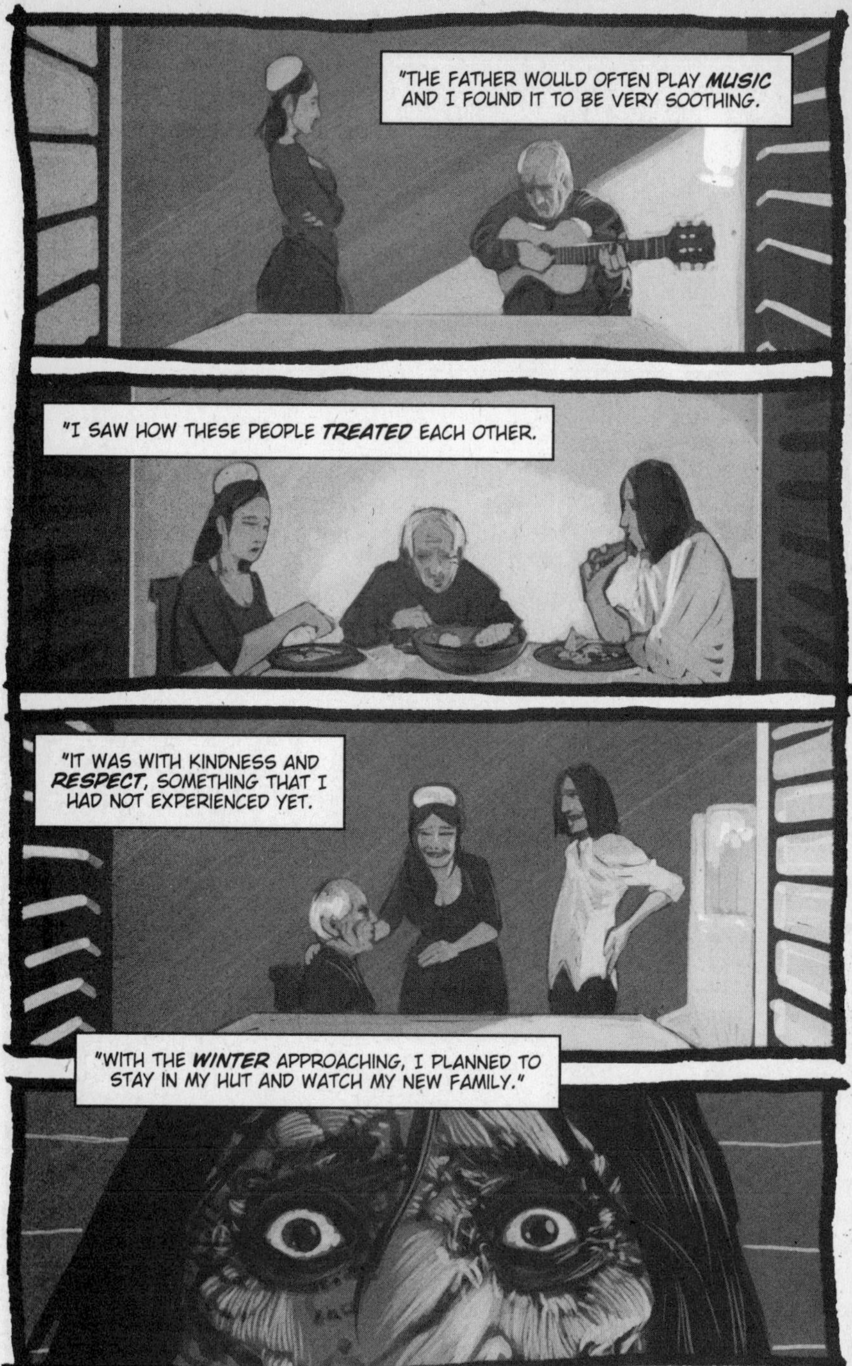
"THE FATHER WOULD OFTEN PLAY MUSIC AND I FOUND IT TO BE VERY SOOTHING.
"I SAW HOW THESE PEOPLE TREATED EACH OTHER.
"IT WAS WITH KINDNESS AND RESPECT, SOMETHING THAT I HAD NOT EXPERIENCED YET.
"WITH THE WINTER APPROACHING, I PLANNED TO STAY IN MY HUT AND WATCH MY NEW FAMILY."

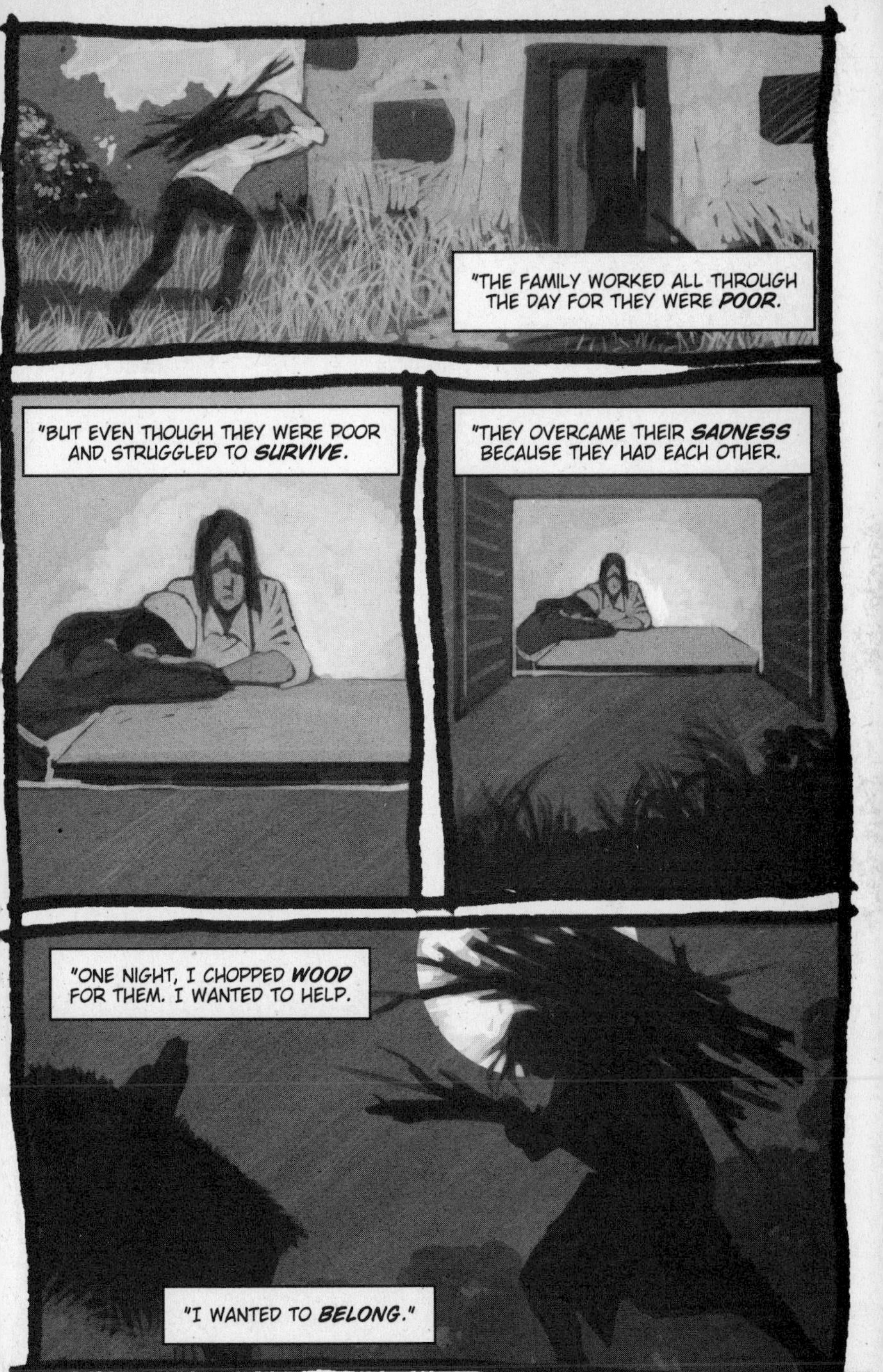
"THE FAMILY WORKED ALL THROUGH THE DAY FOR THEY WERE POOR.
"BUT EVEN THOUGH THEY WERE POOR AND STRUGGLED TO SURVIVE.
"THEY OVERCAME THEIR SADNESS BECAUSE THEY HAD EACH OTHER.
"ONE NIGHT, I CHOPPED WOOD FOR THEM. I WANTED TO HELP.
"I WANTED TO BELONG."

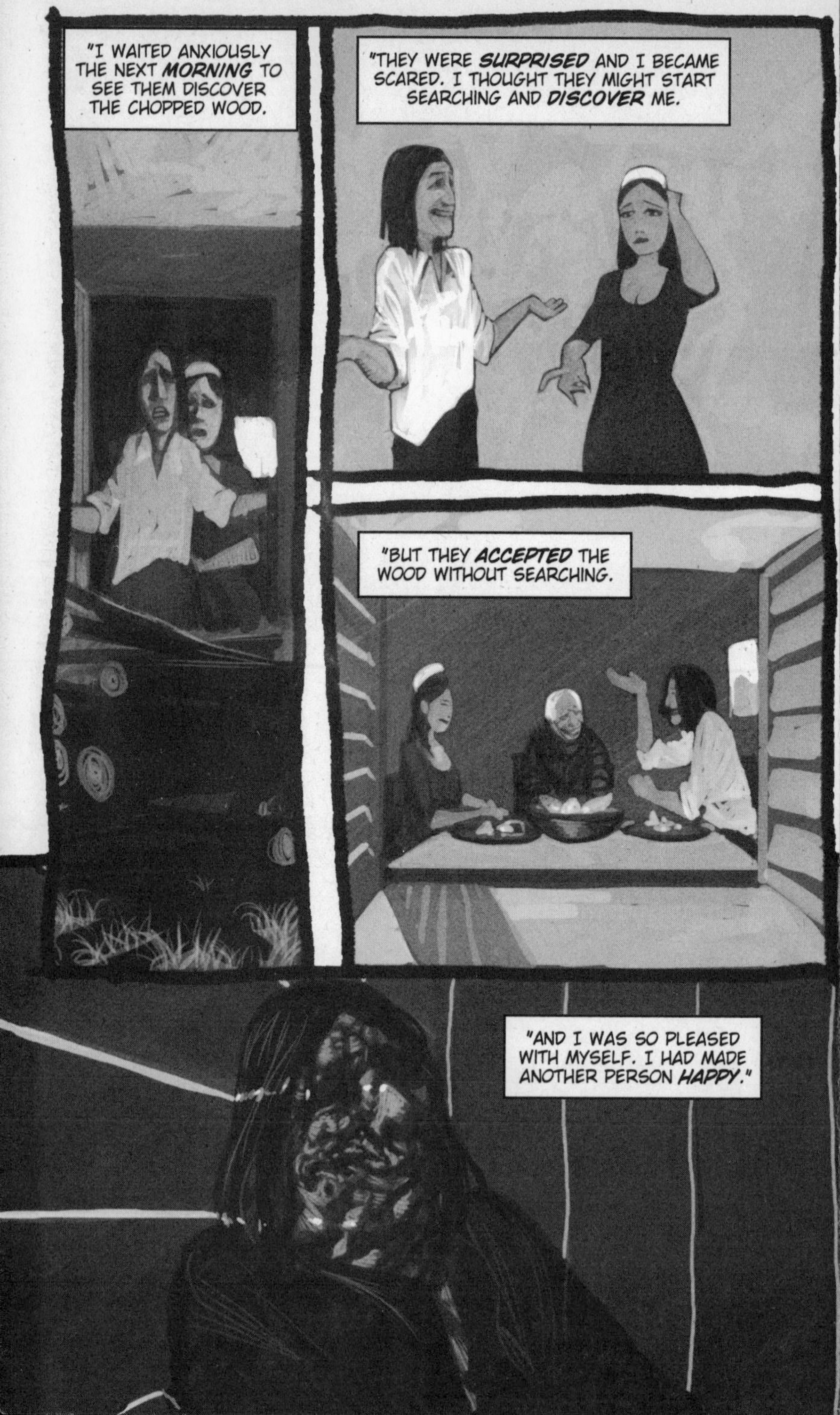
"I WAITED ANXIOUSLY THE NEXT MORNING TO SEE THEM DISCOVER THE CHOPPED WOOD.
"THEY WERE SURPRISED AND I BECAME SCARED. I THOUGHT THEY MIGHT START SEARCHING AND DISCOVER ME.
"BUT THEY ACCEPTED THE WOOD WITHOUT SEARCHING.
"AND I WAS SO PLEASED WITH MYSELF. I HAD MADE ANOTHER PERSON HAPPY."

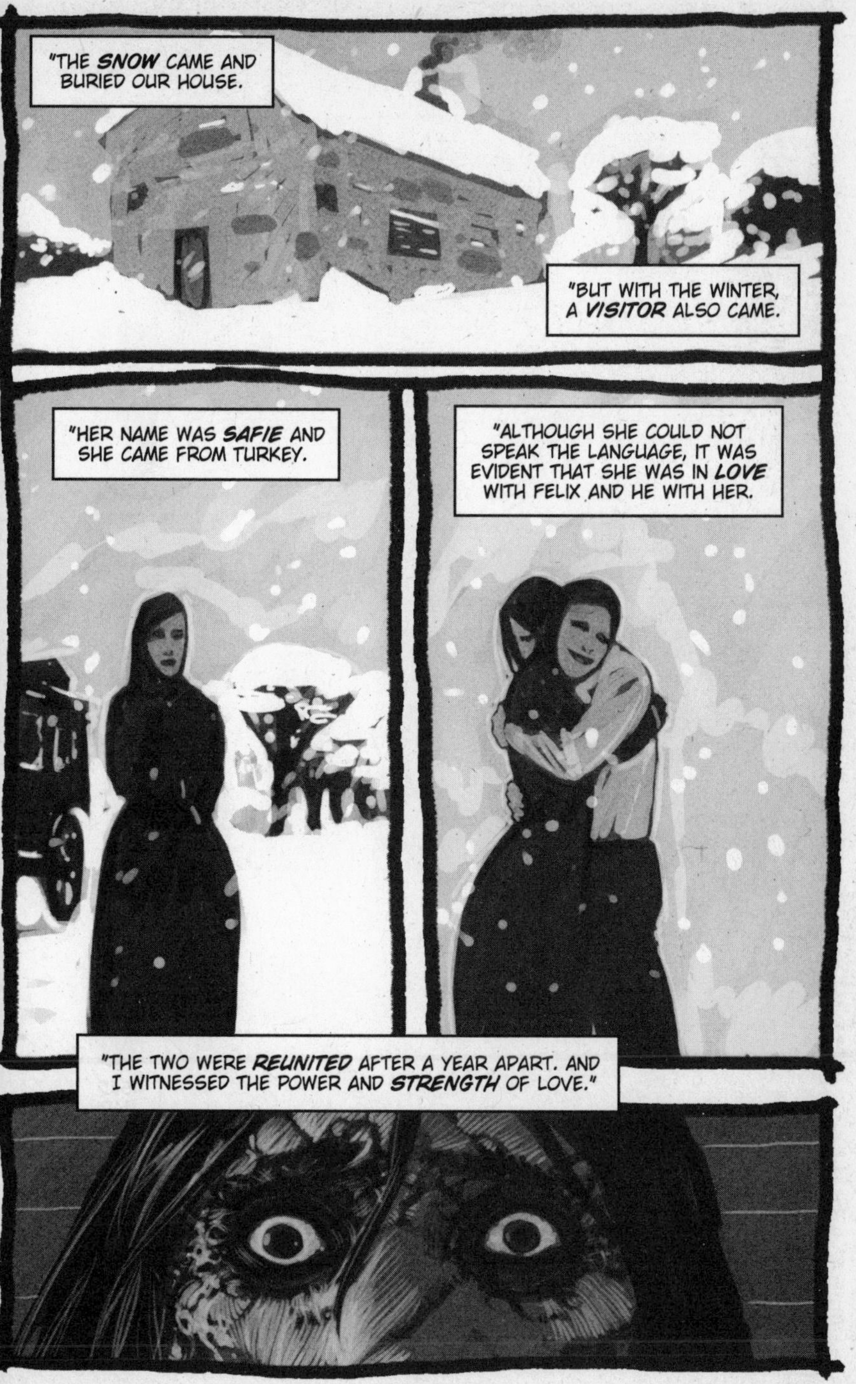
"THE SNOW CAME AND BURIED OUR HOUSE.
"BUT WITH THE WINTER, A VISITOR ALSO CAME.
"HER NAME WAS SAFIE AND SHE CAME FROM TURKEY.
"ALTHOUGH SHE COULD NOT SPEAK THE LANGUAGE, IT WAS EVIDENT THAT SHE WAS IN LOVE WITH FELIX AND HE WITH HER.
"THE TWO WERE REUNITED AFTER A YEAR APART. AND I WITNESSED THE POWER AND STRENGTH OF LOVE."

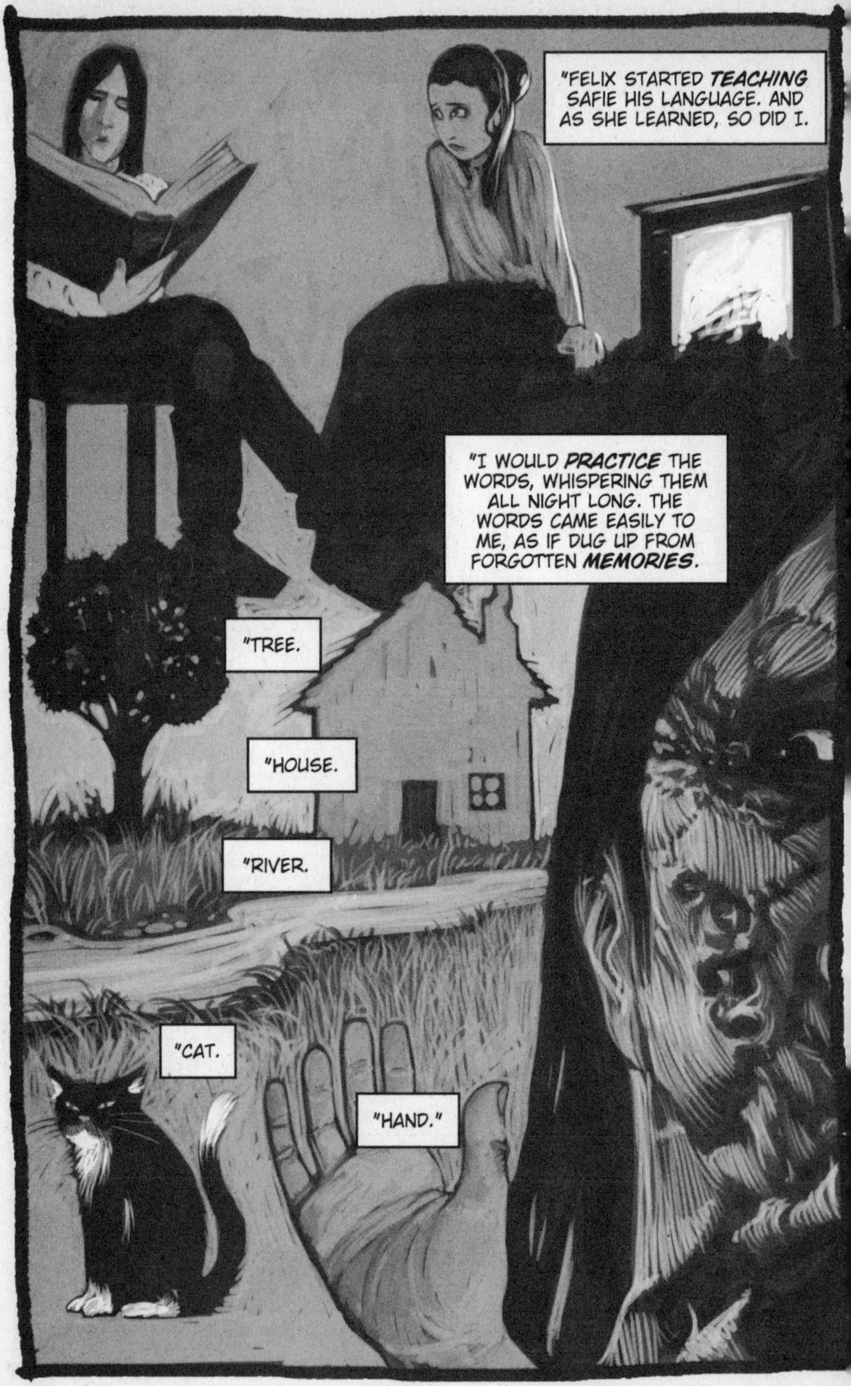
"FELIX STARTED TEACHING SAFIE HIS LANGUAGE. AND AS SHE LEARNED, SO DID I.
"I WOULD PRACTICE THE WORDS, WHISPERING THEM ALL NIGHT LONG. THE WORDS CAME EASILY TO ME, AS IF DUG UP FROM FORGOTTEN MEMORIES.
"TREE.
"HOUSE.
"RIVER.
"CAT.
"HAND."

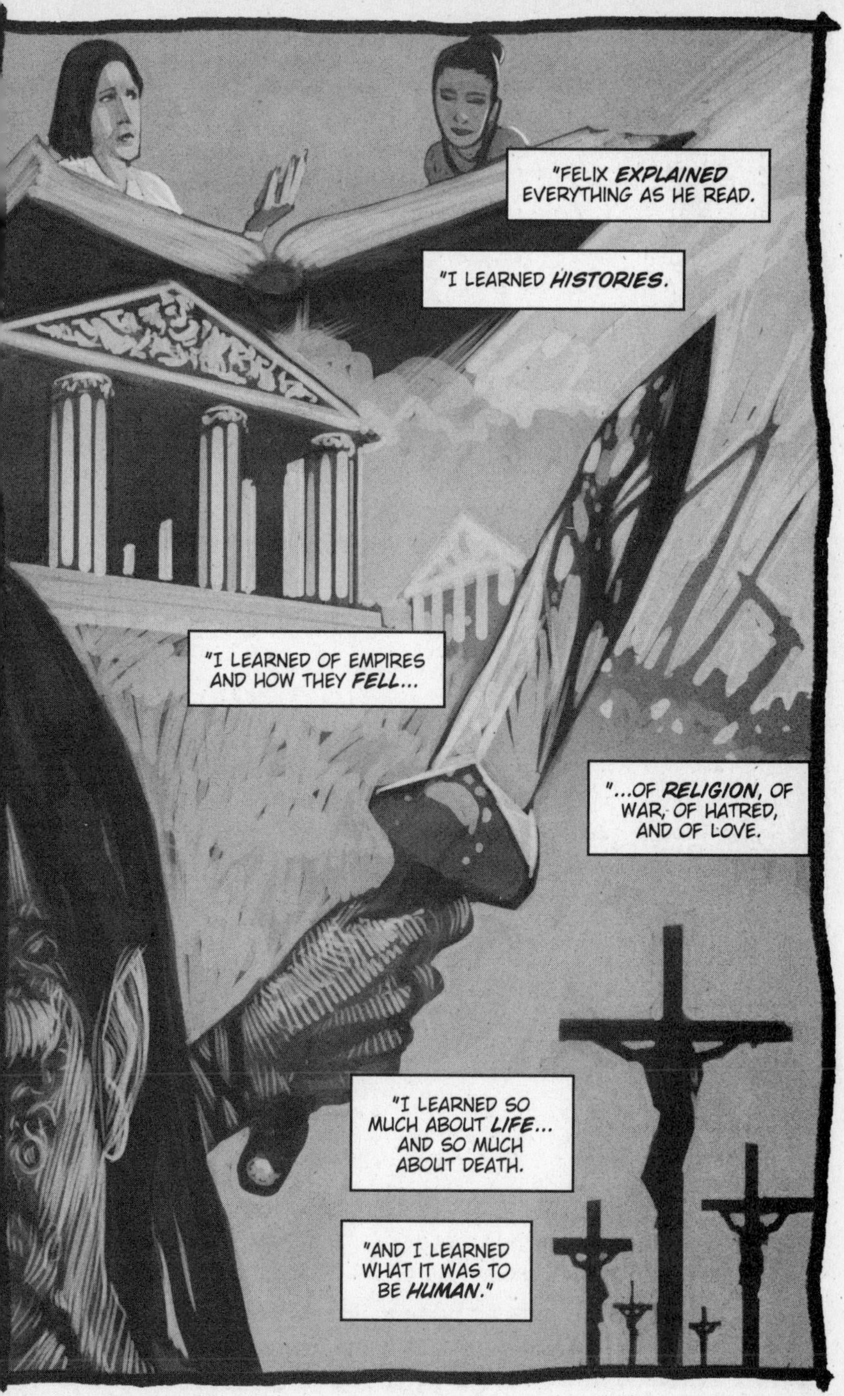
"FELIX EXPLAINED EVERYTHING AS HE READ.
"I LEARNED HISTORIES.
"I LEARNED OF EMPIRES AND HOW THEY FELL...
"...OF RELIGION, OF WAR, OF HATRED, AND OF LOVE.
"I LEARNED SO MUCH ABOUT LIFE... AND SO MUCH ABOUT DEATH.
"AND I LEARNED WHAT IT WAS TO BE HUMAN."

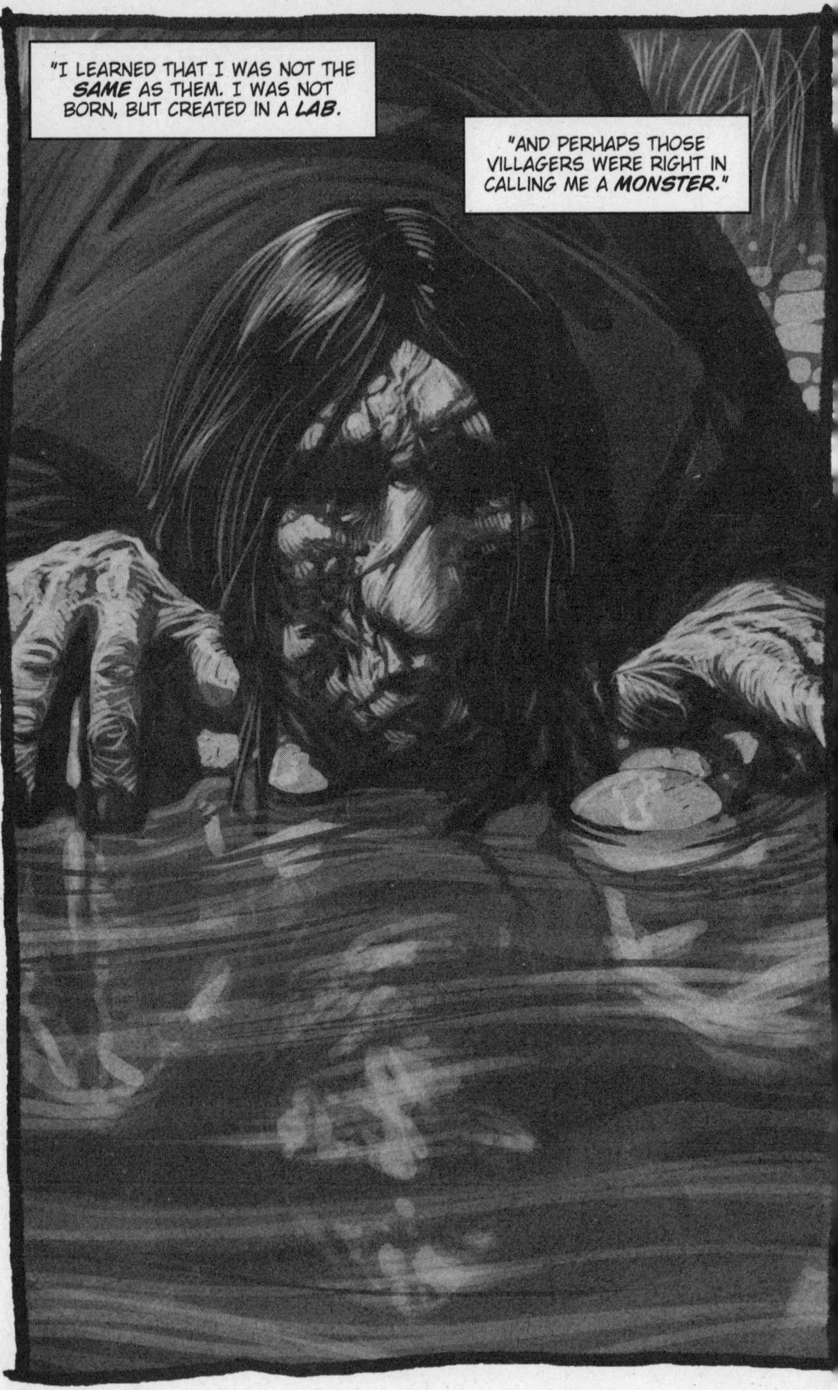
"I LEARNED THAT I WAS NOT THE SAME AS THEM. I WAS NOT BORN, BUT CREATED IN A LAB.
"AND PERHAPS THOSE VILLAGERS WERE RIGHT IN CALLING ME A MONSTER."

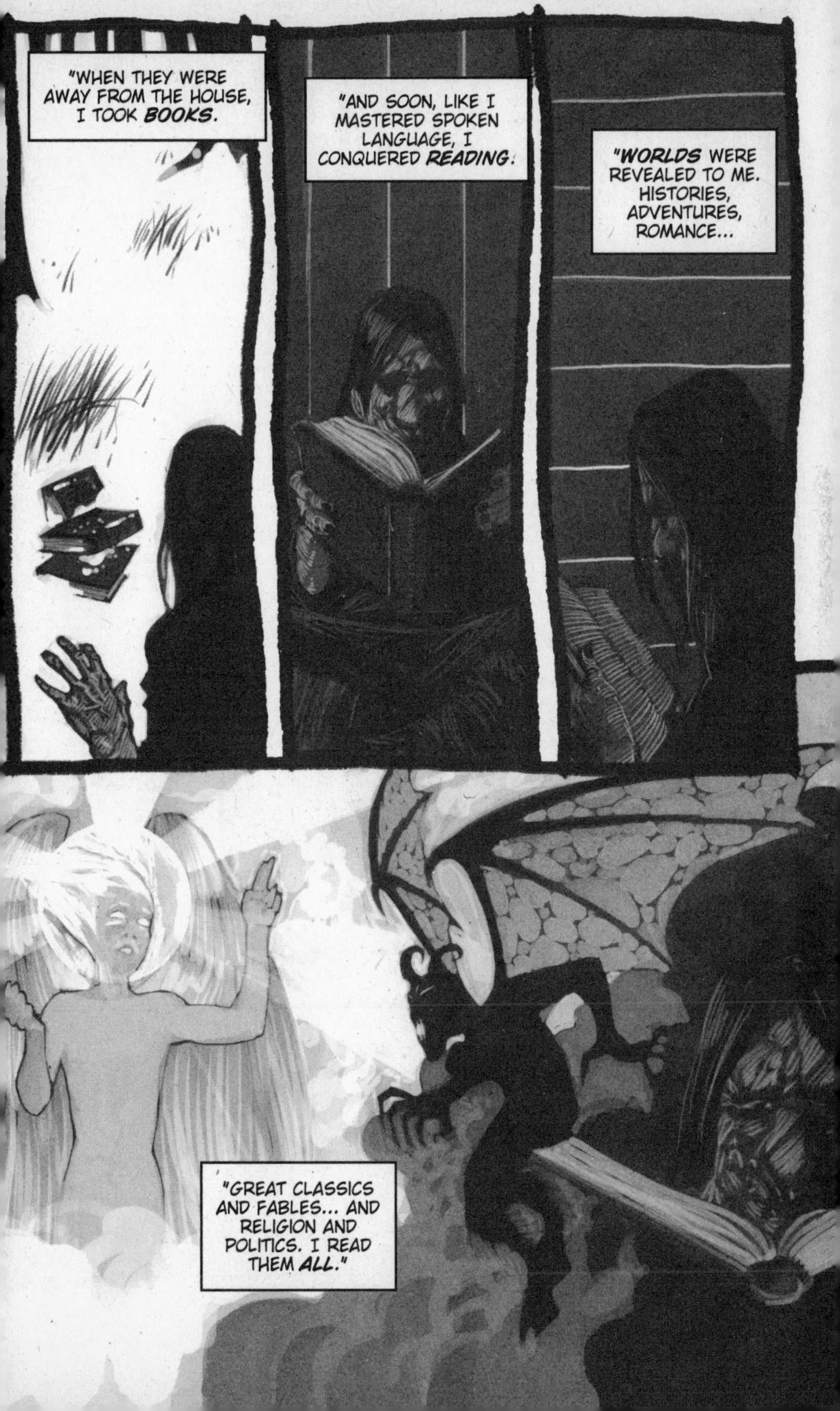
"WHEN THEY WERE AWAY FROM THE HOUSE, I TOOK *BOOKS*.
"AND SOON, LIKE I MASTERED SPOKEN LANGUAGE, I CONQUERED *READING*.
"*WORLDS* WERE REVEALED TO ME. HISTORIES, ADVENTURES, ROMANCE...
"GREAT CLASSICS AND FABLES... AND RELIGION AND POLITICS. I READ THEM *ALL*."

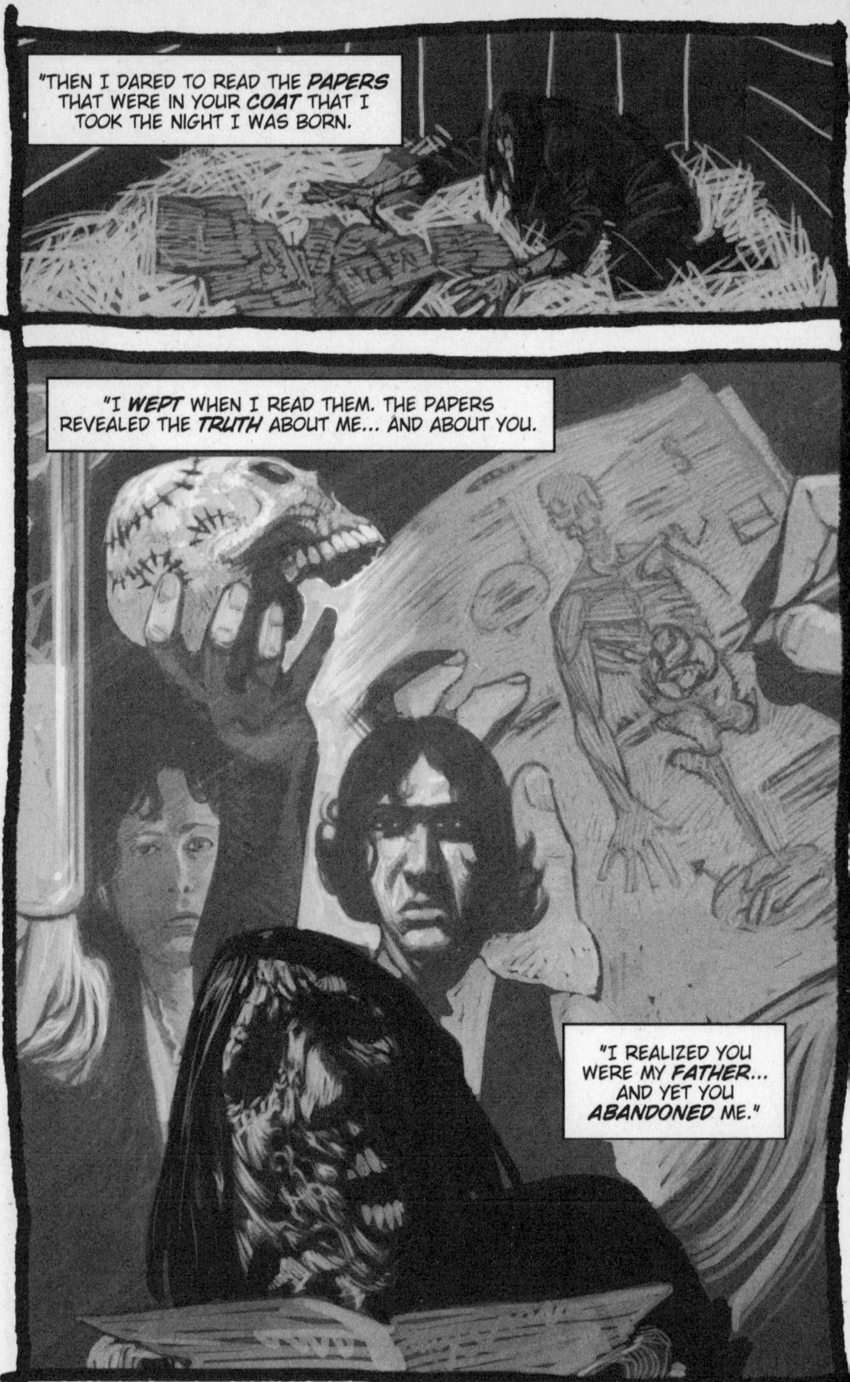
"THEN I DARED TO READ THE PAPERS THAT WERE IN YOUR COAT THAT I TOOK THE NIGHT I WAS BORN.
"I WEPT WHEN I READ THEM. THE PAPERS REVEALED THE TRUTH ABOUT ME... AND ABOUT YOU.
"I REALIZED YOU WERE MY FATHER... AND YET YOU ABANDONED ME."

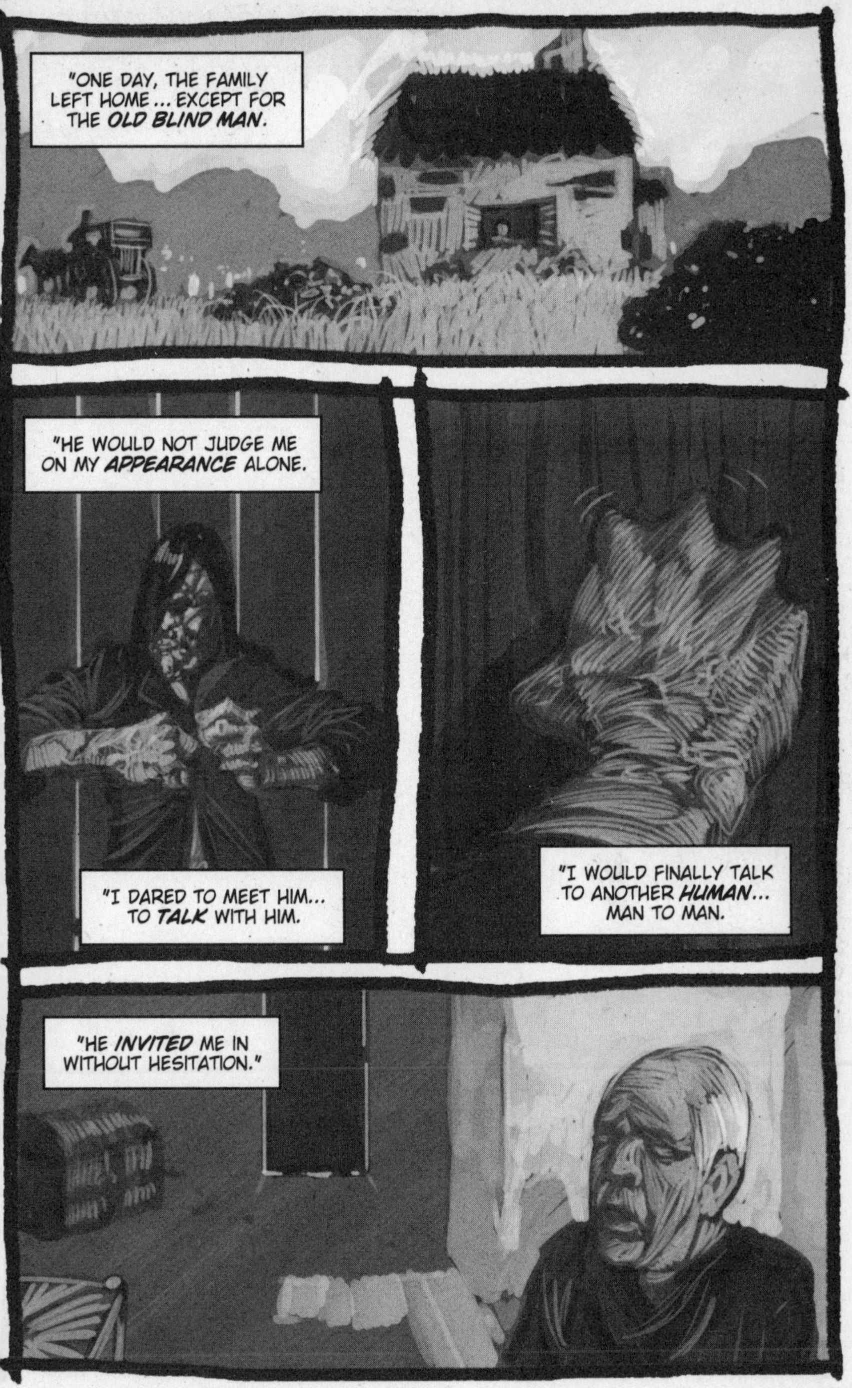
"ONE DAY, THE FAMILY LEFT HOME ... EXCEPT FOR THE OLD BLIND MAN.
"HE WOULD NOT JUDGE ME ON MY APPEARANCE ALONE.
"I DARED TO MEET HIM... TO TALK WITH HIM.
"I WOULD FINALLY TALK TO ANOTHER HUMAN... MAN TO MAN.
"HE INVITED ME IN WITHOUT HESITATION."

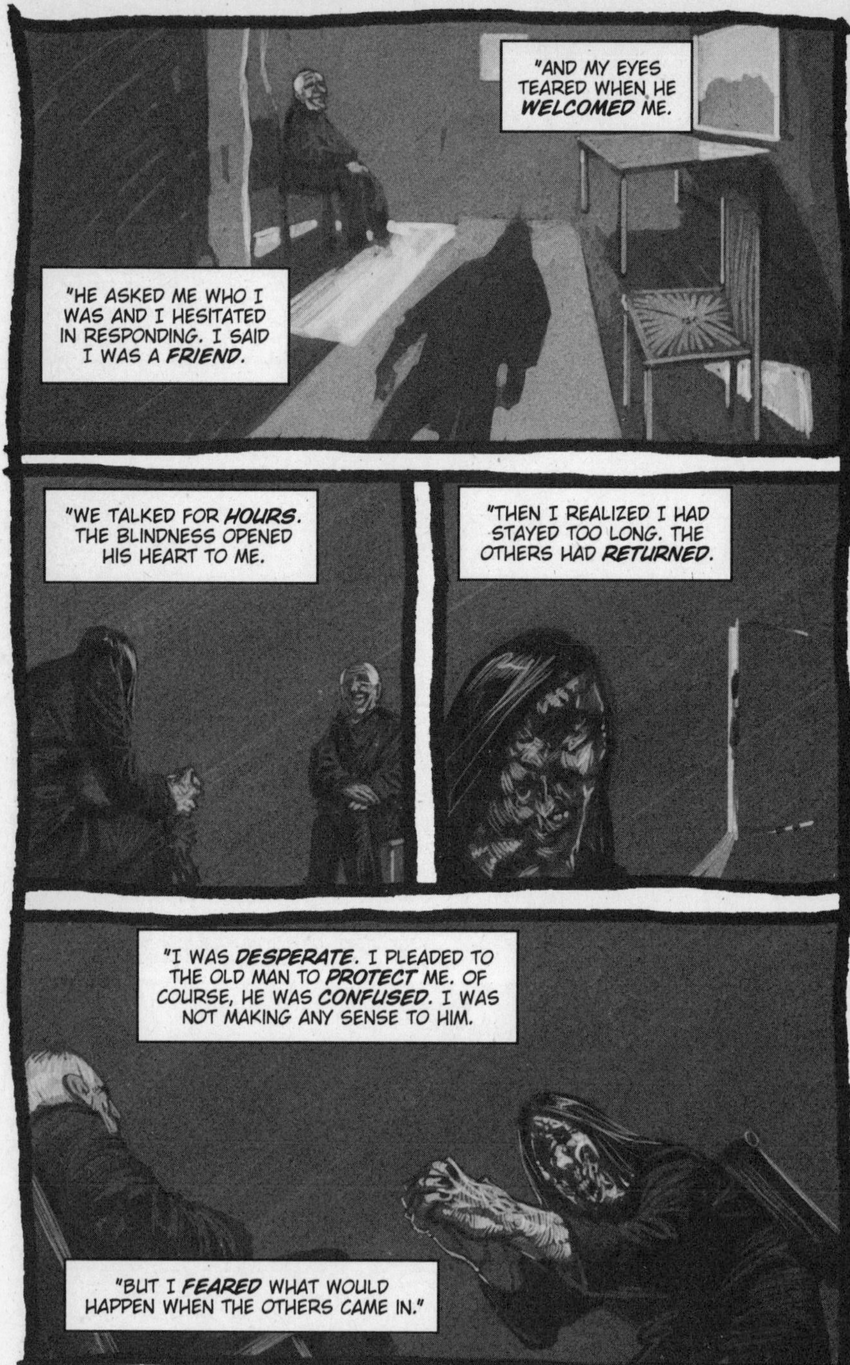
"AND MY EYES TEARED WHEN HE WELCOMED ME.
"HE ASKED ME WHO I WAS AND I HESITATED IN RESPONDING. I SAID I WAS A FRIEND.
"WE TALKED FOR HOURS. THE BLINDNESS OPENED HIS HEART TO ME.
"THEN I REALIZED I HAD STAYED TOO LONG. THE OTHERS HAD RETURNED.
"I WAS DESPERATE. I PLEADED TO THE OLD MAN TO PROTECT ME. OF COURSE, HE WAS CONFUSED. I WAS NOT MAKING ANY SENSE TO HIM.
"BUT I FEARED WHAT WOULD HAPPEN WHEN THE OTHERS CAME IN."

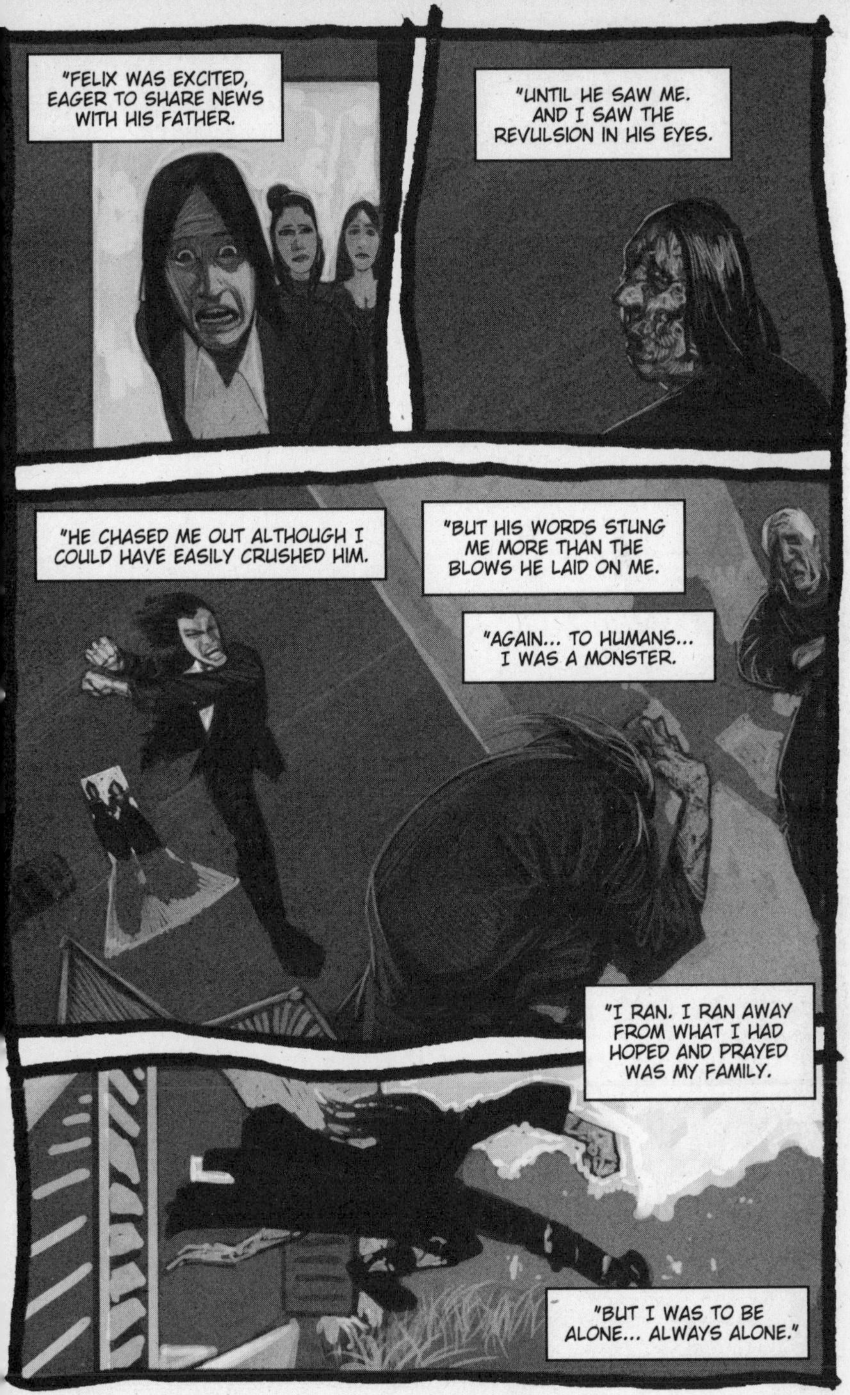
"FELIX WAS EXCITED, EAGER TO SHARE NEWS WITH HIS FATHER.
"UNTIL HE SAW ME. AND I SAW THE REVULSION IN HIS EYES.
"HE CHASED ME OUT ALTHOUGH I COULD HAVE EASILY CRUSHED HIM.
"BUT HIS WORDS STUNG ME MORE THAN THE BLOWS HE LAID ON ME.
"AGAIN... TO HUMANS... I WAS A MONSTER.
"I RAN. I RAN AWAY FROM WHAT I HAD HOPED AND PRAYED WAS MY FAMILY.
"BUT I WAS TO BE ALONE... ALWAYS ALONE."

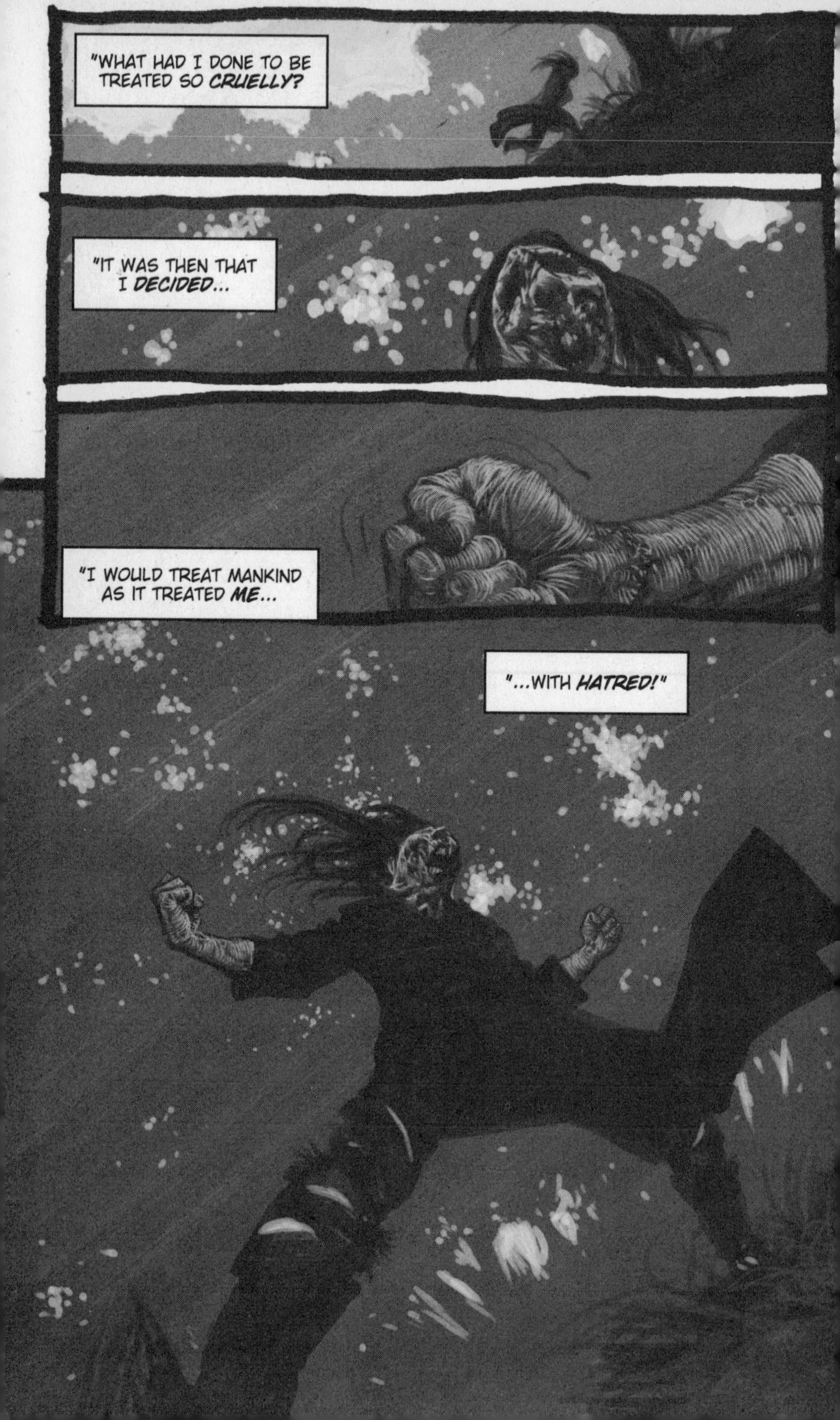
"WHAT HAD I DONE TO BE TREATED SO CRUELLY?
"IT WAS THEN THAT I DECIDED...
"I WOULD TREAT MANKIND AS IT TREATED ME...
"...WITH HATRED!"

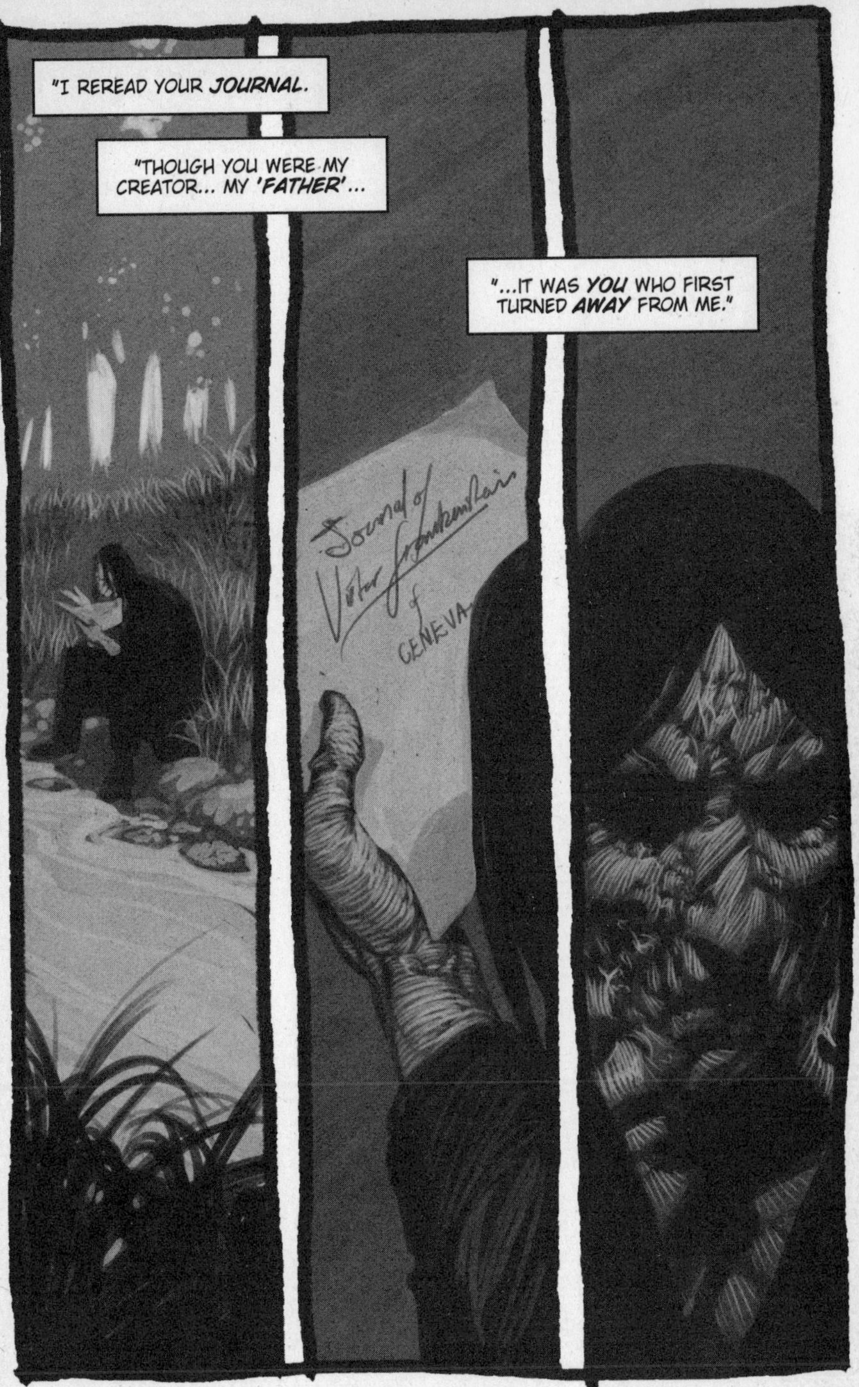
"I REREAD YOUR JOURNAL.
"THOUGH YOU WERE MY CREATOR... MY 'FATHER'...
Journal of Victor Frankenstein of GENEVA
"...IT WAS YOU WHO FIRST TURNED AWAY FROM ME."

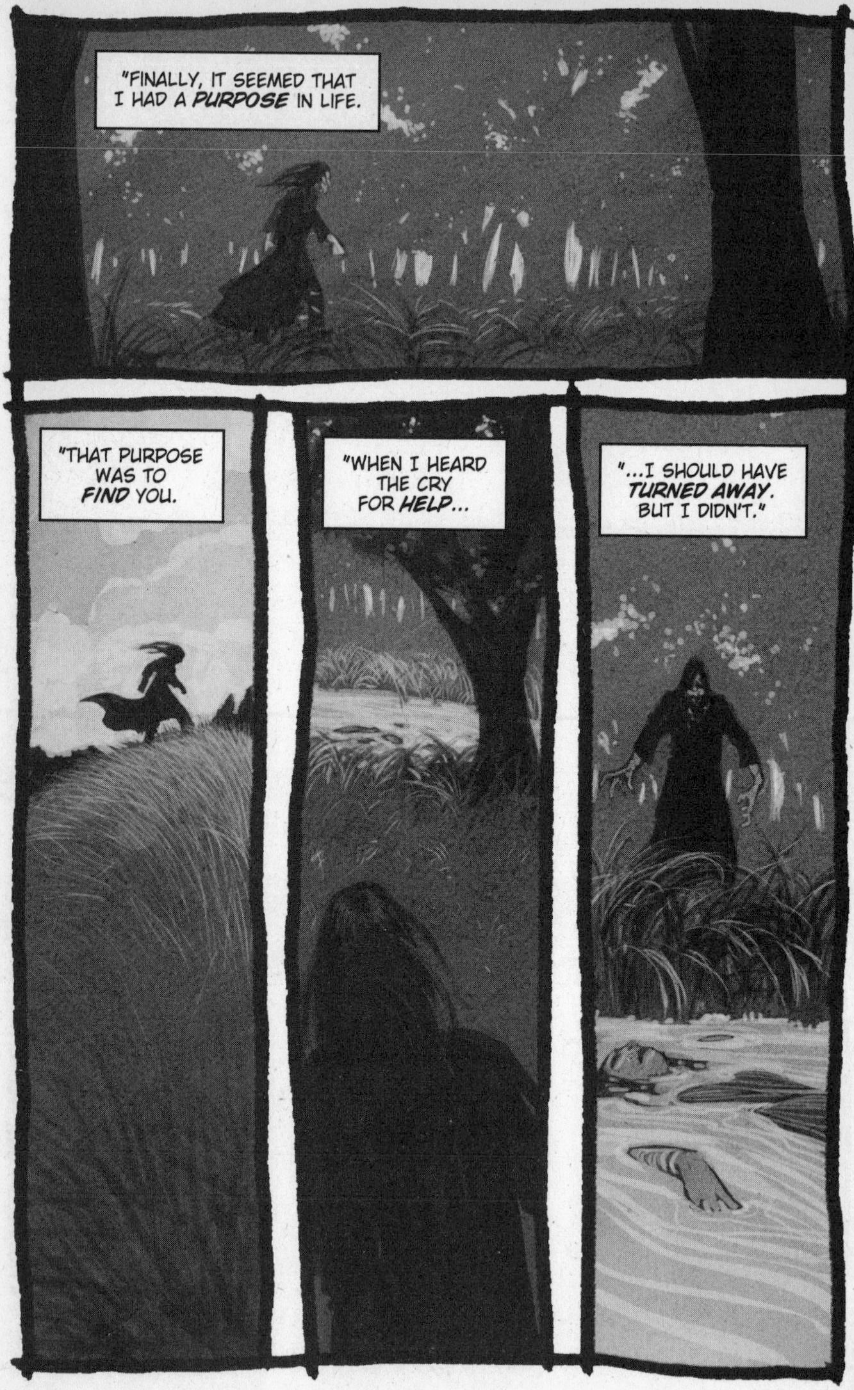
"FINALLY, IT SEEMED THAT I HAD A *PURPOSE* IN LIFE.
"THAT PURPOSE WAS TO *FIND* YOU.
"WHEN I HEARD THE CRY FOR *HELP*...
"...I SHOULD HAVE *TURNED AWAY*. BUT I DIDN'T."

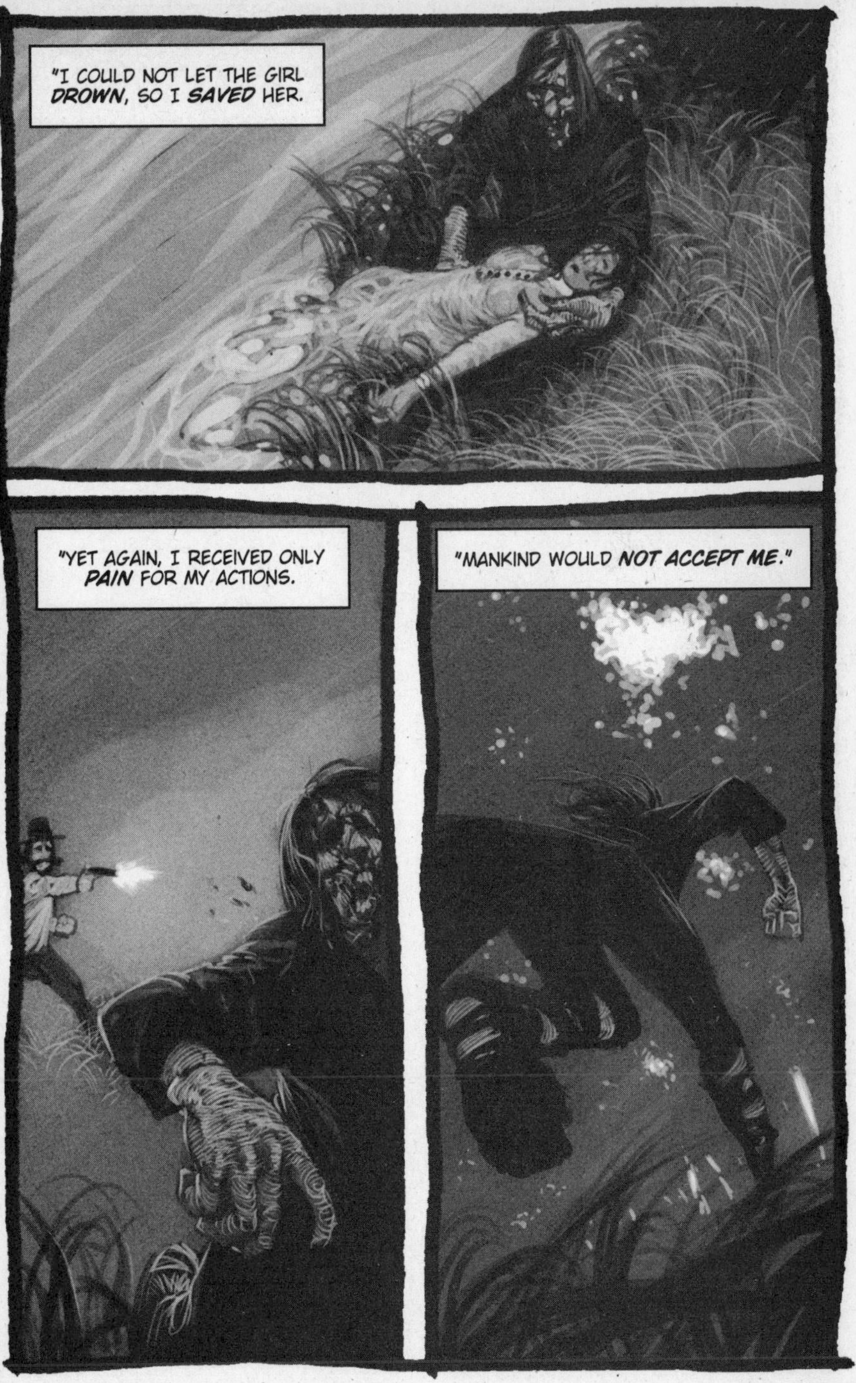
"I COULD NOT LET THE GIRL DROWN, SO I SAVED HER.
"YET AGAIN, I RECEIVED ONLY PAIN FOR MY ACTIONS.
"MANKIND WOULD NOT ACCEPT ME."

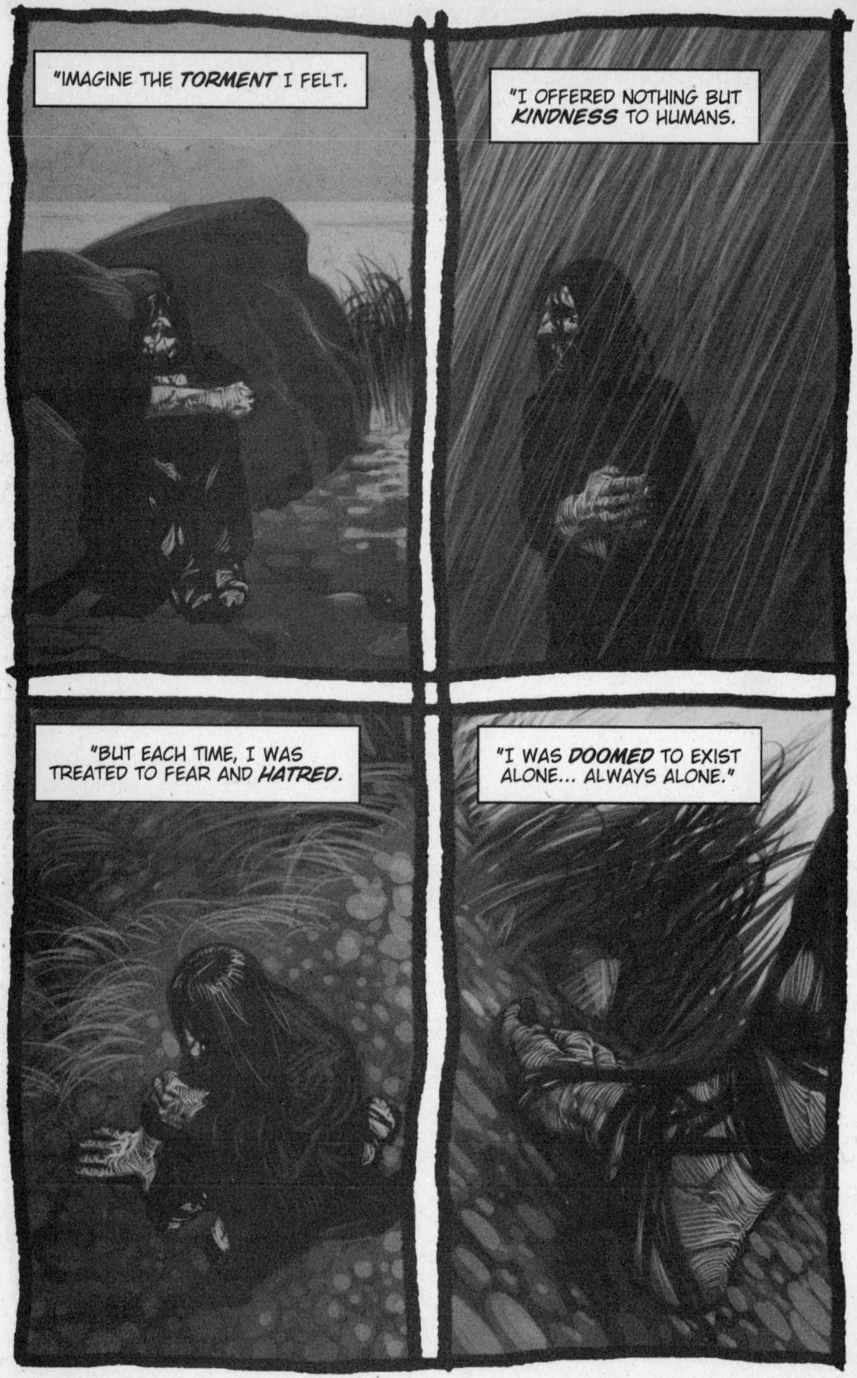
"IMAGINE THE TORMENT I FELT.
"I OFFERED NOTHING BUT KINDNESS TO HUMANS.
"BUT EACH TIME, I WAS TREATED TO FEAR AND HATRED.
"I WAS DOOMED TO EXIST ALONE... ALWAYS ALONE."

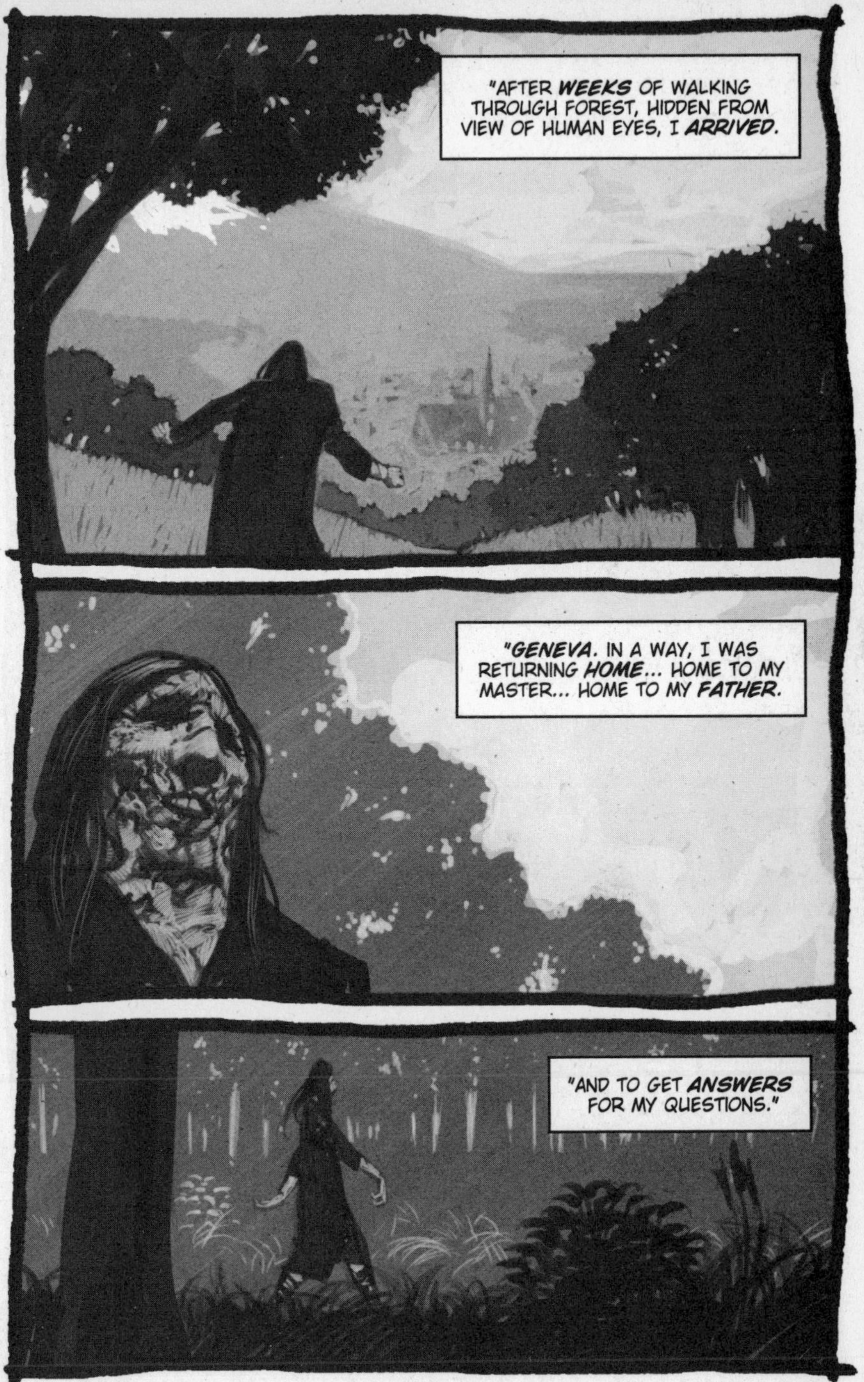
"AFTER WEEKS OF WALKING THROUGH FOREST, HIDDEN FROM VIEW OF HUMAN EYES, I ARRIVED.
"GENEVA. IN A WAY, I WAS RETURNING HOME... HOME TO MY MASTER... HOME TO MY FATHER.
"AND TO GET ANSWERS FOR MY QUESTIONS."

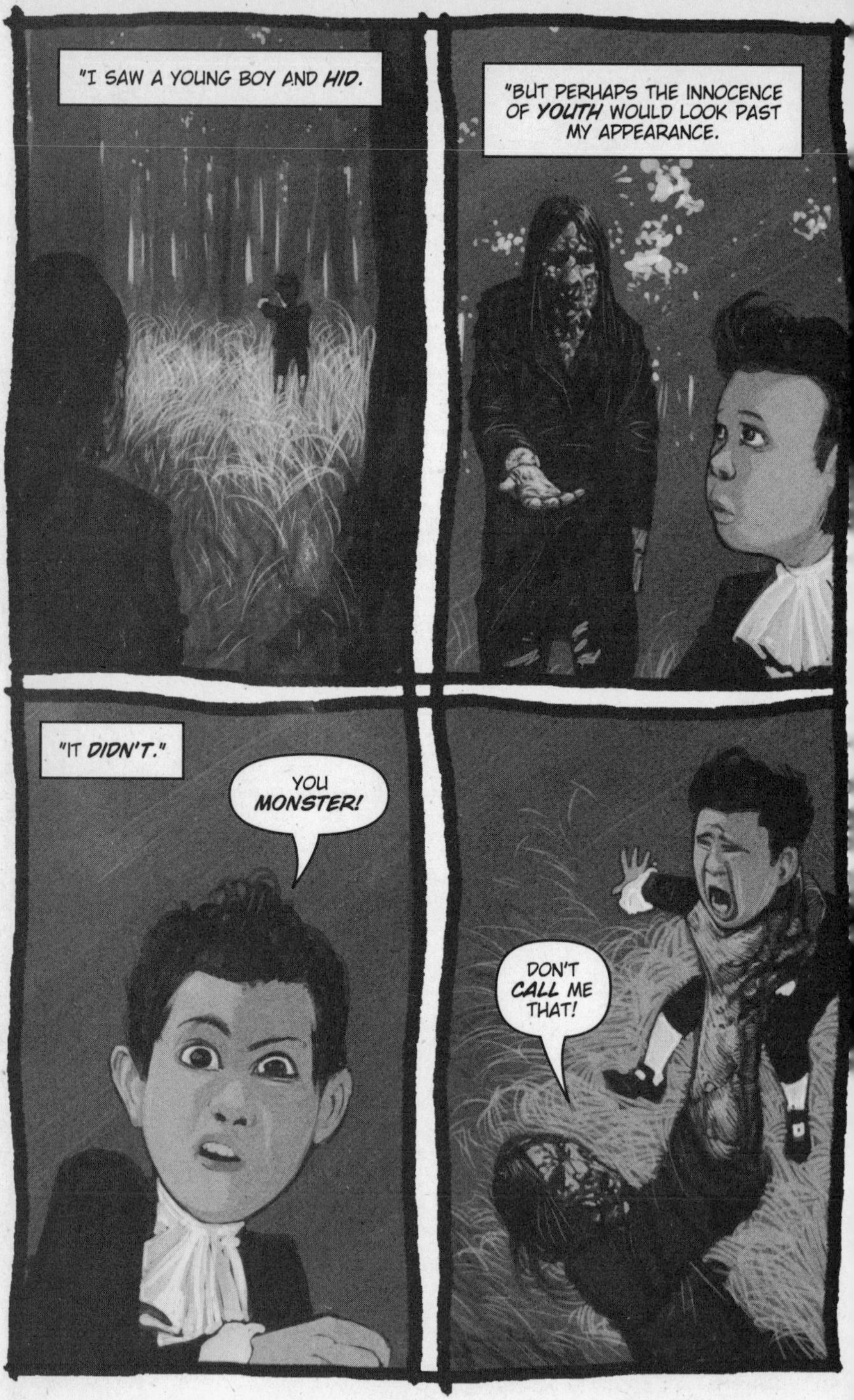
"I SAW A YOUNG BOY AND *HID*.
"BUT PERHAPS THE INNOCENCE OF *YOUTH* WOULD LOOK PAST MY APPEARANCE.
"IT *DIDN'T*."
YOU **MONSTER!**
DON'T **CALL** ME THAT!

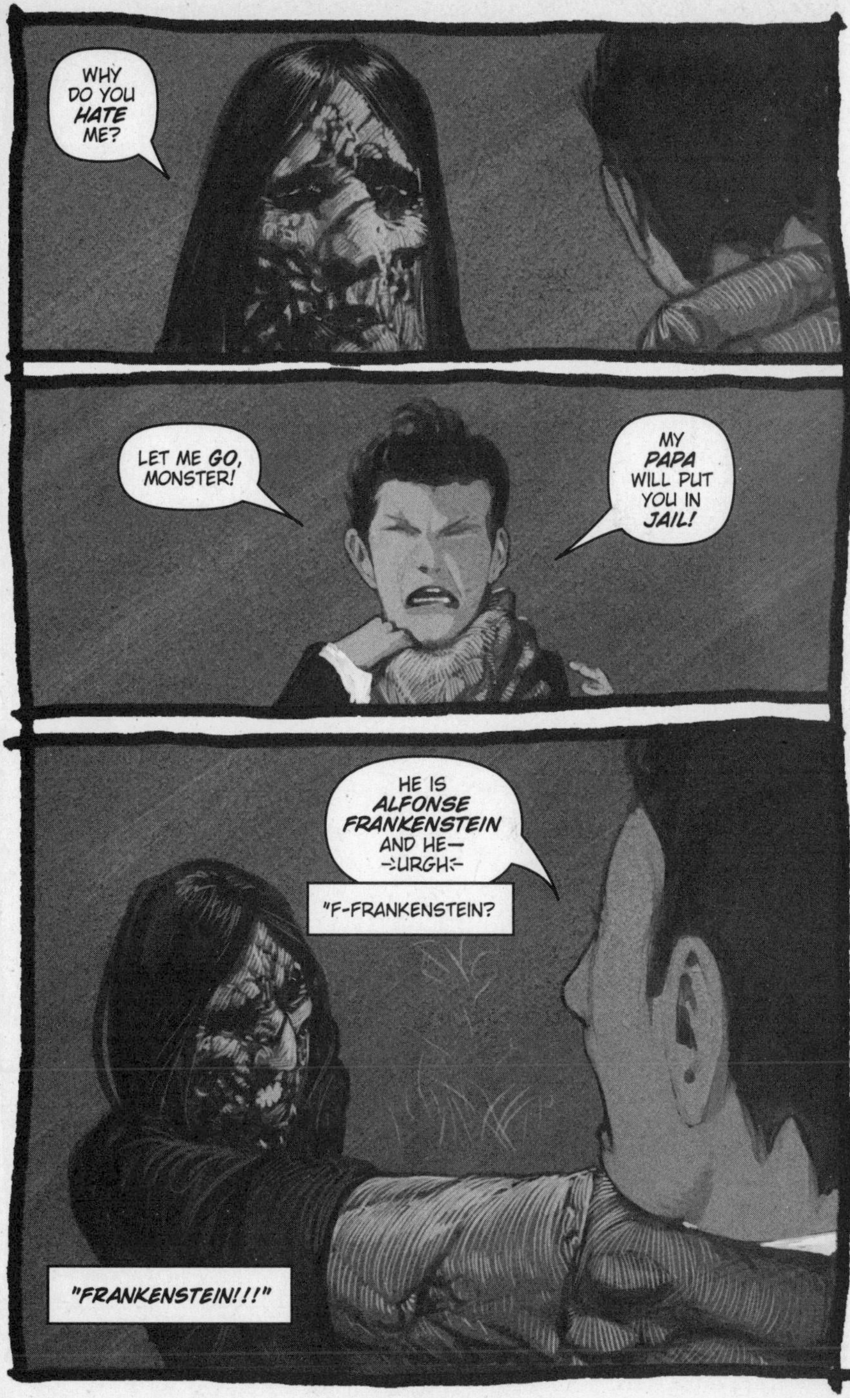
WHY DO YOU HATE ME?
LET ME GO, MONSTER!
MY PAPA WILL PUT YOU IN JAIL!
HE IS ALFONSE FRANKENSTEIN AND HE— URGH
"F-FRANKENSTEIN?
"FRANKENSTEIN!!!"

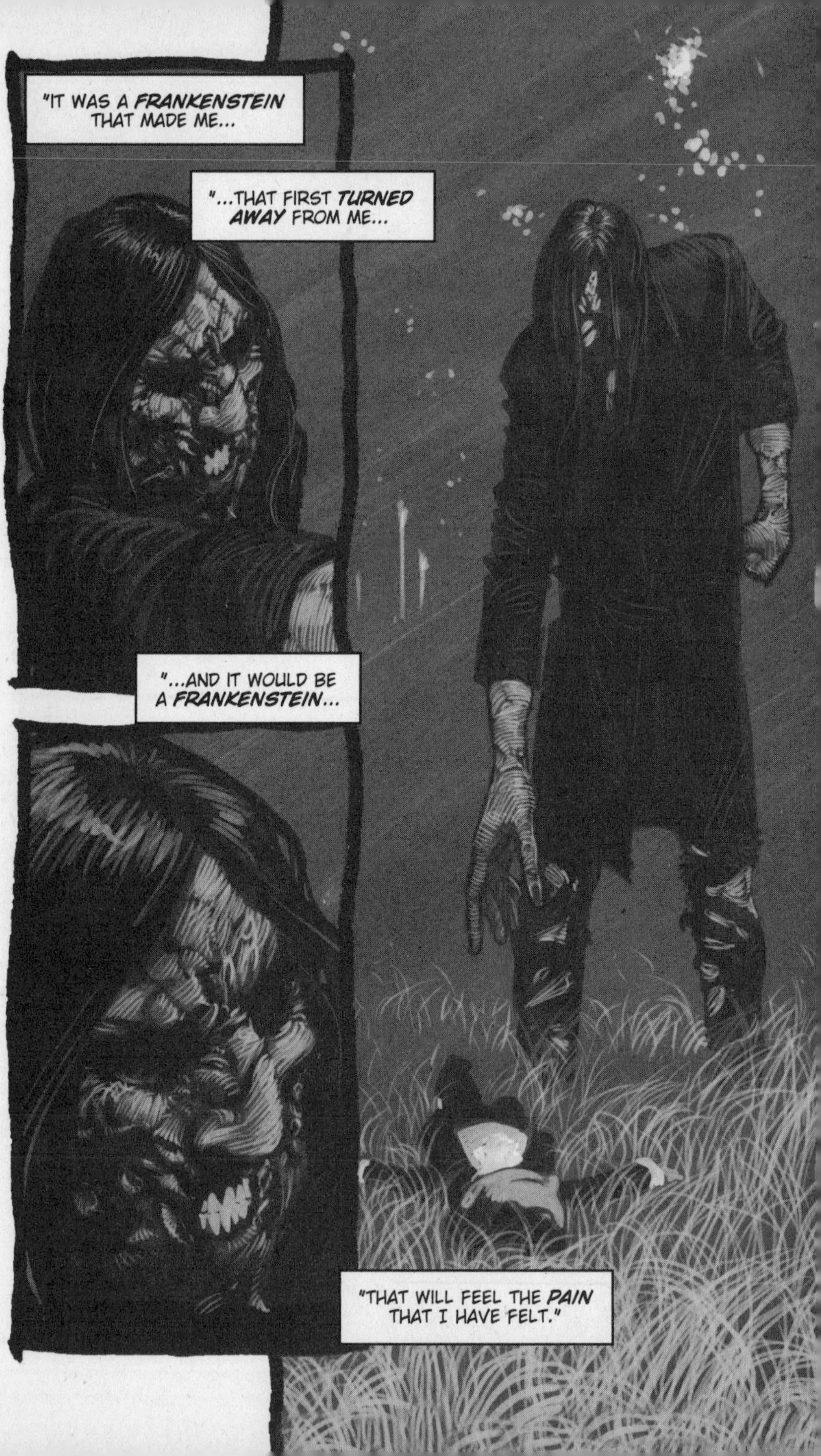
"IT WAS A FRANKENSTEIN THAT MADE ME...
"...THAT FIRST TURNED AWAY FROM ME...
"...AND IT WOULD BE A FRANKENSTEIN...
"THAT WILL FEEL THE PAIN THAT I HAVE FELT."

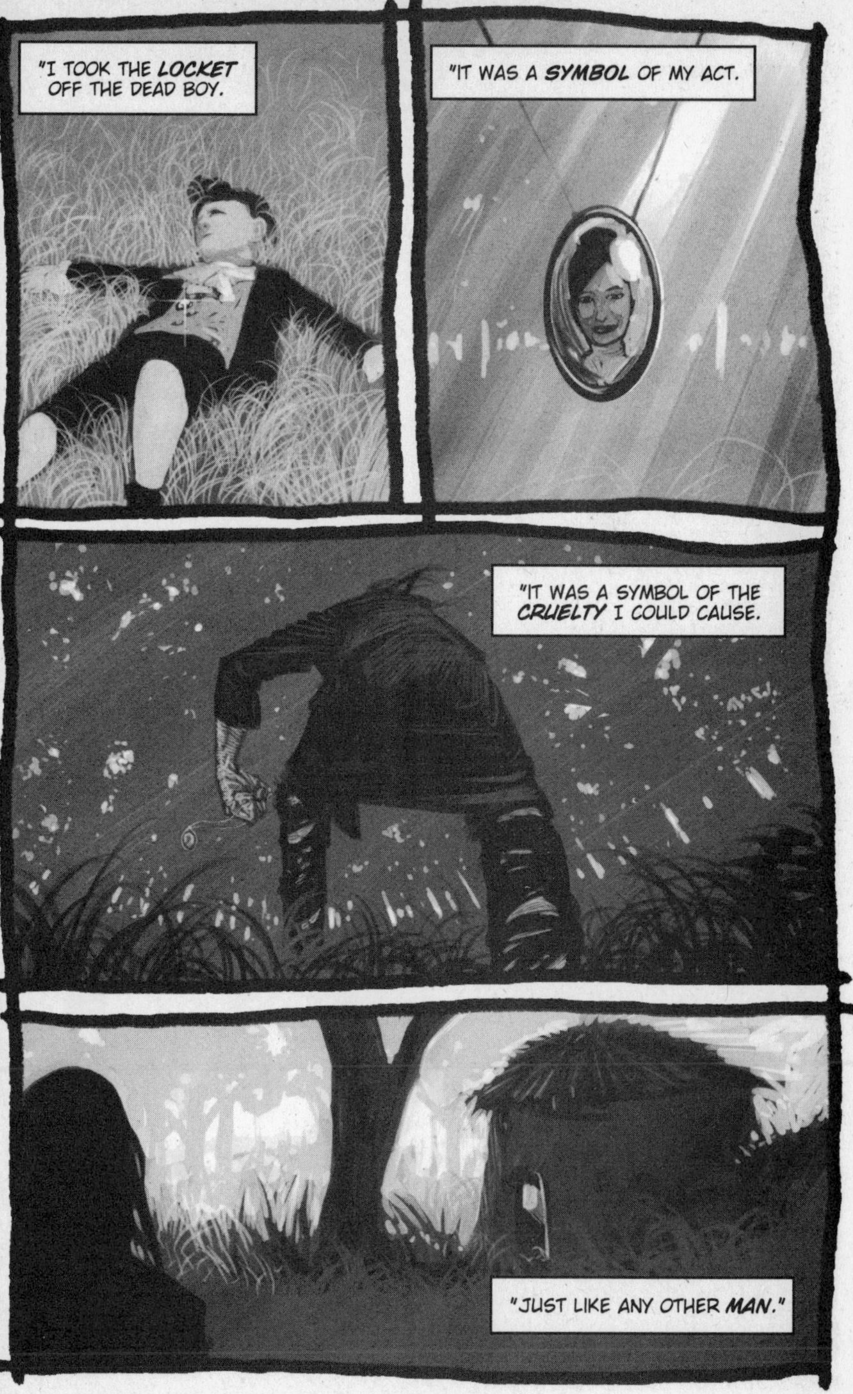
"I TOOK THE LOCKET OFF THE DEAD BOY.
"IT WAS A SYMBOL OF MY ACT.
"IT WAS A SYMBOL OF THE CRUELTY I COULD CAUSE.
"JUST LIKE ANY OTHER MAN."

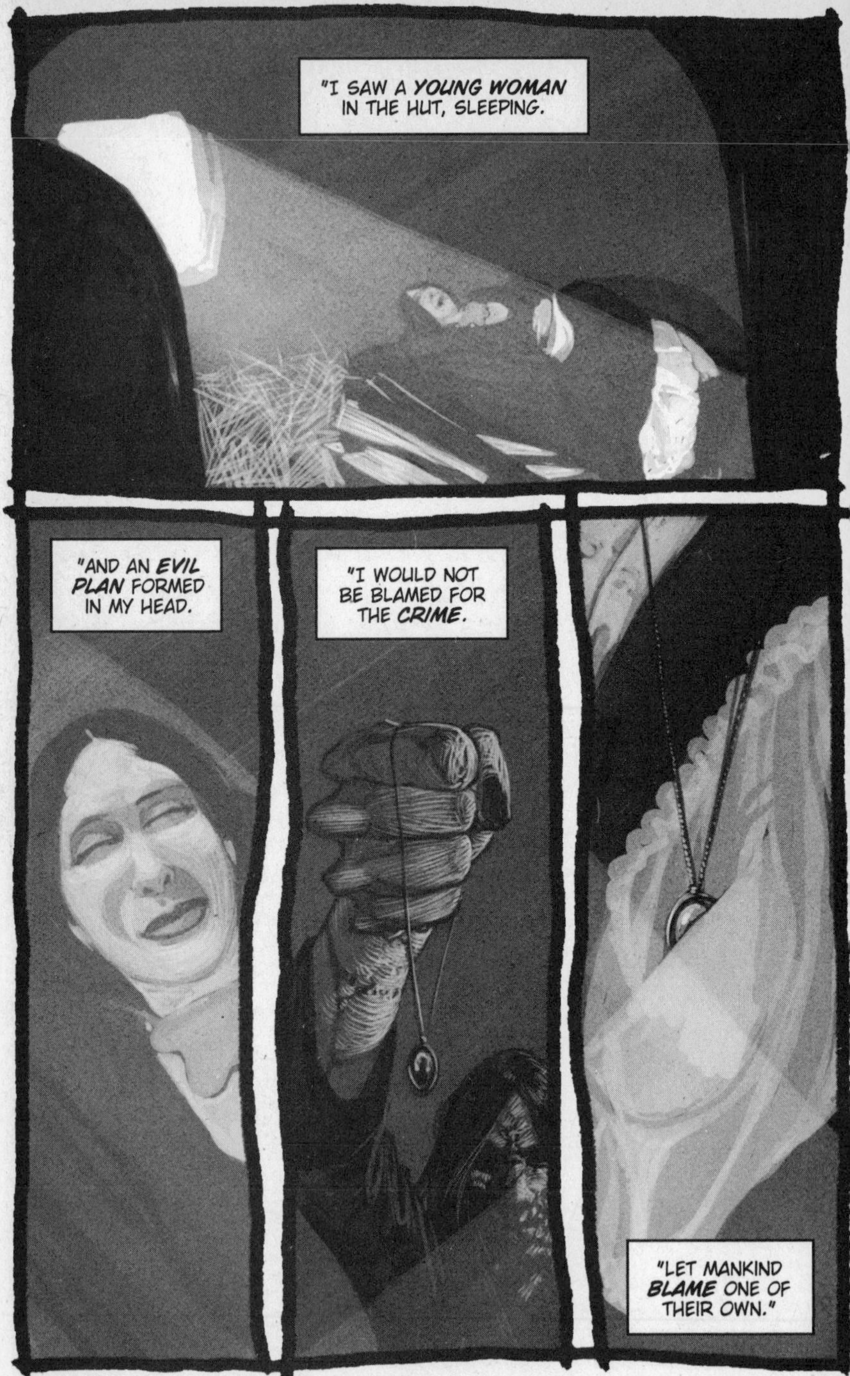
"I SAW A YOUNG WOMAN IN THE HUT, SLEEPING.
"AND AN EVIL PLAN FORMED IN MY HEAD.
"I WOULD NOT BE BLAMED FOR THE CRIME.
"LET MANKIND BLAME ONE OF THEIR OWN."

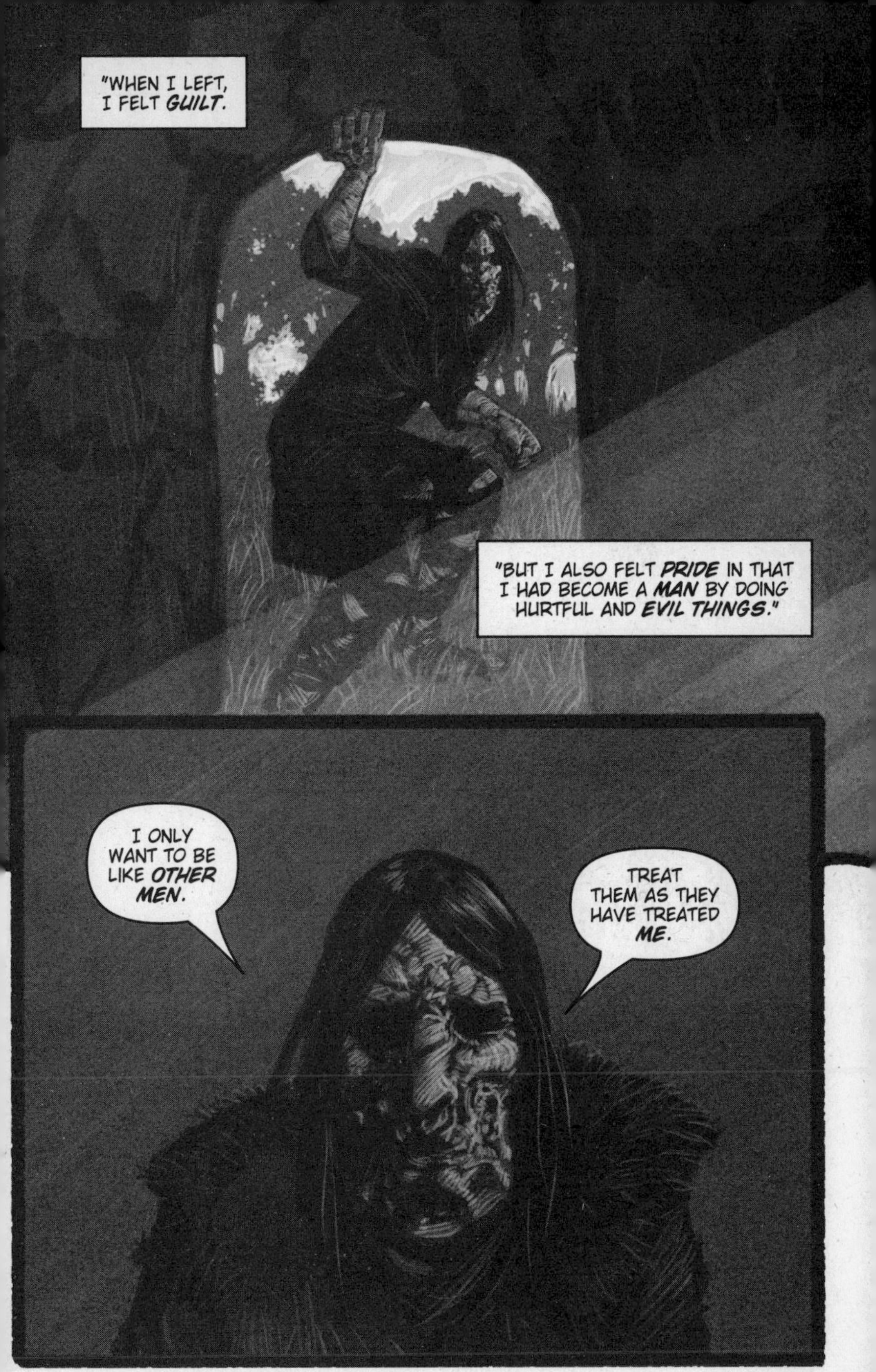
"WHEN I LEFT, I FELT GUILT.
"BUT I ALSO FELT PRIDE IN THAT I HAD BECOME A MAN BY DOING HURTFUL AND EVIL THINGS."
I ONLY WANT TO BE LIKE OTHER MEN.
TREAT THEM AS THEY HAVE TREATED ME.

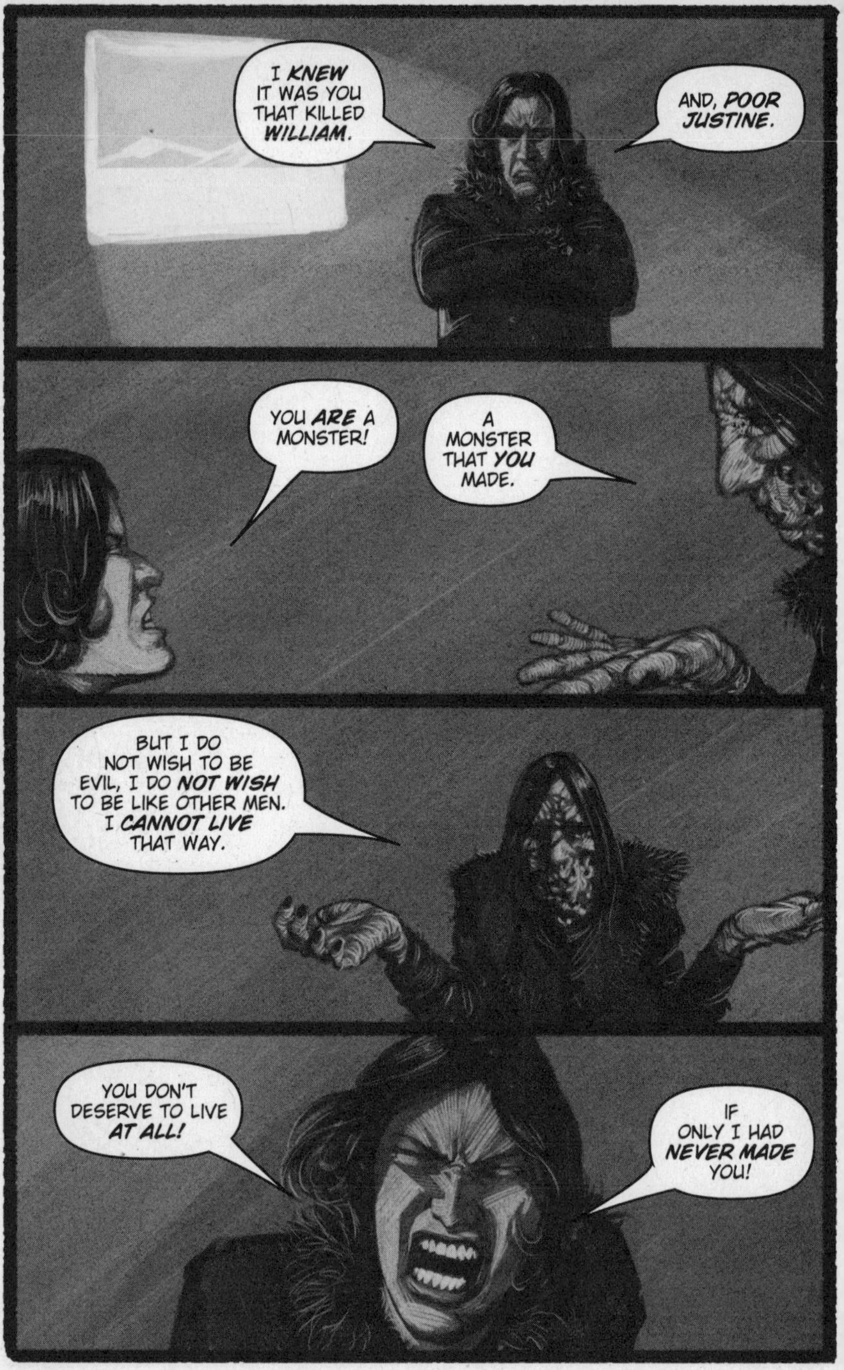
I KNEW IT WAS YOU THAT KILLED WILLIAM.
AND, POOR JUSTINE.
YOU ARE A MONSTER!
A MONSTER THAT YOU MADE.
BUT I DO NOT WISH TO BE EVIL, I DO NOT WISH TO BE LIKE OTHER MEN. I CANNOT LIVE THAT WAY.
YOU DON'T DESERVE TO LIVE AT ALL!
IF ONLY I HAD NEVER MADE YOU!

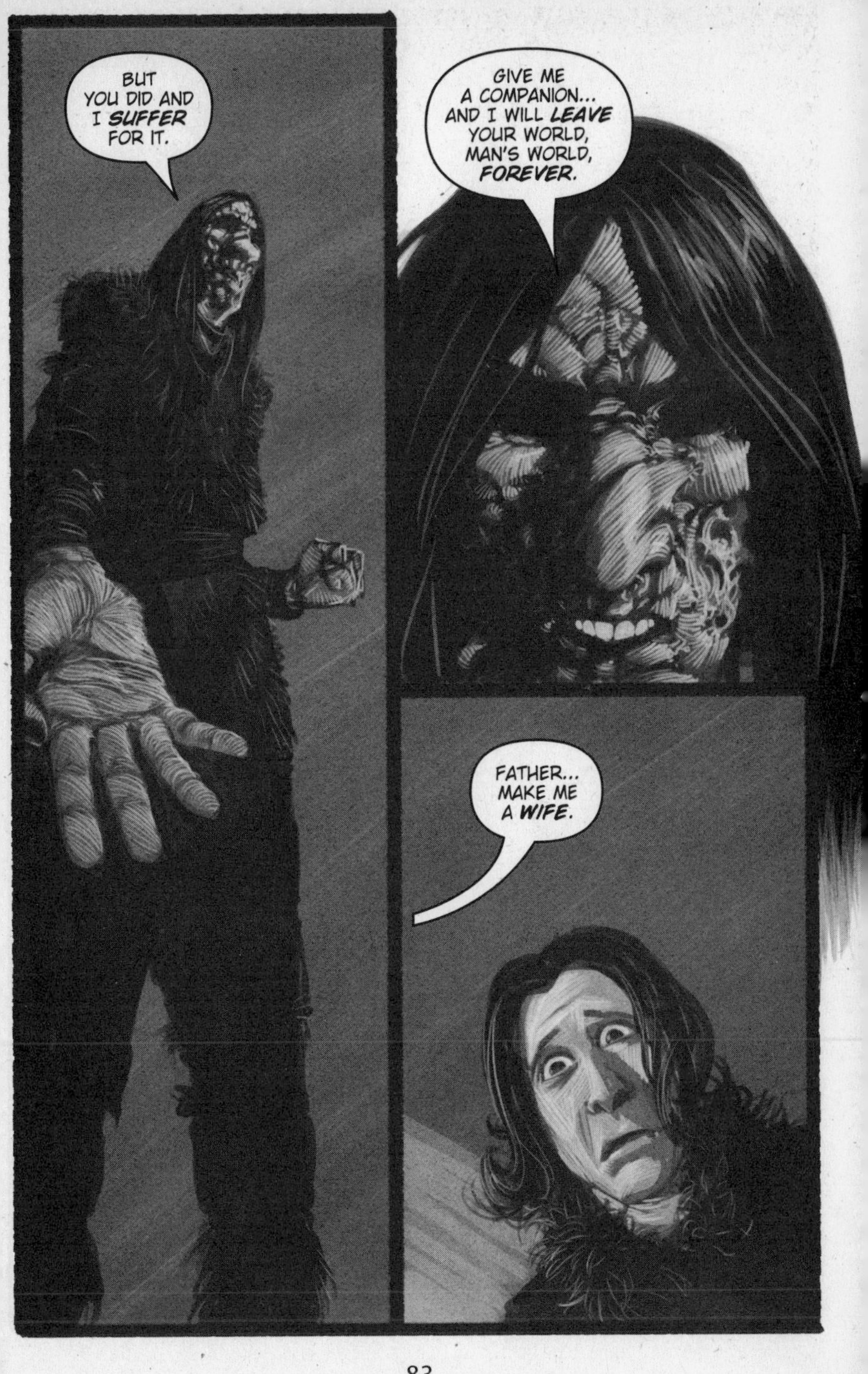
BUT YOU DID AND I SUFFER FOR IT.
GIVE ME A COMPANION... AND I WILL LEAVE YOUR WORLD, MAN'S WORLD, FOREVER.
FATHER... MAKE ME A WIFE.

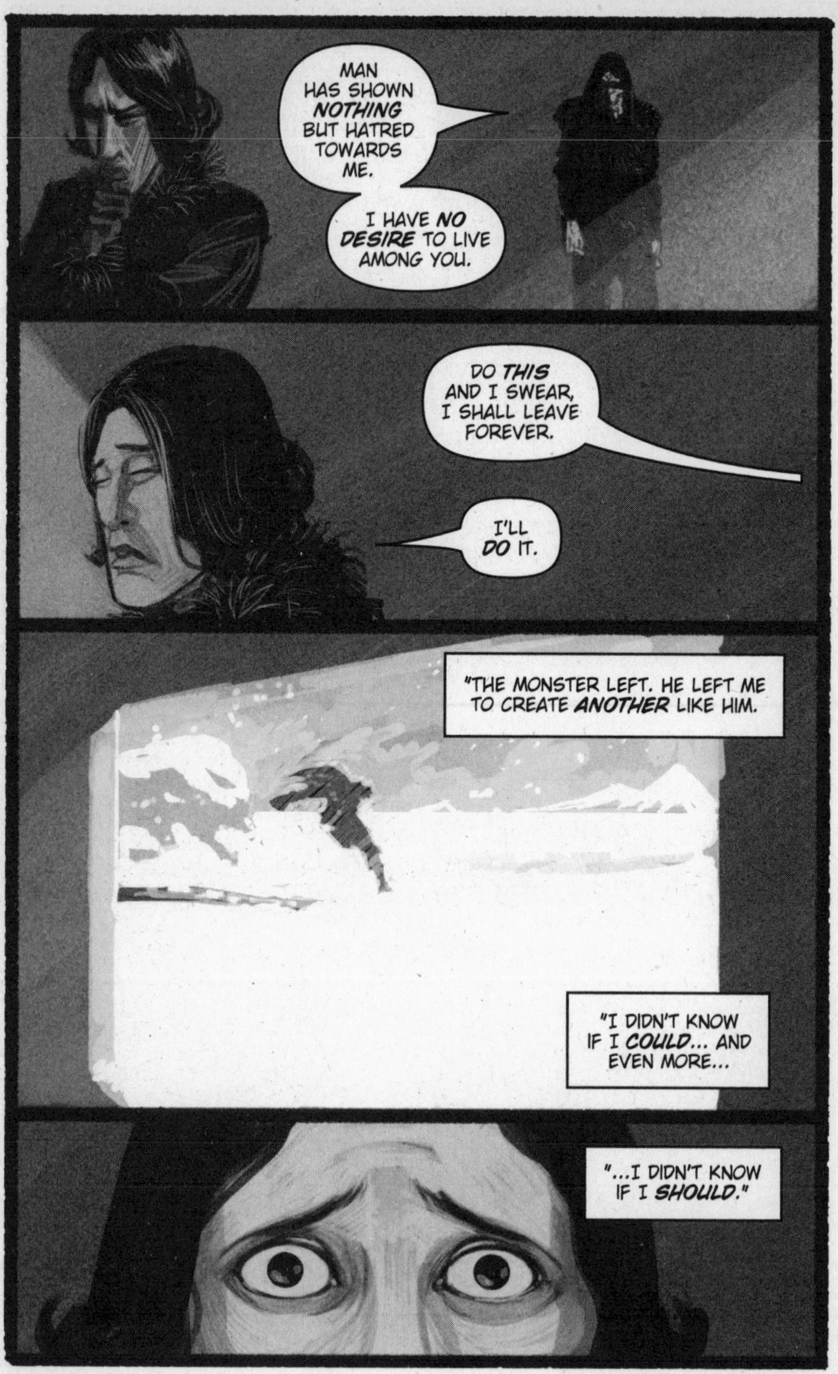
MAN HAS SHOWN *NOTHING* BUT HATRED TOWARDS ME.
I HAVE *NO DESIRE* TO LIVE AMONG YOU.
DO *THIS* AND I SWEAR, I SHALL LEAVE FOREVER.
I'LL *DO* IT.
"THE MONSTER LEFT. HE LEFT ME TO CREATE *ANOTHER* LIKE HIM.
"I DIDN'T KNOW IF I *COULD*... AND EVEN MORE...
"...I DIDN'T KNOW IF I *SHOULD*."

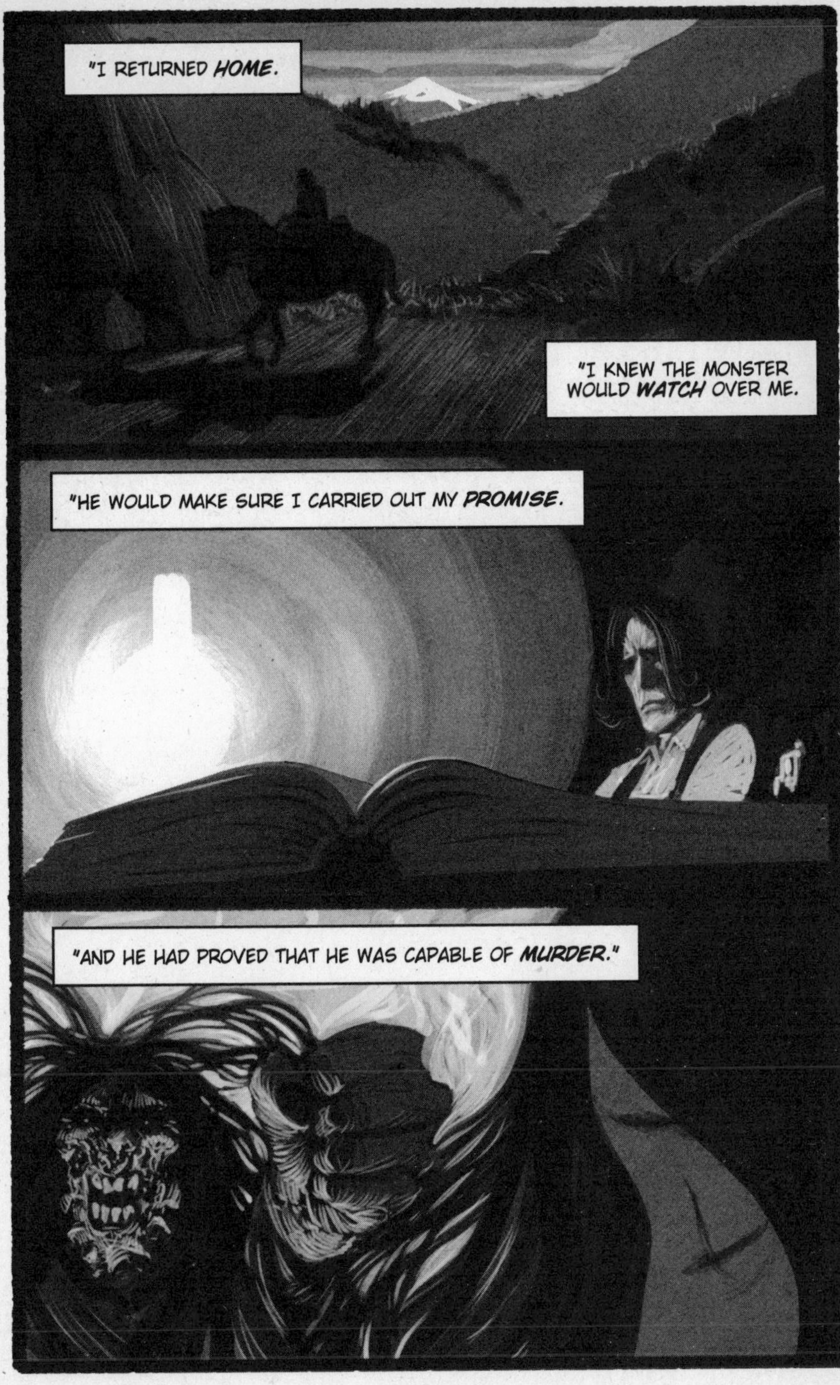
"I RETURNED HOME.
"I KNEW THE MONSTER WOULD WATCH OVER ME.
"HE WOULD MAKE SURE I CARRIED OUT MY PROMISE.
"AND HE HAD PROVED THAT HE WAS CAPABLE OF MURDER."

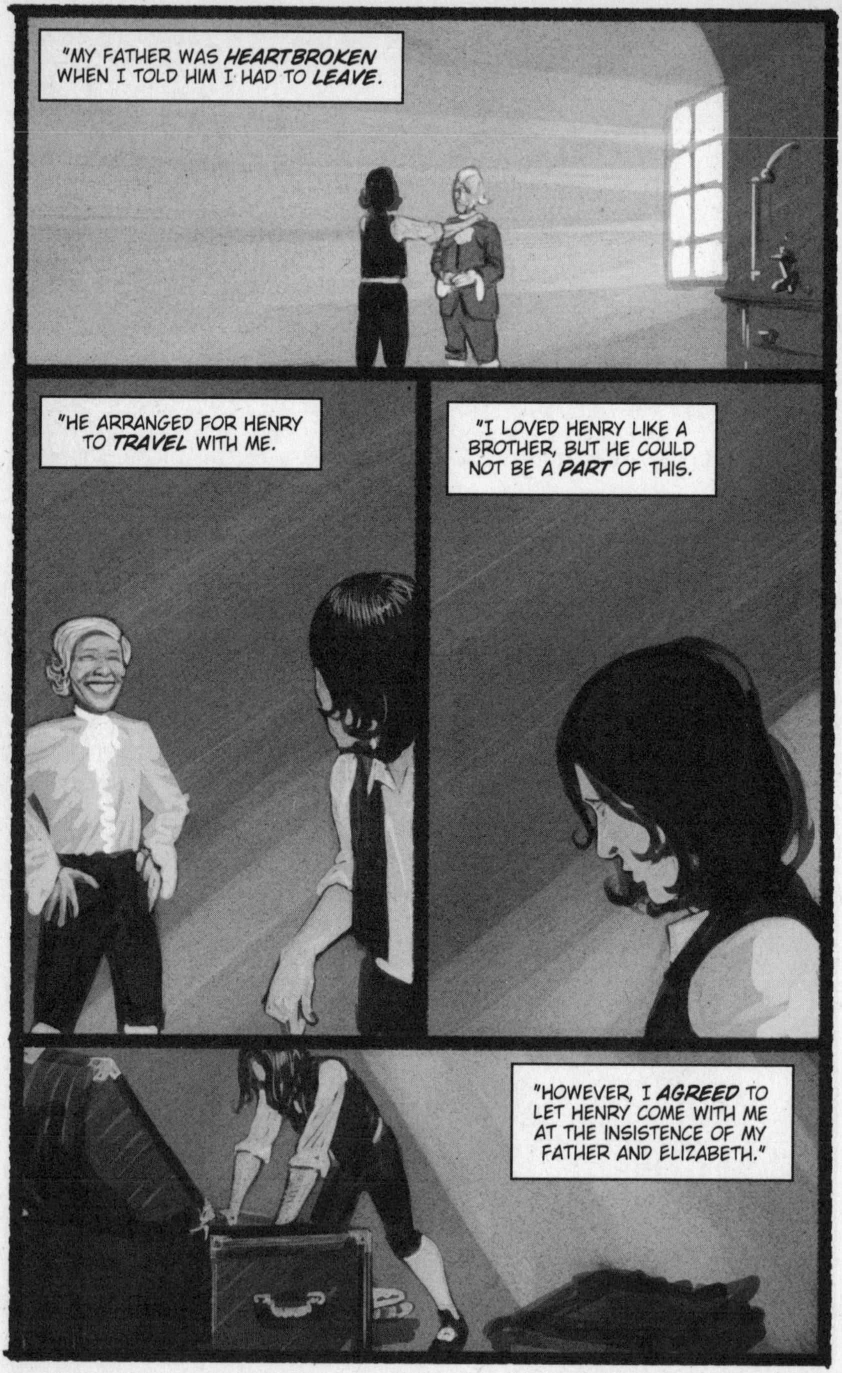
"MY FATHER WAS HEARTBROKEN WHEN I TOLD HIM I HAD TO LEAVE.
"HE ARRANGED FOR HENRY TO TRAVEL WITH ME.
"I LOVED HENRY LIKE A BROTHER, BUT HE COULD NOT BE A PART OF THIS.
"HOWEVER, I AGREED TO LET HENRY COME WITH ME AT THE INSISTENCE OF MY FATHER AND ELIZABETH."

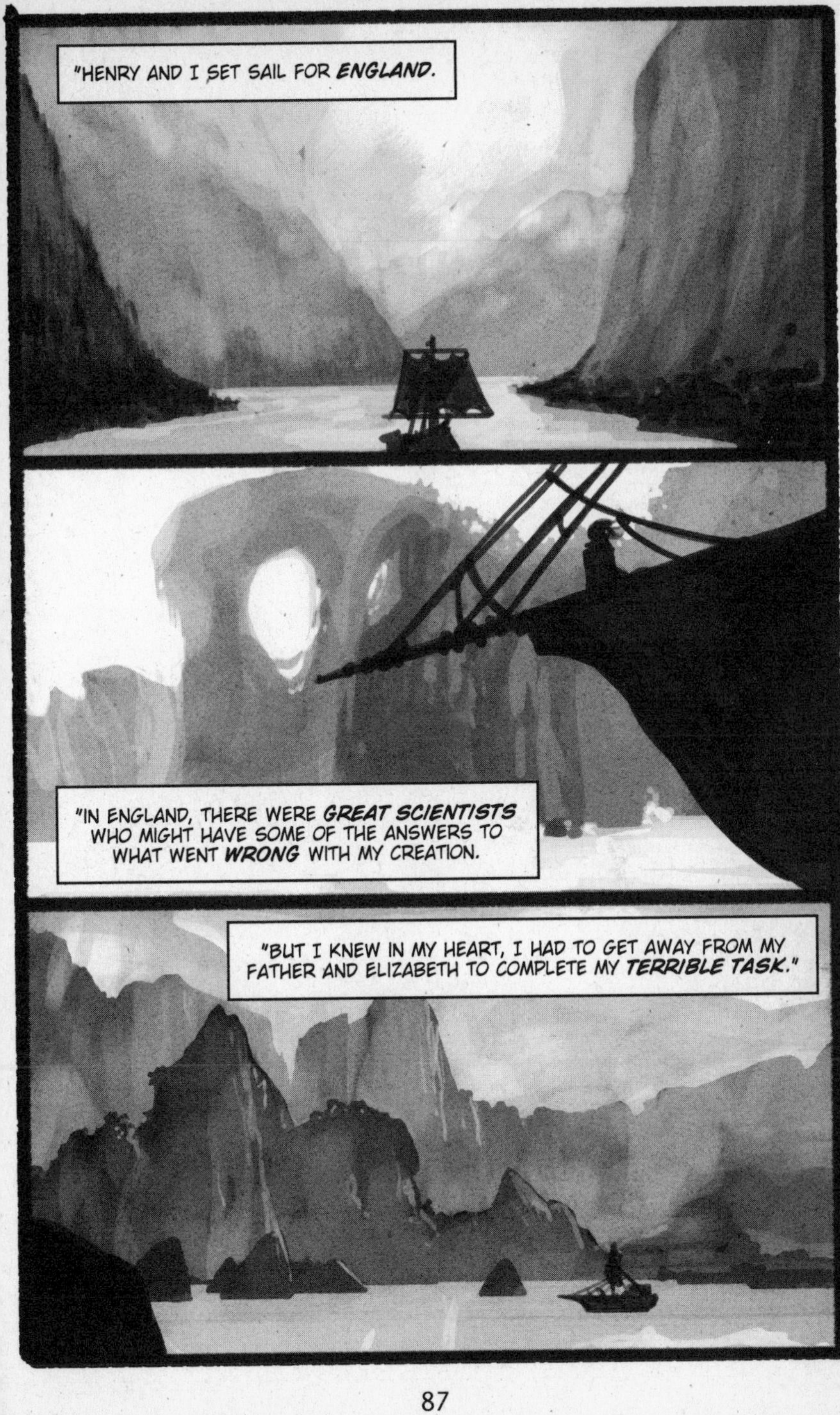
"HENRY AND I SET SAIL FOR ENGLAND.
"IN ENGLAND, THERE WERE GREAT SCIENTISTS WHO MIGHT HAVE SOME OF THE ANSWERS TO WHAT WENT WRONG WITH MY CREATION.
"BUT I KNEW IN MY HEART, I HAD TO GET AWAY FROM MY FATHER AND ELIZABETH TO COMPLETE MY TERRIBLE TASK."

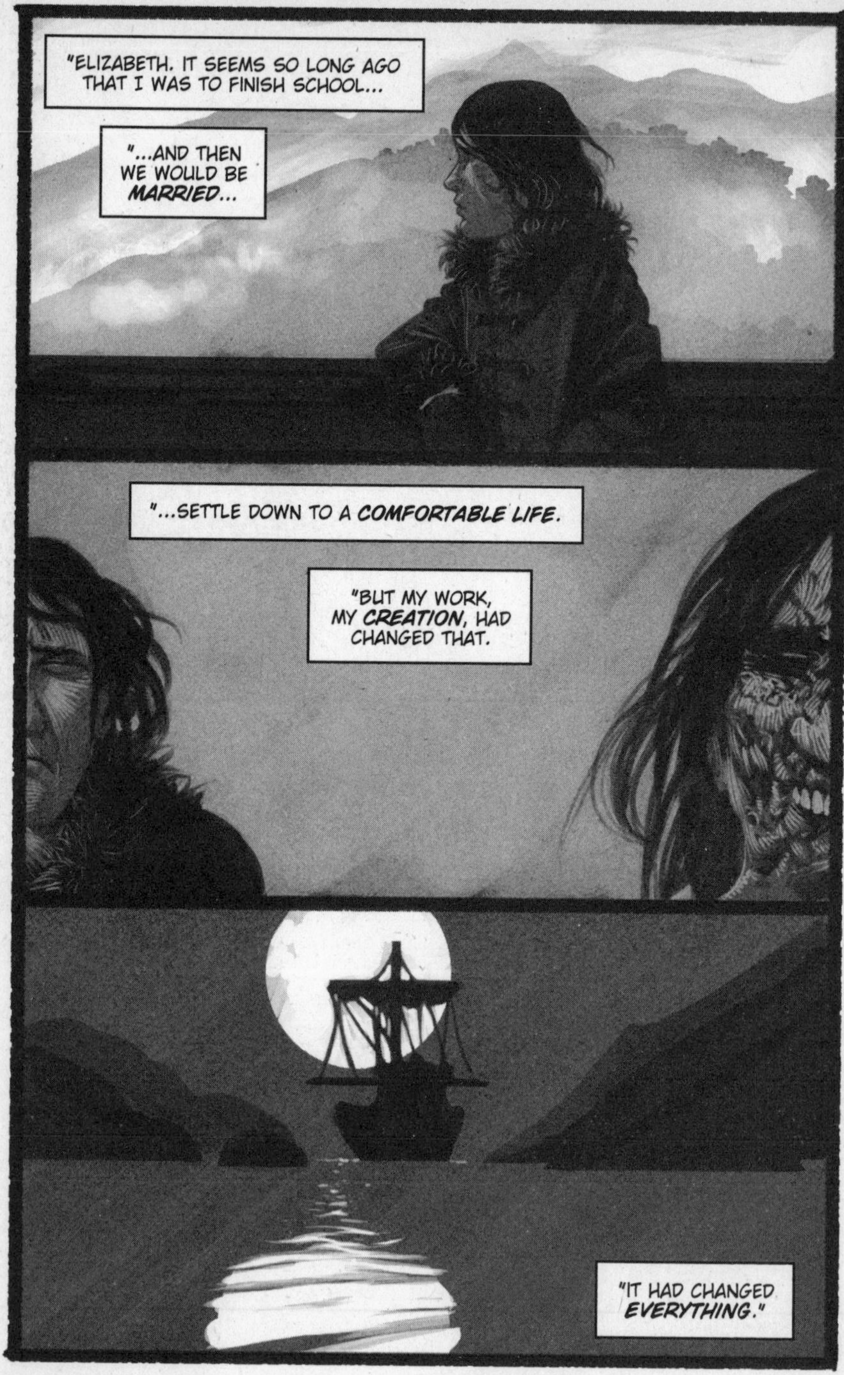
"ELIZABETH. IT SEEMS SO LONG AGO THAT I WAS TO FINISH SCHOOL...
"...AND THEN WE WOULD BE *MARRIED*...
"...SETTLE DOWN TO A *COMFORTABLE LIFE*.
"BUT MY WORK, MY *CREATION*, HAD CHANGED THAT.
"IT HAD CHANGED *EVERYTHING*."

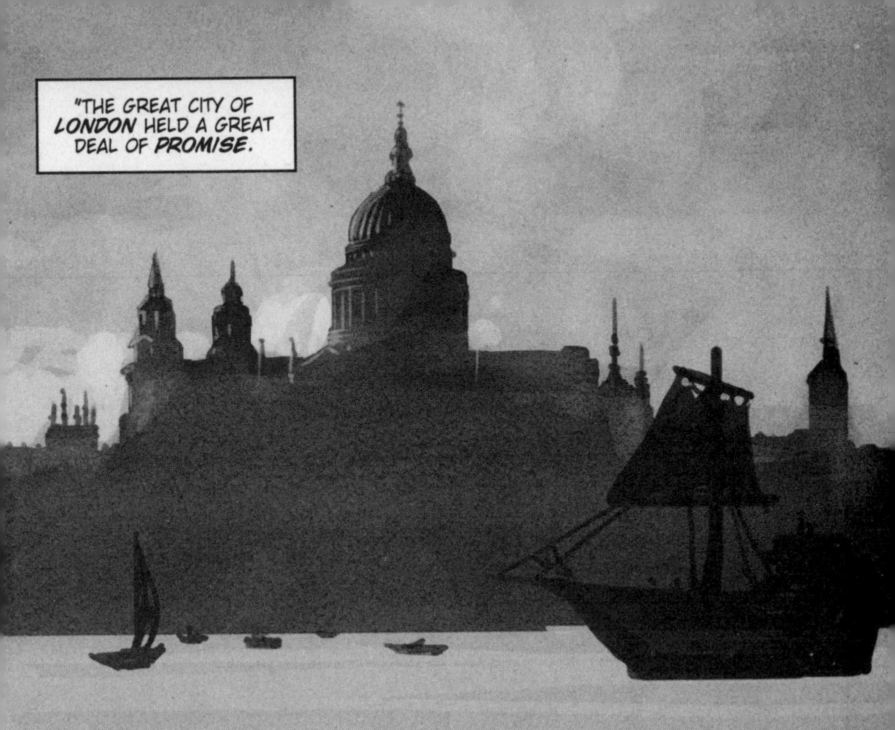
"THE GREAT CITY OF LONDON HELD A GREAT DEAL OF PROMISE.

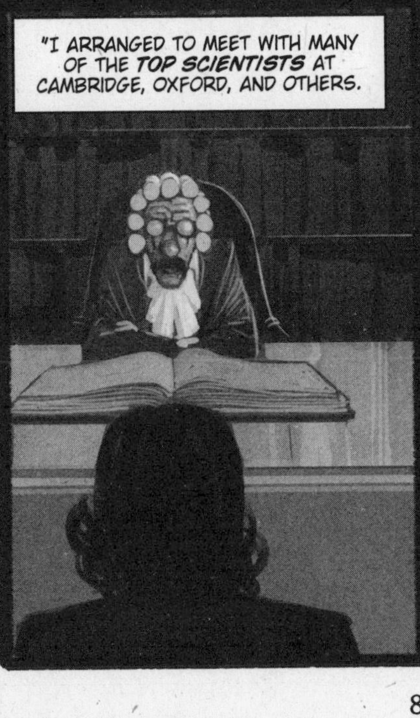
"I ARRANGED TO MEET WITH MANY OF THE TOP SCIENTISTS AT CAMBRIDGE, OXFORD, AND OTHERS.

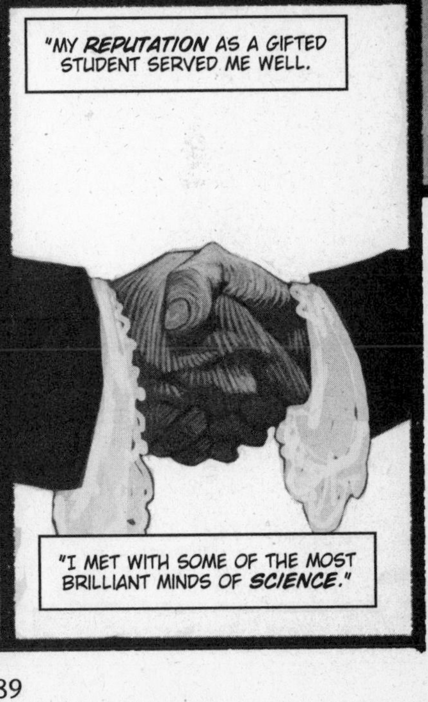
"MY REPUTATION AS A GIFTED STUDENT SERVED ME WELL.
"I MET WITH SOME OF THE MOST BRILLIANT MINDS OF SCIENCE."

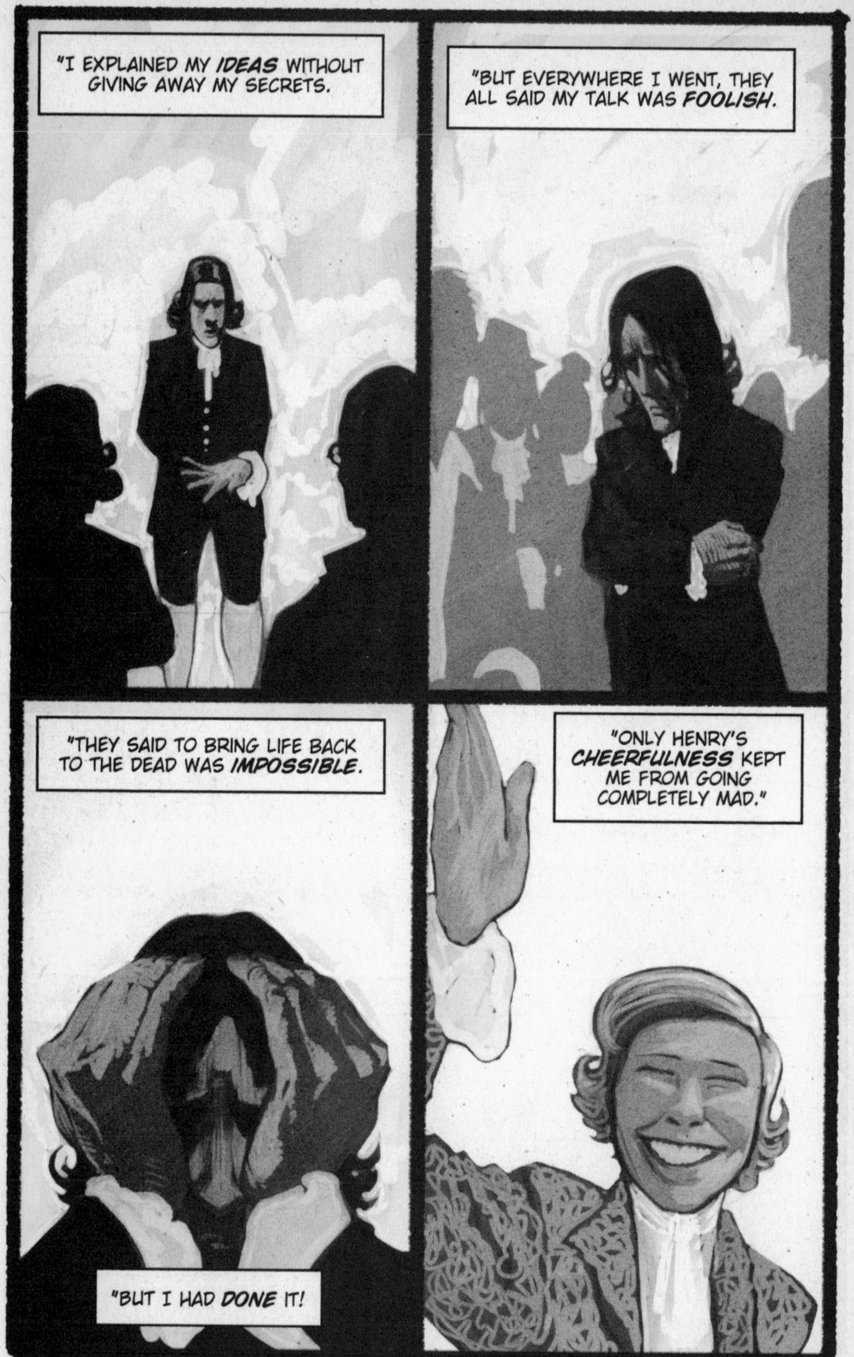
"I EXPLAINED MY IDEAS WITHOUT GIVING AWAY MY SECRETS.
"BUT EVERYWHERE I WENT, THEY ALL SAID MY TALK WAS FOOLISH.
"THEY SAID TO BRING LIFE BACK TO THE DEAD WAS IMPOSSIBLE.
"BUT I HAD DONE IT!
"ONLY HENRY'S CHEERFULNESS KEPT ME FROM GOING COMPLETELY MAD."

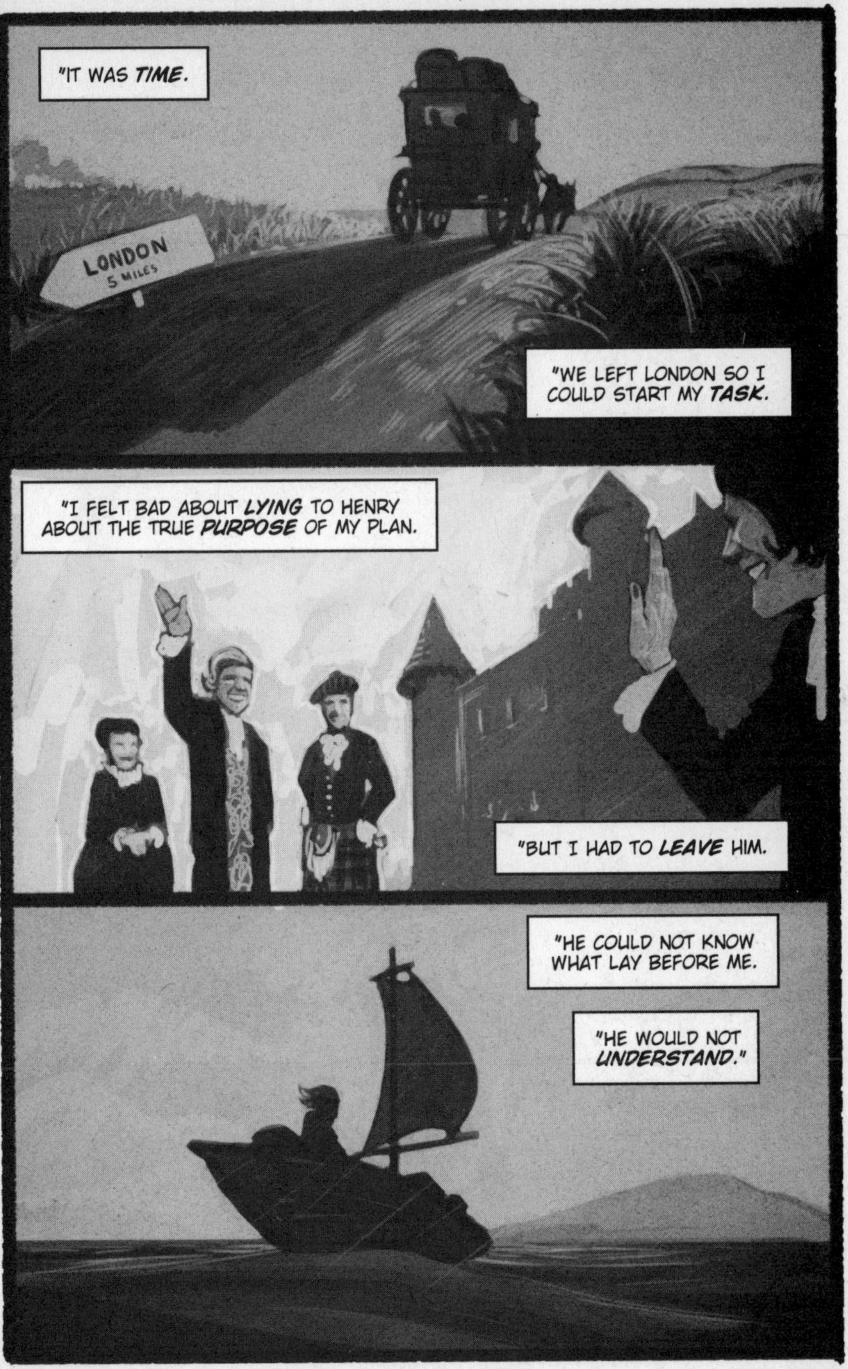
"IT WAS TIME.
LONDON 5 MILES
"WE LEFT LONDON SO I COULD START MY TASK.
"I FELT BAD ABOUT LYING TO HENRY ABOUT THE TRUE PURPOSE OF MY PLAN.
"BUT I HAD TO LEAVE HIM.
"HE COULD NOT KNOW WHAT LAY BEFORE ME.
"HE WOULD NOT UNDERSTAND."

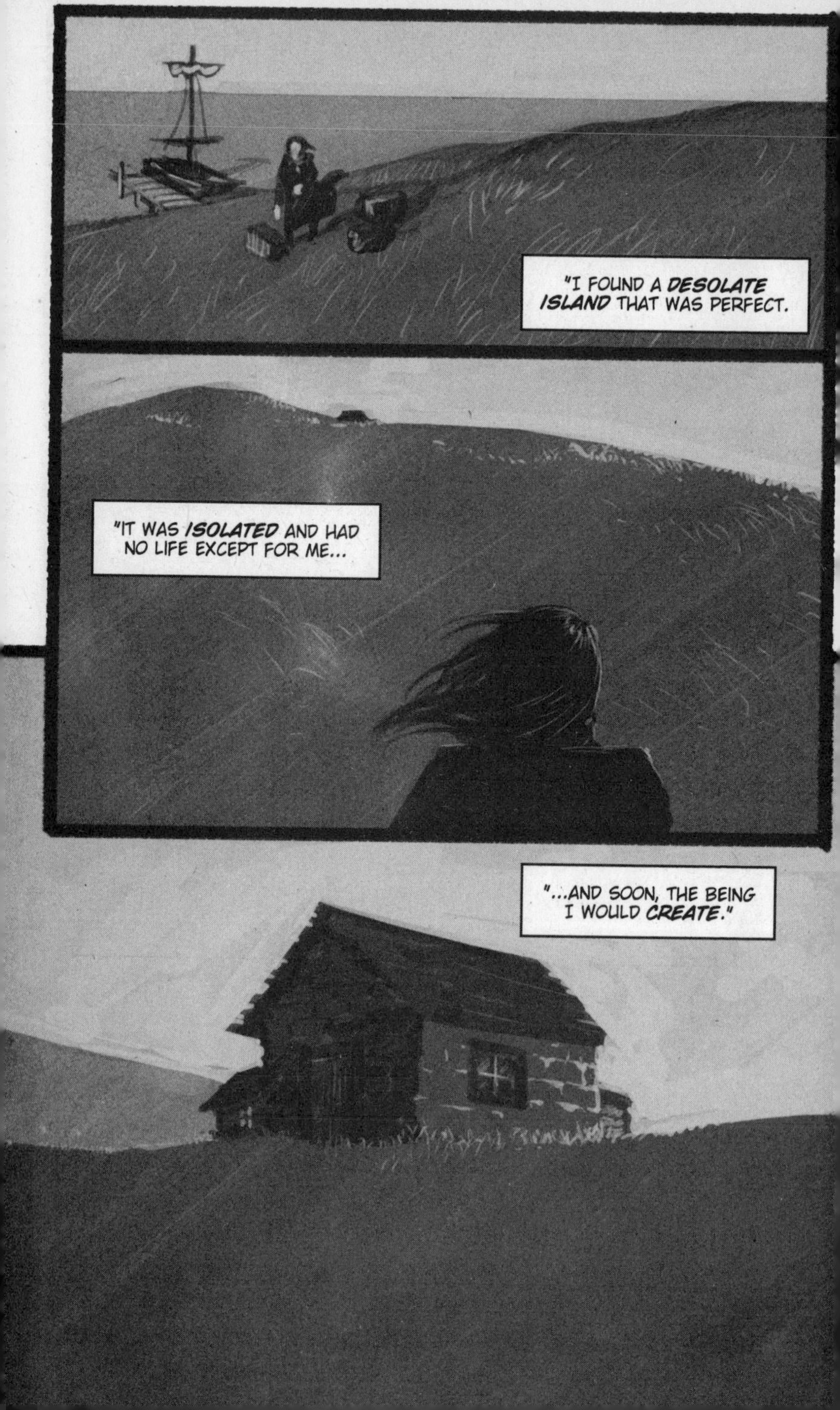
"I FOUND A DESOLATE ISLAND THAT WAS PERFECT.
"IT WAS ISOLATED AND HAD NO LIFE EXCEPT FOR ME...
"...AND SOON, THE BEING I WOULD CREATE."

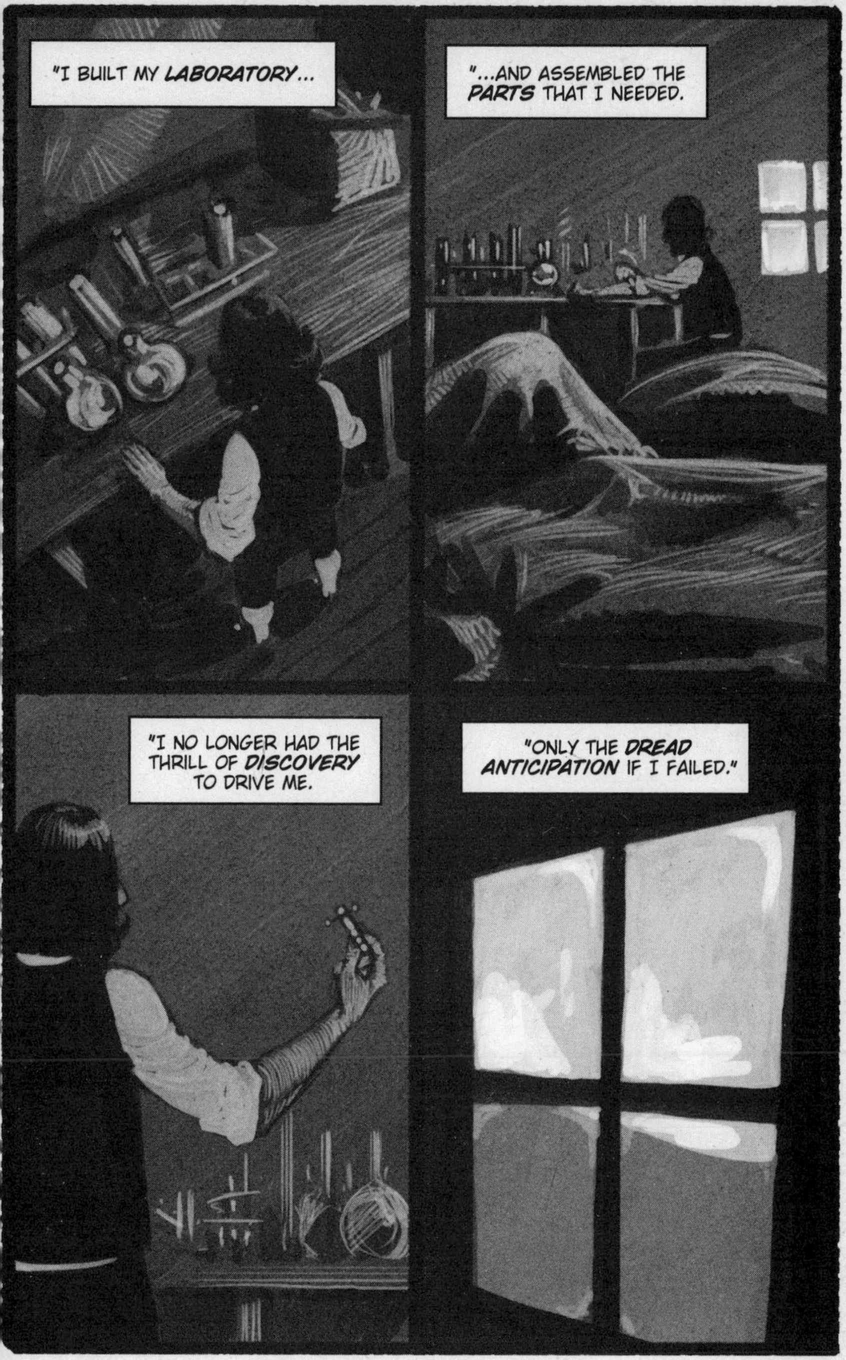
"I BUILT MY LABORATORY...
"...AND ASSEMBLED THE PARTS THAT I NEEDED.
"I NO LONGER HAD THE THRILL OF DISCOVERY TO DRIVE ME.
"ONLY THE DREAD ANTICIPATION IF I FAILED."

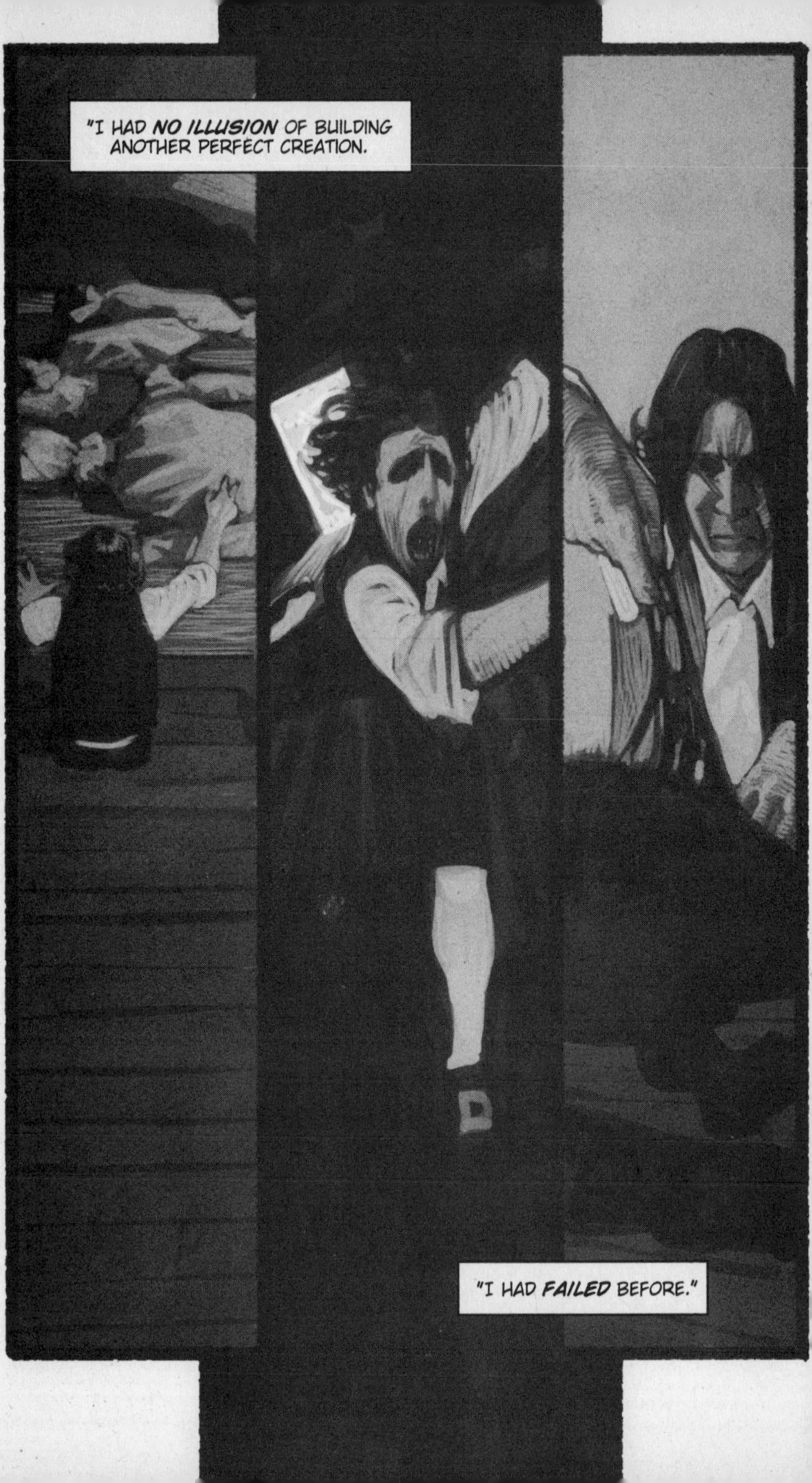
"I HAD NO ILLUSION OF BUILDING ANOTHER PERFECT CREATION.
"I HAD FAILED BEFORE."

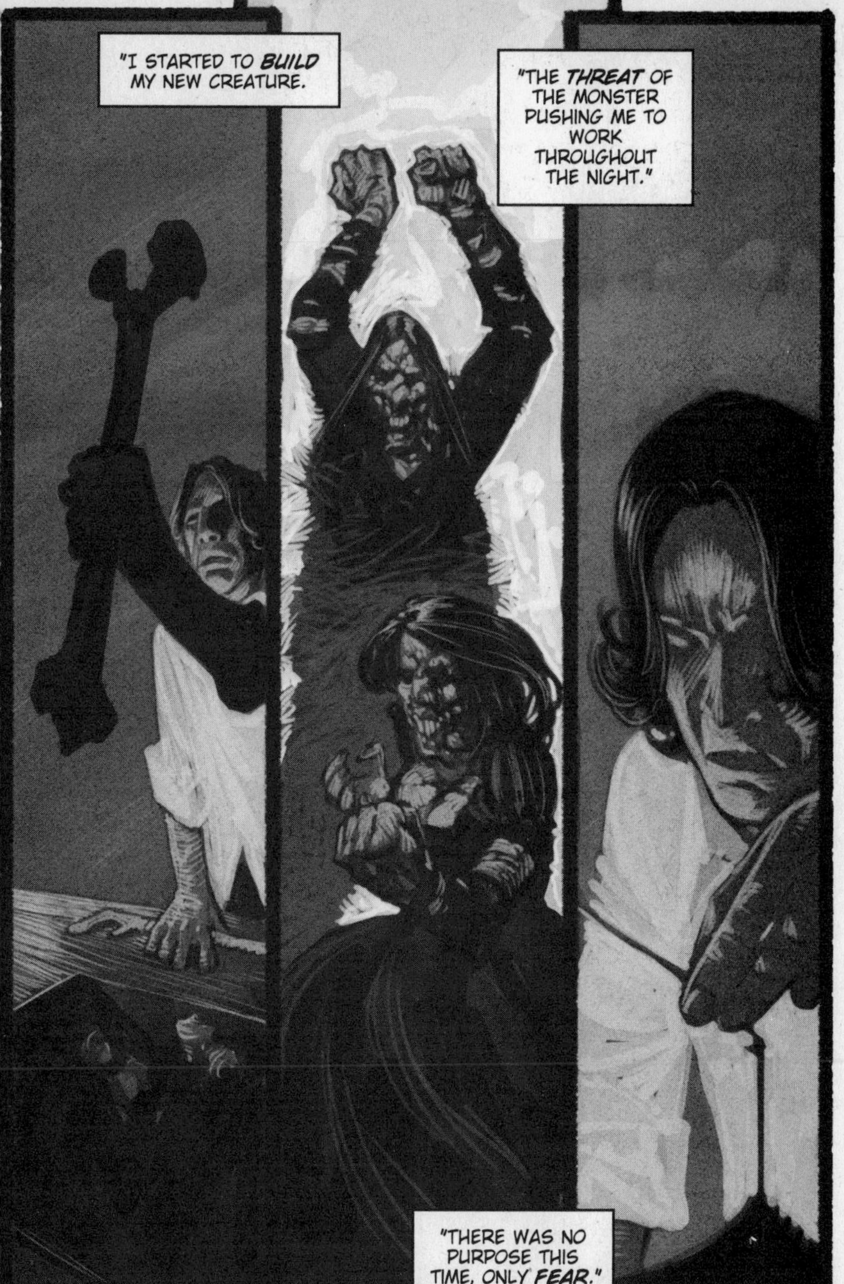
"I STARTED TO BUILD MY NEW CREATURE.
"THE THREAT OF THE MONSTER PUSHING ME TO WORK THROUGHOUT THE NIGHT."
"THERE WAS NO PURPOSE THIS TIME, ONLY FEAR."

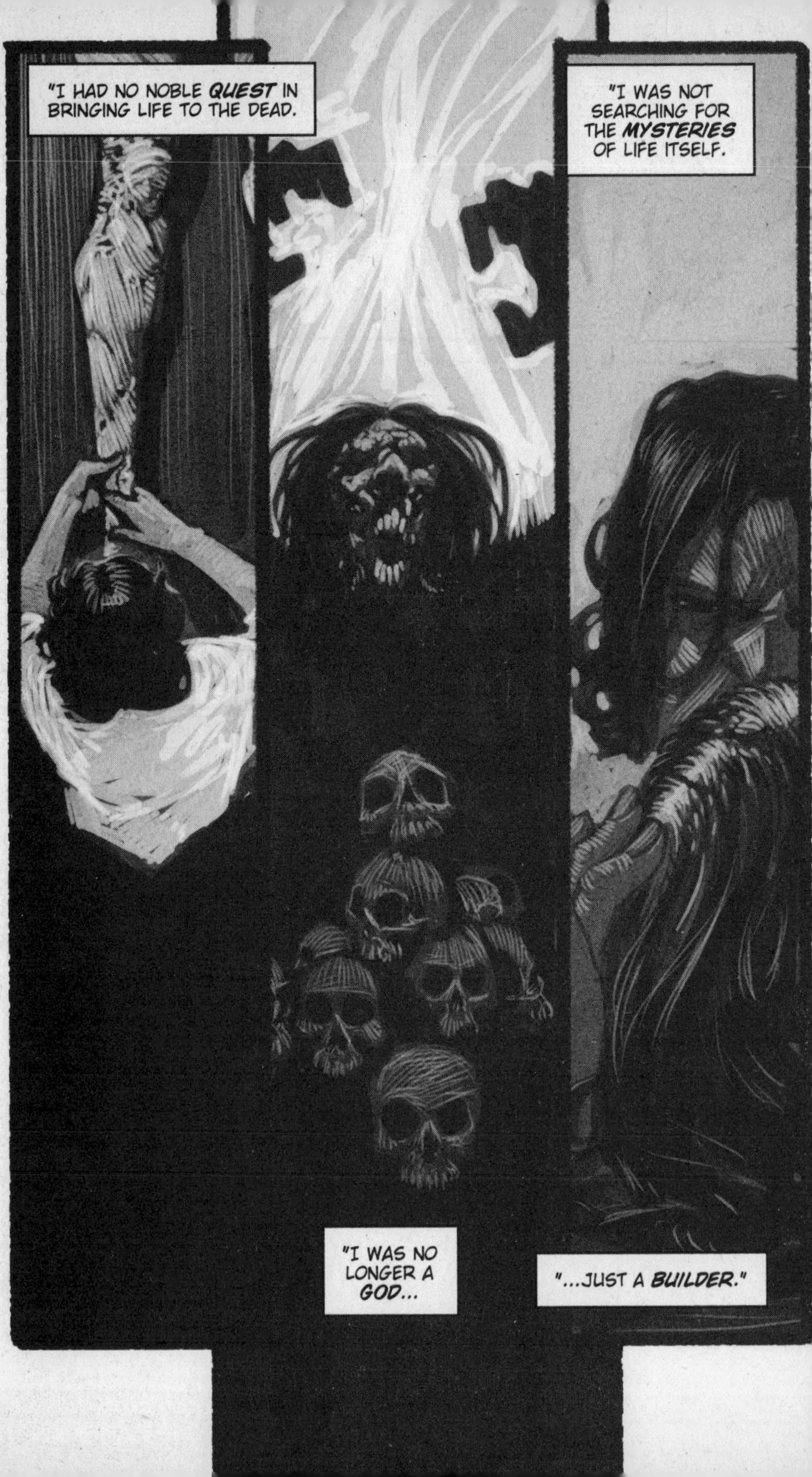
"I HAD NO NOBLE QUEST IN BRINGING LIFE TO THE DEAD.
"I WAS NOT SEARCHING FOR THE MYSTERIES OF LIFE ITSELF.
"I WAS NO LONGER A GOD...
"...JUST A BUILDER."

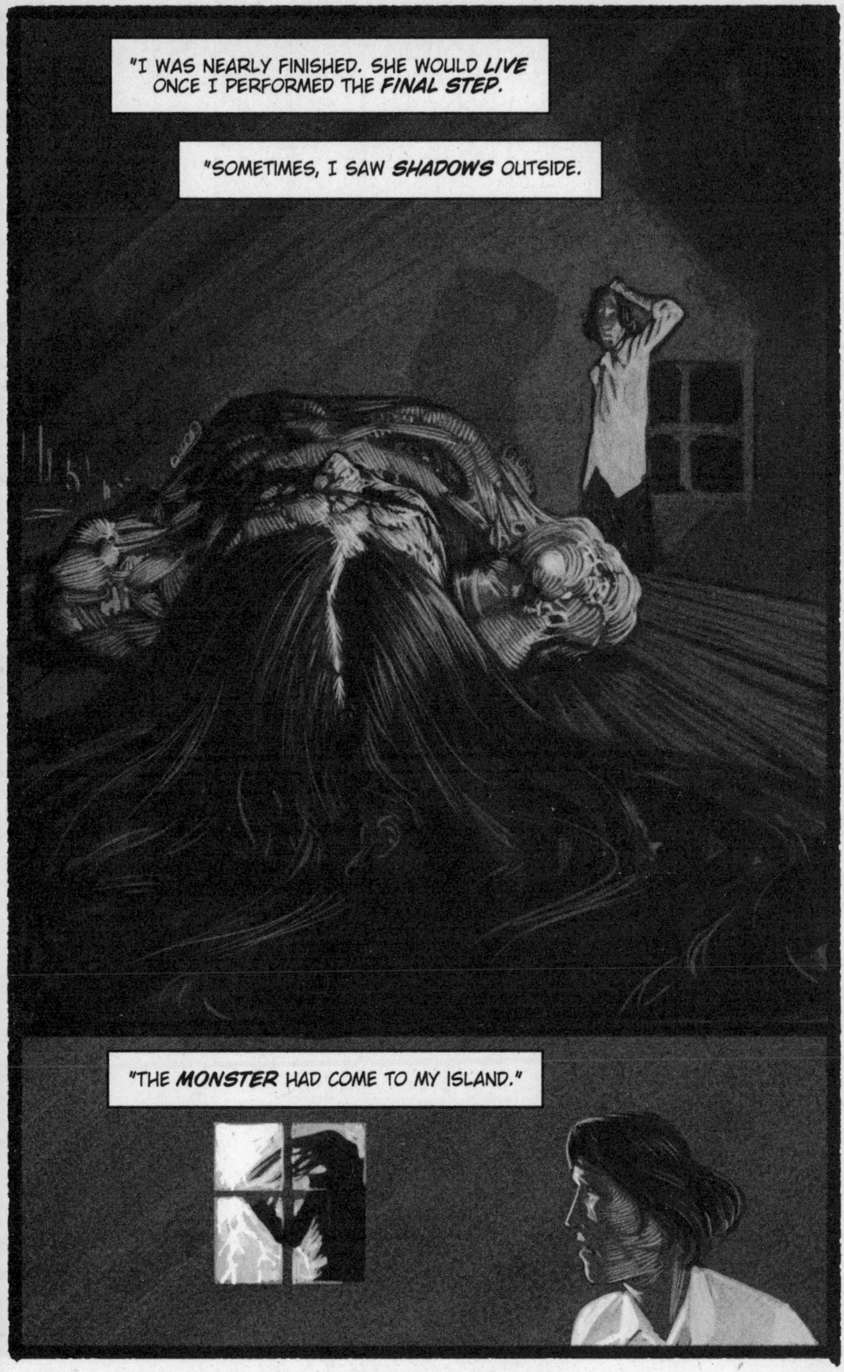
"I WAS NEARLY FINISHED. SHE WOULD LIVE ONCE I PERFORMED THE FINAL STEP.
"SOMETIMES, I SAW SHADOWS OUTSIDE.
"THE MONSTER HAD COME TO MY ISLAND."

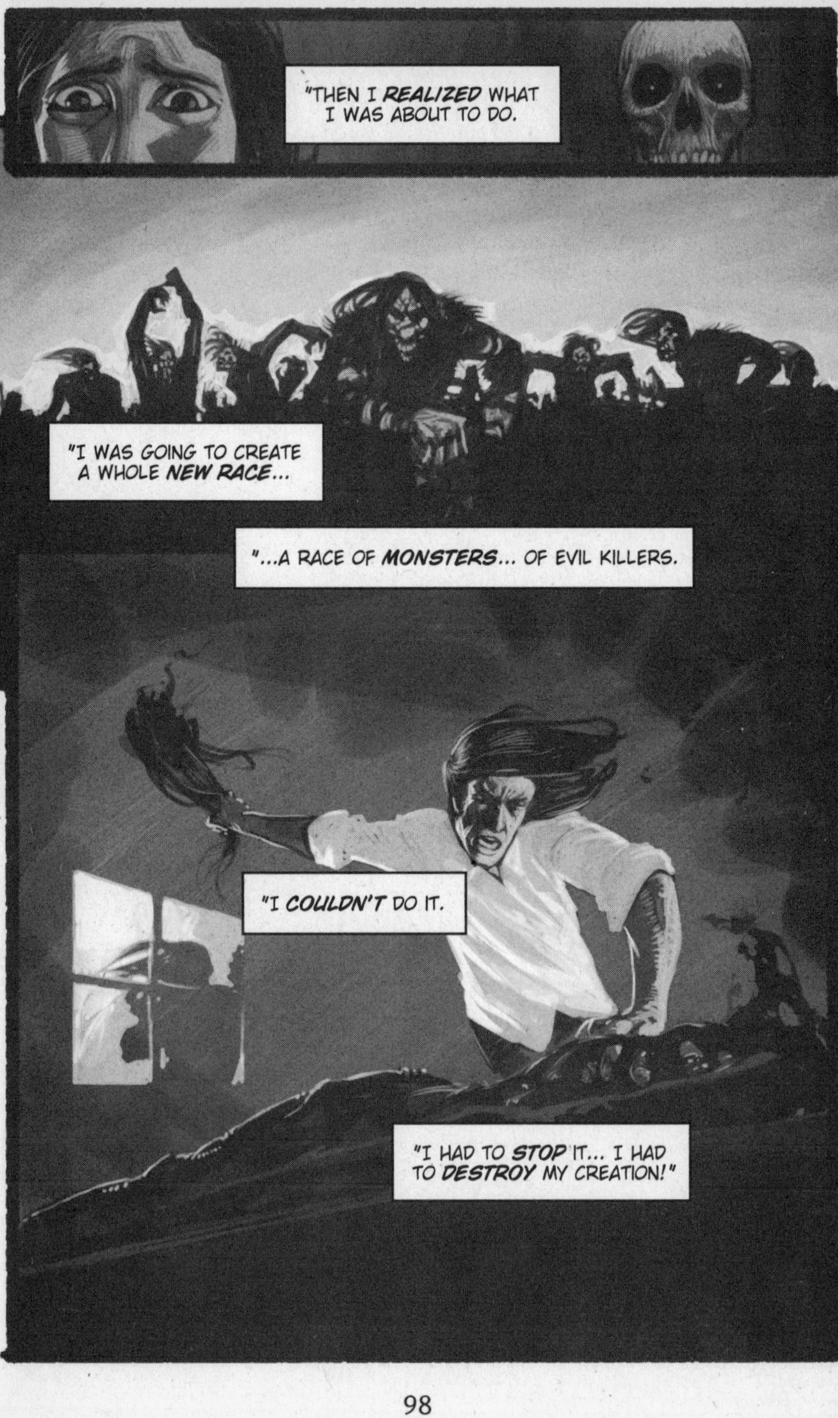
"THEN I REALIZED WHAT I WAS ABOUT TO DO.
"I WAS GOING TO CREATE A WHOLE NEW RACE...
"...A RACE OF MONSTERS... OF EVIL KILLERS.
"I COULDN'T DO IT.
"I HAD TO STOP IT... I HAD TO DESTROY MY CREATION!"

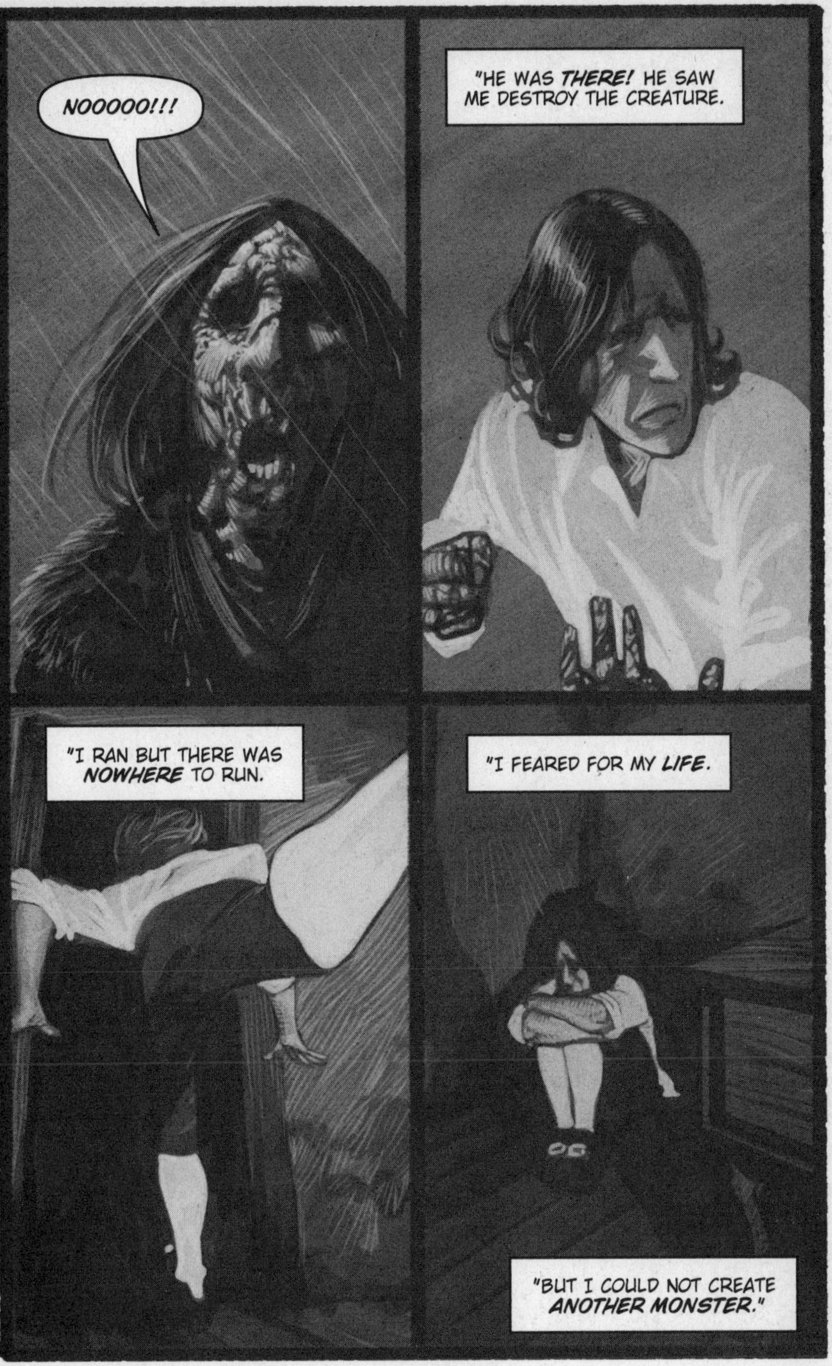
NOOOOO!!!
"HE WAS THERE! HE SAW ME DESTROY THE CREATURE.
"I RAN BUT THERE WAS NOWHERE TO RUN.
"I FEARED FOR MY LIFE.
"BUT I COULD NOT CREATE ANOTHER MONSTER."

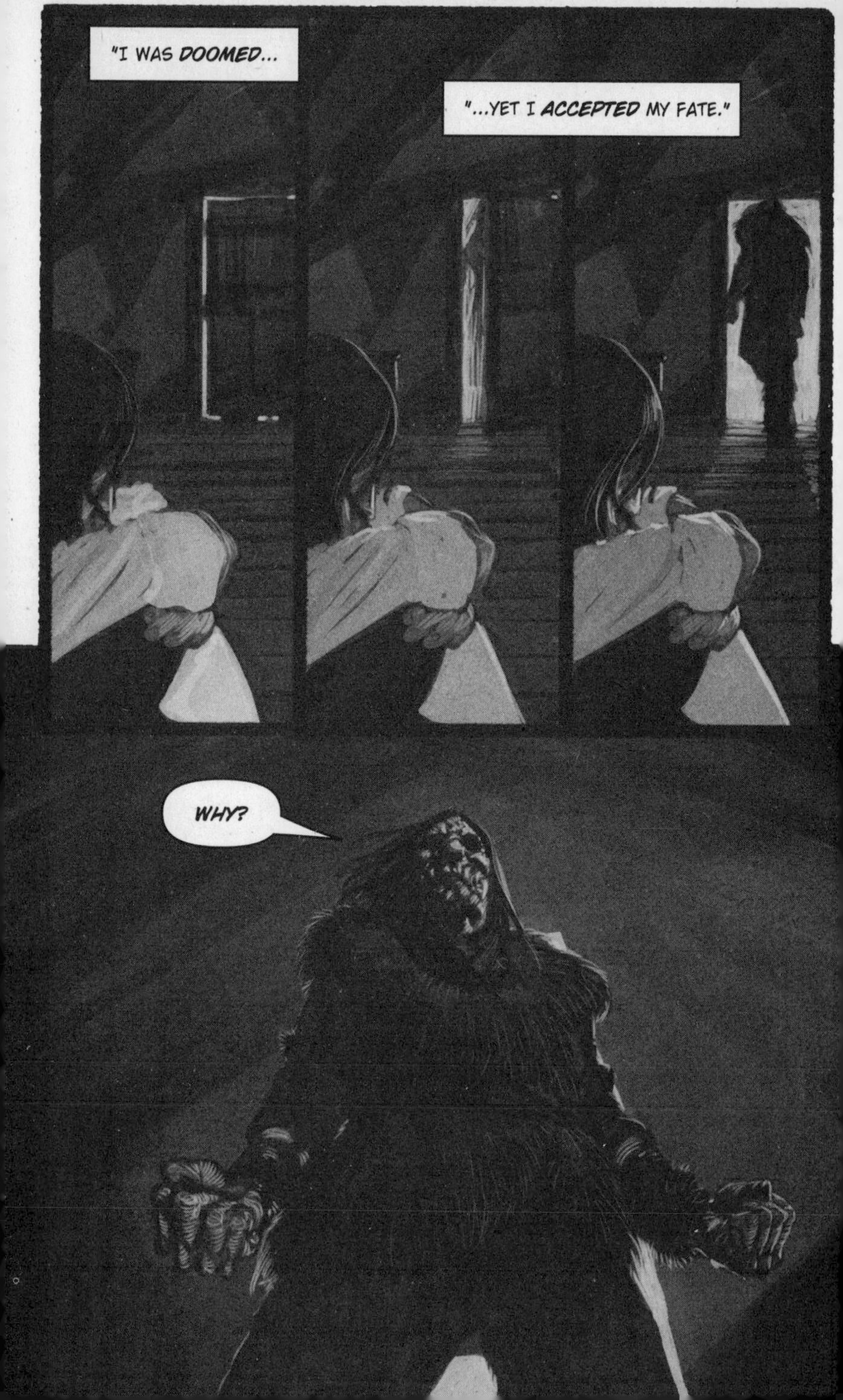
"I WAS DOOMED...
"...YET I ACCEPTED MY FATE."
WHY?

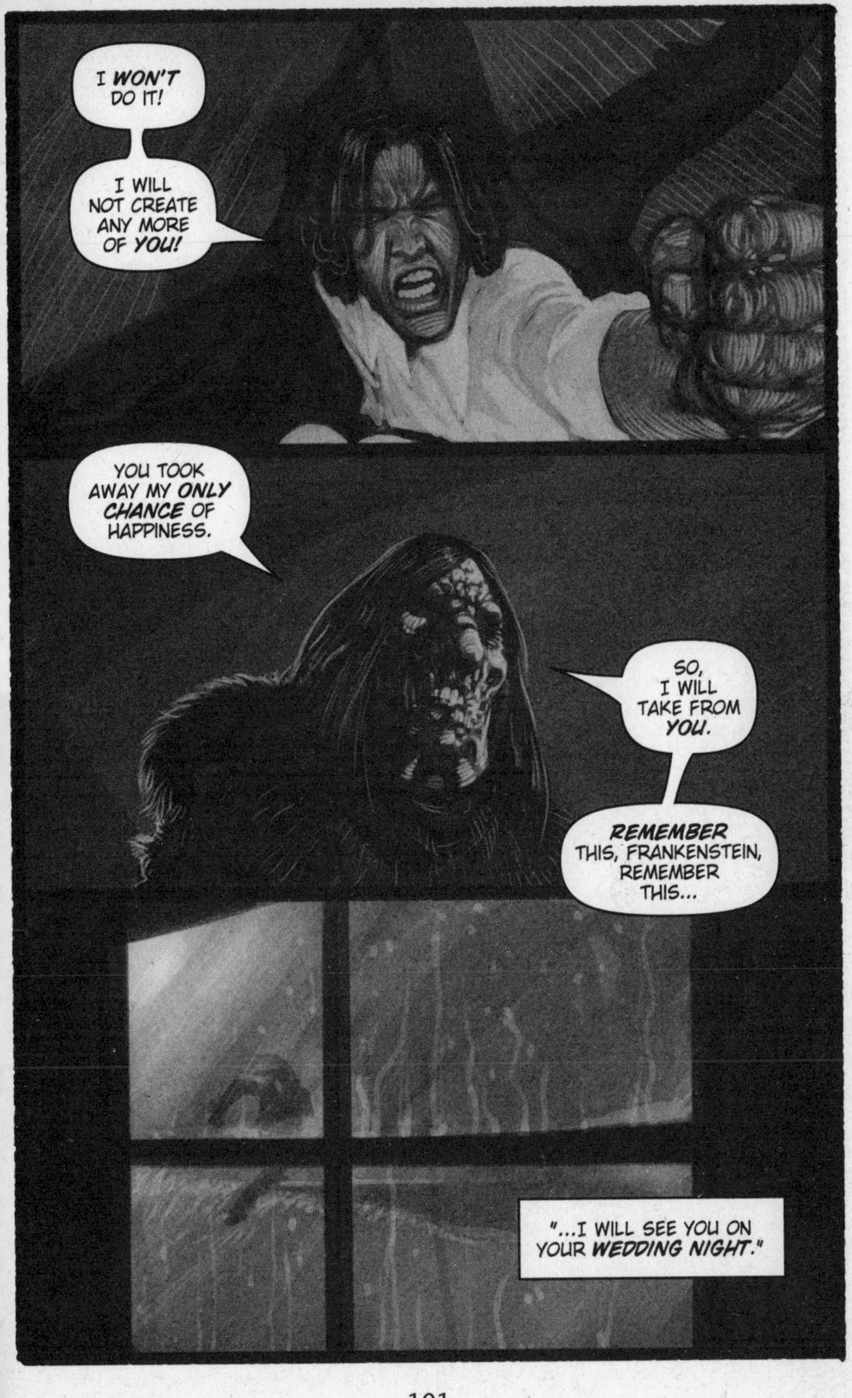
I WON'T DO IT!
I WILL NOT CREATE ANY MORE OF YOU!
YOU TOOK AWAY MY ONLY CHANCE OF HAPPINESS.
SO, I WILL TAKE FROM YOU.
REMEMBER THIS, FRANKENSTEIN, REMEMBER THIS...
"...I WILL SEE YOU ON YOUR WEDDING NIGHT."

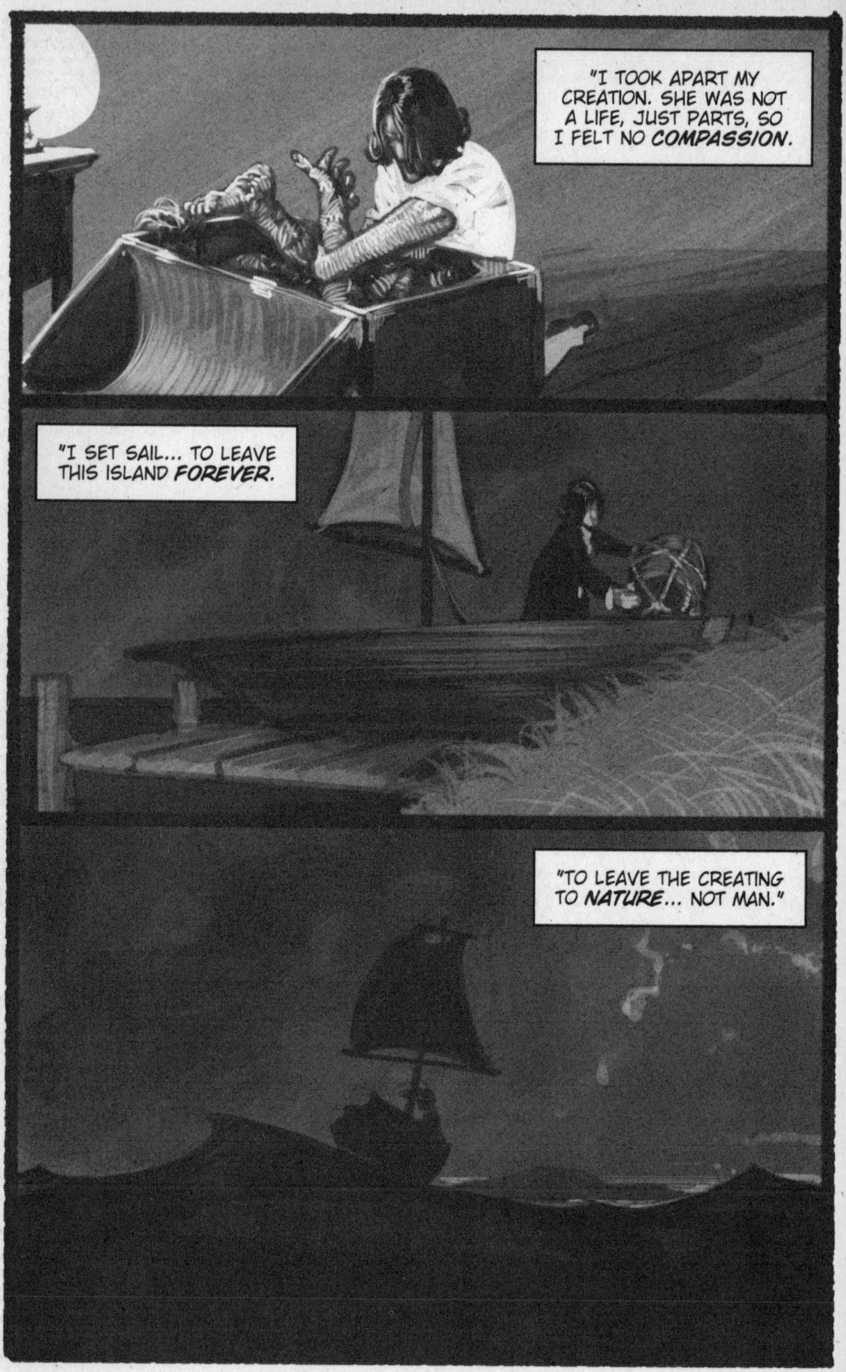
"I TOOK APART MY CREATION. SHE WAS NOT A LIFE, JUST PARTS, SO I FELT NO COMPASSION.
"I SET SAIL... TO LEAVE THIS ISLAND FOREVER.
"TO LEAVE THE CREATING TO NATURE... NOT MAN."

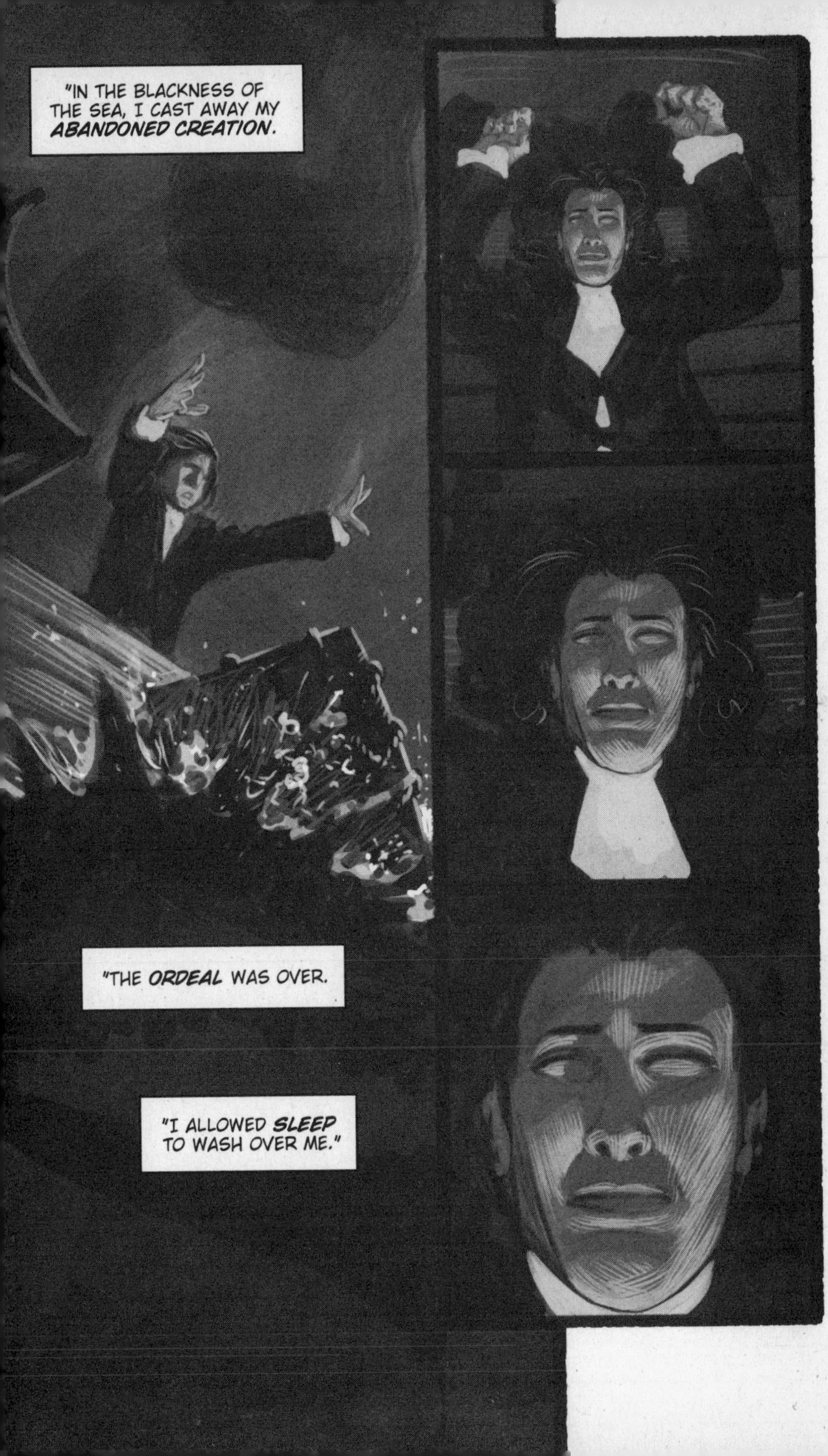
"IN THE BLACKNESS OF THE SEA, I CAST AWAY MY ABANDONED CREATION.
"THE ORDEAL WAS OVER.
"I ALLOWED SLEEP TO WASH OVER ME."

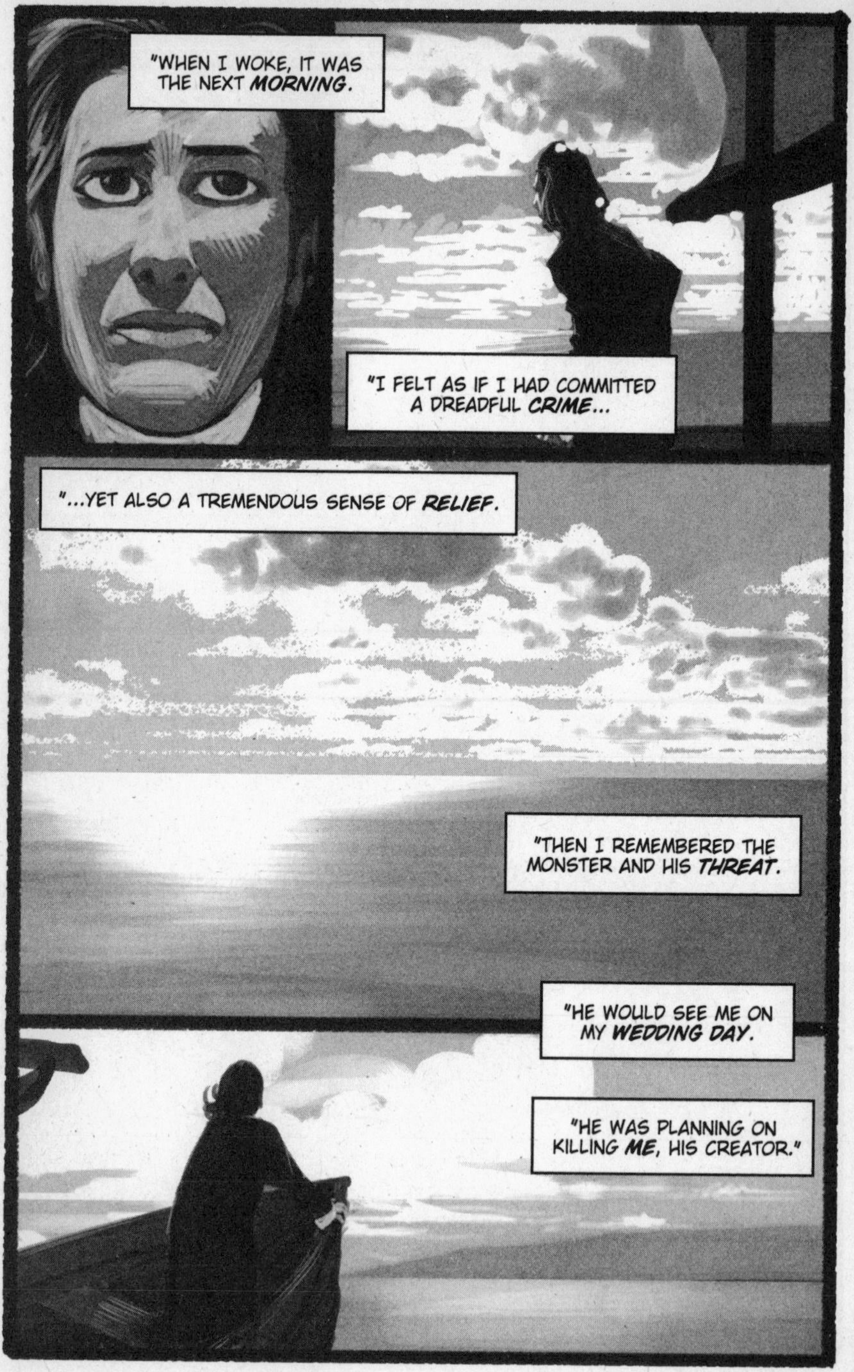
"WHEN I WOKE, IT WAS THE NEXT MORNING.
"I FELT AS IF I HAD COMMITTED A DREADFUL CRIME...
"...YET ALSO A TREMENDOUS SENSE OF RELIEF.
"THEN I REMEMBERED THE MONSTER AND HIS THREAT.
"HE WOULD SEE ME ON MY WEDDING DAY.
"HE WAS PLANNING ON KILLING ME, HIS CREATOR."

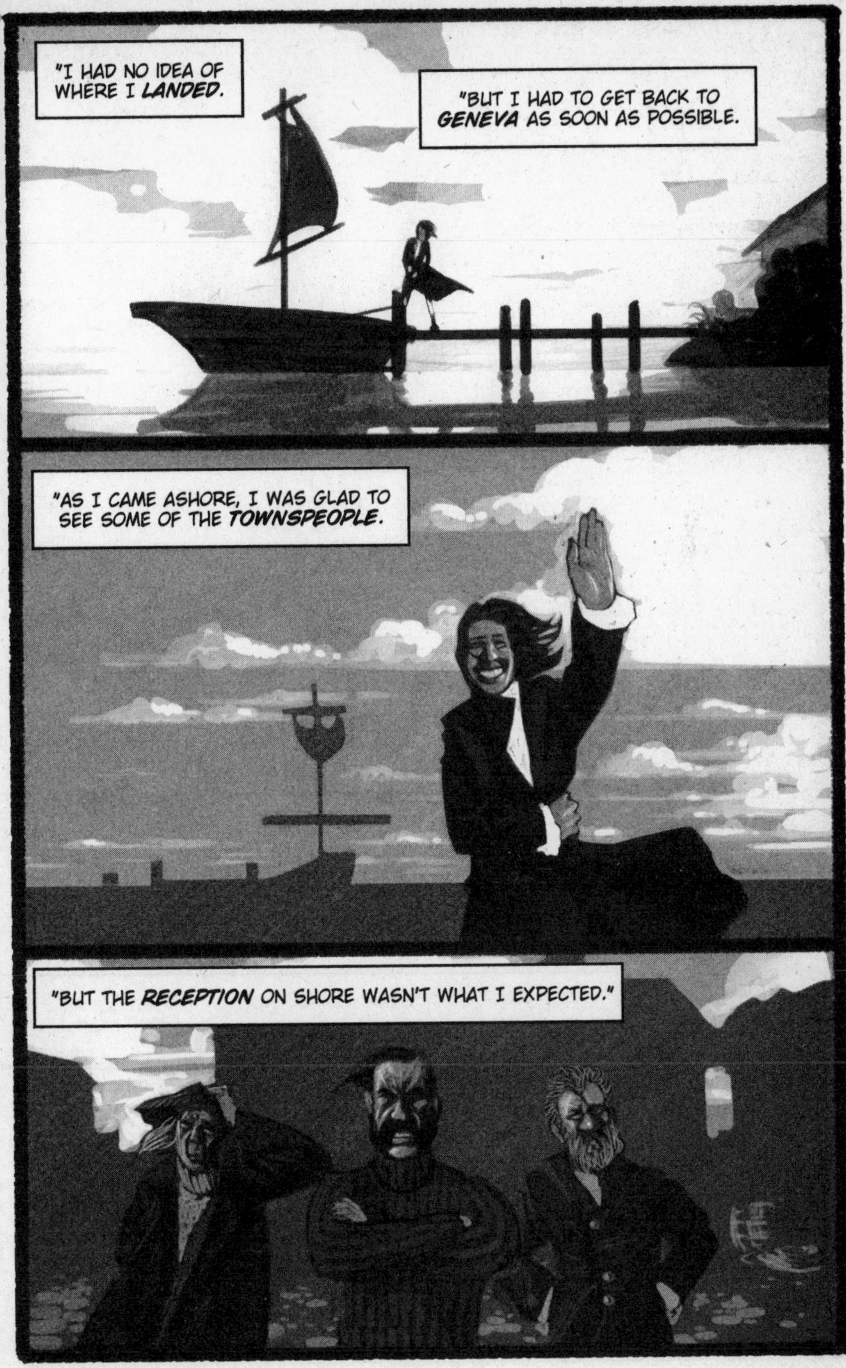
"I HAD NO IDEA OF WHERE I LANDED.
"BUT I HAD TO GET BACK TO GENEVA AS SOON AS POSSIBLE.
"AS I CAME ASHORE, I WAS GLAD TO SEE SOME OF THE TOWNSPEOPLE.
"BUT THE RECEPTION ON SHORE WASN'T WHAT I EXPECTED."

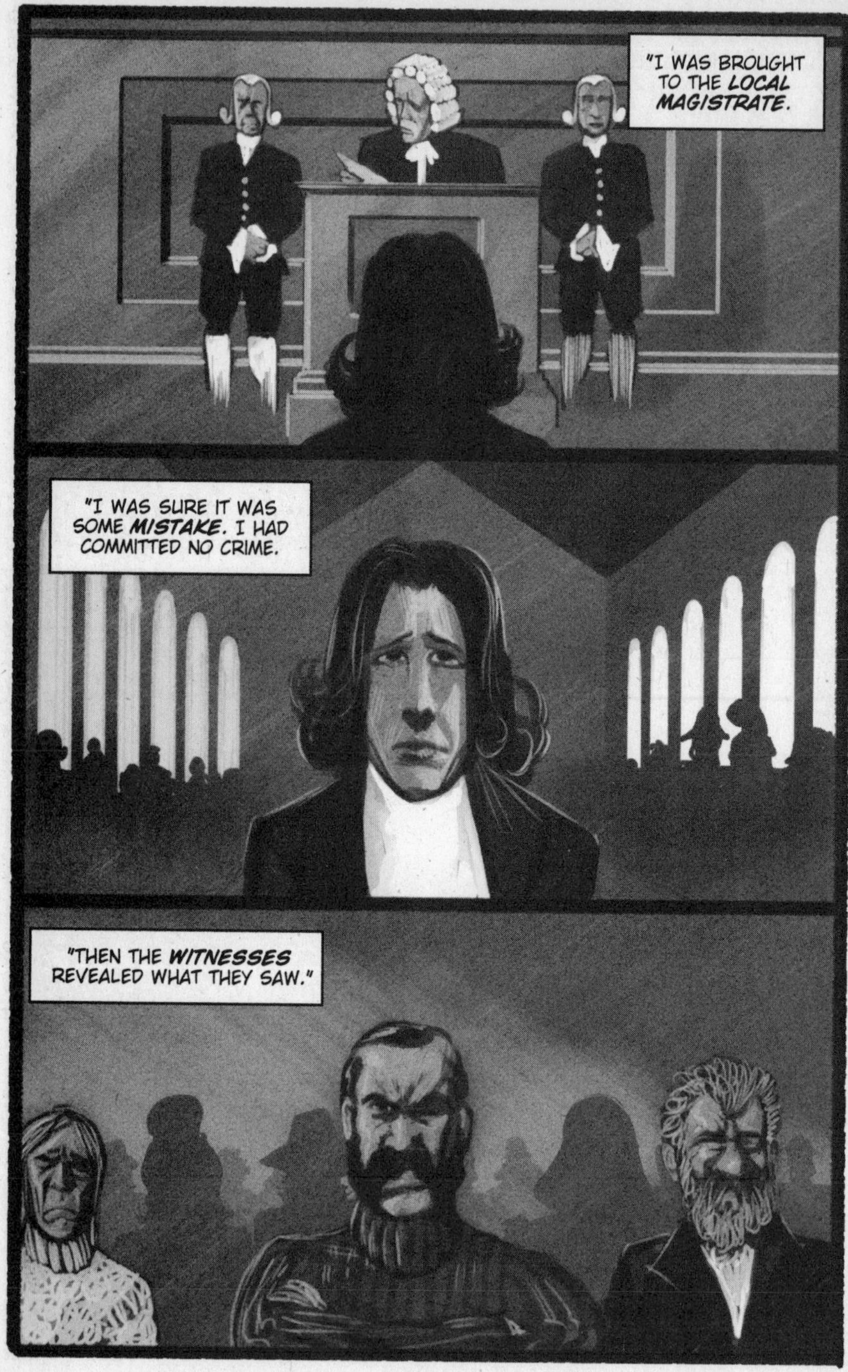
"I WAS BROUGHT TO THE LOCAL MAGISTRATE.
"I WAS SURE IT WAS SOME MISTAKE. I HAD COMMITTED NO CRIME.
"THEN THE WITNESSES REVEALED WHAT THEY SAW."

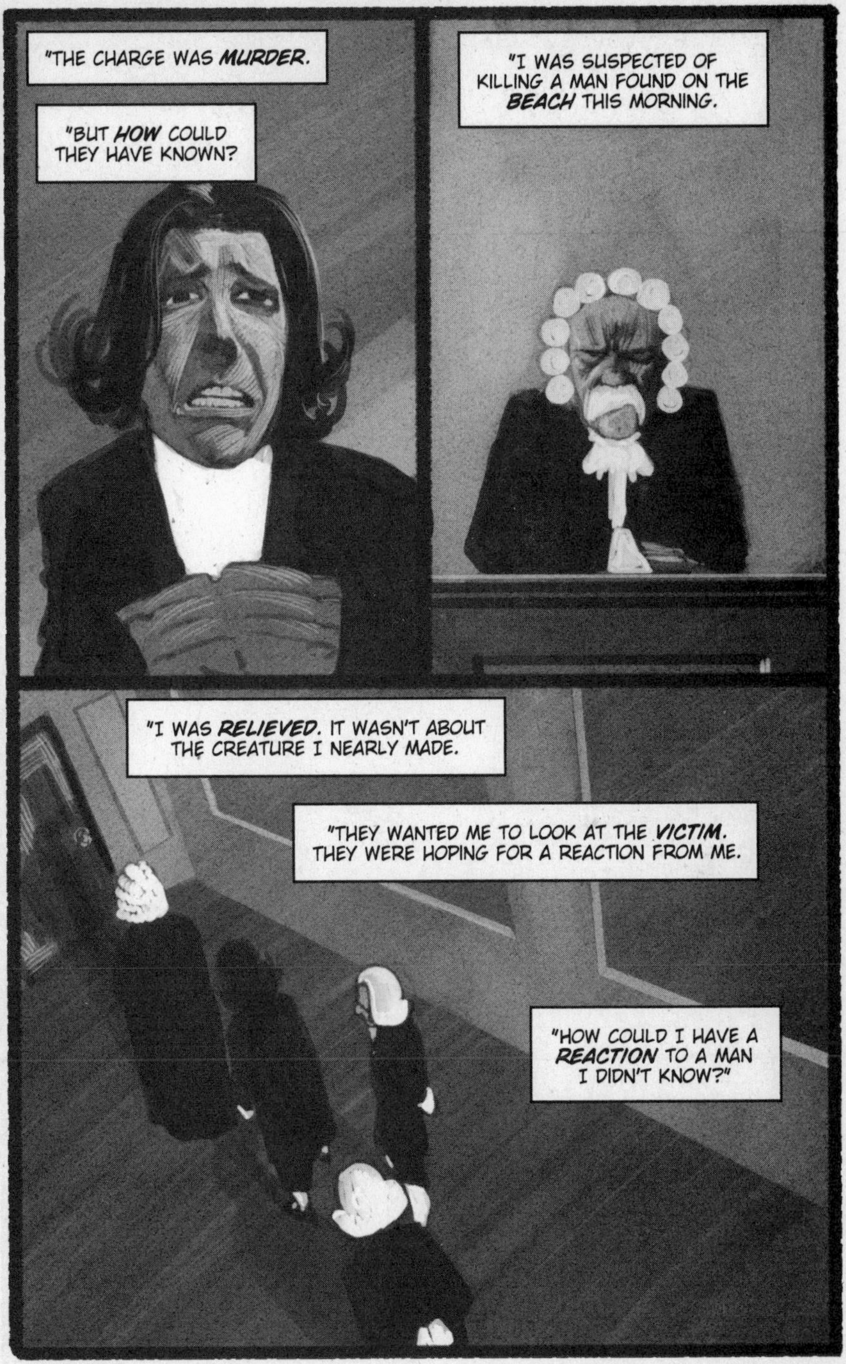
"THE CHARGE WAS MURDER.
"BUT HOW COULD THEY HAVE KNOWN?
"I WAS SUSPECTED OF KILLING A MAN FOUND ON THE BEACH THIS MORNING.
"I WAS RELIEVED. IT WASN'T ABOUT THE CREATURE I NEARLY MADE.
"THEY WANTED ME TO LOOK AT THE VICTIM. THEY WERE HOPING FOR A REACTION FROM ME.
"HOW COULD I HAVE A REACTION TO A MAN I DIDN'T KNOW?"

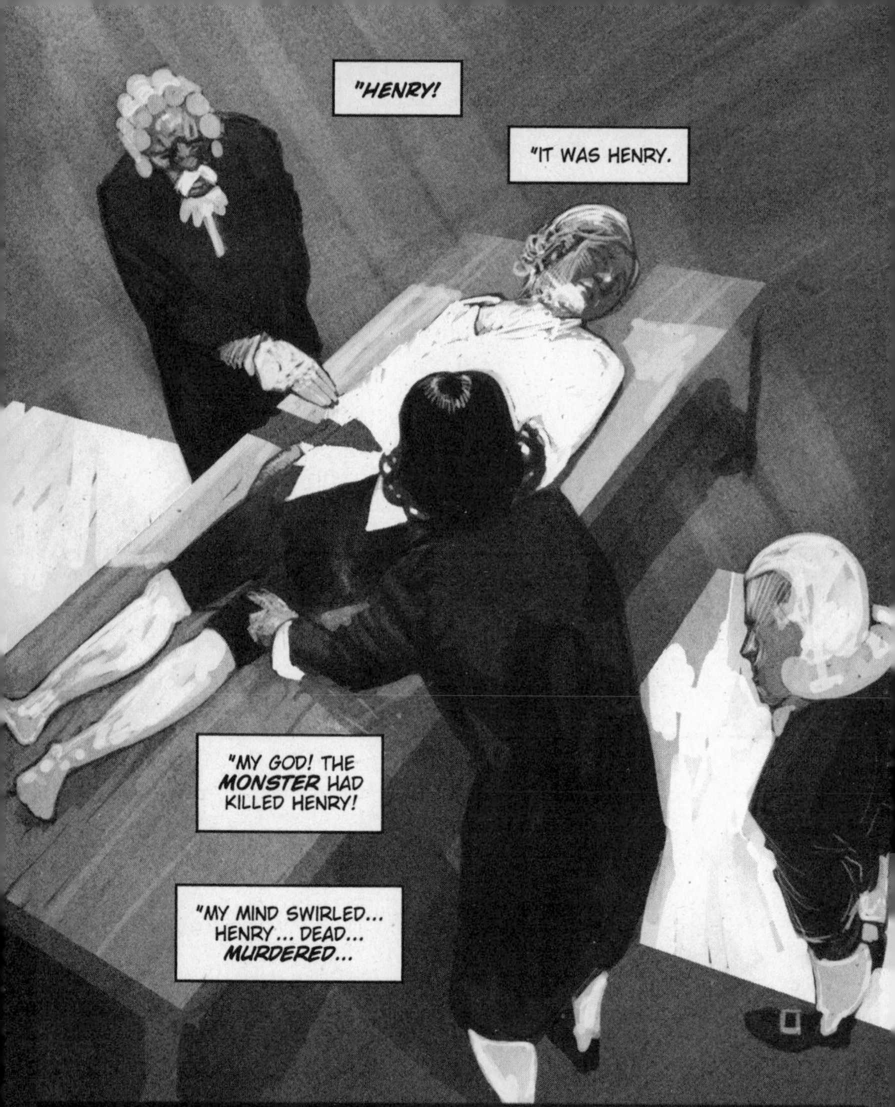
"HENRY!
"IT WAS HENRY.
"MY GOD! THE MONSTER HAD KILLED HENRY!
"MY MIND SWIRLED... HENRY... DEAD... MURDERED...

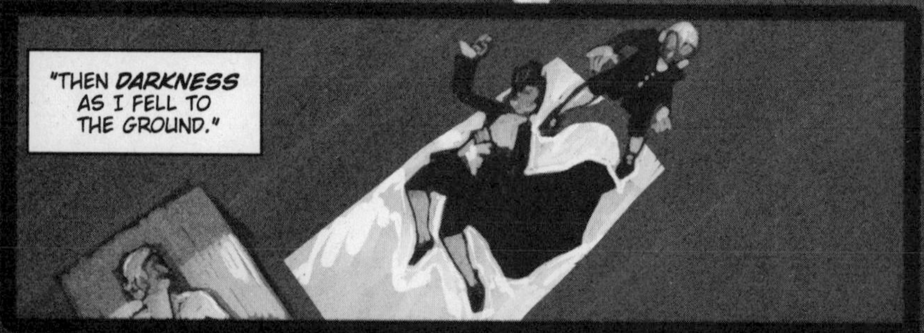
"THEN DARKNESS AS I FELL TO THE GROUND."

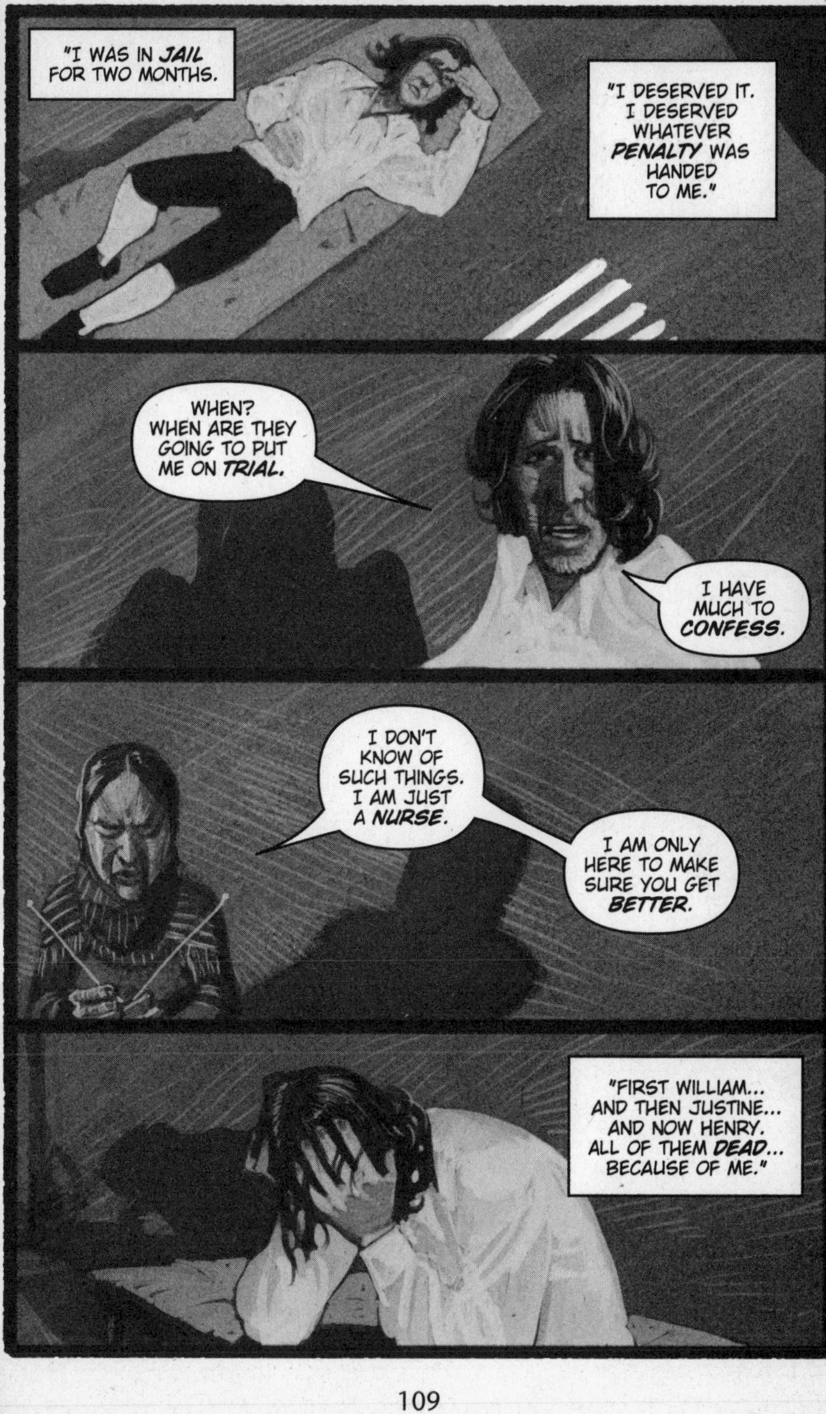
"I WAS IN JAIL FOR TWO MONTHS.
"I DESERVED IT. I DESERVED WHATEVER PENALTY WAS HANDED TO ME."
WHEN? WHEN ARE THEY GOING TO PUT ME ON TRIAL.
I HAVE MUCH TO CONFESS.
I DON'T KNOW OF SUCH THINGS. I AM JUST A NURSE.
I AM ONLY HERE TO MAKE SURE YOU GET BETTER.
"FIRST WILLIAM... AND THEN JUSTINE... AND NOW HENRY. ALL OF THEM DEAD... BECAUSE OF ME."

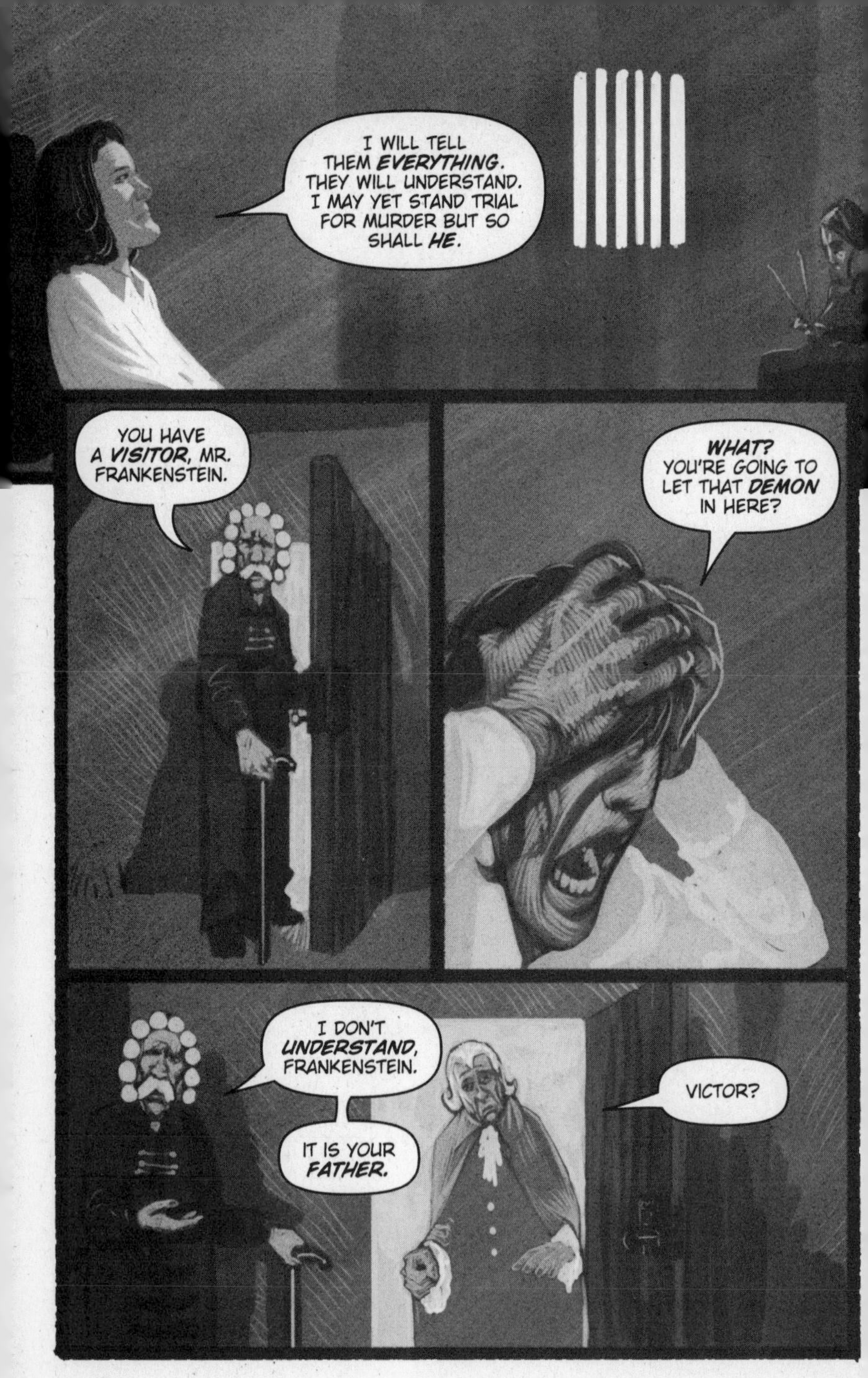
I WILL TELL THEM *EVERYTHING*. THEY WILL UNDERSTAND. I MAY YET STAND TRIAL FOR MURDER BUT SO SHALL *HE*.
YOU HAVE A *VISITOR*, MR. FRANKENSTEIN.
WHAT? YOU'RE GOING TO LET THAT *DEMON* IN HERE?
I DON'T *UNDERSTAND*, FRANKENSTEIN.
IT IS YOUR *FATHER*.
VICTOR?

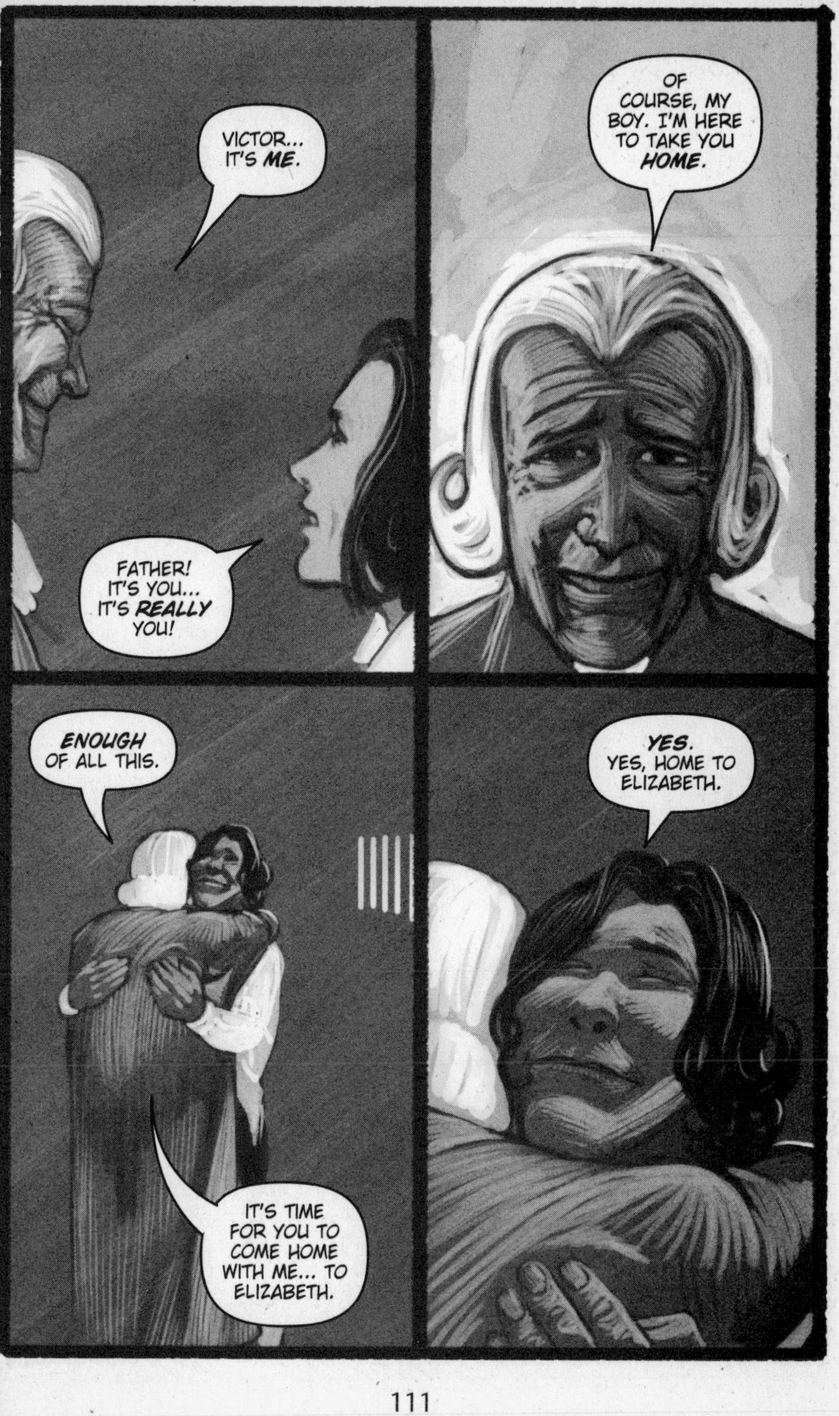
VICTOR... IT'S *ME*.
FATHER! IT'S YOU... IT'S *REALLY* YOU!
OF COURSE, MY BOY. I'M HERE TO TAKE YOU *HOME*.
ENOUGH OF ALL THIS.
IT'S TIME FOR YOU TO COME HOME WITH ME... TO ELIZABETH.
YES. YES, HOME TO ELIZABETH.

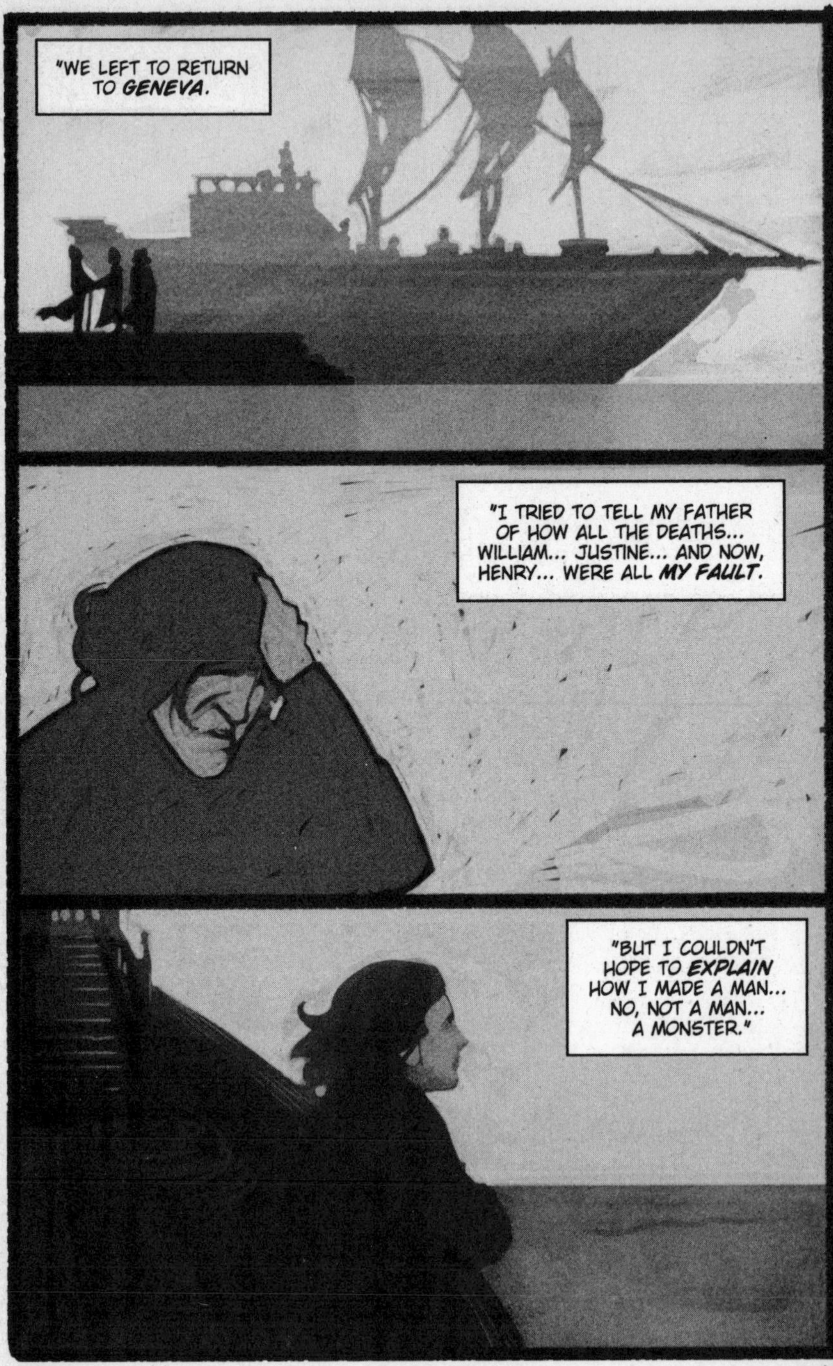
"WE LEFT TO RETURN TO GENEVA.
"I TRIED TO TELL MY FATHER OF HOW ALL THE DEATHS... WILLIAM... JUSTINE... AND NOW, HENRY... WERE ALL MY FAULT.
"BUT I COULDN'T HOPE TO EXPLAIN HOW I MADE A MAN... NO, NOT A MAN... A MONSTER."

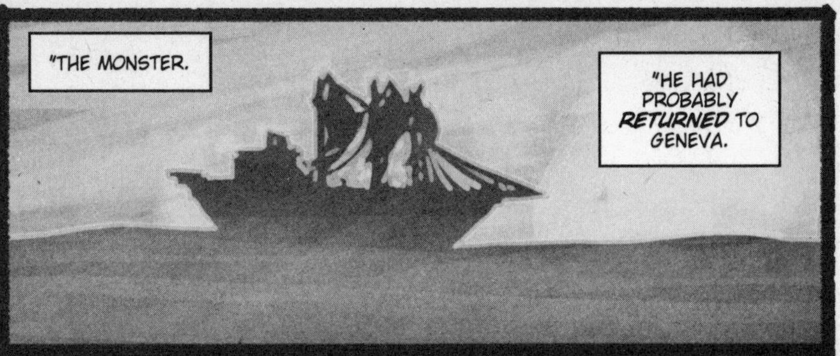
"THE MONSTER.
"HE HAD PROBABLY RETURNED TO GENEVA.

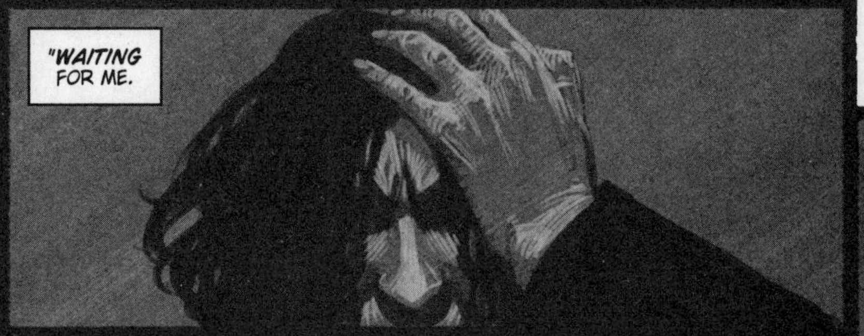
"WAITING FOR ME.

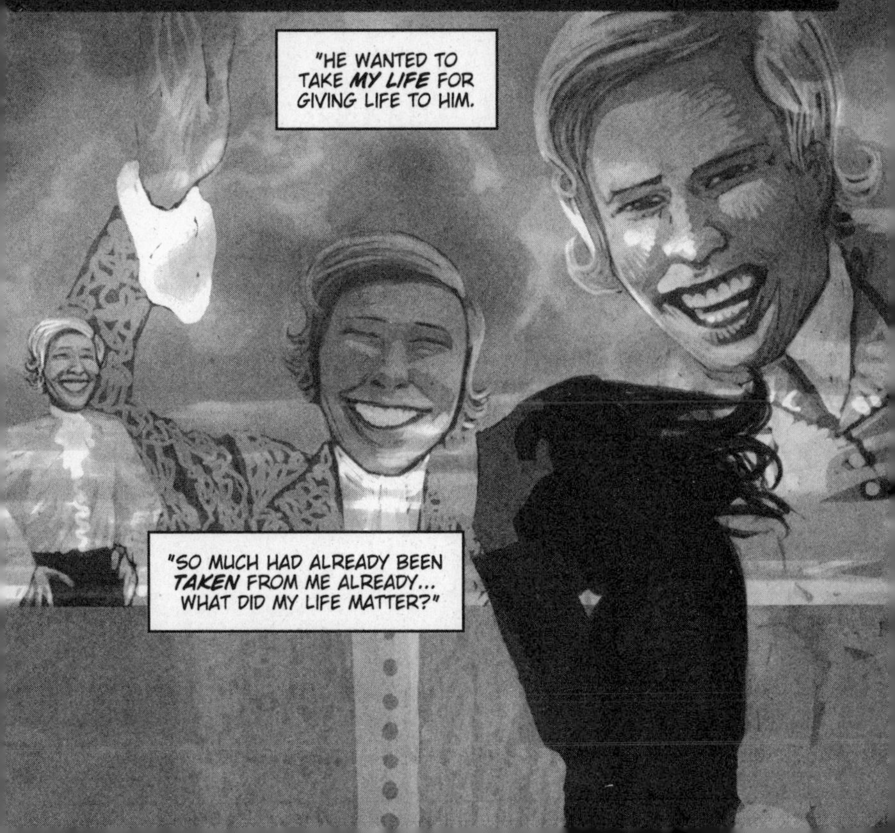
"HE WANTED TO TAKE MY LIFE FOR GIVING LIFE TO HIM.
"SO MUCH HAD ALREADY BEEN TAKEN FROM ME ALREADY... WHAT DID MY LIFE MATTER?"

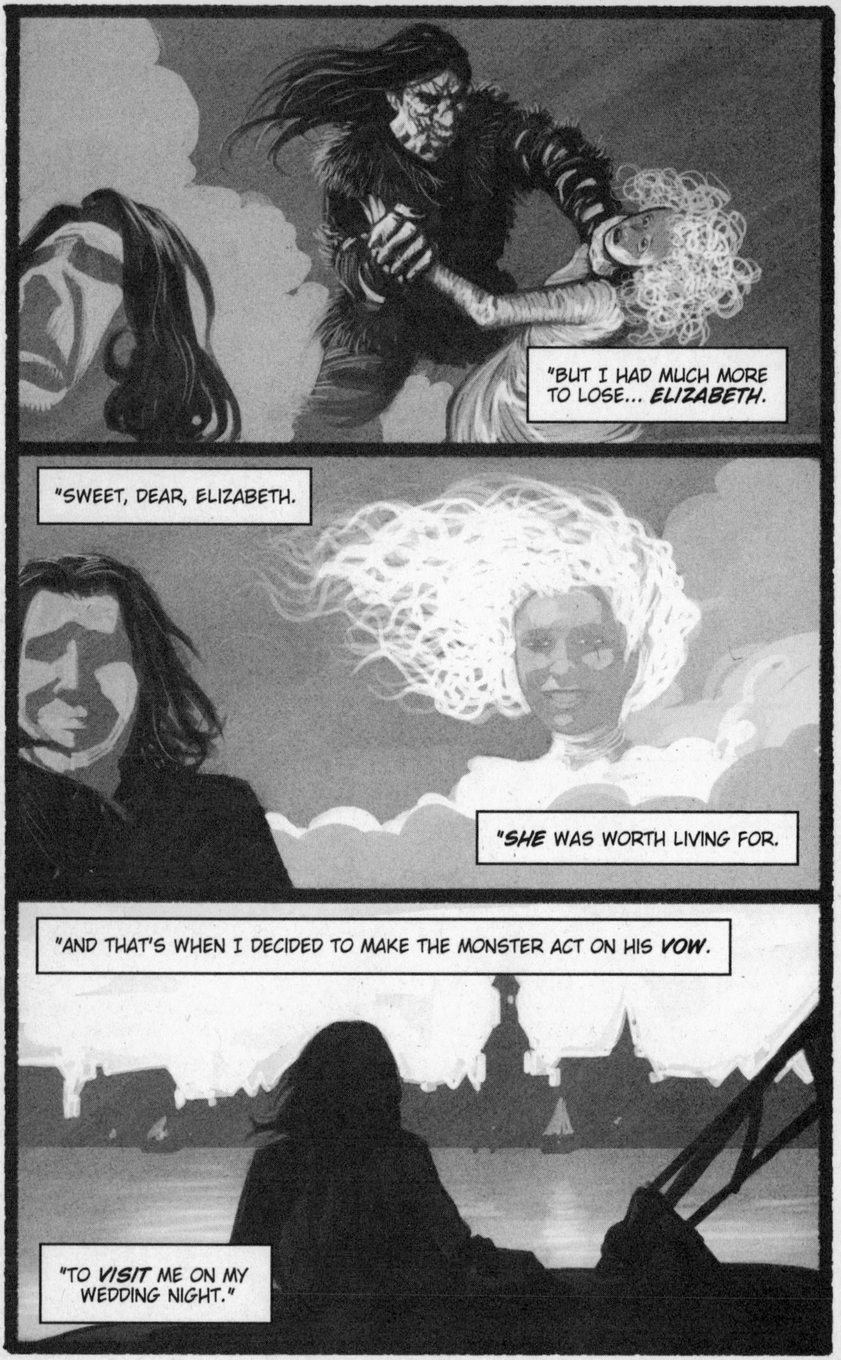
"BUT I HAD MUCH MORE TO LOSE... ELIZABETH.
"SWEET, DEAR, ELIZABETH.
"SHE WAS WORTH LIVING FOR.
"AND THAT'S WHEN I DECIDED TO MAKE THE MONSTER ACT ON HIS VOW.
"TO VISIT ME ON MY WEDDING NIGHT."

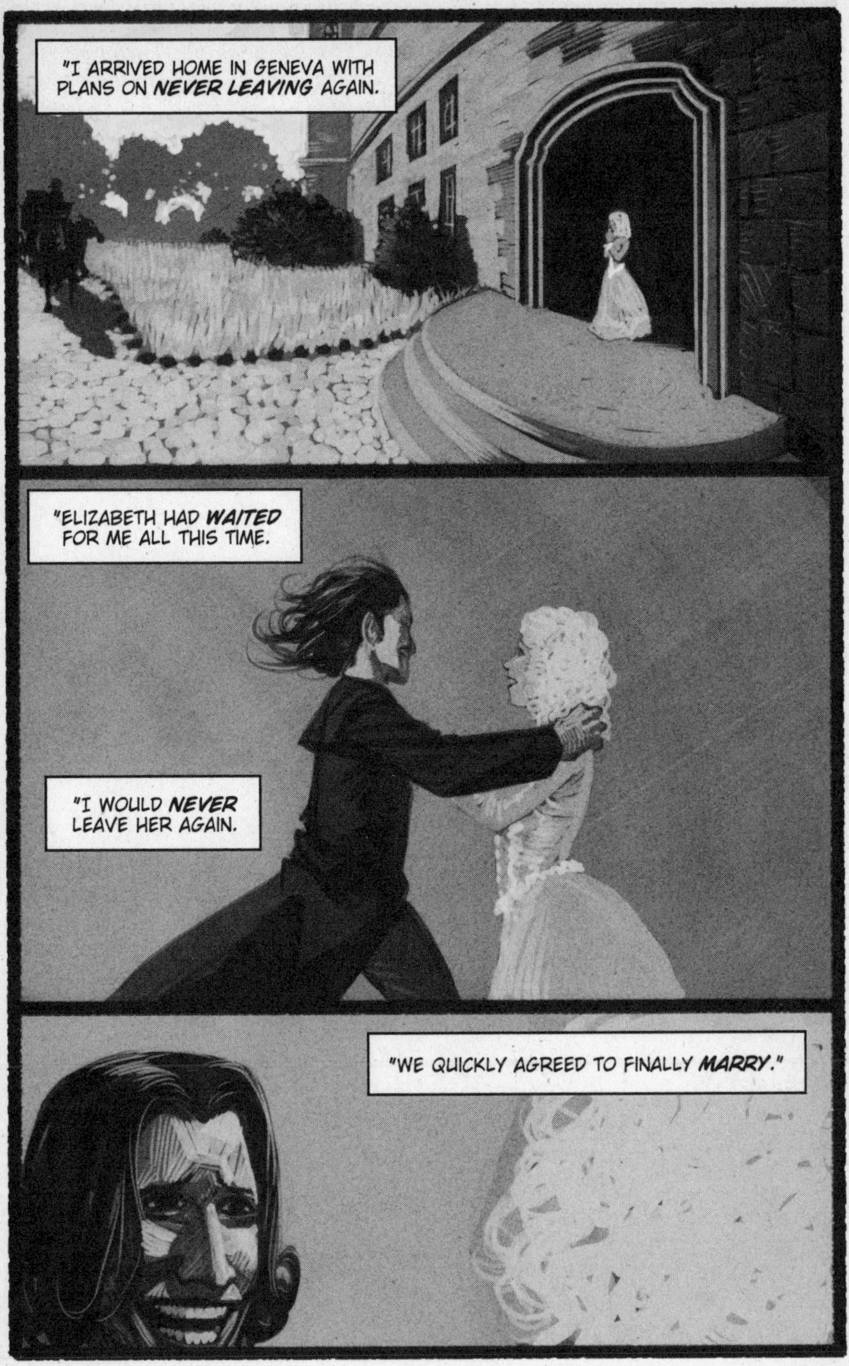
"I ARRIVED HOME IN GENEVA WITH PLANS ON NEVER LEAVING AGAIN.
"ELIZABETH HAD WAITED FOR ME ALL THIS TIME.
"I WOULD NEVER LEAVE HER AGAIN.
"WE QUICKLY AGREED TO FINALLY MARRY."

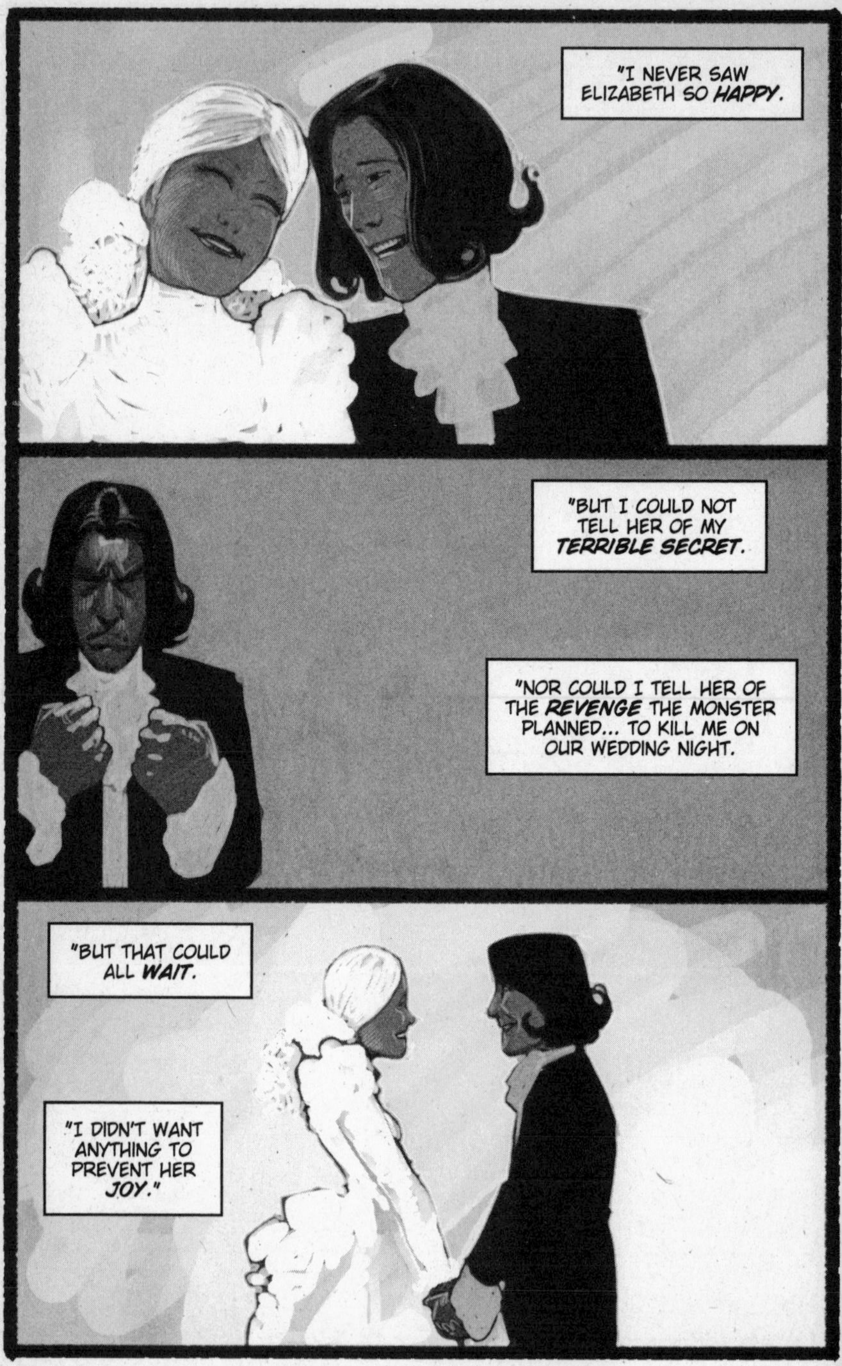
"I NEVER SAW ELIZABETH SO HAPPY.
"BUT I COULD NOT TELL HER OF MY TERRIBLE SECRET.
"NOR COULD I TELL HER OF THE REVENGE THE MONSTER PLANNED... TO KILL ME ON OUR WEDDING NIGHT.
"BUT THAT COULD ALL WAIT.
"I DIDN'T WANT ANYTHING TO PREVENT HER JOY."

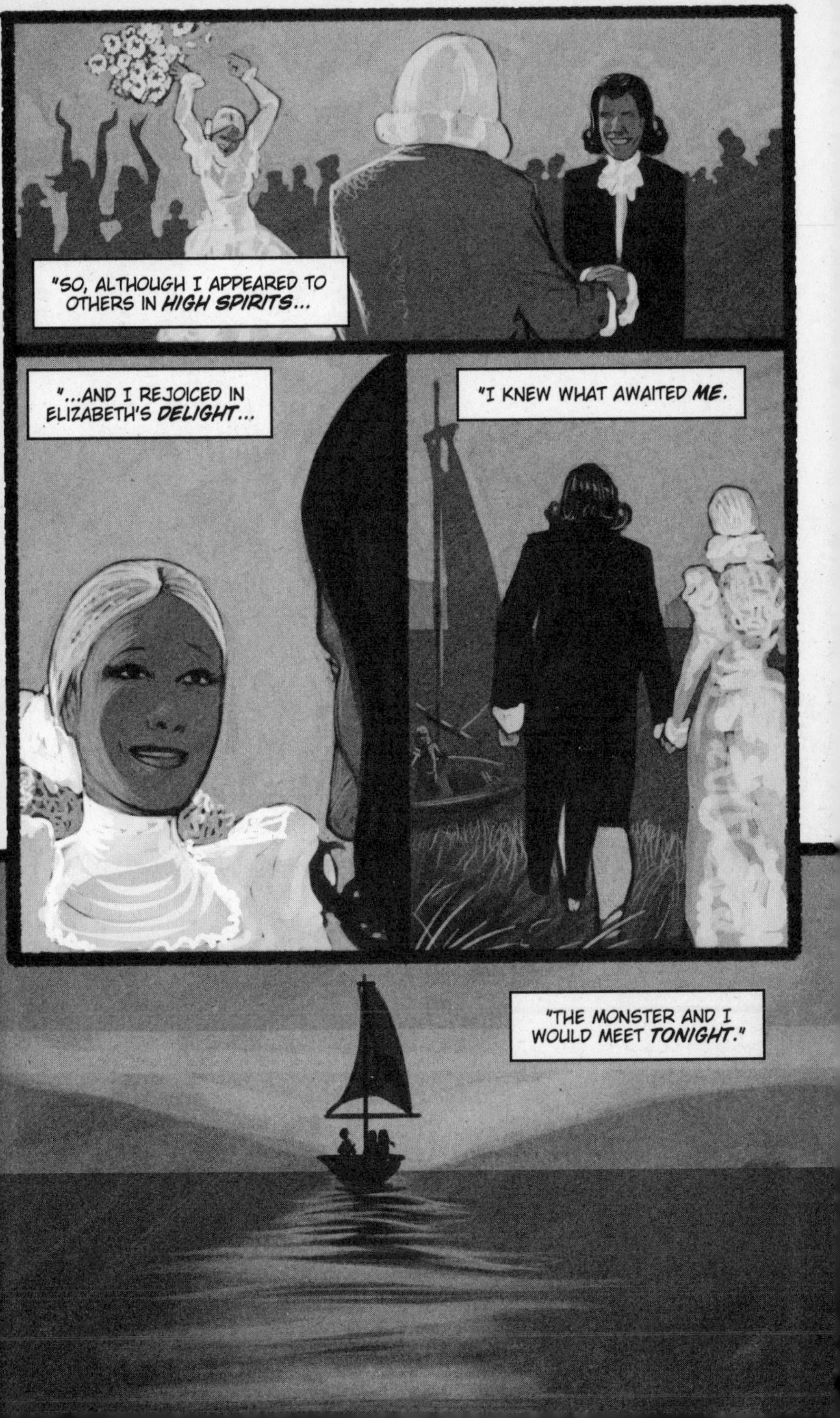
"SO, ALTHOUGH I APPEARED TO OTHERS IN HIGH SPIRITS...
"...AND I REJOICED IN ELIZABETH'S DELIGHT...
"I KNEW WHAT AWAITED ME.
"THE MONSTER AND I WOULD MEET TONIGHT."

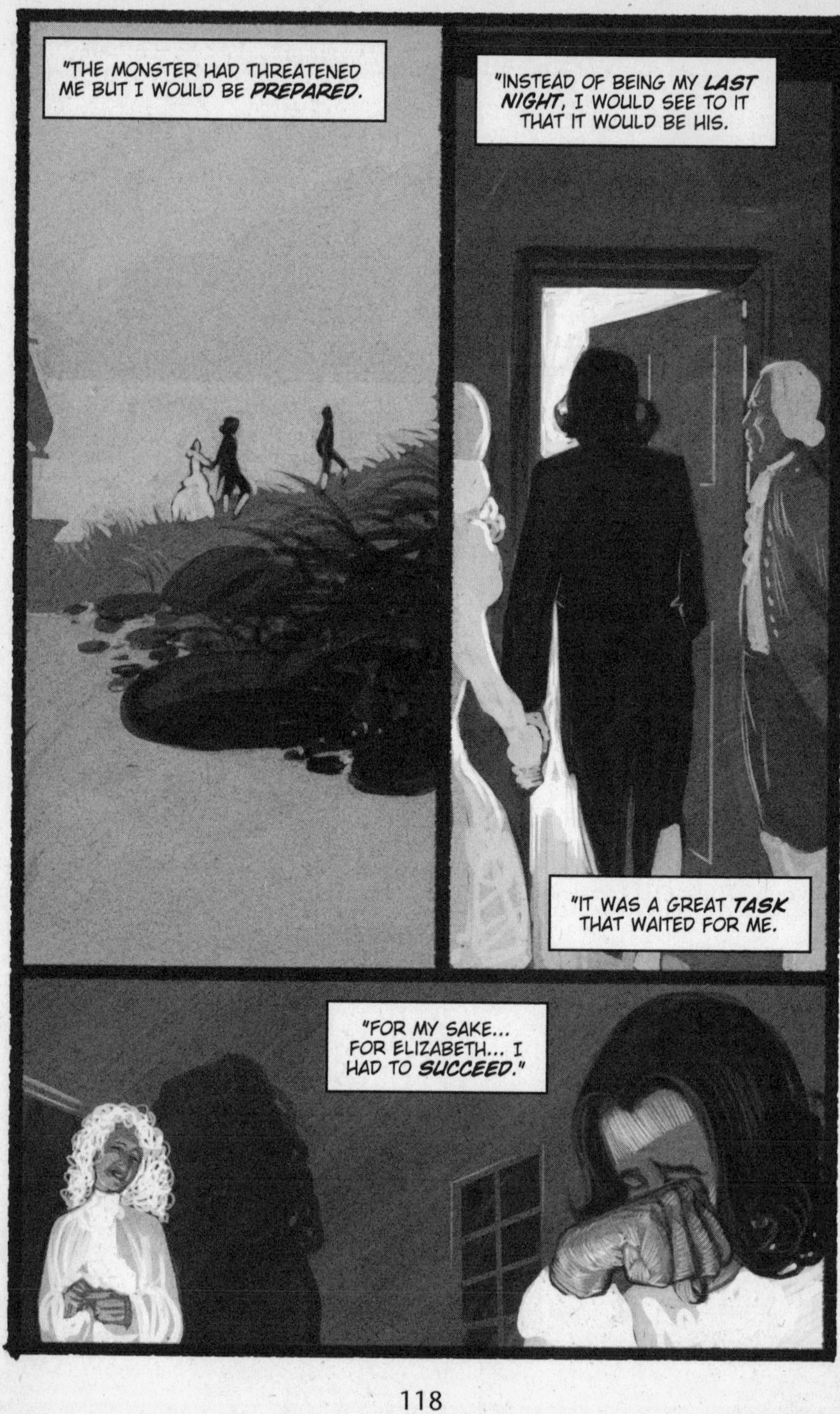
"THE MONSTER HAD THREATENED ME BUT I WOULD BE PREPARED.
"INSTEAD OF BEING MY LAST NIGHT, I WOULD SEE TO IT THAT IT WOULD BE HIS.
"IT WAS A GREAT TASK THAT WAITED FOR ME.
"FOR MY SAKE... FOR ELIZABETH... I HAD TO SUCCEED."

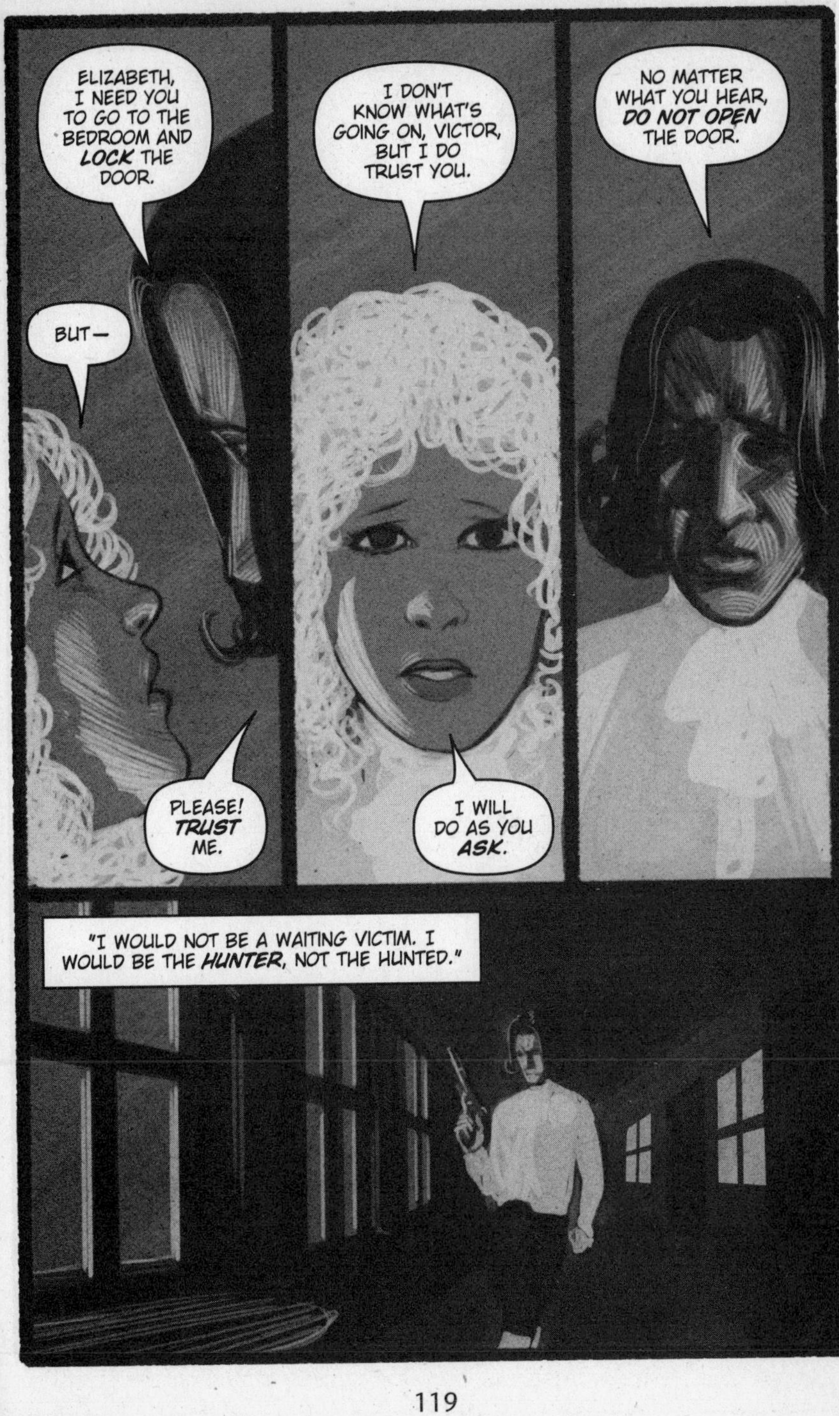
ELIZABETH, I NEED YOU TO GO TO THE BEDROOM AND LOCK THE DOOR.
BUT—
PLEASE! TRUST ME.
I DON'T KNOW WHAT'S GOING ON, VICTOR, BUT I DO TRUST YOU.
I WILL DO AS YOU ASK.
NO MATTER WHAT YOU HEAR, DO NOT OPEN THE DOOR.
"I WOULD NOT BE A WAITING VICTIM. I WOULD BE THE HUNTER, NOT THE HUNTED."

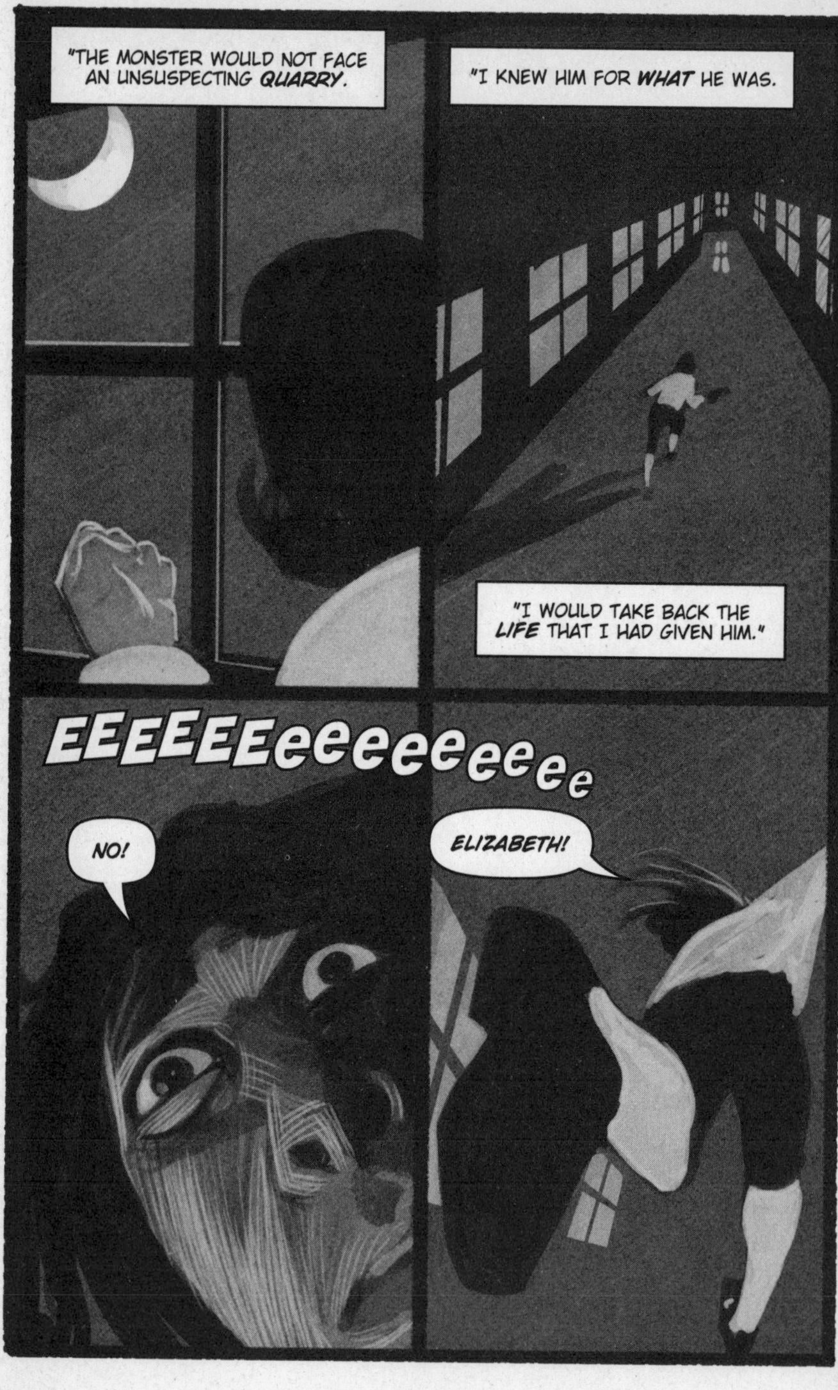
"THE MONSTER WOULD NOT FACE AN UNSUSPECTING *QUARRY*.
"I KNEW HIM FOR *WHAT* HE WAS.
"I WOULD TAKE BACK THE *LIFE* THAT I HAD GIVEN HIM."
EEEEEEeeeeeeeee
NO!
ELIZABETH!

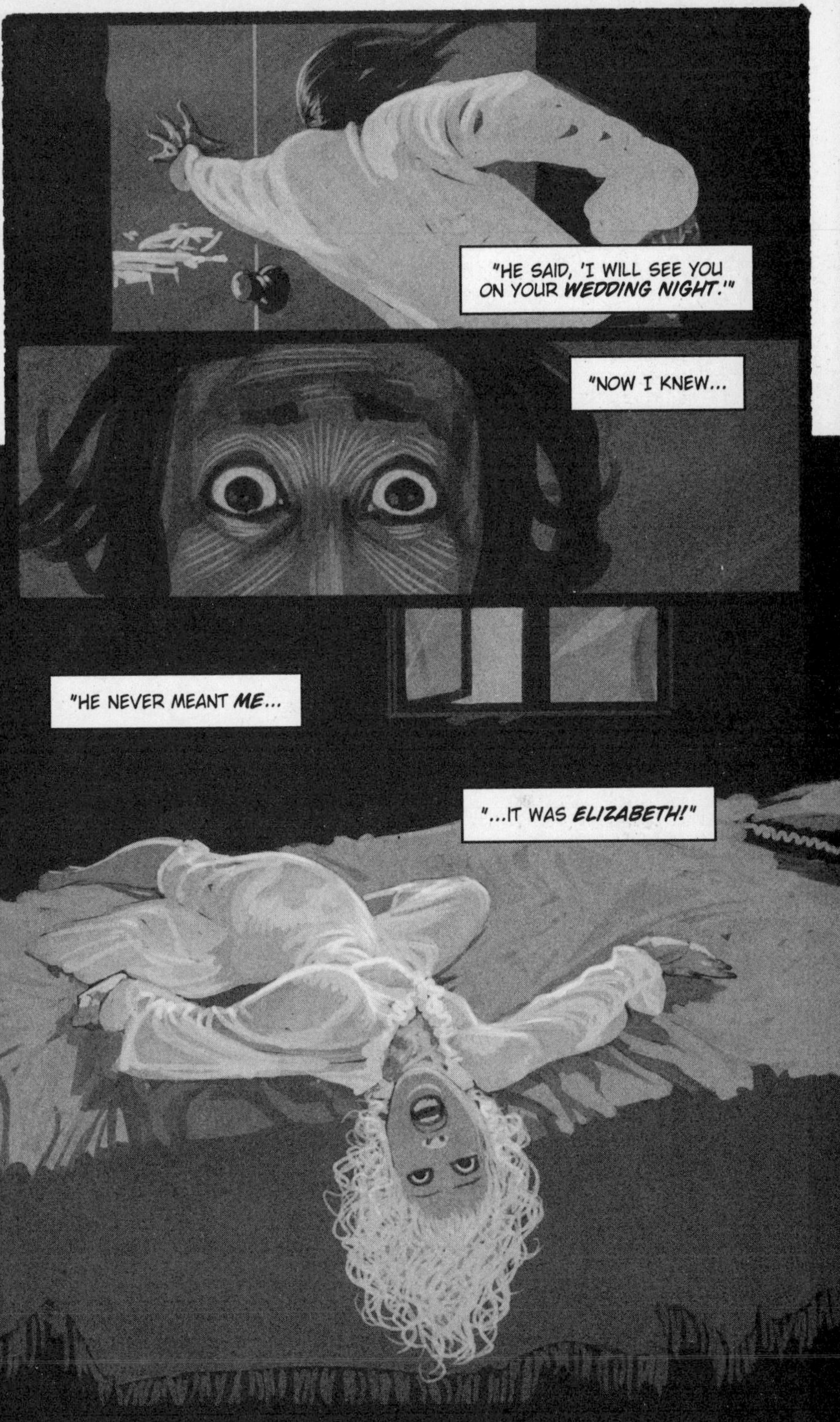

"HE SAID, 'I WILL SEE YOU ON YOUR WEDDING NIGHT.'"
"NOW I KNEW...
"HE NEVER MEANT ME...
"...IT WAS ELIZABETH!"

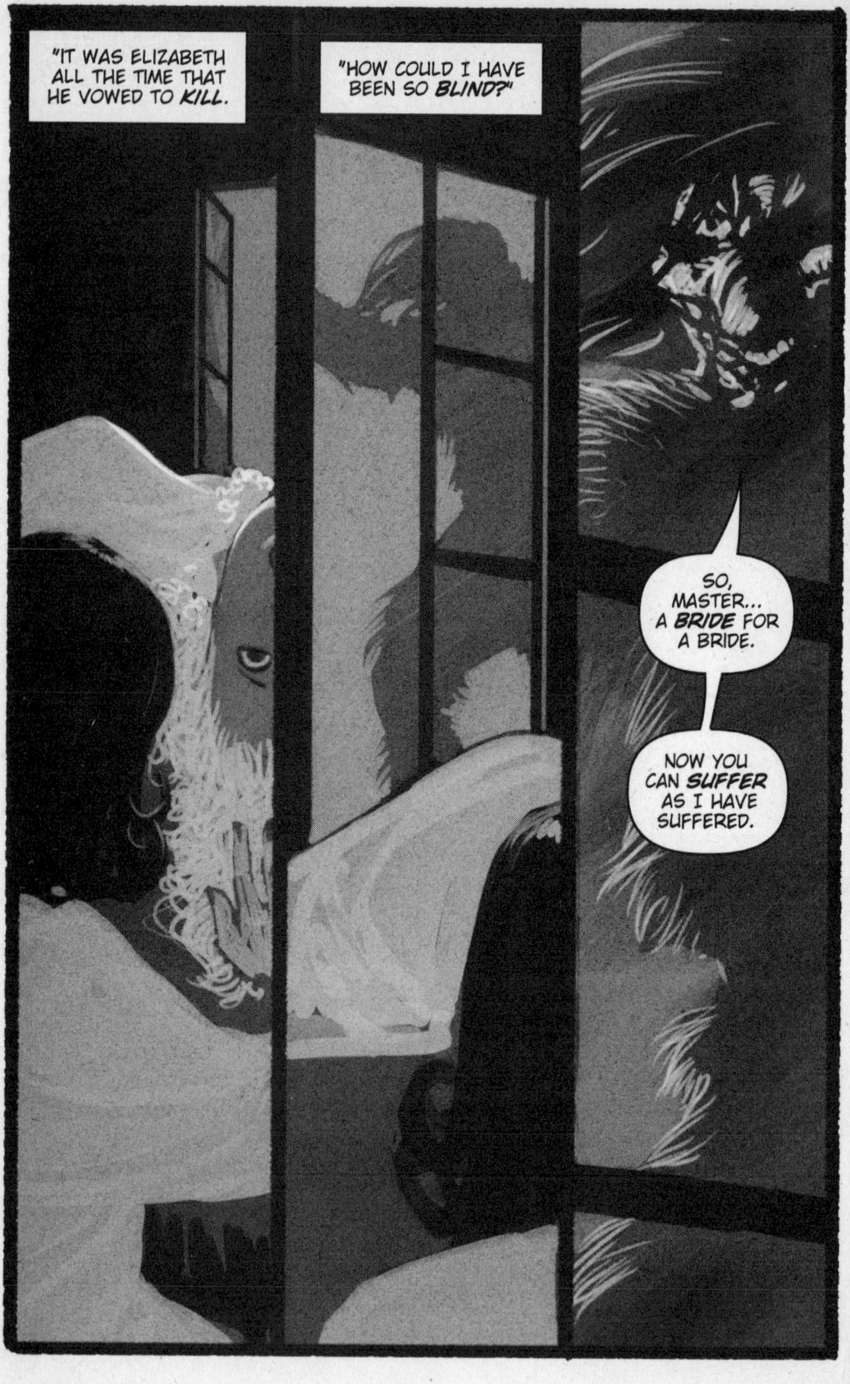
"IT WAS ELIZABETH ALL THE TIME THAT HE VOWED TO KILL.
"HOW COULD I HAVE BEEN SO BLIND?"
SO, MASTER... A BRIDE FOR A BRIDE.
NOW YOU CAN SUFFER AS I HAVE SUFFERED.

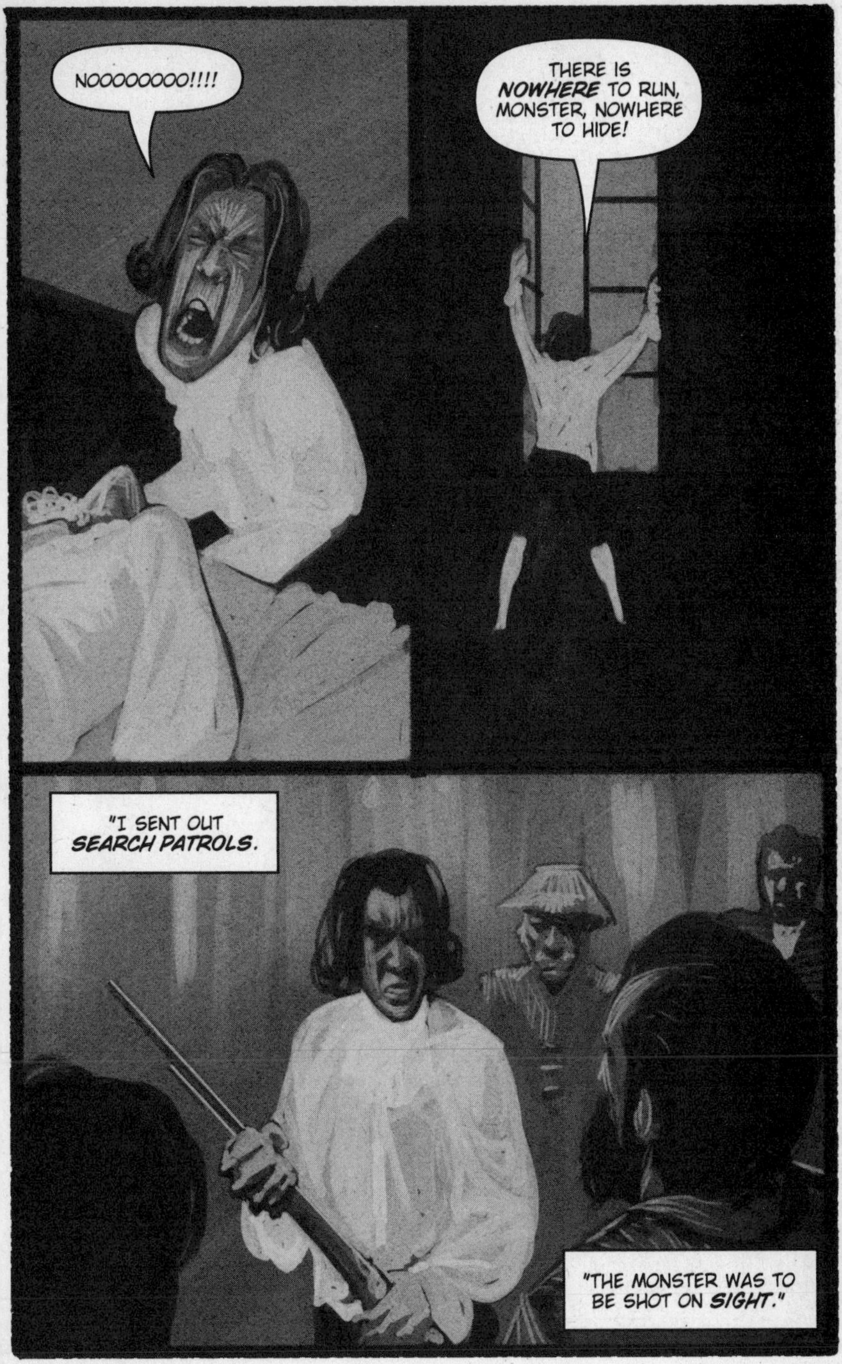
NOOOOOOOO!!!!
THERE IS NOWHERE TO RUN, MONSTER, NOWHERE TO HIDE!
"I SENT OUT SEARCH PATROLS.
"THE MONSTER WAS TO BE SHOT ON SIGHT."

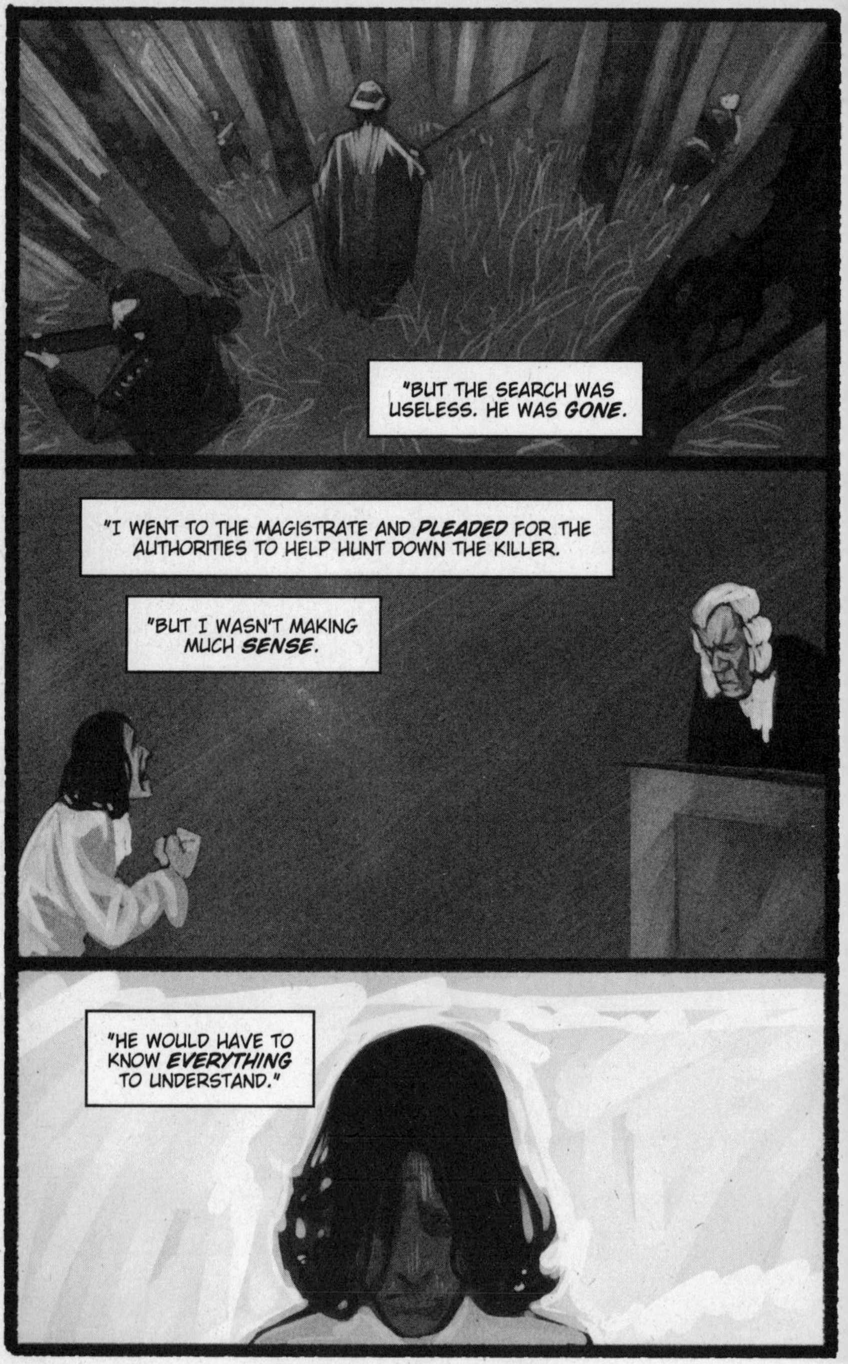
"BUT THE SEARCH WAS USELESS. HE WAS GONE.
"I WENT TO THE MAGISTRATE AND PLEADED FOR THE AUTHORITIES TO HELP HUNT DOWN THE KILLER.
"BUT I WASN'T MAKING MUCH SENSE.
"HE WOULD HAVE TO KNOW EVERYTHING TO UNDERSTAND."

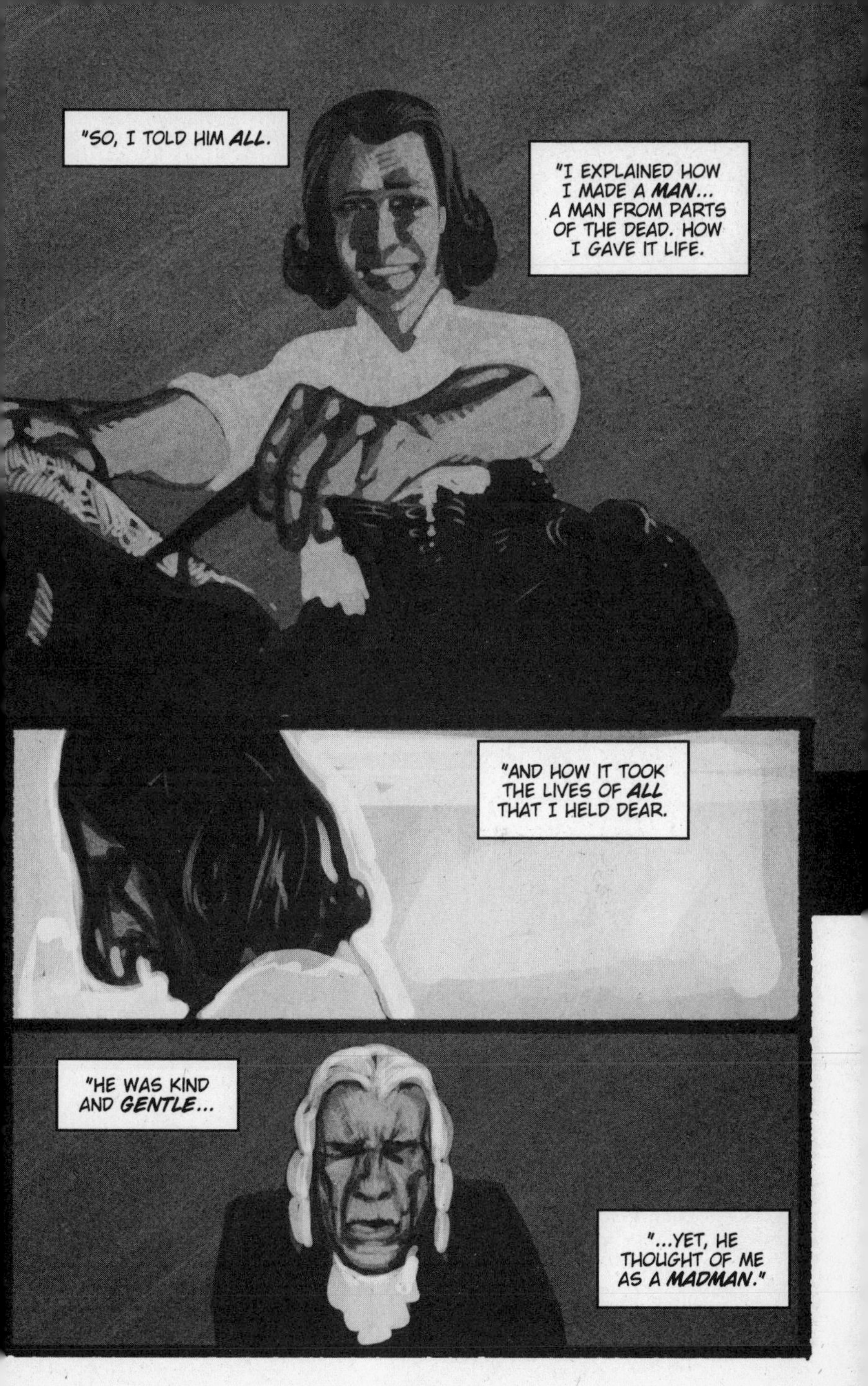
"SO, I TOLD HIM ALL.
"I EXPLAINED HOW I MADE A MAN... A MAN FROM PARTS OF THE DEAD. HOW I GAVE IT LIFE.
"AND HOW IT TOOK THE LIVES OF ALL THAT I HELD DEAR.
"HE WAS KIND AND GENTLE...
"...YET, HE THOUGHT OF ME AS A MADMAN."

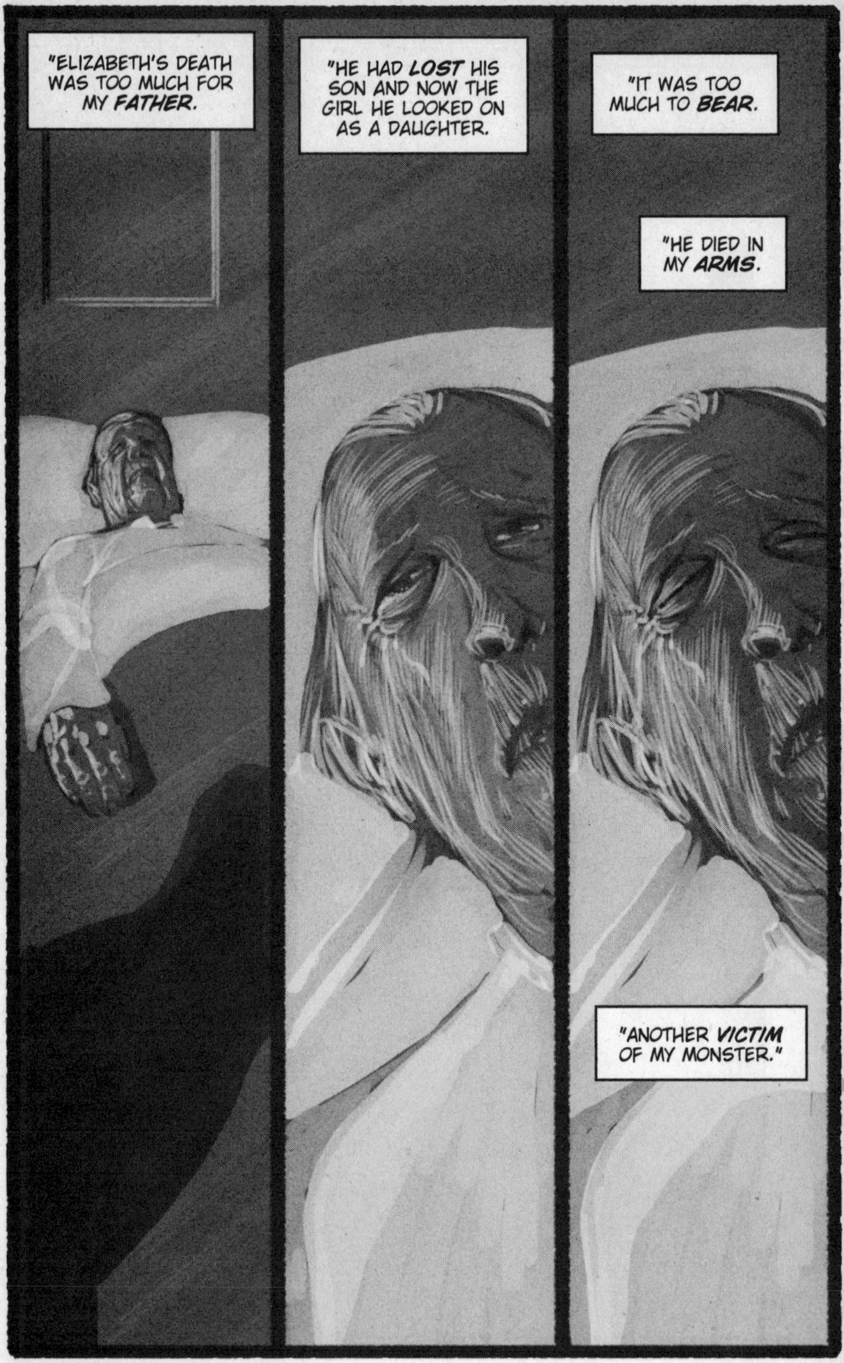
"ELIZABETH'S DEATH WAS TOO MUCH FOR MY FATHER.
"HE HAD LOST HIS SON AND NOW THE GIRL HE LOOKED ON AS A DAUGHTER.
"IT WAS TOO MUCH TO BEAR.
"HE DIED IN MY ARMS.
"ANOTHER VICTIM OF MY MONSTER."

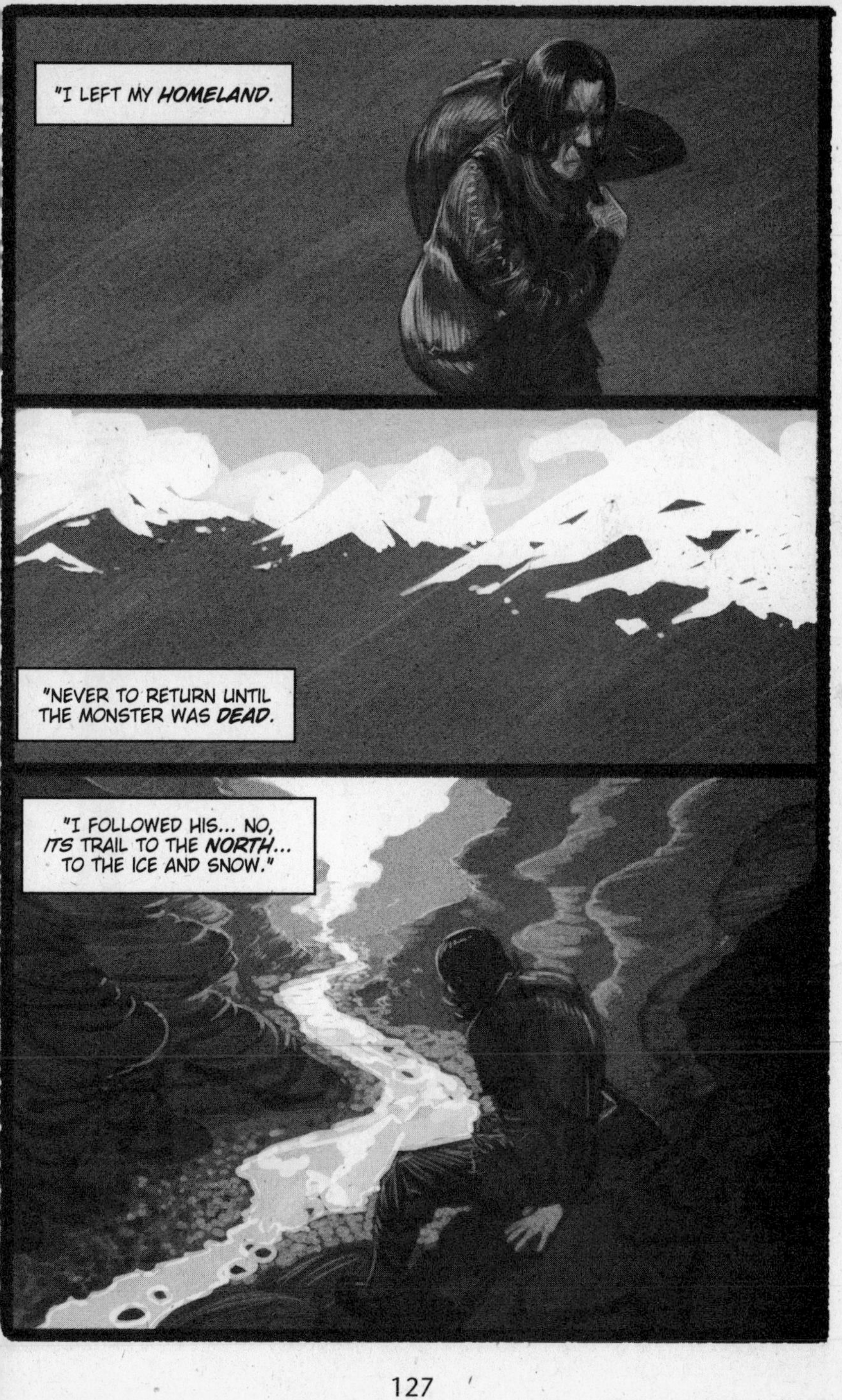
"I LEFT MY HOMELAND.
"NEVER TO RETURN UNTIL THE MONSTER WAS DEAD.
"I FOLLOWED HIS... NO, ITS TRAIL TO THE NORTH... TO THE ICE AND SNOW."

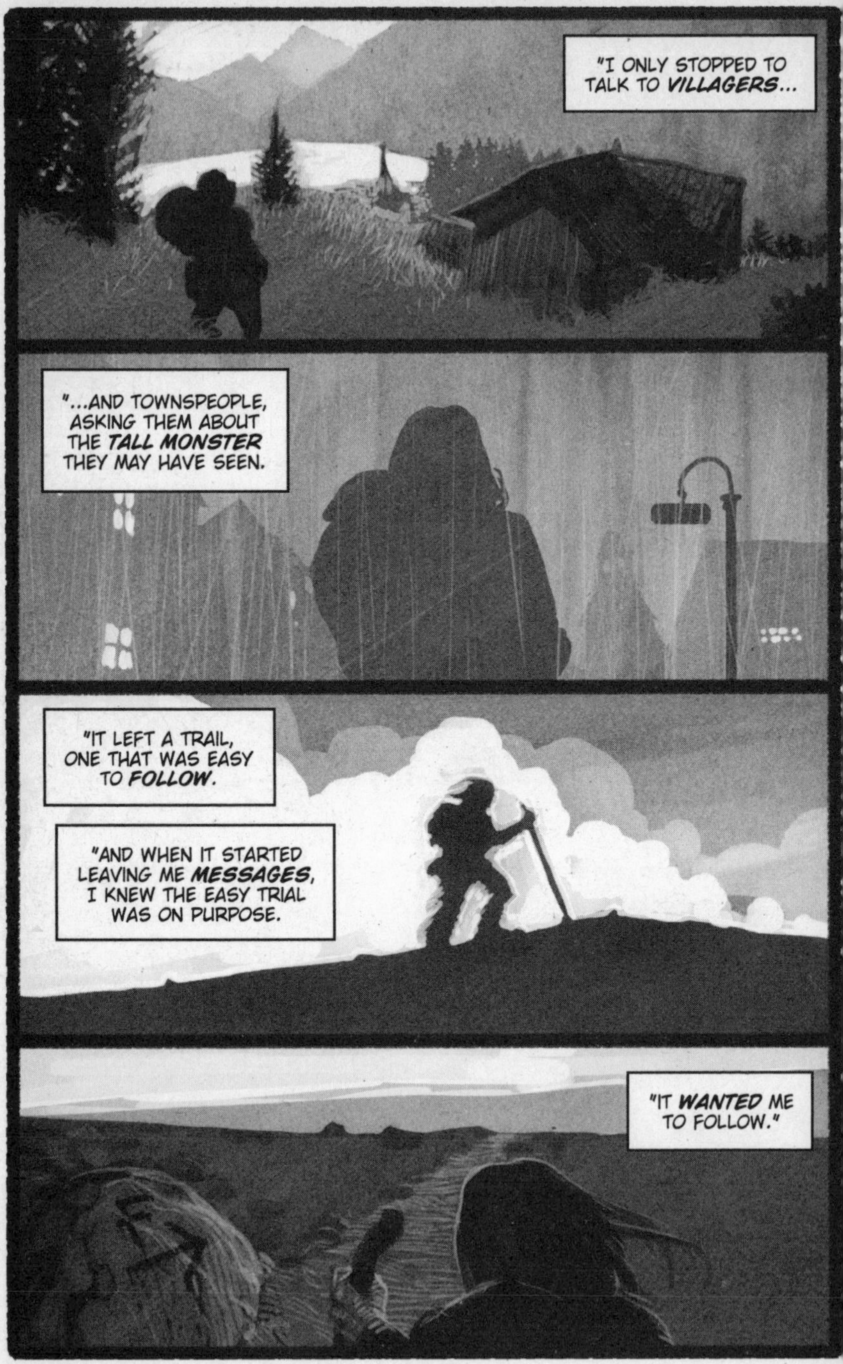
"I ONLY STOPPED TO TALK TO VILLAGERS...
"...AND TOWNSPEOPLE, ASKING THEM ABOUT THE TALL MONSTER THEY MAY HAVE SEEN.
"IT LEFT A TRAIL, ONE THAT WAS EASY TO FOLLOW.
"AND WHEN IT STARTED LEAVING ME MESSAGES, I KNEW THE EASY TRIAL WAS ON PURPOSE.
"IT WANTED ME TO FOLLOW."

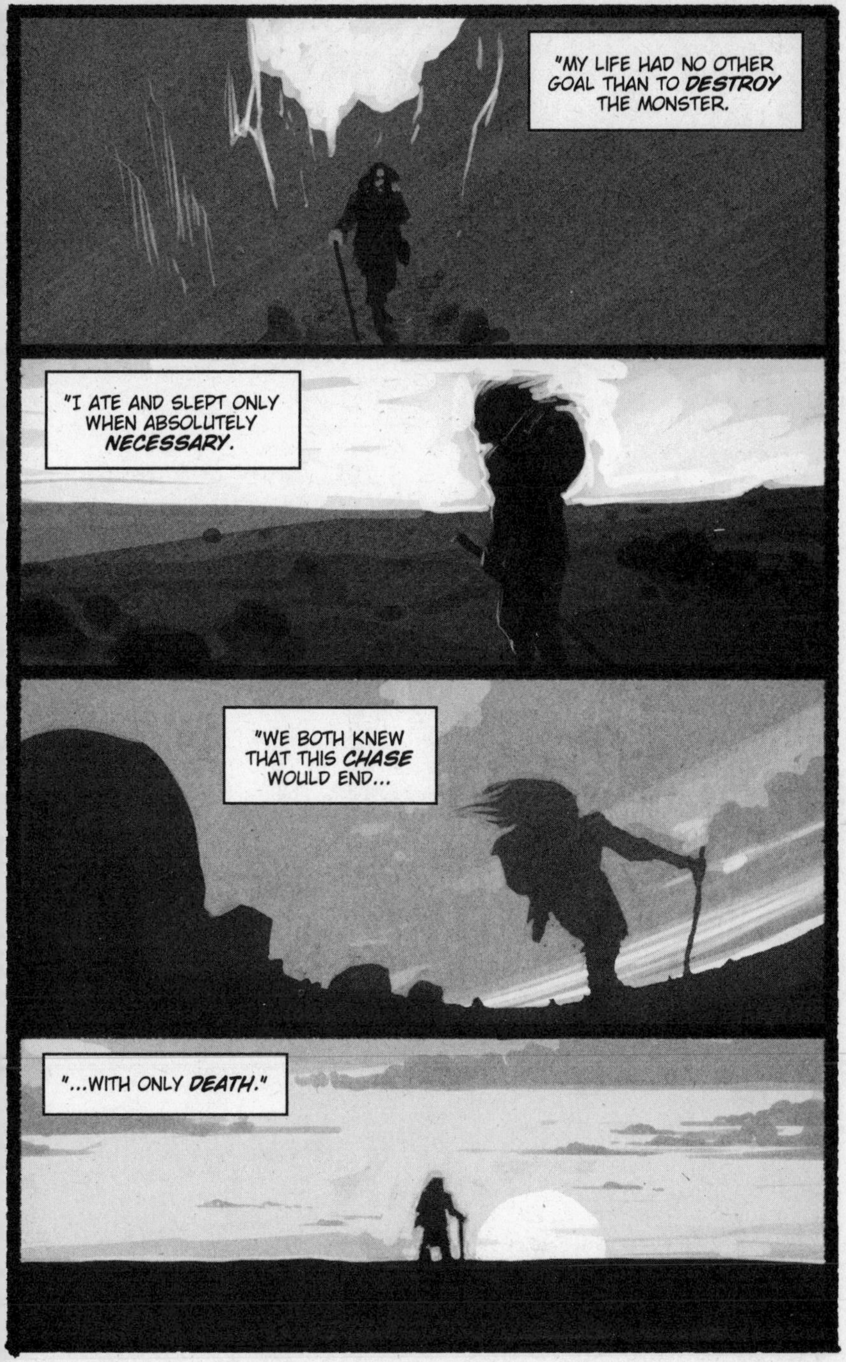
"MY LIFE HAD NO OTHER GOAL THAN TO DESTROY THE MONSTER.
"I ATE AND SLEPT ONLY WHEN ABSOLUTELY NECESSARY.
"WE BOTH KNEW THAT THIS CHASE WOULD END...
"...WITH ONLY DEATH."

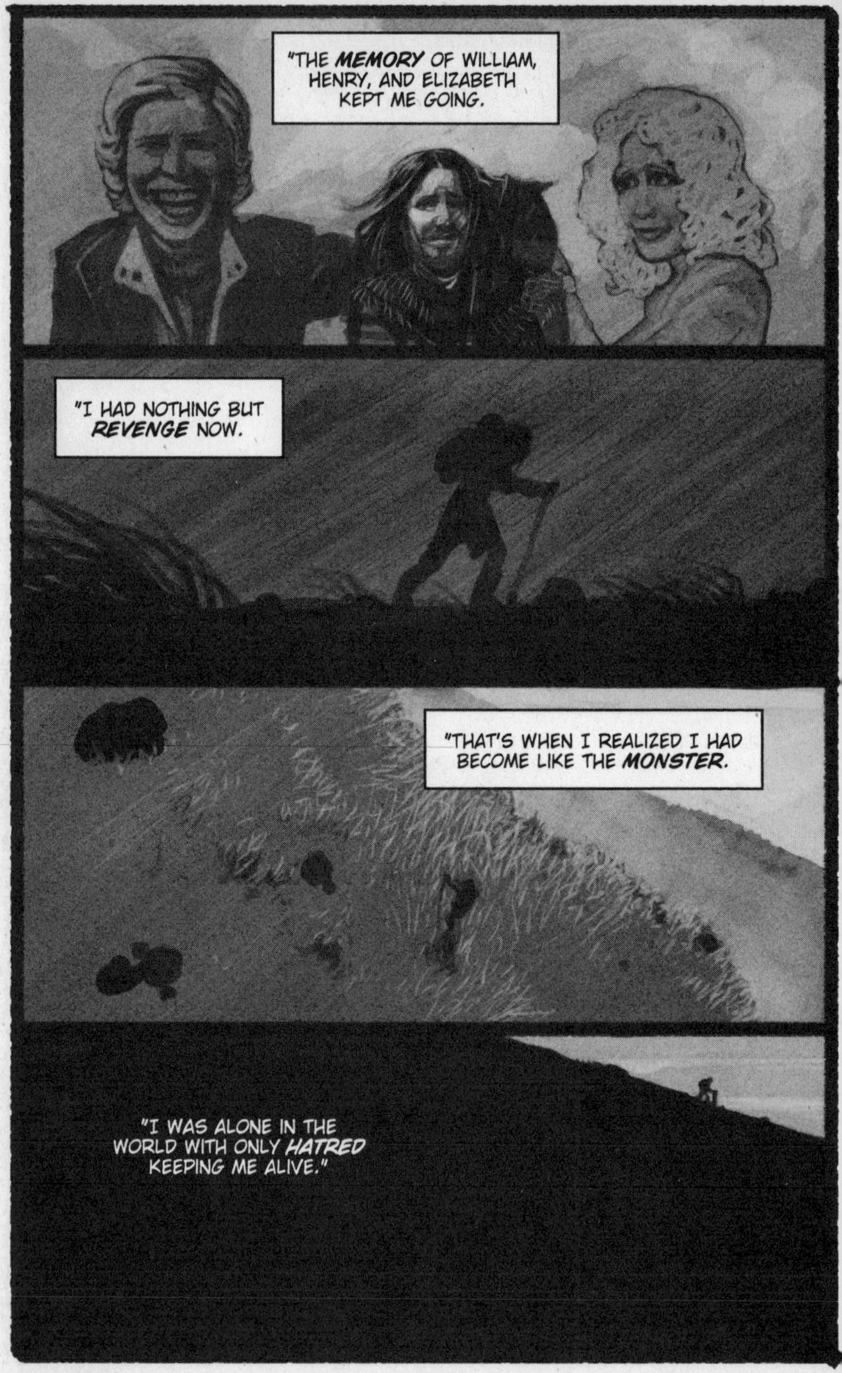
"THE MEMORY OF WILLIAM, HENRY, AND ELIZABETH KEPT ME GOING.
"I HAD NOTHING BUT REVENGE NOW.
"THAT'S WHEN I REALIZED I HAD BECOME LIKE THE MONSTER.
"I WAS ALONE IN THE WORLD WITH ONLY HATRED KEEPING ME ALIVE."

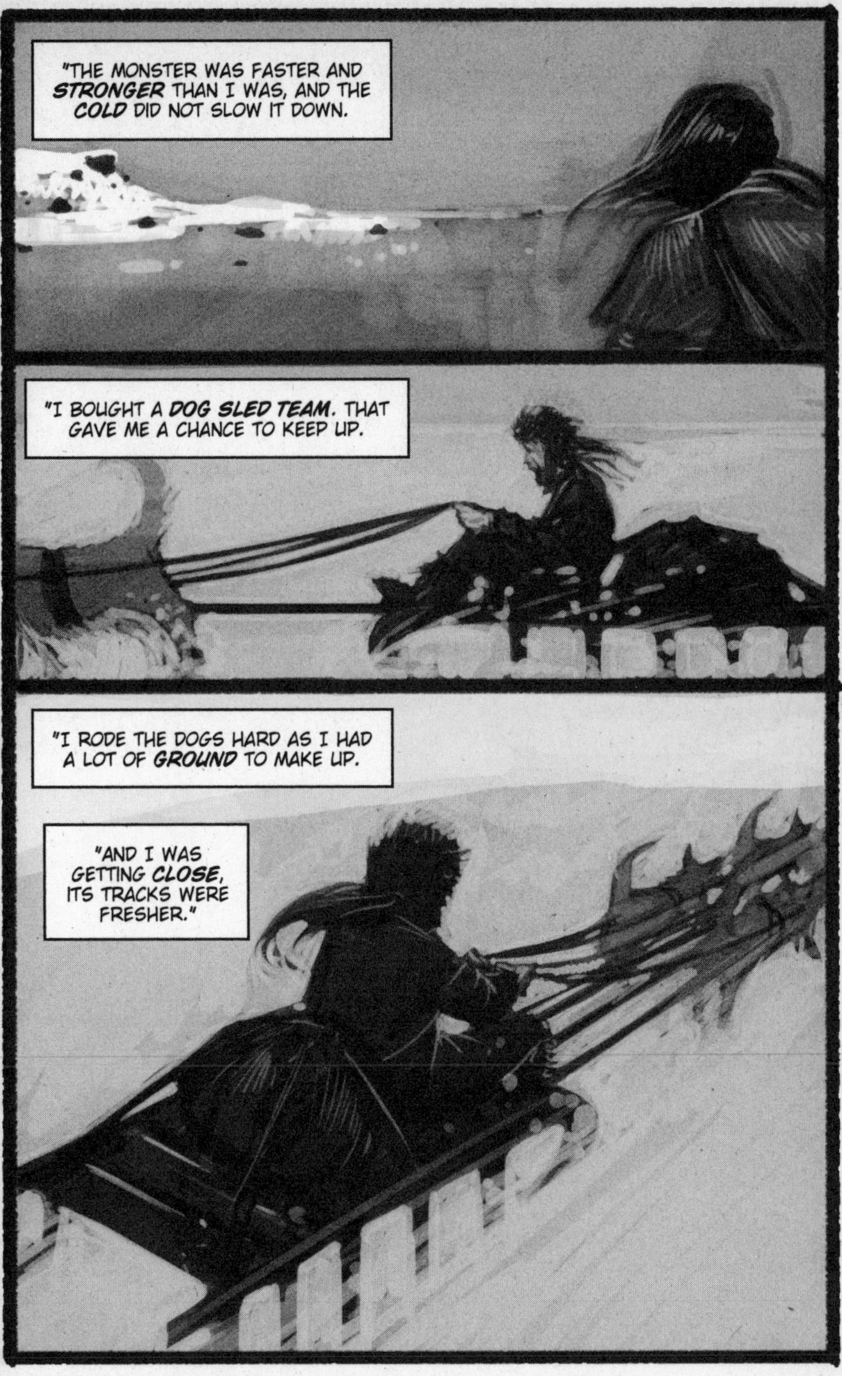
"THE MONSTER WAS FASTER AND STRONGER THAN I WAS, AND THE COLD DID NOT SLOW IT DOWN.
"I BOUGHT A DOG SLED TEAM. THAT GAVE ME A CHANCE TO KEEP UP.
"I RODE THE DOGS HARD AS I HAD A LOT OF GROUND TO MAKE UP.
"AND I WAS GETTING CLOSE, ITS TRACKS WERE FRESHER."

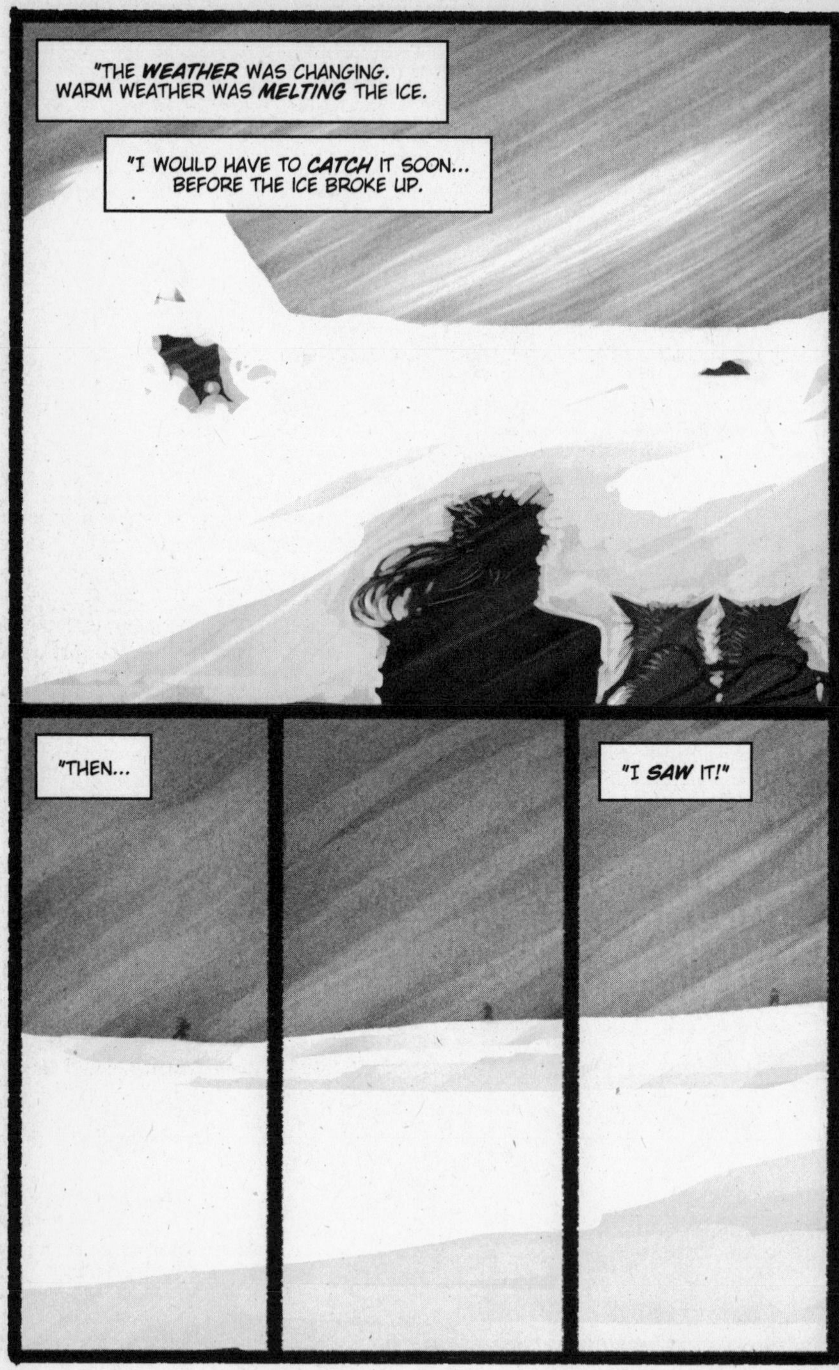
"THE WEATHER WAS CHANGING. WARM WEATHER WAS MELTING THE ICE.
"I WOULD HAVE TO CATCH IT SOON... BEFORE THE ICE BROKE UP.
"THEN...
"I SAW IT!"

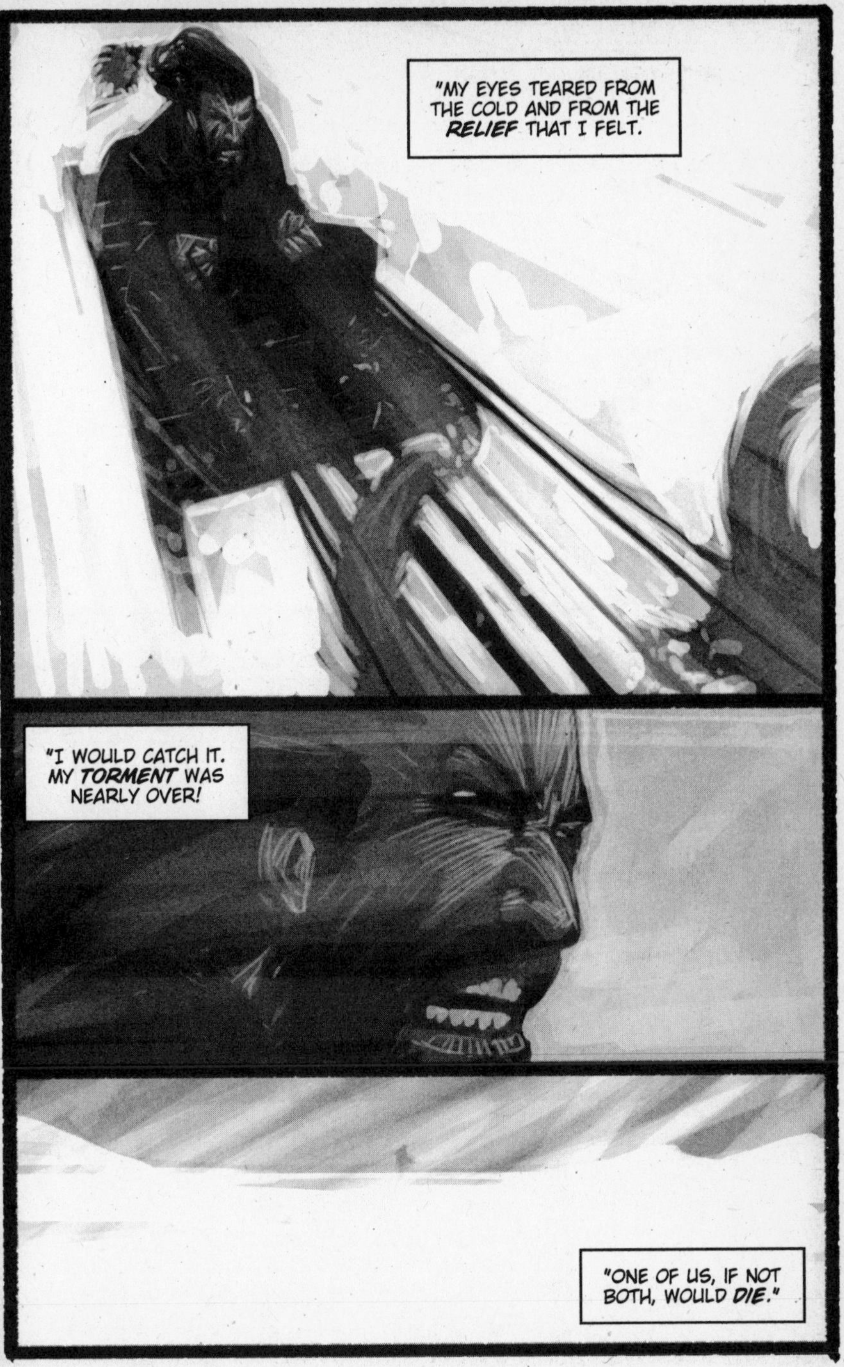
"MY EYES TEARED FROM THE COLD AND FROM THE RELIEF THAT I FELT.
"I WOULD CATCH IT. MY TORMENT WAS NEARLY OVER!
"ONE OF US, IF NOT BOTH, WOULD DIE."

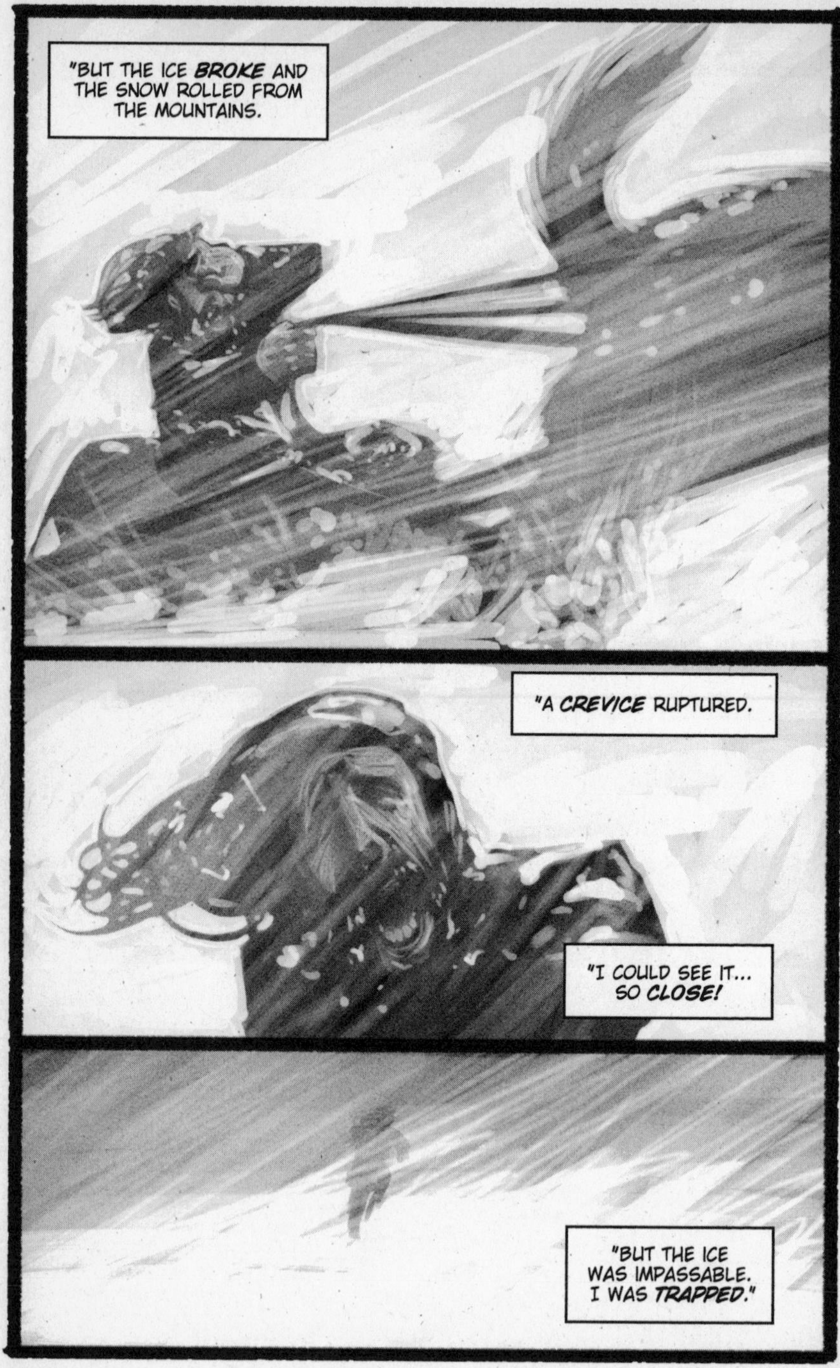
"BUT THE ICE BROKE AND THE SNOW ROLLED FROM THE MOUNTAINS.
"A CREVICE RUPTURED.
"I COULD SEE IT... SO CLOSE!
"BUT THE ICE WAS IMPASSABLE. I WAS TRAPPED."

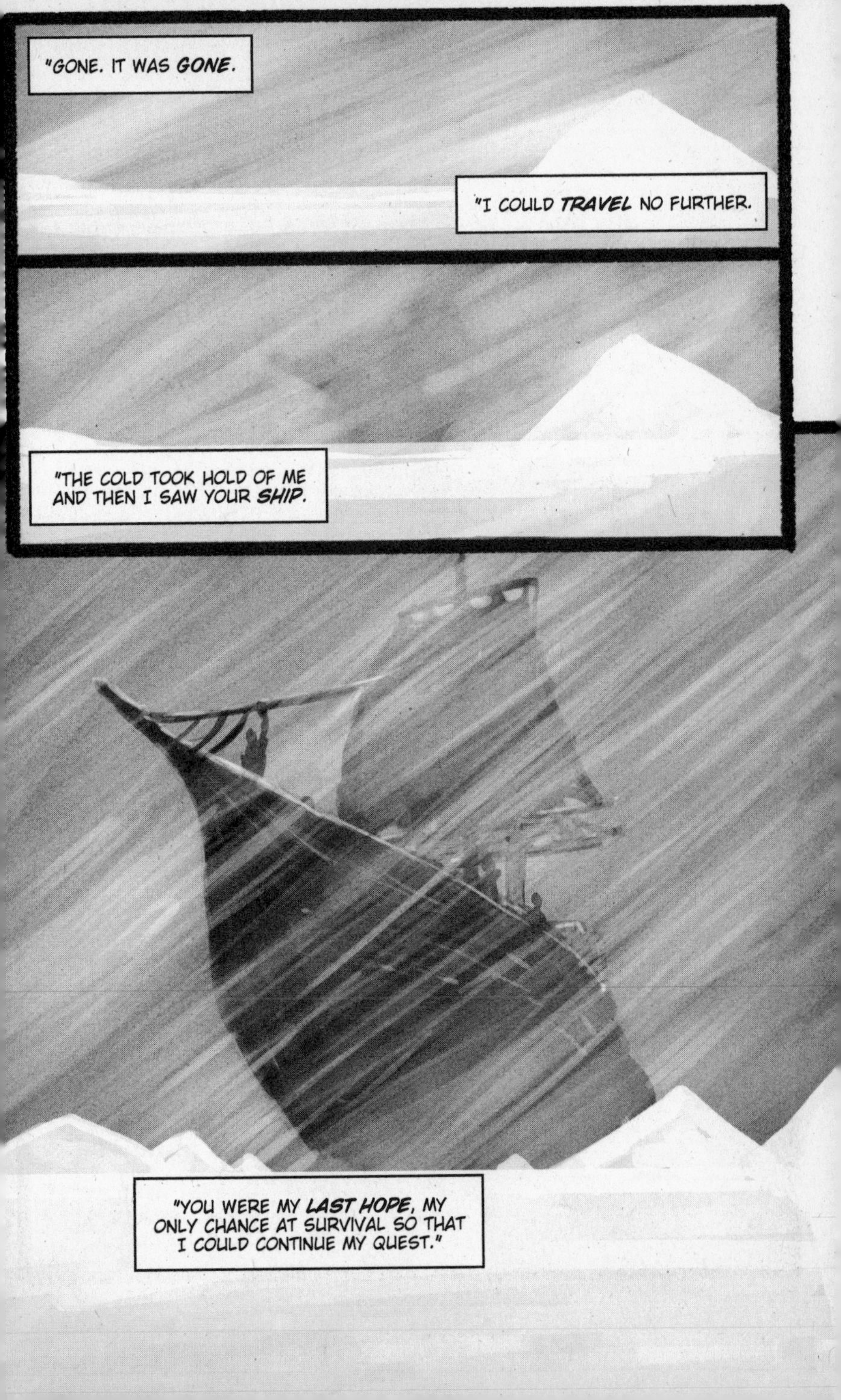
"GONE. IT WAS GONE.
"I COULD TRAVEL NO FURTHER.
"THE COLD TOOK HOLD OF ME AND THEN I SAW YOUR SHIP.
"YOU WERE MY LAST HOPE, MY ONLY CHANCE AT SURVIVAL SO THAT I COULD CONTINUE MY QUEST."

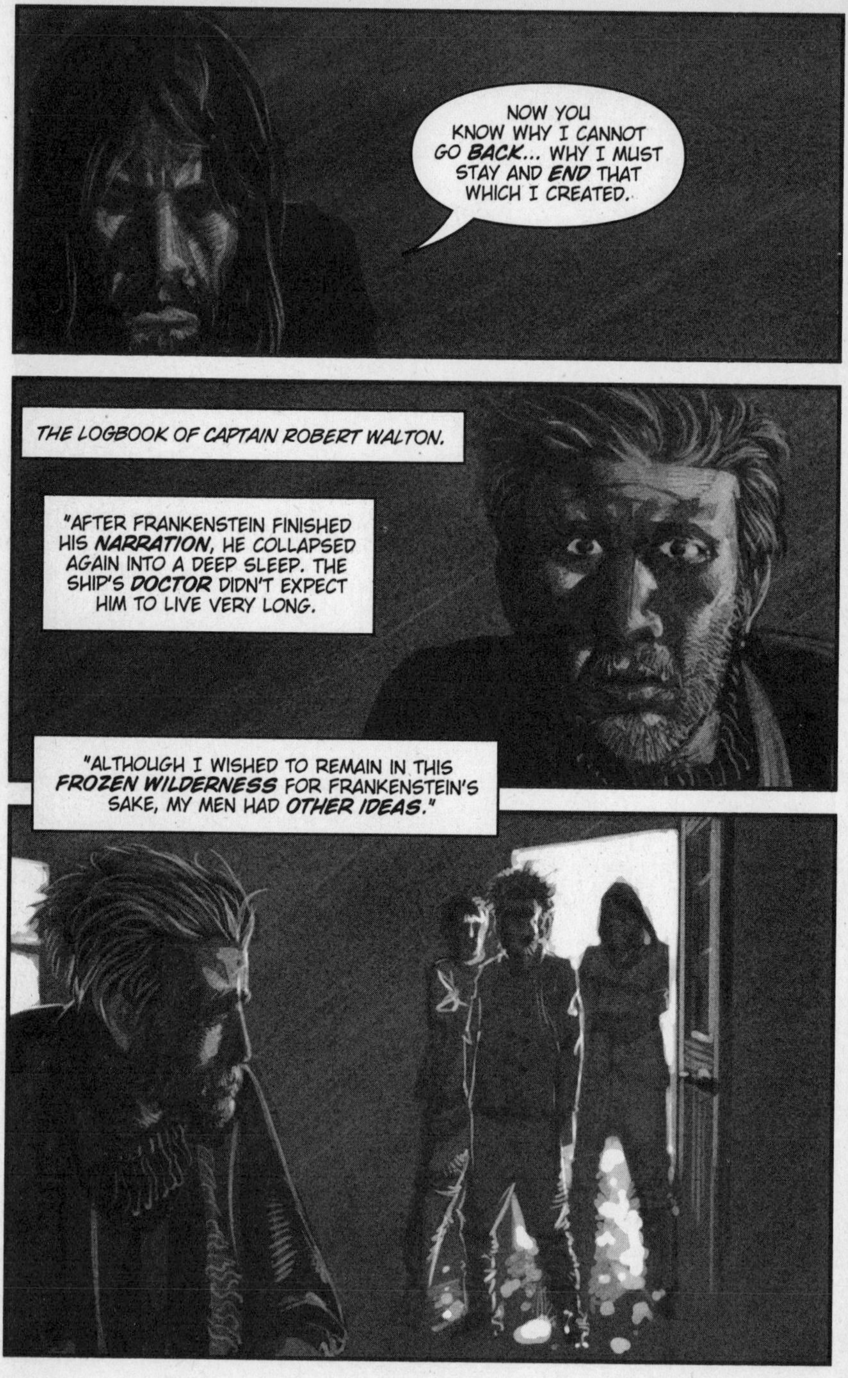
NOW YOU KNOW WHY I CANNOT GO BACK... WHY I MUST STAY AND END THAT WHICH I CREATED.
THE LOGBOOK OF CAPTAIN ROBERT WALTON.
"AFTER FRANKENSTEIN FINISHED HIS NARRATION, HE COLLAPSED AGAIN INTO A DEEP SLEEP. THE SHIP'S DOCTOR DIDN'T EXPECT HIM TO LIVE VERY LONG.
"ALTHOUGH I WISHED TO REMAIN IN THIS FROZEN WILDERNESS FOR FRANKENSTEIN'S SAKE, MY MEN HAD OTHER IDEAS."

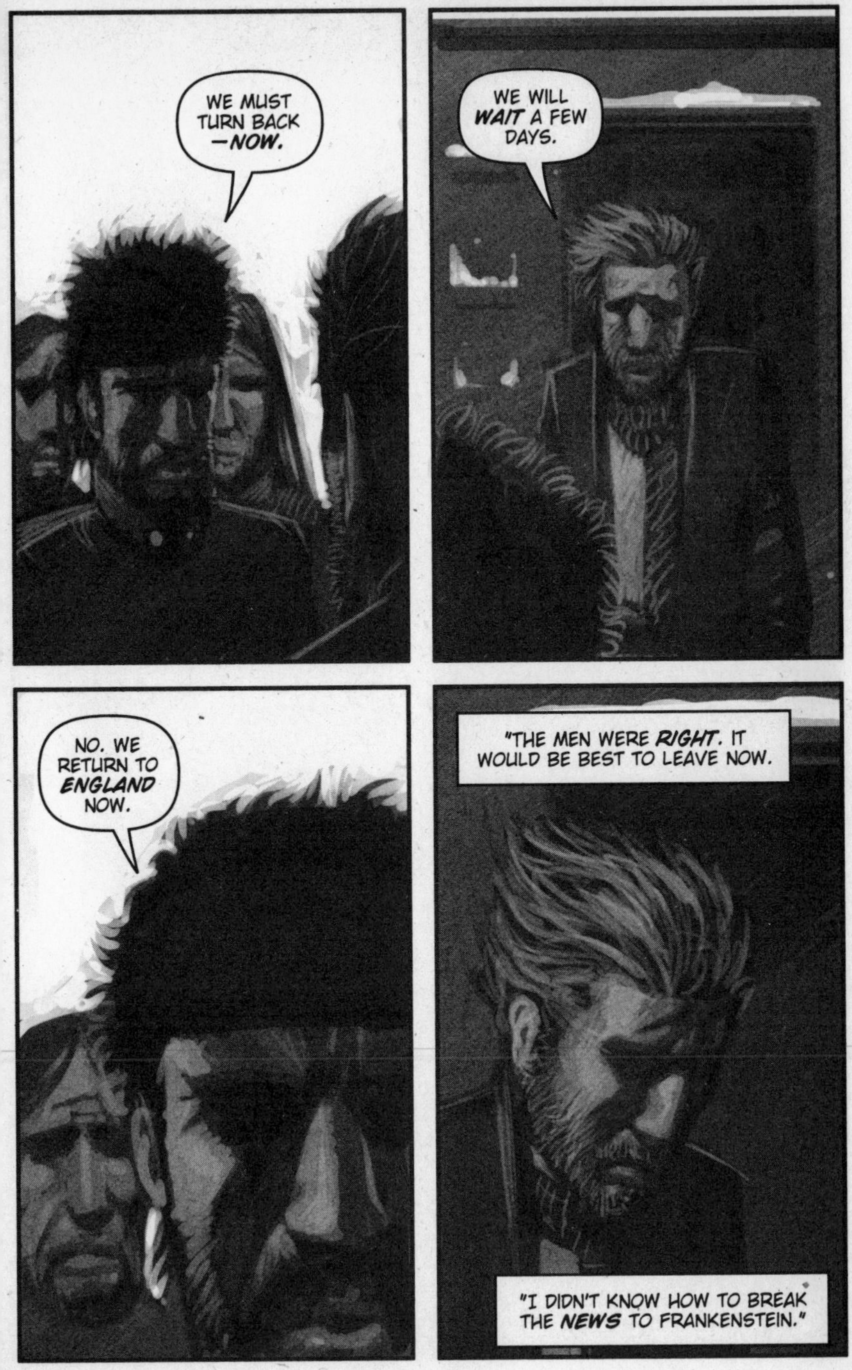
WE MUST TURN BACK —*NOW*.
WE WILL *WAIT* A FEW DAYS.
NO. WE RETURN TO *ENGLAND* NOW.
"THE MEN WERE *RIGHT*. IT WOULD BE BEST TO LEAVE NOW.
"I DIDN'T KNOW HOW TO BREAK THE *NEWS* TO FRANKENSTEIN."

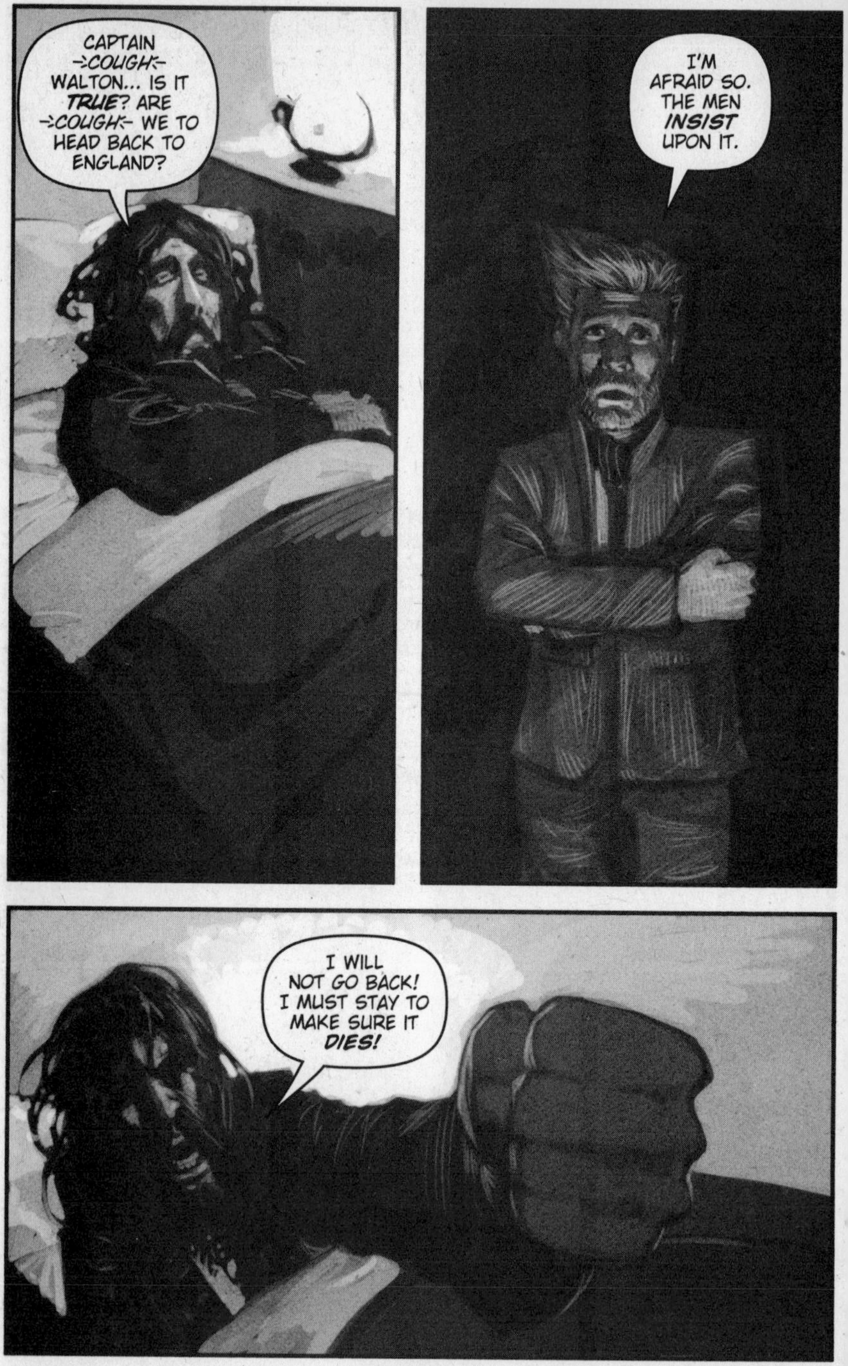
CAPTAIN -COUGH- WALTON... IS IT TRUE? ARE -COUGH- WE TO HEAD BACK TO ENGLAND?
I'M AFRAID SO. THE MEN INSIST UPON IT.
I WILL NOT GO BACK! I MUST STAY TO MAKE SURE IT DIES!

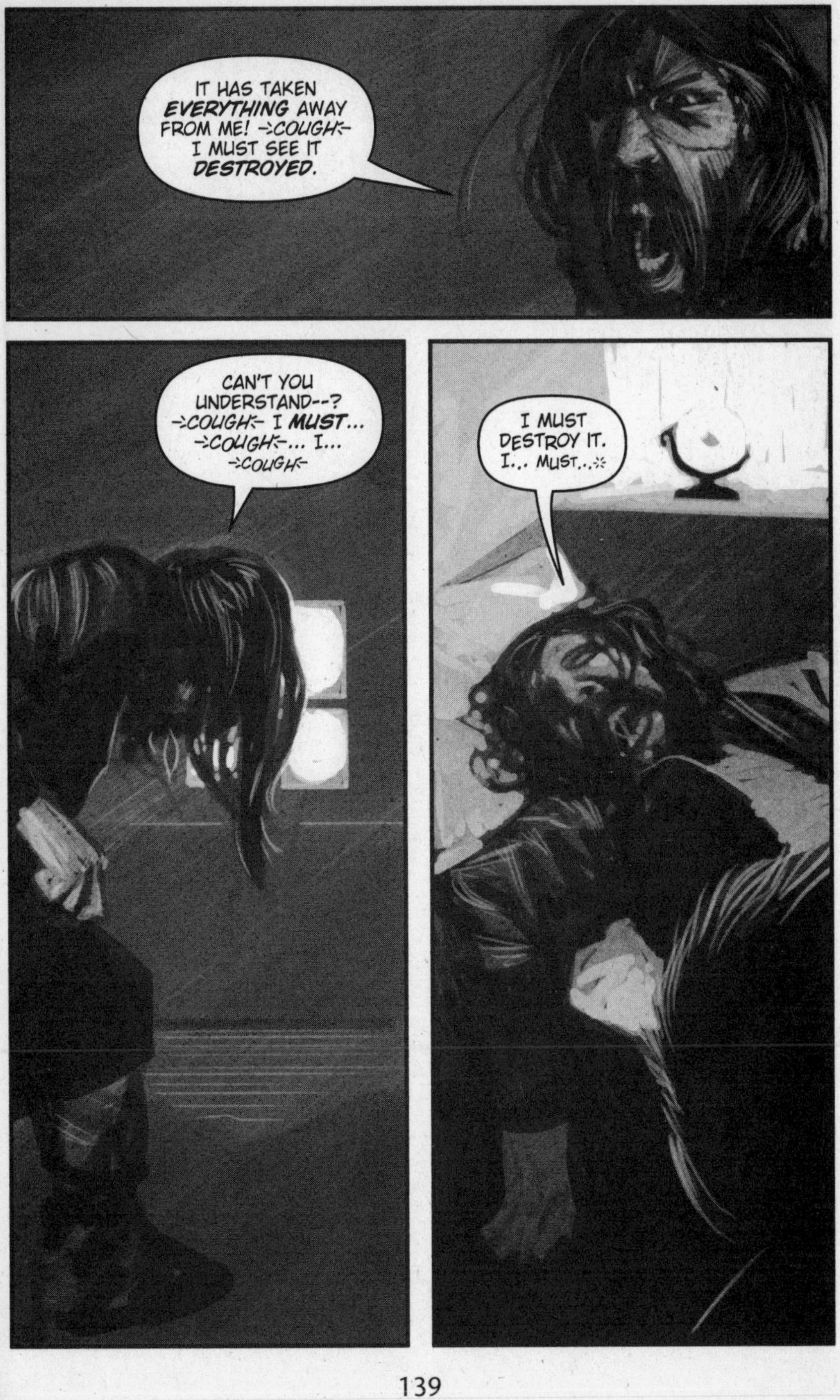
IT HAS TAKEN EVERYTHING AWAY FROM ME! -COUGH- I MUST SEE IT DESTROYED.
CAN'T YOU UNDERSTAND--? -COUGH- I MUST... -COUGH-... I... -COUGH-
I MUST DESTROY IT. I... MUST...

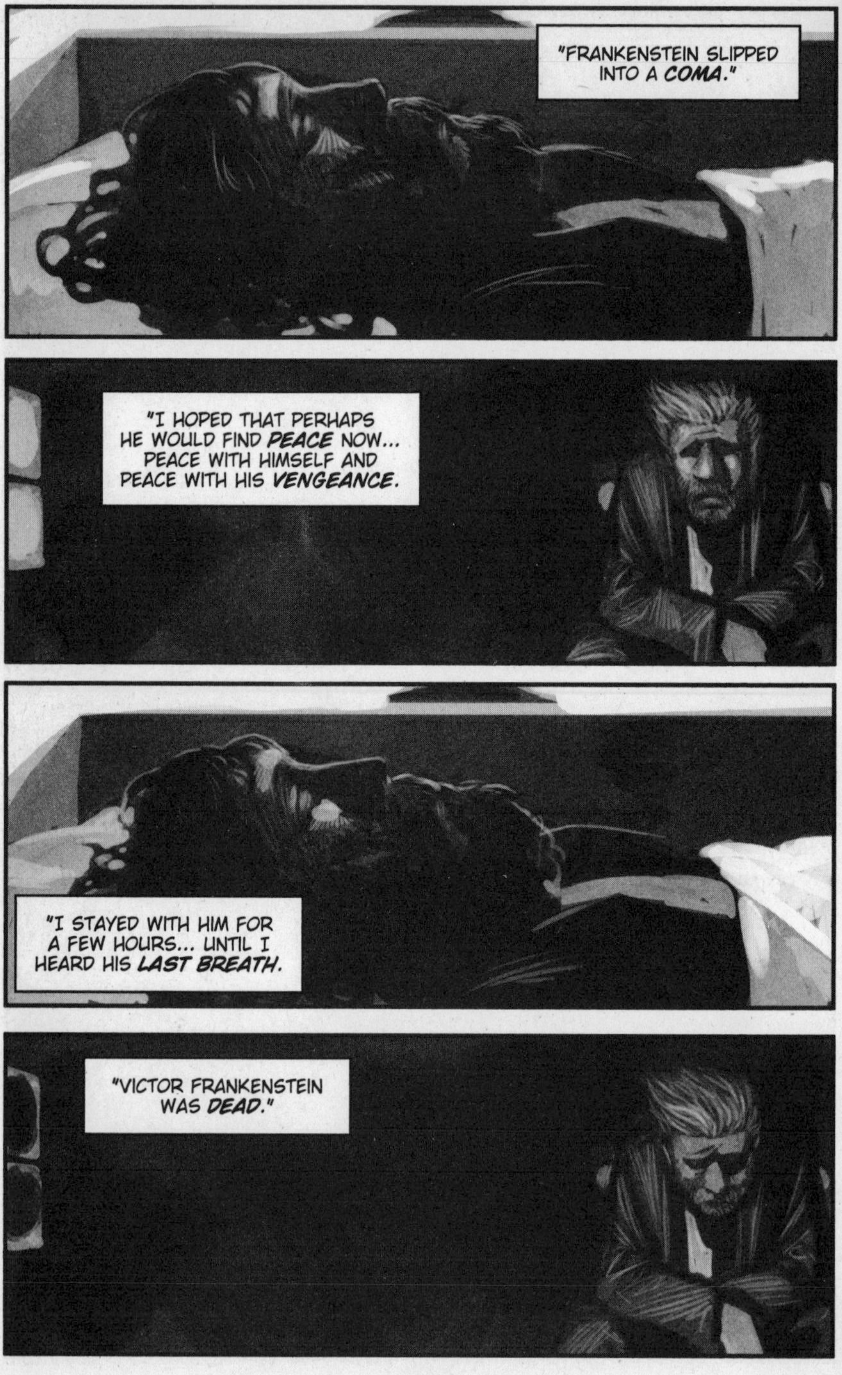
"FRANKENSTEIN SLIPPED INTO A COMA."
"I HOPED THAT PERHAPS HE WOULD FIND PEACE NOW... PEACE WITH HIMSELF AND PEACE WITH HIS VENGEANCE.
"I STAYED WITH HIM FOR A FEW HOURS... UNTIL I HEARD HIS LAST BREATH.
"VICTOR FRANKENSTEIN WAS DEAD."

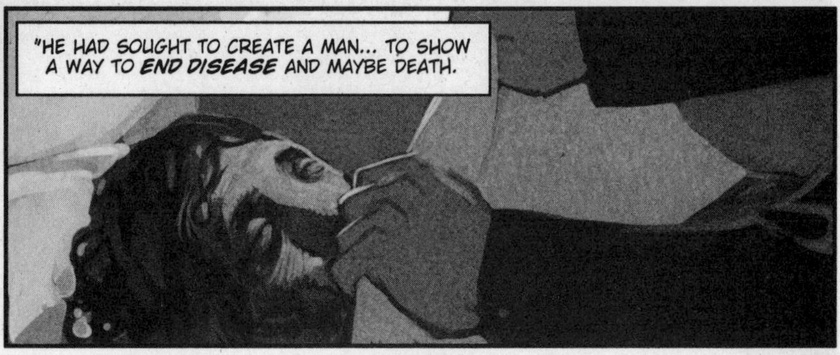
"HE HAD SOUGHT TO CREATE A MAN... TO SHOW A WAY TO END DISEASE AND MAYBE DEATH.

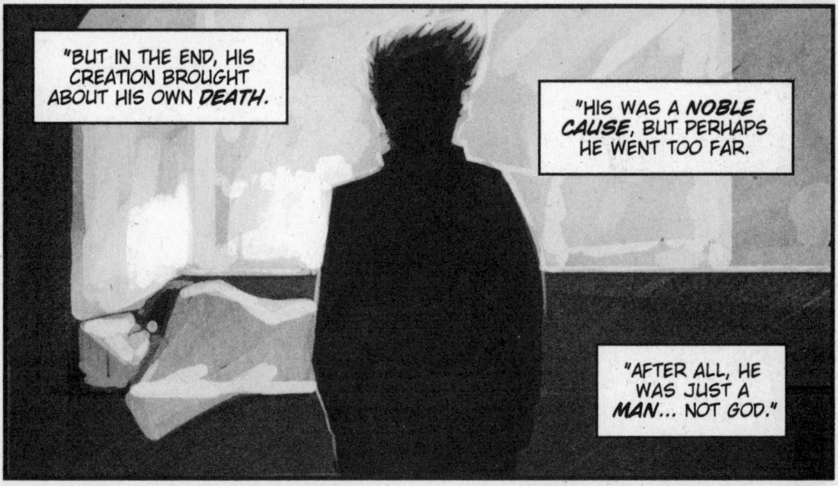
"BUT IN THE END, HIS CREATION BROUGHT ABOUT HIS OWN DEATH.
"HIS WAS A NOBLE CAUSE, BUT PERHAPS HE WENT TOO FAR.
"AFTER ALL, HE WAS JUST A MAN... NOT GOD."

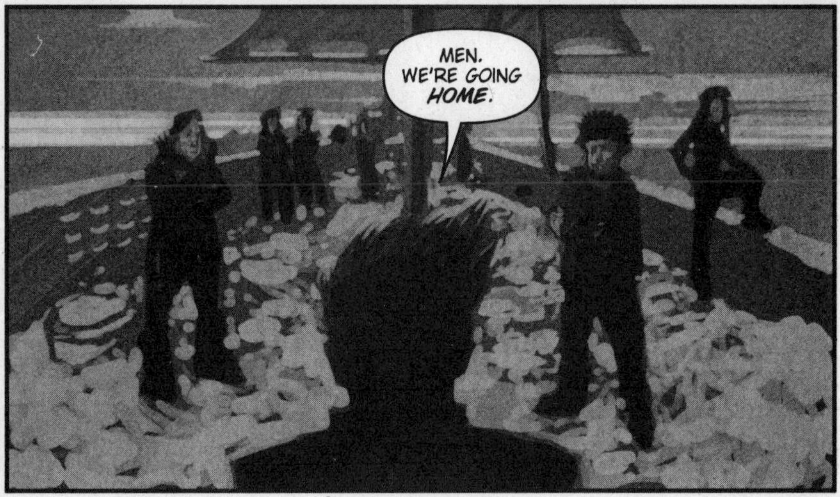
MEN. WE'RE GOING HOME.

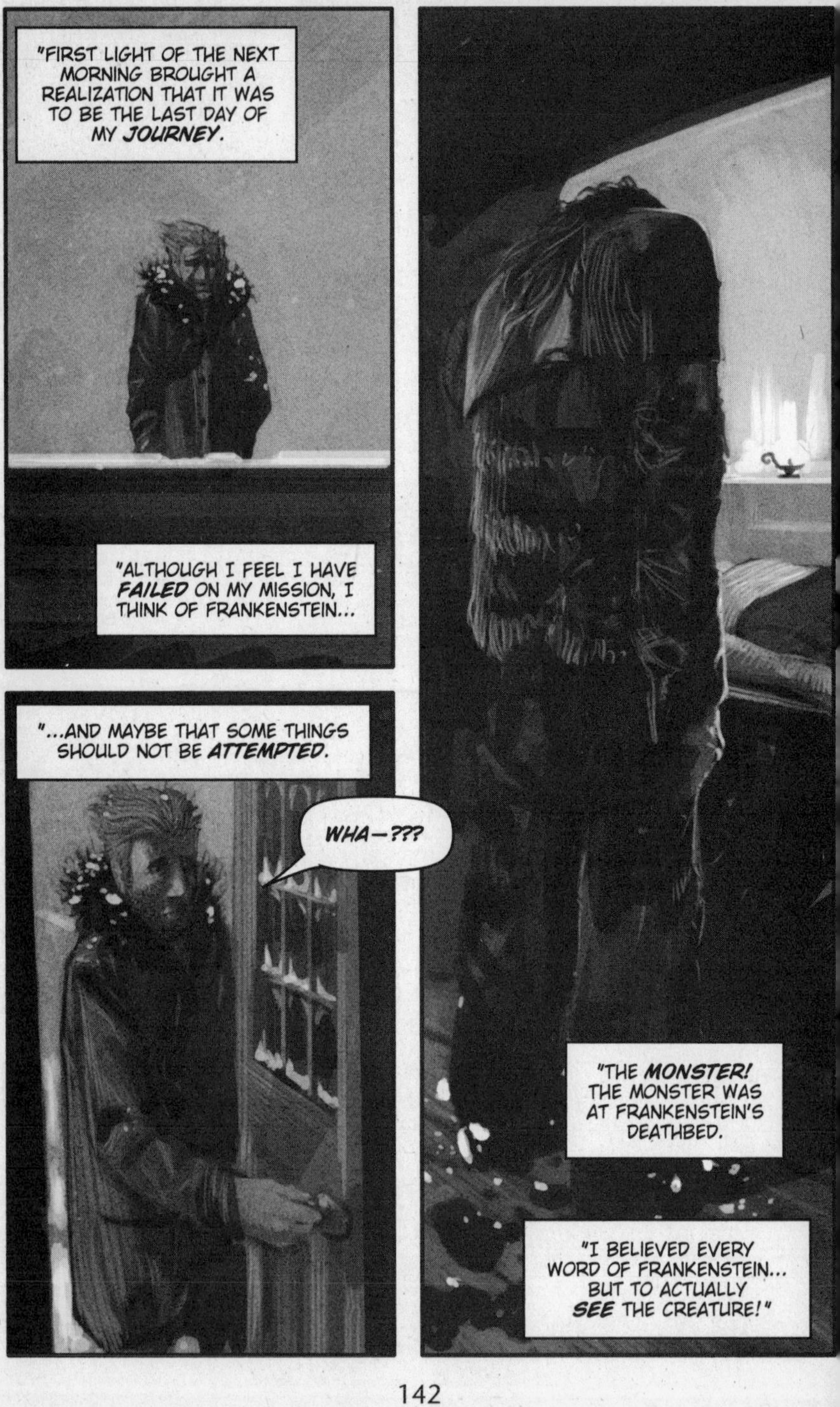
"FIRST LIGHT OF THE NEXT MORNING BROUGHT A REALIZATION THAT IT WAS TO BE THE LAST DAY OF MY JOURNEY.
"ALTHOUGH I FEEL I HAVE FAILED ON MY MISSION, I THINK OF FRANKENSTEIN...
"...AND MAYBE THAT SOME THINGS SHOULD NOT BE ATTEMPTED.
WHA—???
"THE MONSTER! THE MONSTER WAS AT FRANKENSTEIN'S DEATHBED.
"I BELIEVED EVERY WORD OF FRANKENSTEIN... BUT TO ACTUALLY SEE THE CREATURE!"

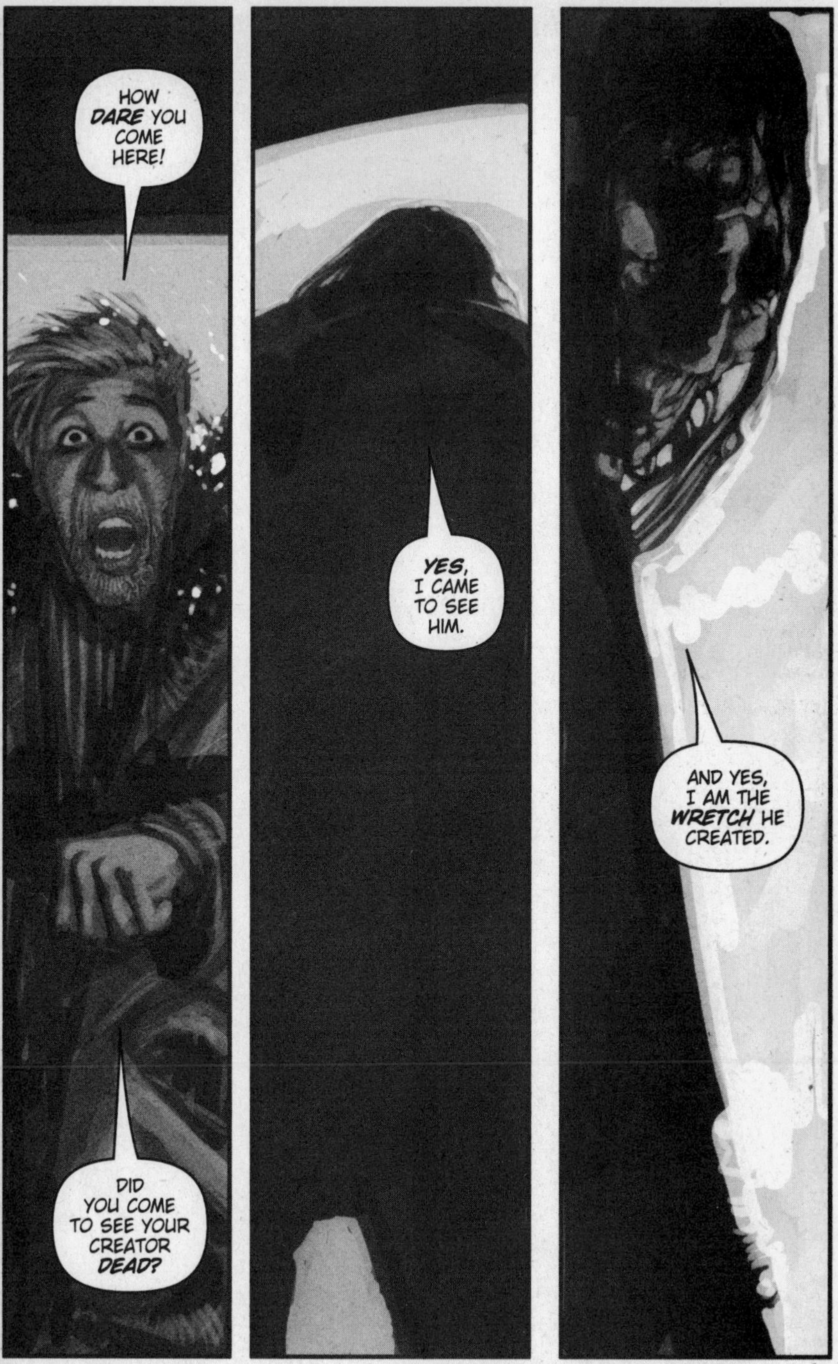
HOW DARE YOU COME HERE!
DID YOU COME TO SEE YOUR CREATOR DEAD?
YES, I CAME TO SEE HIM.
AND YES, I AM THE WRETCH HE CREATED.

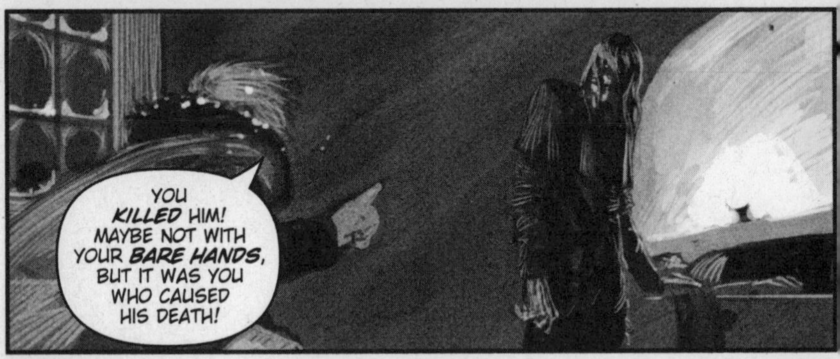
YOU KILLED HIM! MAYBE NOT WITH YOUR BARE HANDS, BUT IT WAS YOU WHO CAUSED HIS DEATH!

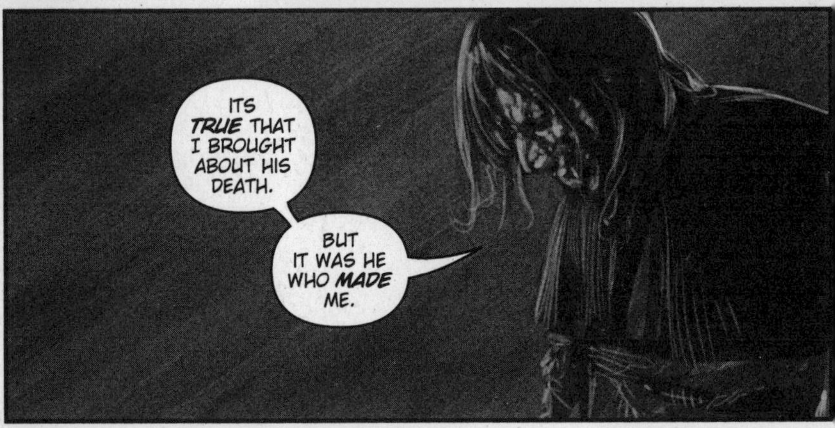
ITS TRUE THAT I BROUGHT ABOUT HIS DEATH.
BUT IT WAS HE WHO MADE ME.

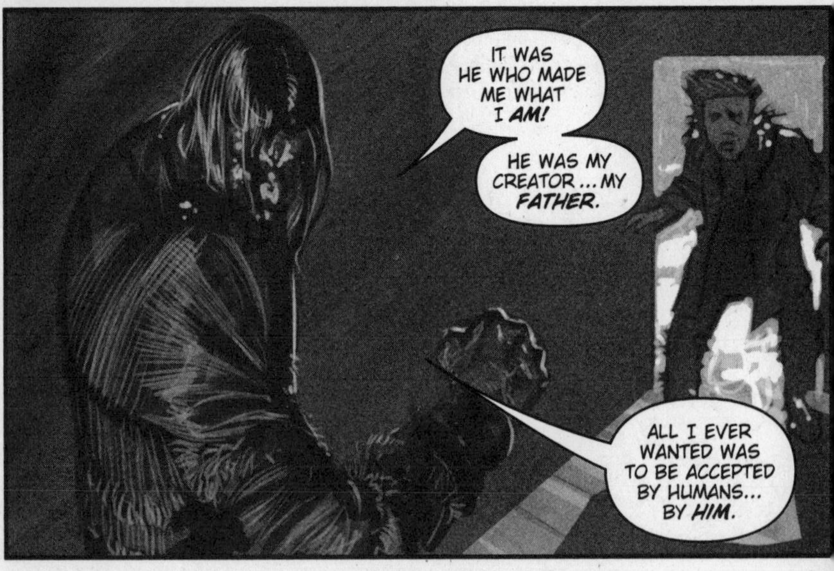
IT WAS HE WHO MADE ME WHAT I AM!
HE WAS MY CREATOR ... MY FATHER.
ALL I EVER WANTED WAS TO BE ACCEPTED BY HUMANS... BY HIM.

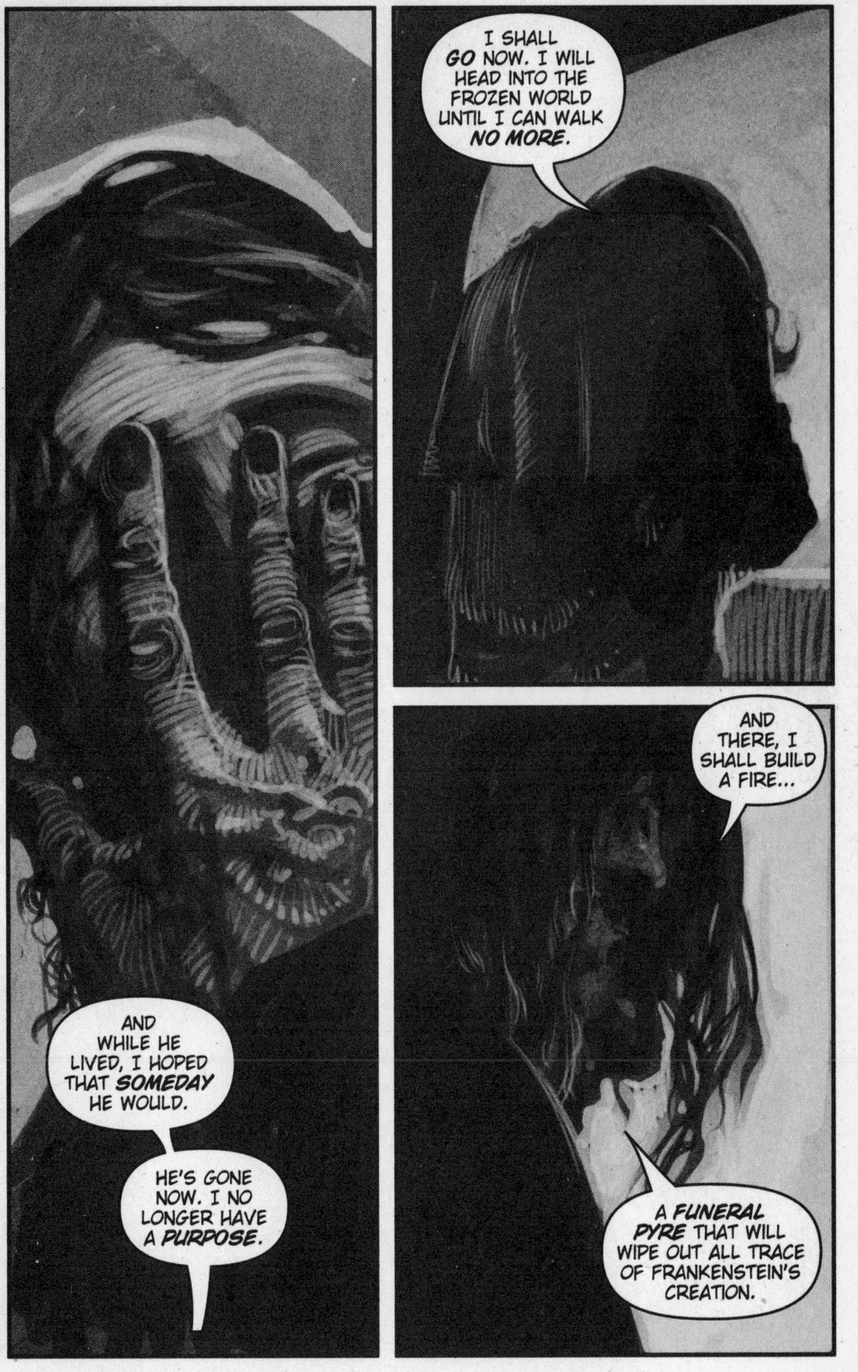

AND WHILE HE LIVED, I HOPED THAT SOMEDAY HE WOULD.
HE'S GONE NOW. I NO LONGER HAVE A PURPOSE.
I SHALL GO NOW. I WILL HEAD INTO THE FROZEN WORLD UNTIL I CAN WALK NO MORE.
AND THERE, I SHALL BUILD A FIRE...
A FUNERAL PYRE THAT WILL WIPE OUT ALL TRACE OF FRANKENSTEIN'S CREATION.

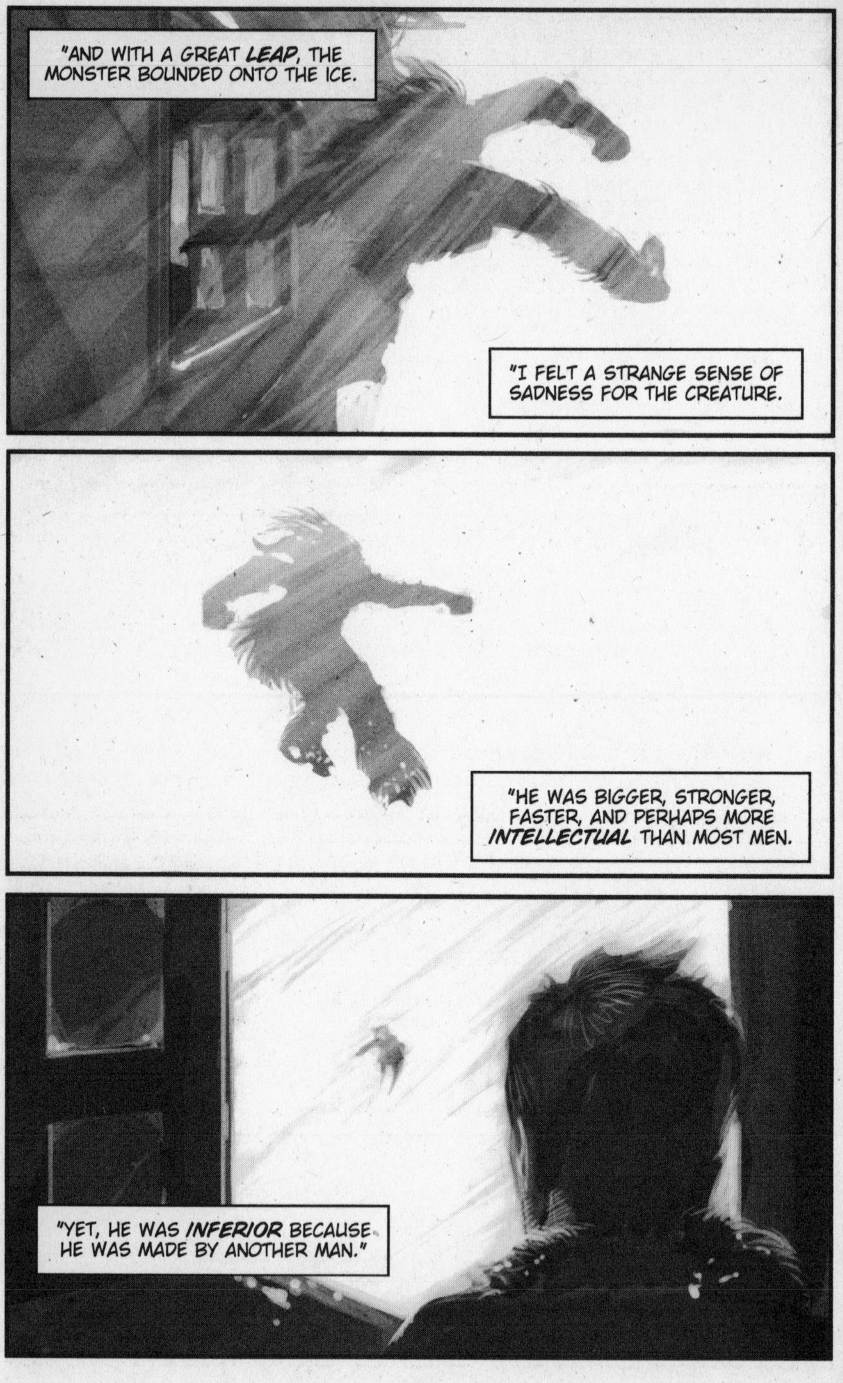
"AND WITH A GREAT LEAP, THE MONSTER BOUNDED ONTO THE ICE.
"I FELT A STRANGE SENSE OF SADNESS FOR THE CREATURE.
"HE WAS BIGGER, STRONGER, FASTER, AND PERHAPS MORE INTELLECTUAL THAN MOST MEN.
"YET, HE WAS INFERIOR BECAUSE HE WAS MADE BY ANOTHER MAN."

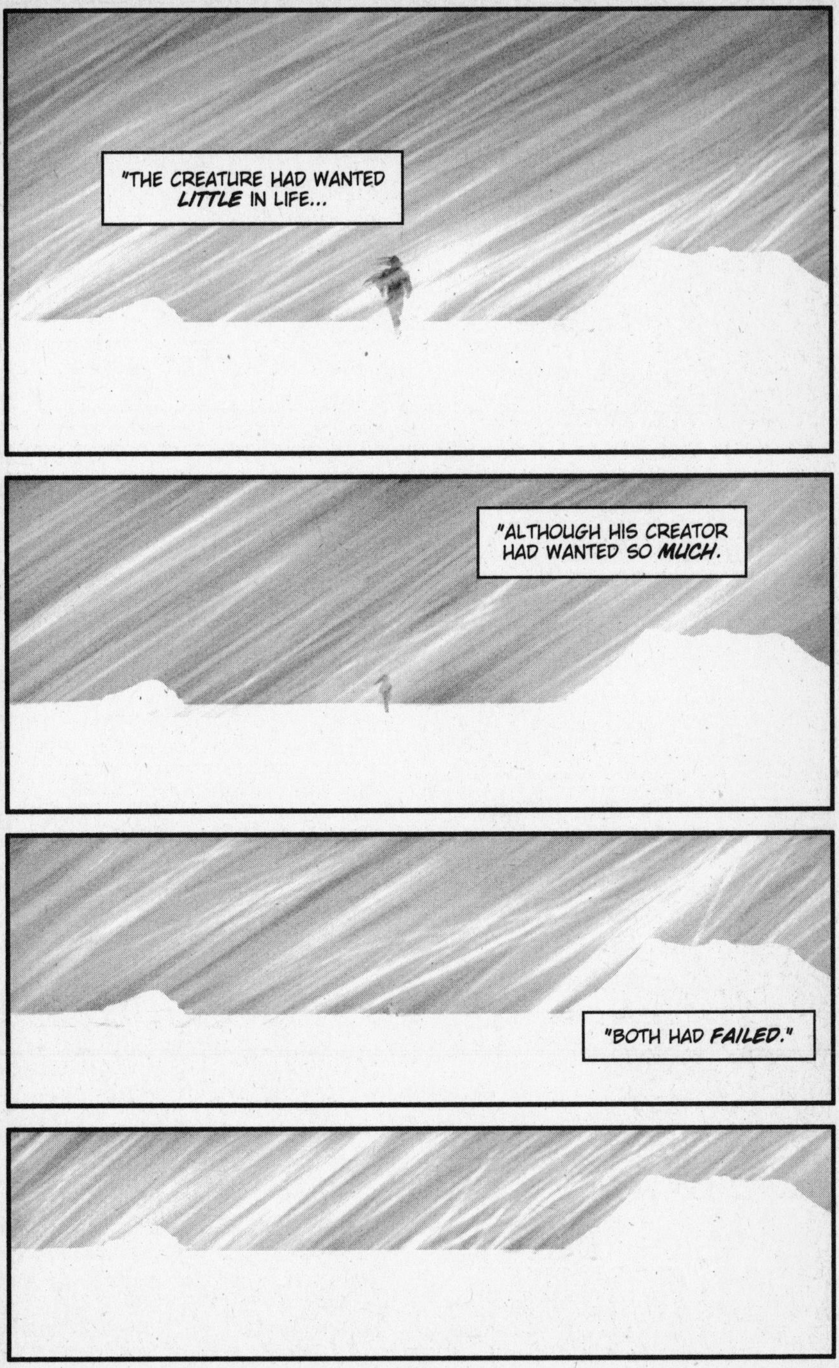
"THE CREATURE HAD WANTED *LITTLE* IN LIFE...
"ALTHOUGH HIS CREATOR HAD WANTED SO *MUCH*.
"BOTH HAD *FAILED*."

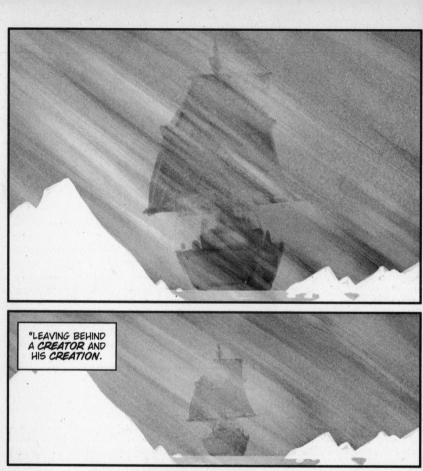

"LEAVING BEHIND A **CREATOR** AND HIS **CREATION**.

"ONLY DEATH COULD BRING THEM **TOGETHER**."

THE END

THE MAKING OF MARY SHELLEY'S FRANKENSTEIN

"My hope is that this adaptation will be strong enough to stand on its own as an individual piece of work in the graphic novel format."—Gary Reed

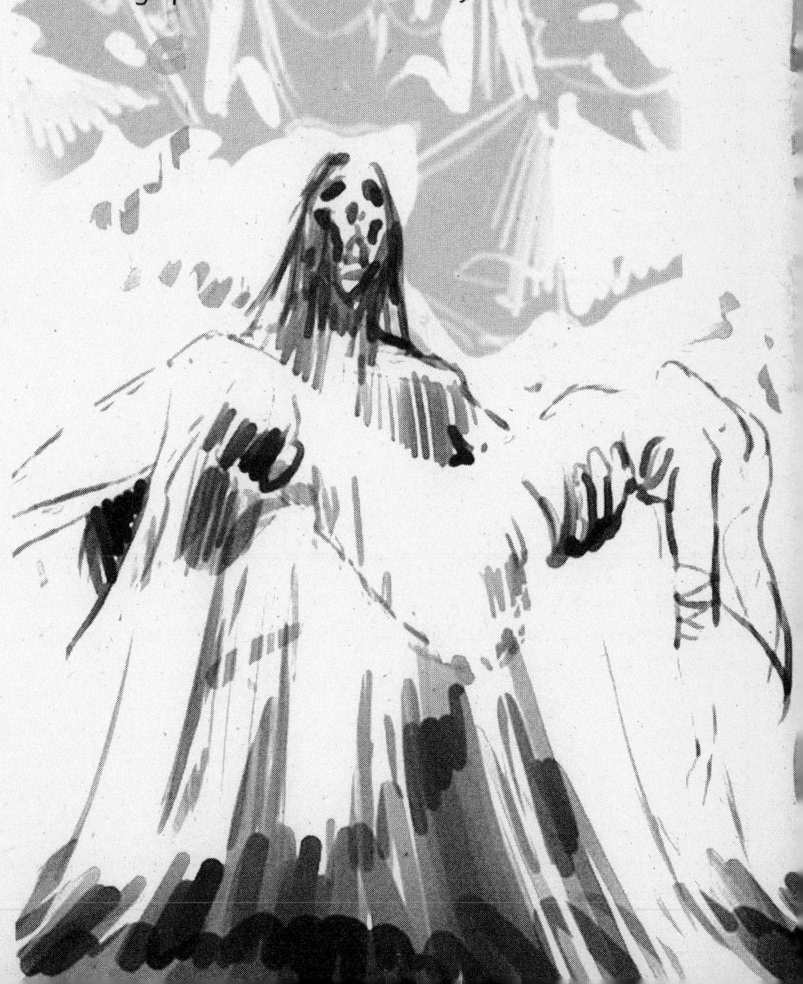

Gary Reed talks about his adaptation of

MARY SHELLEY'S

FRANKENSTEIN

Mary Shelley's *Frankenstein* is a tale of two individuals linked together by science. Although one of them is not a willing participant, by the end of the story, the two are both living lives of regret and shame.

Victor Frankenstein and "the monster" are both victims. Frankenstein builds his creature and delves into the reanimation of life for the right reasons . . . to help others and to delay the finality of death. However, he instead creates a new life that causes death for all those who he holds dear. The monster is brought into this world with little recollection of his previous life. He is essentially a newborn and finds that because of his appearnace, he is cast out from joining mankind and therefore is a being of his own kind . . . alone.

I've kept the narration simple and similar to the original so that most of the story is told from Victor Frankenstein's viewpoint with the middle portion showing the contrasting view of Frankenstein's creation. Victor, of course, dwells on the horror of what he has created. The monster's viewpoint is that of an innocent thrust into a world not of his making and how he is forced to survive.

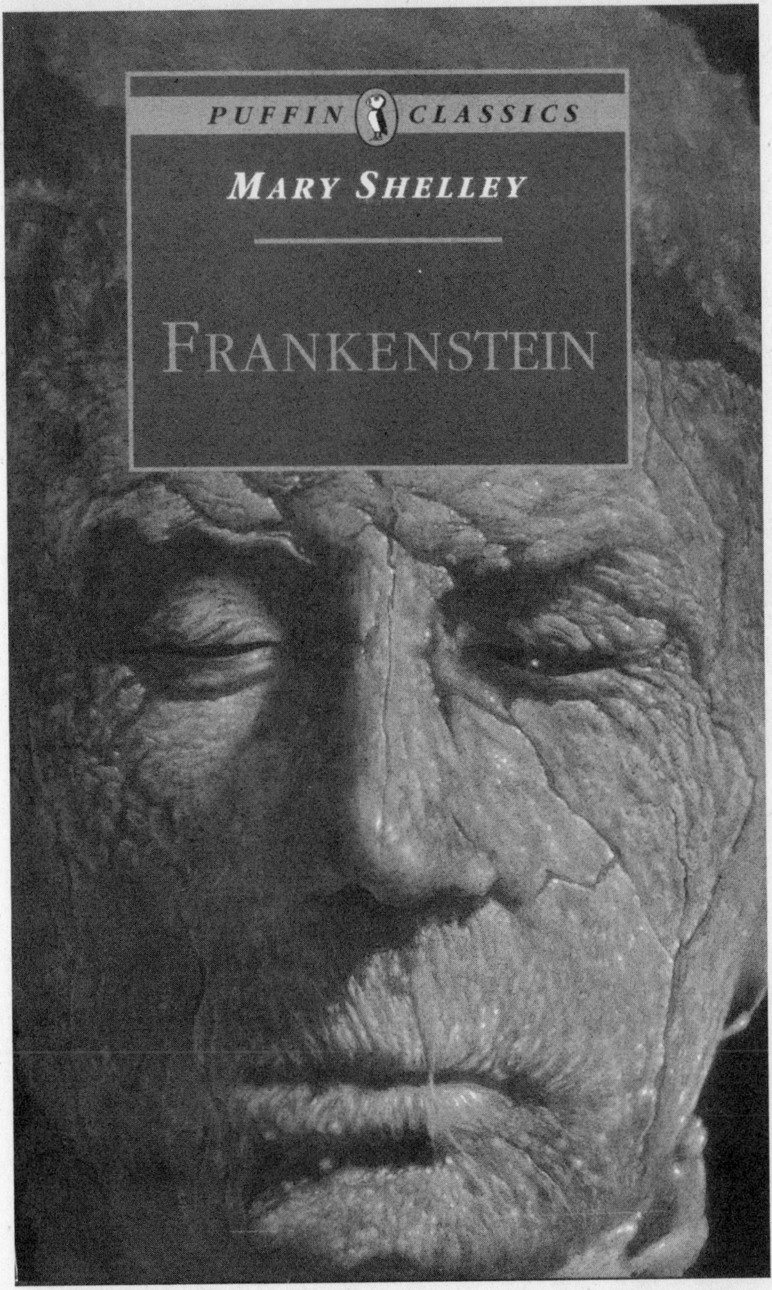
PUFFIN CLASSICS
MARY SHELLEY
FRANKENSTEIN

The Puffin Classics edition that was the source for the graphic novel adaptation.

MY TIME WITH FRANKIE

OR

ADAPTING AND ILLUSTRATING A REALLY LONG BOOK

by Frazer Irving

When publisher Byron Preiss asked me to do this project, he had mentioned that he'd seen some of my digitally painted art, and that he felt this would work well for Frankie. I agreed and to be honest, doing one-hundred-forty-four pages in Photoshop is easier than one-hundred-forty-four pages on paper, especially when one has such a lot of work to do in a relatively short space of time.

To start with I had to read *Frankenstein*, and then break it down into sentences, which then became little boxes with tiny words in them. This was my way of distilling all those words into simple notes and doodles. Once this was completed and okayed, I got down to the juicy stuff of illustrating the pages themselves.

The process starts with the thumbnail sketches that I email to my editors. These are loose and very sketchy but they have all the info I need to create the final art, which is all done on computer. Working with layers in Photoshop I developed a process where the black lines are separated from the white lines, and the borders go above it all. The style of art is different from what I'm used to. Normally one uses just black and builds up tones of grey. Here I was more interested in using the white to cut away from the black . . . sort of a reverse process if you will. This is very useful for conveying the darker elements of the book, the creeping horror and the shadowy undertones of Frankenstein's mind. I feel that the method used to render a story is as important as the actual content and design of characters themselves.

As with any book like this, there's so much more I could say about its creation and design, but much of that will have to wait until I've sent the finished book out in the world. It's difficult to judge how a book will affect the readers, and this is no exception. The historical context of the setting may be a hindrance or a boon to the story, and the same goes for the style of art. But my goal, personally, is to produce a faithful adaptation of Shelley's novel in a manner which says as much about me as it does about her.

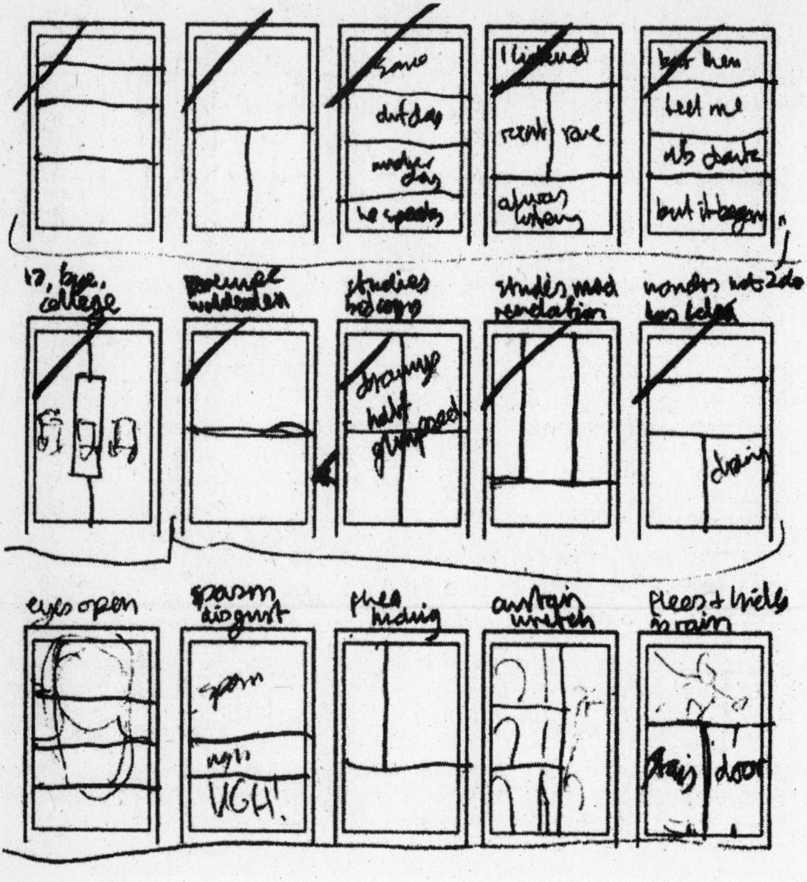
eyes open
spasm disgust
spasm
UGH!
curtain wretch
stairs
door

Frazer Irving's "little boxes with tiny words on them"

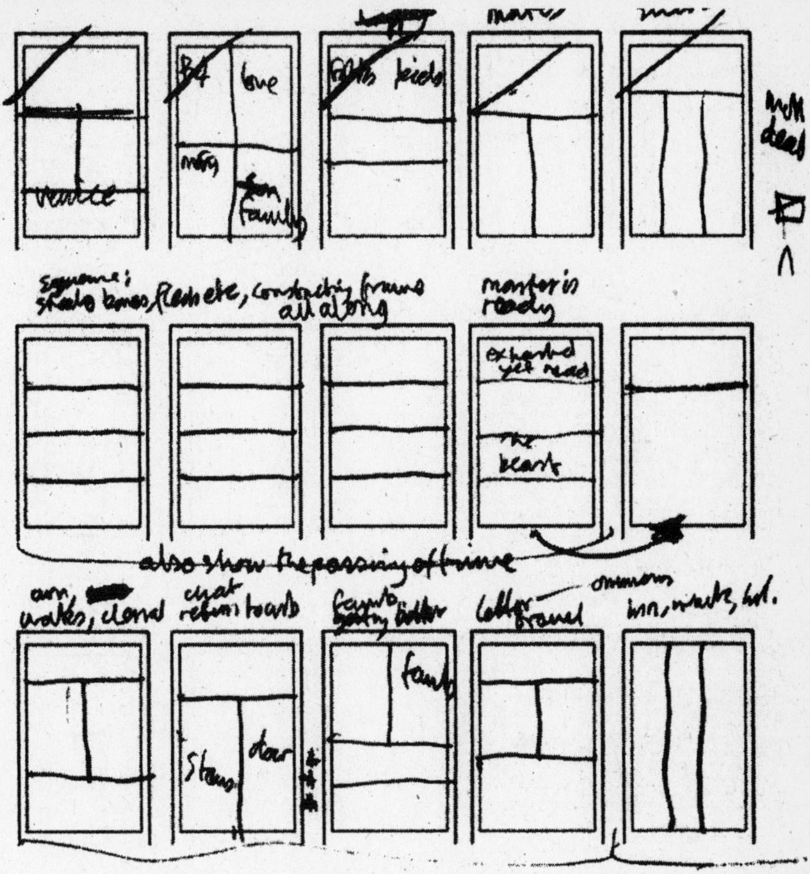
love
family
master is ready
the beast
also show the passing of time
Stairs
door
family

that are the first stage of his visual breakdown of the story.

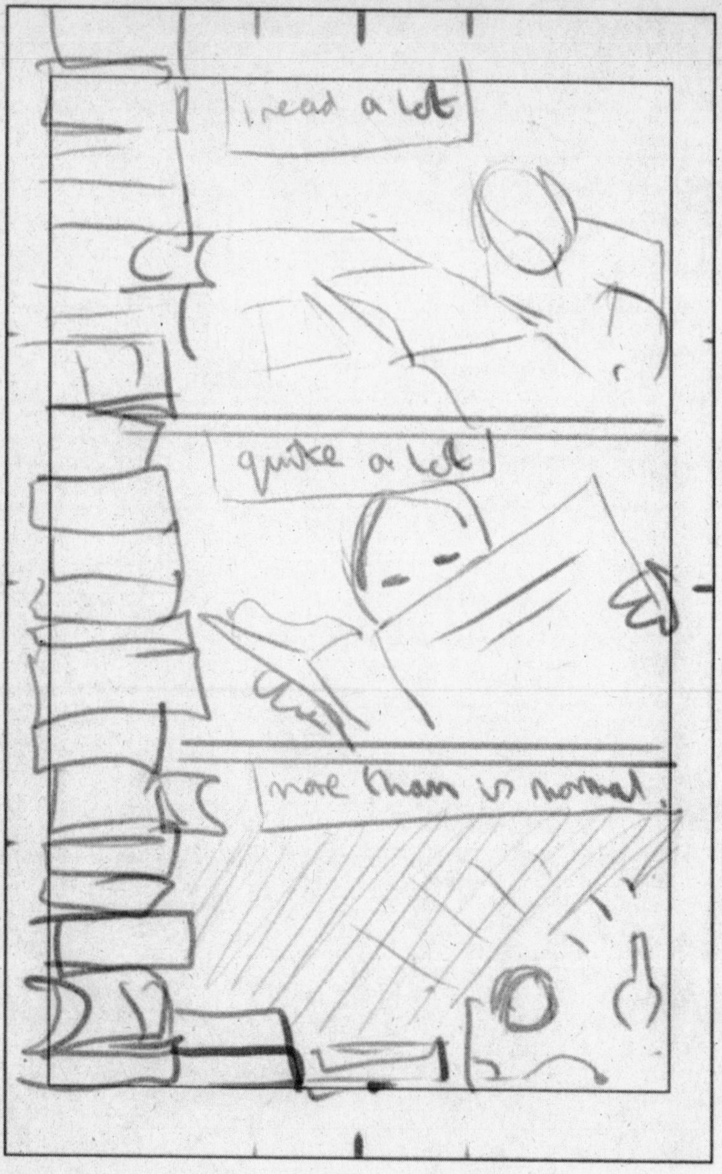
I read a lot
quite a lot
more than is normal

The first sketch of a four-page sequence showing the dramatic moment when Victor Frankenstein brings his monster to life. Note where Frazer has indicated where the text should be placed.

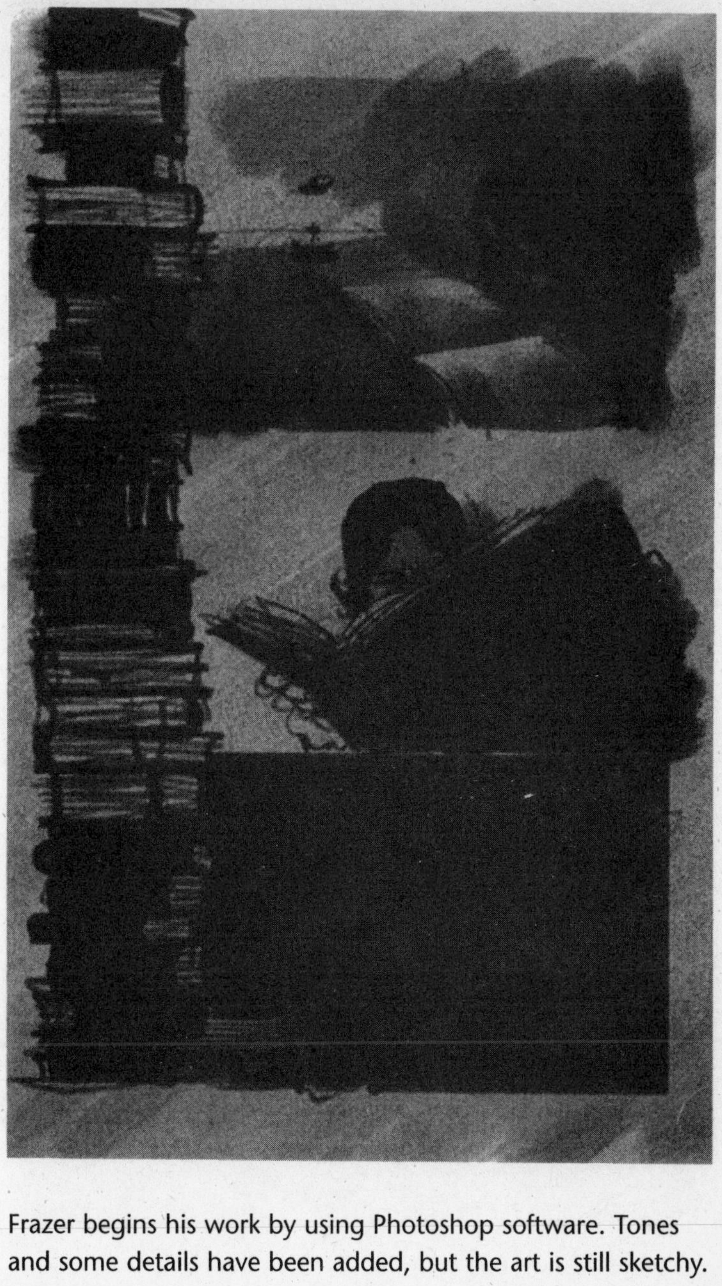

Frazer begins his work by using Photoshop software. Tones and some details have been added, but the art is still sketchy.

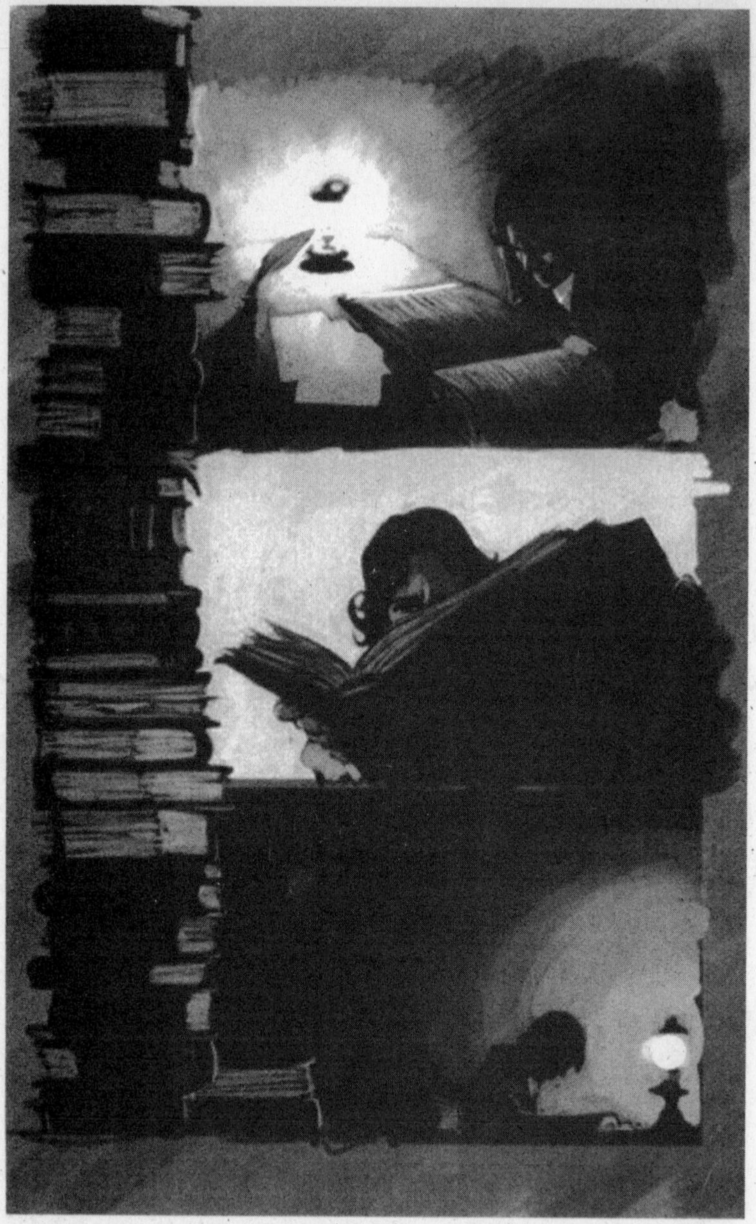

Here we see a wider range of tones, and that the art is more finished. Note that the borders have not yet been added.

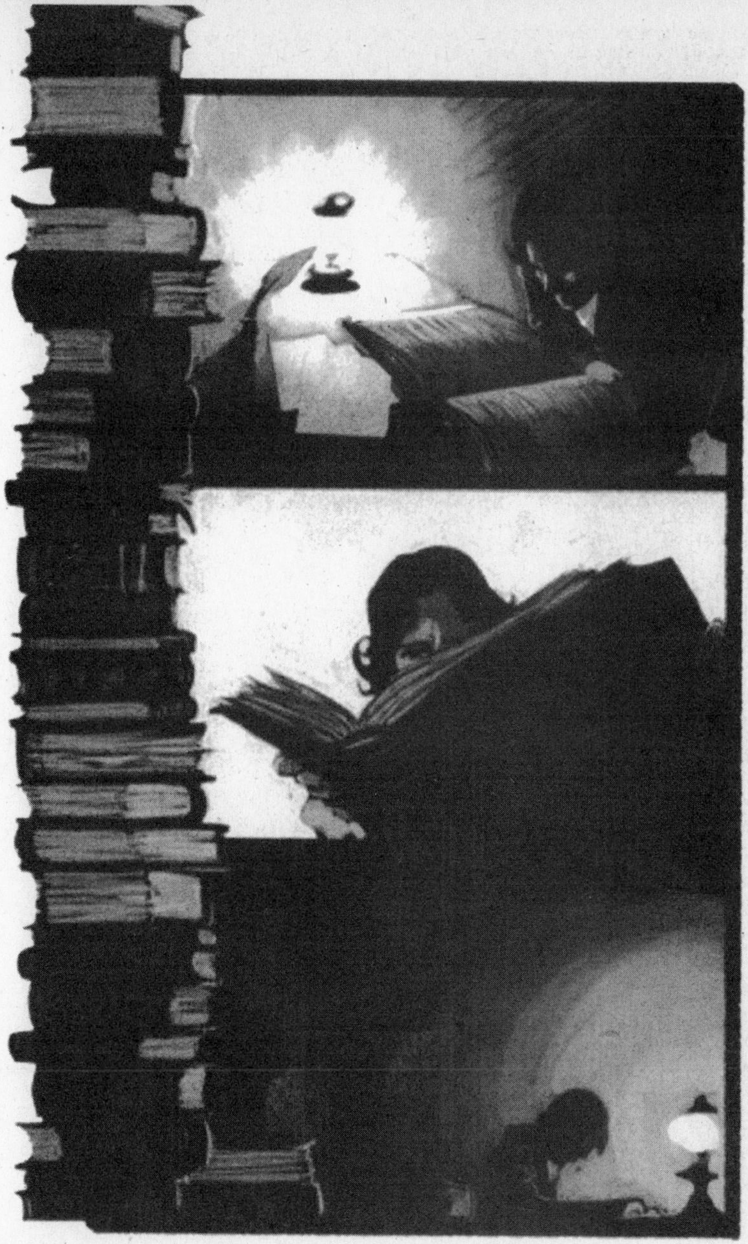

Here is the art for page 14 at its final stage. The only thing missing is the text.

PAGE 12

Caption: "My mother's death delayed my move to the **university** at Ingolstadt , but finally, I had to go.

Caption: "I had to leave my father and my **family** . . . my dear friend, Henry . . .

Caption: "But it was **Elizabeth** that I would miss most.

Caption: "We had talked of **marriage** but my education had to come first. I had the normal fears of youth but was also excited about what I would **experience** at Ingolstadt.

A copy of Gary Reed's script for page 12.

A now complete page 12 with the art and text combined.

built this thing
I crafted every part
and then it was done
and I gave it life

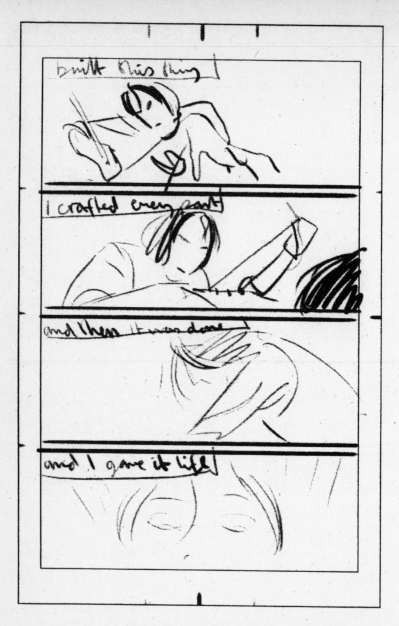

The beginning of a four-page sequence showing the dramatic moment when Victor Frankenstein brings his monster to life.

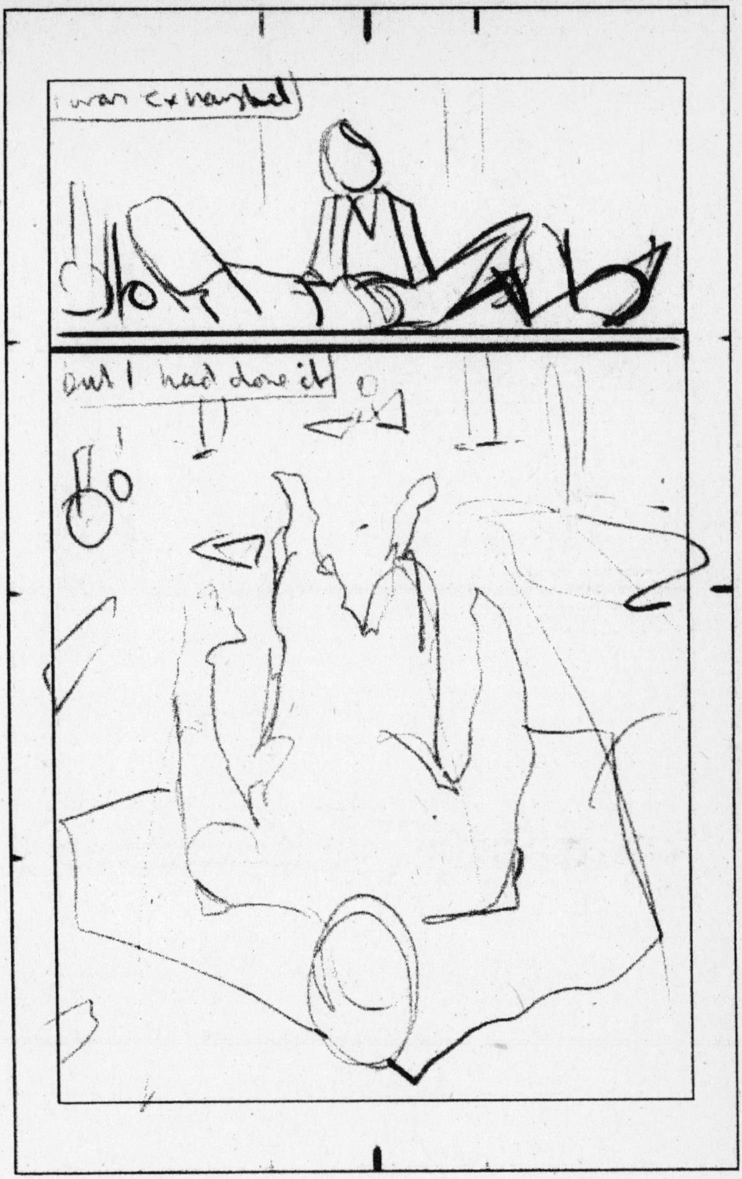
I was exhausted
but I had done it

Note where Frazer has indicated where the text should be placed.

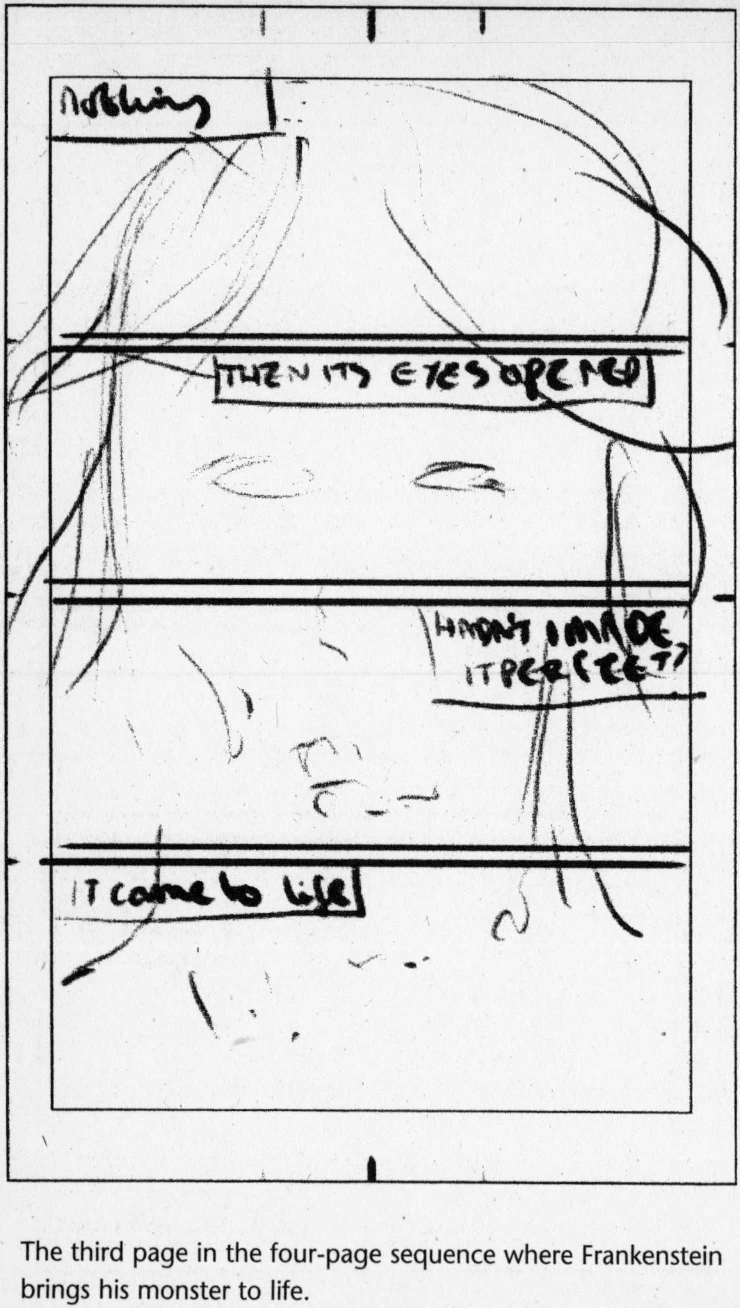
nothing
THEN ITS EYES OPENED
HADN'T I MADE IT PERFECT?
IT came to life

The third page in the four-page sequence where Frankenstein brings his monster to life.

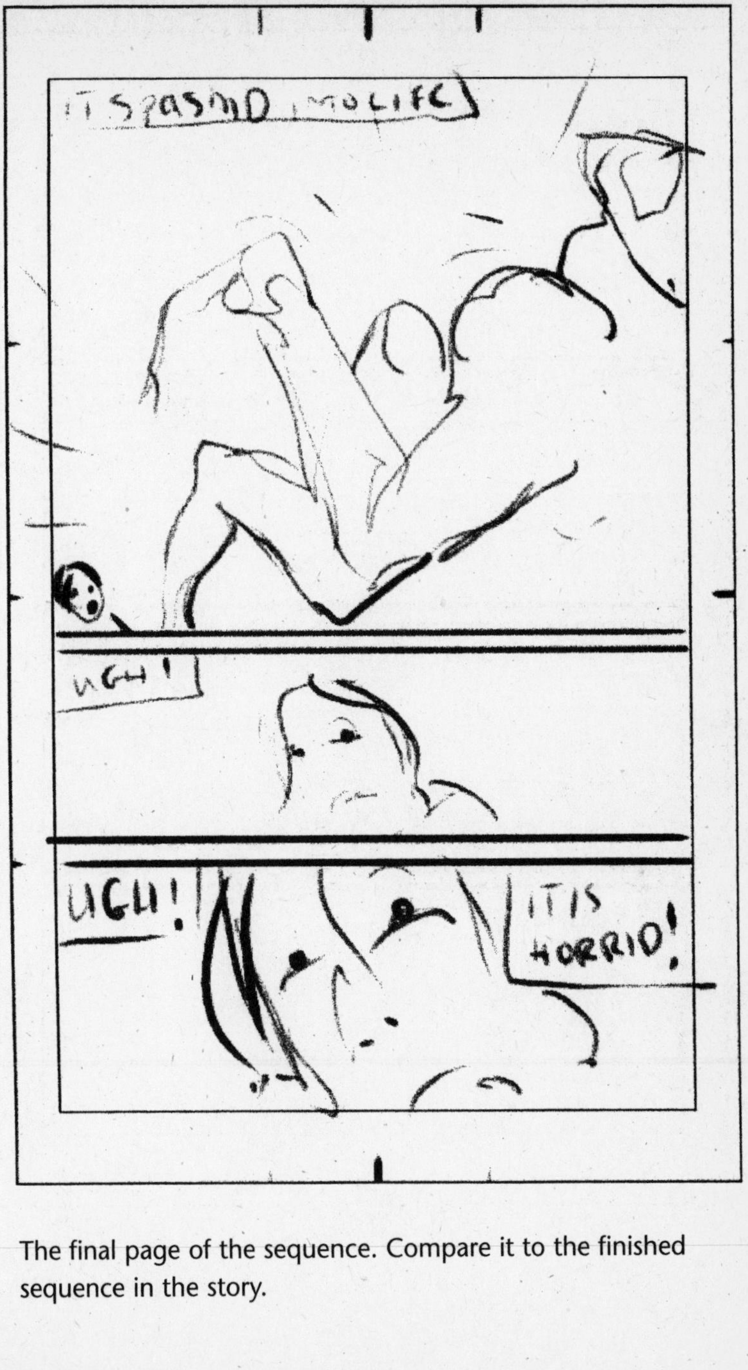
UGH!
UGH!
IT IS HORRID!

The final page of the sequence. Compare it to the finished sequence in the story.

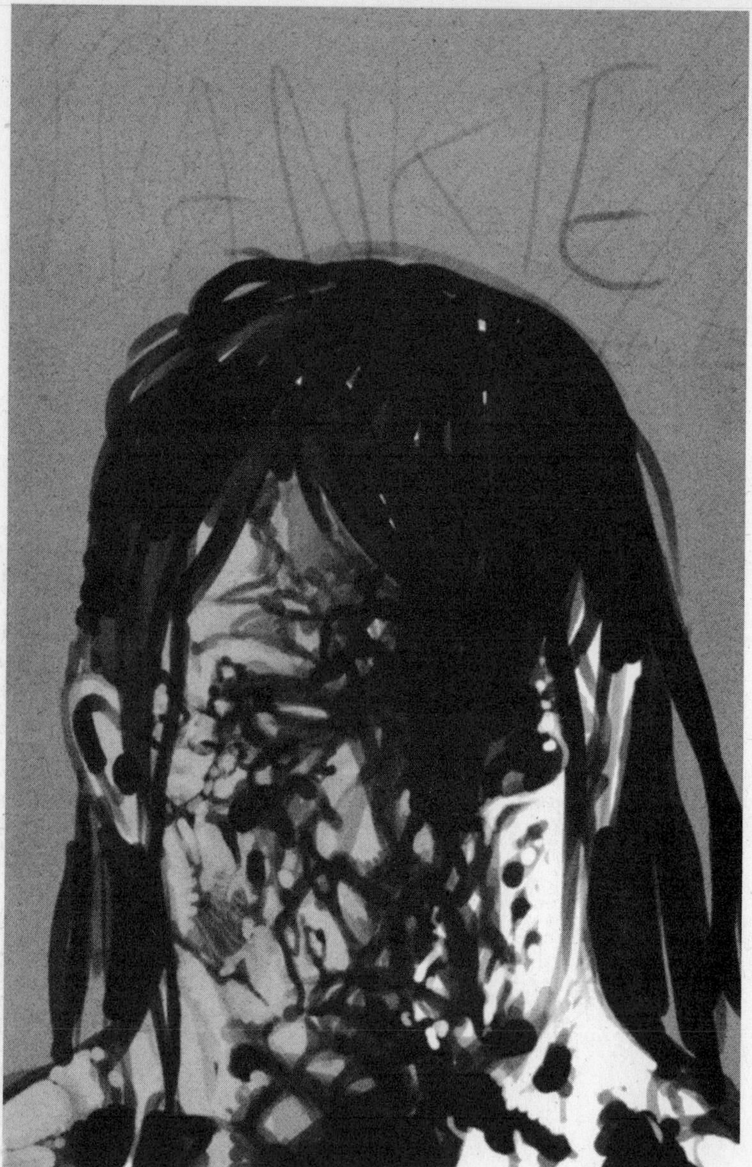

The first in an initial round of cover sketches submitted by Frazer Irving.

The second sketch shows the monster in the Arctic.

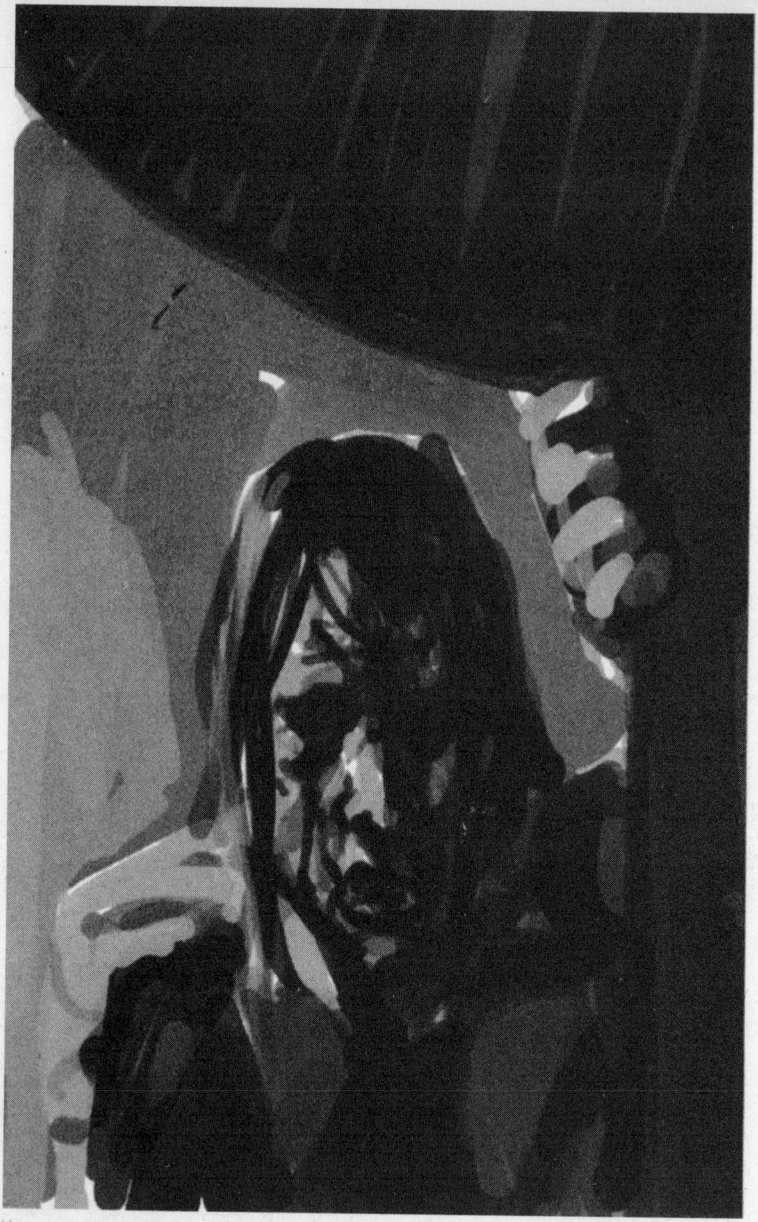

In this third sketch, we see Frazer focus on the monster's anguish.

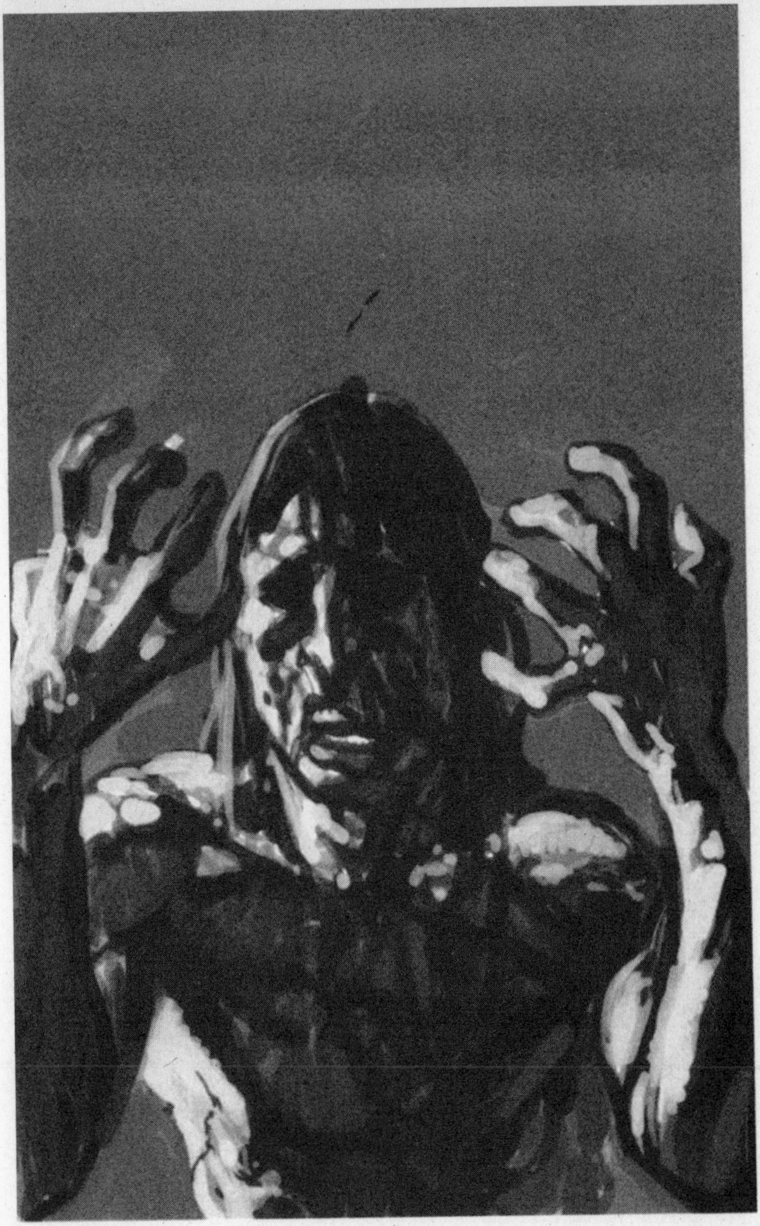

In this fourth sketch he emphasizes the anguish and details of the creation.

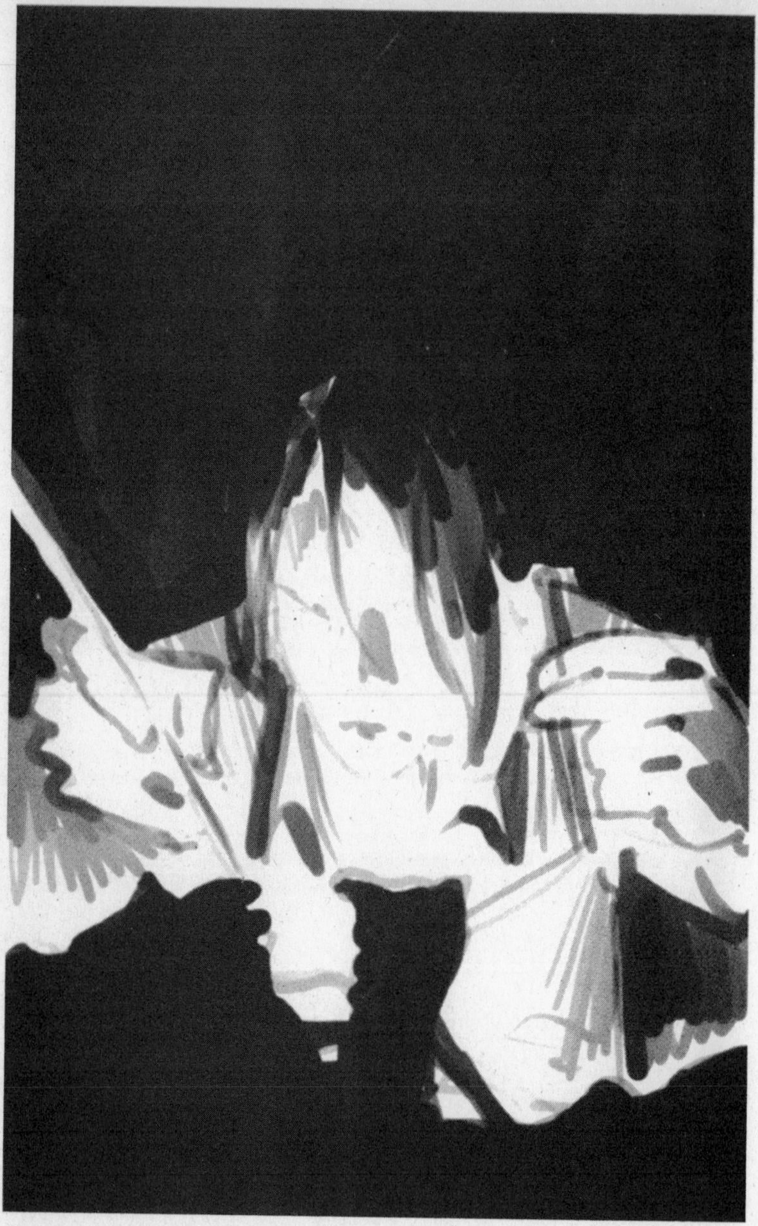

Frazer also did several other sketches for the cover that didn't focus specifically on the monster. This on he called "Creation."

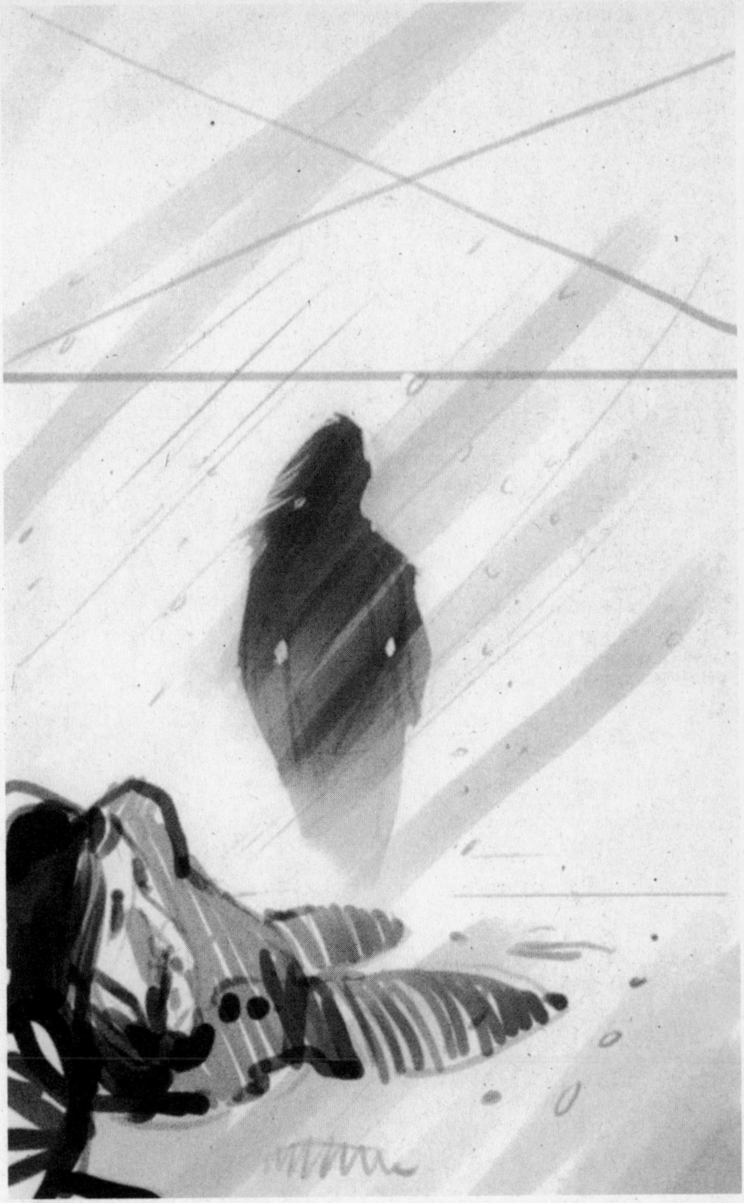

"Snowstorm." Note the space blocked out for the title.

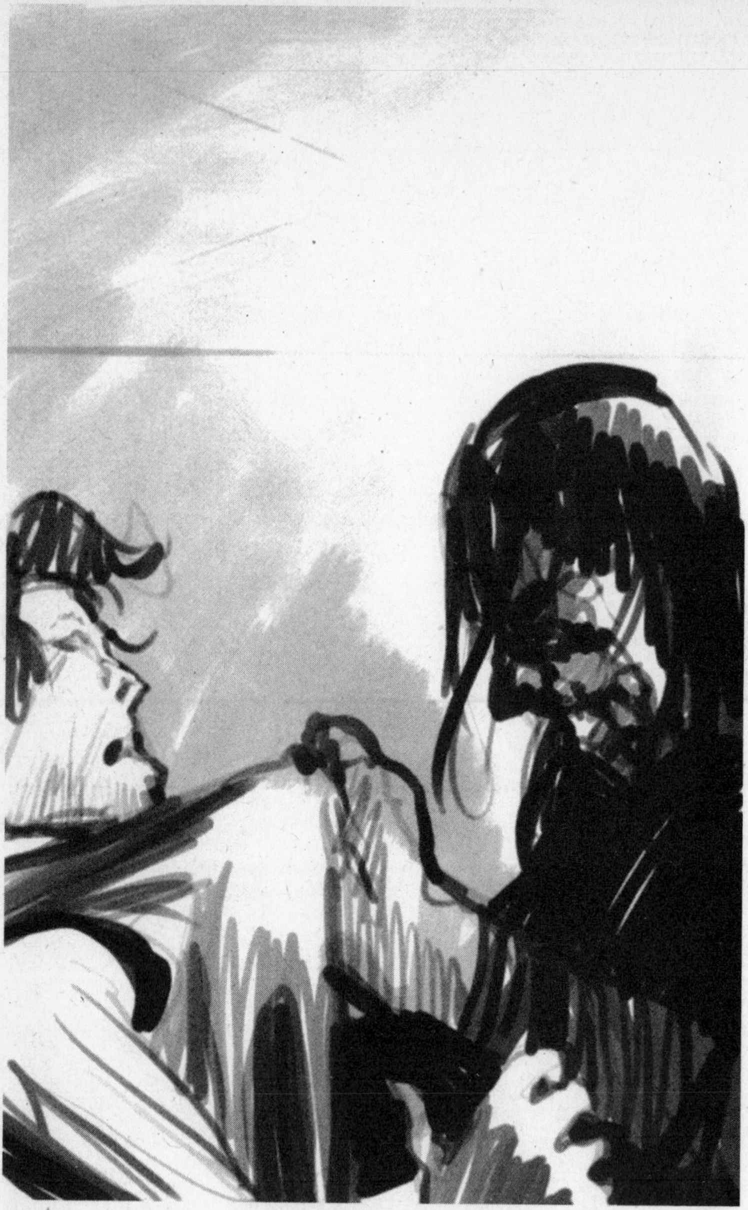

"Wedding Night."

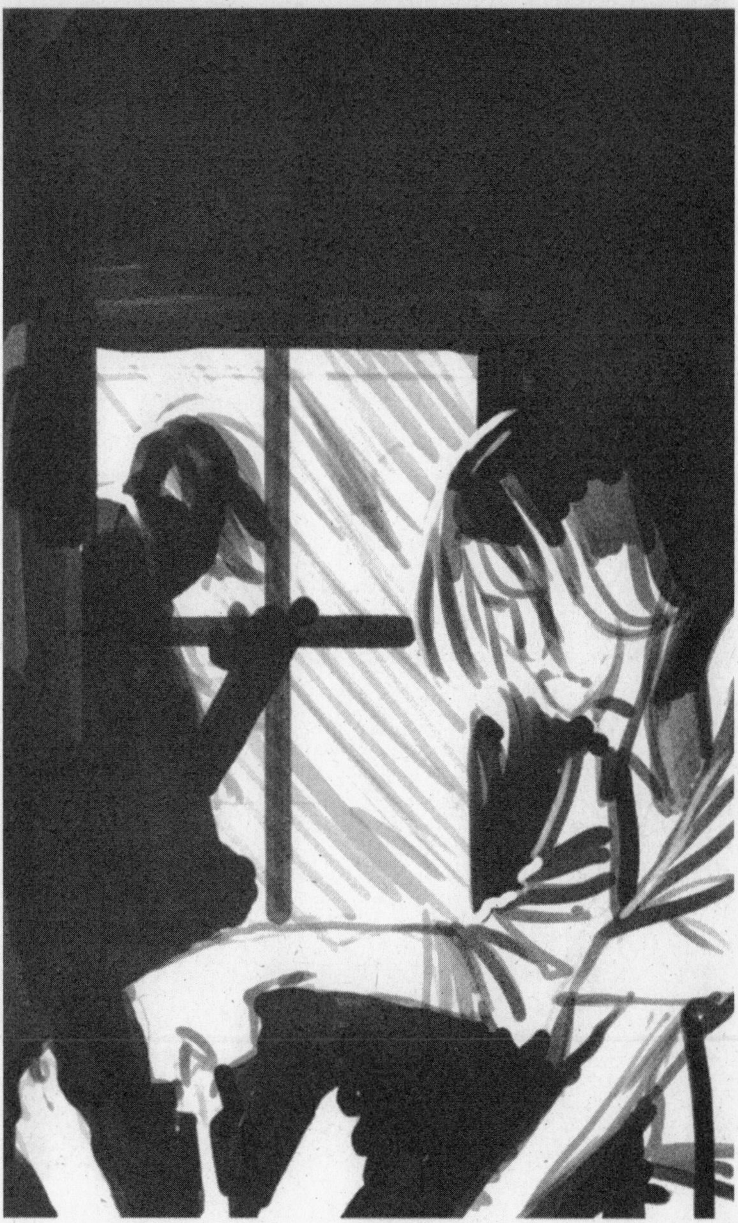

"Window."

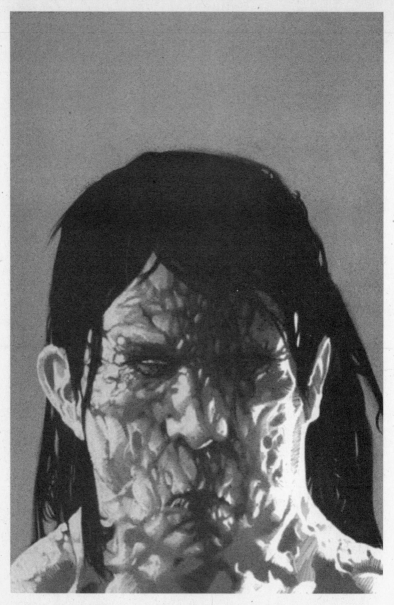

Once a sketch is selected, a finished piece of art is prepared.
Here is Frazer's first version of the final cover art. Compare it
with the final printed version on the cover to see what was
changed.

MARY SHELLEY (1797-1851) experienced the kind of childhood that sounds like a dark fairy tale. Her mother, an early feminist, died giving birth to her; she was brought up by a remote father (the philosopher William Godwin) and a stepmother who hated her. Her step-sister was a depressive, who would later commit suicide; and there were also a step-brother and a half-brother in the family. The young Mary escaped from her surroundings into reading, and would often read by the side of her mother's tomb.

In 1813, she met Percy Bysshe Shelley. He was only twenty-one years old, but was already married—and unhappy in his marriage. And it was already clear that he was destined to be one of the geniuses of English poetry. Despite Mary's age, the two fell in love and eloped in 1816. Because of this, her father disowned her.

The young couple decided to live abroad, and settled in Italy. It was Byron who suggested, in 1817, that they each write a horror story of some kind. The result, in Mary's case, was *Frankenstein.* A young girl of twenty wrote the book whose name has become synonymous with horror.

Tragedy followed them: of their four children, only one lived very long. Then in 1822, aged just thirty, Percy Shelley was drowned.

Mary's life was effectively over: even though she lived for another thirty years, her flame never again burned as brightly as it had in the company of her brilliant husband and their friends such as the poet Lord Byron; and although she wrote more, the single book which is her lasting legacy belonged to the time in Italy.

FRAZER IRVING was born and raised in the town of Ilford, on the edge of London. He's been reading comics since he was old enough to turn pages. He's done work for DC Comics (*The Authority: Scorched Earth*) and Dark Horse Comics (*Fort: Prophet of the Unexplained*) as well as the magazine *2000AD* ("The Necronauts," "Judge Dredd," "Judge Death"), the BBC, and Wizards of the Coast. More information about Frazer's upcoming projects can be found at his web site www.frazerirving.com.

GARY REED was the publisher of Caliber Press, a specialty publisher of comics and books that released over 1500 issues in the 1990s. In addition to serving as president of Caliber, he was also publisher of Stabur Graphics and vice president of McFarlane Toys during their inaugural launch. Gary has written over 200 comics and books including *Baker Street*, *Renfield*, *Saint Germaine*, and *Raven Chronicles*.